Praise for *The Intelligencer*

"This is terrific—an intelligent, graceful, sophisticated novel that packs a real thriller's punch. Think *Shakespeare in Love* meets James Bond."
—Lee Child, bestselling author of *The Enemy*

"A spellbinding first novel . . . an imaginative story that weaves together 16th-century English politics, modern-day high-tech espionage, and globe-trotting adventures into a tough, thrilling, and thoroughly exciting ride through history. . . . Silbert deftly keeps us guessing till the last secret is revealed. This thriller heralds the debut of a new author with a real talent for spinning a memorable mystery."
—*Book-of-the-Month Club* (Main Selection)

"The pace is quick and the action fascinating . . . a fun mystery with bonuses."
—*Library Journal*

"Silbert brings hands-on experience as a private eye to her entertaining debut thriller, which shifts deftly between the present and the late 16th century. . . . [T]he tale moves at a refreshing clip, and Silbert provides plenty of engaging back story about Elizabethan history, ciphers, Iranian jails, the poison of the Australian blue-ringed octopus and much more."
—*Publishers Weekly*

"An artful and ingenious blend of Elizabethan history and twenty-first century espionage by a gifted and insightful observer of the age-old dark side of intelligence."
—Jack Devine, former Acting Director for Operations at the CIA

"Forget Shakespeare. Christopher Marlowe is the true man of mystery to former Elizabethan scholars like Leslie Silbert, who studied literature at Oxford before going to work for a New York firm of private investigators. . . . Silbert makes a spirited case for the revisionist theory that the romantic 16th-century poet and playwright was not killed in a taproom brawl but dispatched for his spymongering."   —*The New York Times*

"[A] real delight . . . reminiscent of the film *Shakespeare in Love*."
— *Houston Chronicle*

"Silbert moves with ease from the past to the present, and . . . proves that if she's a Charlie's Angel, she must be the smartest one."
— *The Globe and Mail* (Toronto)

"From London to New York, from Elizabethan times to our new millennium, *The Intelligencer* bursts onto the literary scene with an unforgettable tale of espionage and high-level politics played across time and continents. Make sure your electric bill is paid. You'll be up all night reading!"
— Gayle Lynds, bestselling author of *The Coil*

"*The Intelligencer* is rewarding for those looking for something different, and a boon for the historical-mystery fan. If you liked Dan Brown's *The Da Vinci Code*, you'll love this complex brew."
— *Shotsmag Reviews* (United Kingdom)

"Cleverly crafted . . . highest possible recommendation!"
— Murder by the Book's *The Dead Beat* magazine

"[A] page-turner . . . well-paced and well-researched . . . literary interest, history, and suspense are well balanced." — *The Drood Review of Mystery*

"[T]wisting a modern tale around old secrets, codes, ciphers, treachery, and murder . . . it's a winner." — The Poisoned Pen's *Booknews*

"Silbert offers a wonderfully imagined new take on the eternal mystery of Christopher Marlowe's untimely death in this thoroughly enjoyable first novel that will appeal to fans of historical mysteries, biblio-mysteries, and PI novels alike." — Partners & Crime *Partners Picks*

"[A] fun romp through espionage, past and present. And as a bonus, Silbert, an Elizabethan scholar with a particular interest in Marlowe, provides sources to back the theories and the facts laid forth in her book."
— Politics & Prose *Staff Picks*

The Intelligencer

Leslie Silbert

WASHINGTON SQUARE PRESS

New York   London   Toronto   Sydney

Washington Square Press
1230 Avenue of the Americas
New York, NY 10020

ISBN: 0-7434-3292-4
    0-7434-3293-2 (Pbk)

First Washington Square Press trade paperback edition April 2005

10 9 8 7

For information regarding special discounts for bulk purchases,
please contact Simon & Schuster Special Sales
at 1-800-456-6798 or business@simonandschuster.com

Manufactured in the United States of America

Intelligencer: One employed to obtain secret information, an informer, a spy, a secret agent.*

A term first used in the late sixteenth century.

*The Oxford English Dictionary

FOR MY PARENTS

Cast of Characters

*Except for those marked with an asterisk, all are real historical figures, described as they were in 1593.

Present-Day Characters

Jason Avera—paramilitary operative employed by the Slade Group
Hamid Azadi—senior Iranian intelligence officer
Connor Black—paramilitary operative employed by the Slade Group
Vera Carstairs—Oxford student
Edward Cherry—Sotheby's executive
Alexis Cruz—director of central intelligence
Colin Davies—Scotland Yard detective
Luca de Tolomei—wealthy art dealer
Peregrine James—Marchioness of Halifax
Khadar Khan—businessman based in Islamabad
Surina Khan—daughter of Khadar Khan
Max Lewis—database researcher for the Slade Group
Bill Mazur—private investigator in New York City
Cidro Medina—financier
Donovan Morgan—U.S. senator, Kate's father
Kate Morgan—private eye and spy
Jack O'Mara—Kate's best friend
Hannah Rosenberg—rare-book dealer
Andrew Rutherford—Oxford historian
Jeremy Slade—director of the Slade Group
Hugh Sinclair—Oxford detective
Adriana Vandis—Kate's college roommate

You must be proud, bold, pleasant, resolute,
And now and then stab, as occasion serves.
—YOUNG SPENCER, in Marlowe's *Edward II*

The Intelligencer

1

What, will you thus oppose me, luckless stars . . .
That I may vanish o'er the earth in air,
And leave no memory that e'er I was?
No, I will live . . .

— BARABAS, in Marlowe's *The Jew of Malta*

SOUTHWARK, ENGLAND — DUSK, MAY 1593

*H*is rendezvous was set for nightfall and the sun was sinking quickly. The young man had no time to spare. But as he neared London Bridge, the familiar sounds along that particular stretch of the Thames were hard to resist. His pace slowed. His ears perked up. The clamor of the bear-baiting arena beckoned — a chained bear howling as canine jaws tore at its flesh, frenzied dogs shrieking with every swipe of the bear's claws, groundlings hollering out bets and cheering wildly.

Halting midstride, with one tall black boot hovering a few inches above the ground, he tested his resolve. It failed.

He veered off the riverside path and headed toward the arena. En route, a swath of bold colors drew his attention — the canopy of an unfamiliar booth. Curious, he approached. Long scarlet tresses came into view, then the gnarled face of an old woman, smiling with red-stained lips that matched her shiny wig. At first she appeared to be selling decks of playing cards, but after looking him over, she lifted a small sign advertising her forbidden trade: GRIZEL'S TAROT. With his rakish clothing and brown hair hanging loose, it was clear he was no prim city official.

Slapping a few pennies on her table, the young man asked, "Should I put my money on the bear?"

"You would rather hear the bear's fortune than your own?"

He looked away for a moment, as if thoughtful, then turned back with a mischievous smile. "Yes."

"It would be more worth your while to attend to yourself."

"Well, that is a subject I'm fond of." He took a seat.

She laid her battered cards out slowly, several ill-fitting rings sliding along her shriveled fingers. When the tenth card had been carefully placed facedown upon the table, the woman looked up.

"May we skip to the end? I haven't much time."

"Why don't you let Grizel be the judge of that? First, I must know who you are." Near her left hand, five cards were arranged in the shape of a Celtic cross. She picked up the central card. "Your soul." Turning it over, she gazed reverently at the faded image of a man in a red cloak and cap. "The Magician. Manipulator of the natural world . . . loves tricks and illusions. Has a powerful imagination. A master of language, he is most nimble with words."

"Mmm-hmm."

Raising a gray brow at his inarticulate response, she double-checked the card. With a shrug, she set it down, then selected the bottommost card of the cross. "The card of the present moment. Oh, my, the Page of Swords. You have a passionate mind, don't you, my friend? Always searching, seeking to uncover the hidden truth. Indeed, you begin such a quest today."

The young man leaned forward with interest. "Sweet lady, you're good."

Flattered, she began flipping over the cards that formed the remainder of the cross. "The Ten of Coins—in reverse. You like gambling. And risk, grave risk. Toeing the edge of a precipice."

"Keeps life interesting, and my pockets full."

"Outside influences . . . let me see. The Three of Swords—a dangerous triangle, a fierce conflict. Two powerful forces threaten you." Looking up, she noticed that his expression remained calm. "You'd best take heed," she declared sternly. "Danger discovered in this position is real, but it can be survived."

"Threats, conflicts . . . such things are everyday occurrences." He waved his hand dismissively. "If you please, my last card?"

Grumpily she turned to the second formation of cards on her table: a column five cards high. Lifting the top one, she peered at the image for a moment, hesitated, then showed it to him—a hand-painted skeleton, skull on the ground, toe bones in the air. "How could this be? Upside down, the Death card signifies an impending brush with danger, but one that will be survived. Here, in the afterlife position, it seems to mean you will live after your death . . ."

Puzzled, she tilted her head and studied his face.

"Does seem odd, I admit," he said. "Though some have called my *looks* otherworldly, perhaps—"

She scowled, then broke into a toothless grin. "Ah, of course. I forgot who you are, Magician. Now I understand. It is your magic that is to survive. Long after you take your last breath."

The young man bowed his head bashfully. Though Grizel didn't know it, she was talking to London's most popular playmaker, a writer whose deft pen had worked magic upon the theatrical stage. He marveled at her insight. Then his jaw muscle twitched. *A pox on it!* The cursed thought had wormed its way back into his head—the very one he had been chasing away for months. Would he make such magic again? Of course he would. When the time was right, he told himself.

Looking back up, he flashed his mischievous smile once more. "My lady, could you tell me just one thing I do not yet know?"

Grizel tried to frown, but the twinkle in his eye was contagious. Lifting the second highest card in the column on her right, she glanced at it, then slammed it down as if it burned her fingertips.

"What is it?"

Sadly she placed a hand over his. "Barring angelic intervention, you'll not live to see the next moon."

Vaguely startled, he slid his right hand into the pocket of his close-fitting silk doublet. "There's nothing like a second opinion. Particularly when the first suggests your end is nigh. Do not mistake me, you've been a delight, but there's another lady I always consult when it comes to matters of fate." He produced a silver coin. "If it's her face that greets me, I've nothing to worry about."

He tossed the coin up in the air. Glinting now and again, it flipped over a few times before falling into his left palm, landing face up. "Ah, not to worry, Grizel. The queen here says all will be well. And as her dutiful subject, I am honor-bound to take her word over yours."

With a blown kiss and a smile, the young man left the Tarot booth and hurried once more on his way to London Bridge. Tilting his coin to catch the setting sun's orange glow, he looked closely at the metallic image of Queen Elizabeth's face. He winked at her, and as always, she winked back; he'd scratched off a fragment of the silver over her left eye, revealing just a speck of the darker metal beneath. The trick coin, which had more silver plate on one side than the other, was a counterfeit English shilling he'd fashioned with an associate while on a clandestine mission in the Netherlands the previous year. *The fates are fickle. Better to manufacture your luck, than hope for it.*

Luck of any kind was a precious commodity to him. After all, he was not just a writer in search of his muse. Young Christopher Marlowe was a spy in the queen's secret service . . . a spy with no idea that the old crone was right.

2

The silver Daimler pulled to a stop at Eaton Square in Belgravia, an exclusive residential enclave in central London. A young baron stepped out, buttoned his dinner jacket, and reached for the long-stemmed roses resting on the seat. Nodding to his chauffeur, he began strolling past the pillared white homes alongside the fragrant park.

It was a cool evening for spring, and his hat, thin scarf, and gloves appeared entirely appropriate. No one would guess that he wasn't wearing them for warmth. The accessories were intended to prevent anyone in the vicinity from being able to describe him later on, should they even remember seeing him, which was unlikely. An expensively dressed man in this neighborhood, with the right level of self-assurance in his stride, blended in better than camouflaged soldiers moving through a jungle.

A few minutes later, he stood at the door of a five-story townhouse on Wilton Crescent, a street shaped like its name. The lantern-lit façade was curved as well, and ivy hung from the terrace. Pretending to rap on the front door with his left hand, he surreptitiously operated a small handmade pick gun with his right — the delicate maneuvering hidden by the bouquet balanced in the crook of his right arm.

Having inserted the steel needle jutting from the gun's muzzle into the lock, he used his index and middle fingers to adjust the long trigger and manipulate the lock's cylinder pins. Made of walnut and steel with mother-of-pearl inlay, it was a device he'd fashioned himself. It had not been easy to leave his favorite set of antique picks at home, but out in the open like this, there simply wasn't time to manually pick a lock he knew would have at least five internal levers. Pick guns turned a fifteen-minute operation into a matter of seconds. And while he tended to disdain any-thing considered de rigueur among rookie thieves, for this situation, there was little choice.

The lock's tumblers turned, and once inside the foyer, he set down his flowers, slipped his pick gun into the holster strapped to his left fore-arm, then stepped around lightly with his arms in the air. Graceful movements, but the whimsical dance was not what it seemed. A soft chirp sounded, and his right wrist came to an abrupt halt as the electronic device in his platinum cuff link homed in on the hidden security panel. With a short-range electromagnetic pulse, it promptly jammed the system.

For a master thief, breaking into an ordinary home was child's play, particularly when the owner had moved in so recently that sophisticated security measures had yet to be installed. It was like using a top SAS marksman to shoot a seated fat man from point-blank range.

The baron had agreed to do it as a favor for a friend, his only friend who knew the truth: that he was something of a modern-day Robin Hood. Not out of altruism—he simply had an intense dislike for the idle rich. His set. The very people whose company he kept at exclusive social clubs in London, casinos in Monaco, and posh Portofino hotels. He was a silent traitor in the ranks—filching their priceless treasures, quietly selling the items on the black market, then donating the proceeds to exactly those charitable causes that would most gall the involuntary donors. Courtesy of his most recent coup, a conservative Member of Parliament—a known xenophobe—was unwittingly funding a health clinic for destitute immi-grants. The black-clad baron had snatched a Degas statuette while the MP and his wife were in the next room playing cards in their dressing gowns.

Never before had he robbed a home without having been invited in on a previous occasion. Going in blind was always a bad idea, but his friend knew the owner well and had gathered enough information to guarantee that tonight's theft would be a sure thing. There were as yet no pressure pads installed in the floors. No cameras, no wiring in the win-dows. And the safe was somewhere in the study, located on the third floor.

After climbing the stairs, he examined the study's outer wall—the one between himself and the street—the only wall thick enough to contain a safe. Two good-sized windows, nothing behind the single painting. He turned his attention to the floor. With some strategic tapping and a practiced ear, he quickly detected a hollow beneath a corner of the intricately patterned Shiraz rug. Using a letter opener from the homeowner's desk, he pried up a two-foot-square panel of hardwood slats and saw the safe. Around a decade old, it was a steel contraption with a Sargent & Greenleaf combination lock.

"Mr. Sargent? Mr. Greenleaf? Gentlemen, let's see what you've got for me this time." Lowering himself to the floor, the baron settled onto his side and slipped off his gloves, then placed an ear over the safe and a hand on the lock. While rotating the dial, he lightly caressed the safe door with his free hand, attempting to feel and possibly hear when the lock's tumblers came into contact with each other, in order to calculate where the notches for the locking mechanism had been placed on each wheel.

He frowned. There was chaos beneath his fingertips. Far too many pulses. The lock was definitely a manipulation-resistant model. One with dummy notches added to the wheel edges—shallow enough to avoid interfering with the locking process but deep enough to feel similar to legitimate contact points when an expert like himself turned the dial. With a tilt of his head, he dislodged his hat. It slipped to the floor. "Hats off, my demure darlings. You took round one. But round two, I'm afraid, is mine."

Sitting up, he lifted his right trouser leg, opened a Velcro pouch strapped to the inside of his calf, and withdrew several objects: a fine length of plastique with a V-shaped metal liner—a shaped charge fresh from an underground lab in Bratislava—a digital detonator, two coils of wire, and a small lithium battery-operated power supply. He gently arranged the plastique along the right edge of the safe door, placing it directly over each spot where the door's steel bolts entered the frame. Courtesy of his practiced method, the explosive would slice through the bolts without affecting the safe's interior. Toasting these contents would not do at all—the item he was after was highly flammable.

Inserting the detonator, he connected it to the power source and flipped the switch. A fifteen-second count began. Pulling his gloves back on, he used his handkerchief to wipe down the safe, threw his dinner jacket across the square hole in the floor, then moved a rolling file cabinet over it to secure the fabric. *Three, two* . . . The detonation was barely audible, muffled as it was by his jacket's thin Kevlar lining. Wisps of smoke snaked upward as he rolled the cabinet back to its original position. Kneeling, he peered into the hole, grasped the safe's handle, and gingerly pulled it upward.

And there, not even singed, was an old leather-bound manuscript. He'd been told it had been buried for centuries, along with a secret his friend's family seemed desperate to keep. Titillating stuff, to be sure. He would demand the full story before turning over his takings.

He lifted the plain black volume from the safe. It was fairly heavy, about an inch and a half thick, with leather remarkably smooth for something so old. It had no title on the outside, he noticed, nor much in the way of decoration—just thin, single gold leaf stripes glimmering along the edges of the front and back covers and across the five raised bands on the spine. He started to open it, then caught himself. There would be ample time for that later.

With the manuscript salted away in his black rucksack, the baron spun for a quick survey of the room. The sparkle of crystal caught his eye—a dozen decanters on tiered shelving across the room, perched in rows with the formality and precision of a boy's choir. After sniffing the contents of each and replacing the bottles with care, he poured himself a glass. Nothing—not even a getaway—should come between a man and an old cognac. The evening's sport might have been a bore, but the refreshments were exceptional. Lifting the velvety liquid to his lips, he enjoyed what was more of a soft kiss than a sip.

The romantic interlude between connoisseur and cocktail was cut short. Harsh pulses of red light filled his glass. With a quick glance, he saw a whirling light outside the windows, heard the sound of car doors shutting, footsteps coming closer, hushed tones.

Bewilderment wrinkled his brow. Security men on the scene already? Impossible. He'd disabled the simple system effectively, without a doubt. They must be approaching one of the adjacent homes. Maybe the neighbors were having a domestic dispute, or a child had accidentally tripped an alarm.

Softly a door creaked. With a jolt, the baron realized it was the rear entrance of the house he was in. The place was being surrounded. *This* place. But he'd find a way out. Always had.

Though calm, his mind raced over the possibilities. Perhaps the inevitable had finally occurred. Perhaps the police had caught up with him after all these years. Followed him from his home, then called in for backup. He had known it would happen at some point, had meticulously planned his escape and new identity long before.

Thinking the roof his best option, he was moving across the room toward the stairwell when footfalls sounded within the house. From the floor above, from down the hall. Drawing closer. Damn, he thought; he would have to duck out one of these windows, climb to the roof from here. Peering down at the street, he saw two armed men keeping vigil . . . and one of them was looking up. He was trapped.

For a moment, the baron stood stock-still, mesmerized by the sound of his unexpected fate, slowly closing in. With a shake of his head, he realized how greatly he'd underestimated the opposition.

Taking a seat in a leather armchair by the windows, he placed his glass on the table before him. He then removed his left glove, revealing a large square-cut ruby ring. With his right thumb and forefinger, he flipped back the gemstone and gazed at the well of powder hidden beneath — highly potent crystals distilled from the saliva of Australia's blue-ringed octopus. The small, sand-colored creature, which flashed to yellow with bright blue rings when disturbed, possessed venom five hundred times more toxic than cyanide. Having decided long ago that he would sooner die than face prison, he lifted his tongue, positioned the ring just beneath, and tilted back his head. The crystals melted and almost instantaneously penetrated the rich vascular network on the underside of his tongue. Seconds later — faster than if he'd injected it into his arm — the poison was entering his heart.

Grimacing at the bitter taste in his mouth, he took another sip of cognac. How perfectly appropriate, he mused. Bittersweet. The flavor of his ironic demise — Europe's most infamous gentleman thief caught during an ordinary household robbery. In spite of the tremors in his hand, he raised his glass.

His final toast. Punctuated by gunshots.

3

Wrapped in a towel, Kate Morgan was standing in her bedroom eyeing the contents of her closet with a furrowed brow. She had a problem — a business meeting to get to in twenty minutes where she was supposed to look presentable — but it was a warm spring afternoon and there was an eye-grabbing mark on her neck that she needed to hide. Can you get away with wearing a scarf tied around your neck on a day like this without looking like a teenager covering up a hickey? she wondered. Probably not.

Ah-ha! This should do the trick. She pulled a black sleeveless turtleneck from one of her shelves, laid it on her bed, and began to towel-dry her hair.

The hot barrel of the freshly emptied pistol that had been slammed into her neck the night before had left an ugly welt — part bruise, part burn. Kate knew she was lucky. The guy had been aiming to crush her trachea. She'd twisted at the right moment and he missed by a couple of inches, giving her a window to throw a well-placed punch to the face. A painful but effective finishing touch on that assignment. Her boss had insisted she take the following day off, but an urgent matter had come up — with a client who might be unsettled at the sight of seared purple flesh.

Bra, underwear, and slim-fitting top in place, Kate zipped up the skirt of her pinstripe suit. Pulling a comb through her long tangle-prone hair, she searched for the right pair of earrings. Pearls. Nice and demure. Makeup? Maybe a dab of lipstick. She picked up a tube, turned to her mirror, and applied a layer of her favorite shade, Guerlain's Brun Angora—reddish brown flecked with gold. The color worked well with her dark hair, green eyes, and olive skin tone.

Now the jacket. She pushed the middle button through and took a step back to assess her image. After flicking her twisting curls back over her shoulders, she tilted her head to the left and looked at the right side of her neck. The turtleneck did its job well. Good, she thought; you're officially presentable. She glanced at her clock. *You're also late. Time to move.*

Kate slipped into her shoes and reached for her shoulder bag. That's when she noticed the back of her right hand. *Shit. Forgot about that. Oh, well, not much I can do.*

As usual on a perfect spring day in New York, tourists with cameras and ice cream cones filled the Fifth Avenue sidewalks. Kate was slicing her way through the throngs in the direction of Central Park. The canopy of oak and sycamore leaves hanging over the park walls had just come into view—a green wave lapping at the granite shore of the metropolis.

She paused with a cluster of other pedestrians before a red light at Fifty-ninth Street. The clattering of hooves from the horse-drawn carriage depot on her left mingled with the buzz of nearby conversations and the incessant blaring of taxi horns. Thinking wistfully of the T-shirt, spandex shorts, and sneakers she'd been running in the hour before, she shrugged out of her suit jacket.

"Is that all?" a leering bicycle courier called out, cruising toward her.

"For now, but later tonight . . ."

Blowing a kiss at his bewildered expression, she moved forward with the flow of the crowd and dialed her boss.

"Slade," he said.

"It's Kate. I cleaned up and I'm on my way to the Pierre. Who am I meeting?"

"Cidro Medina. Oxford dropout turned finance wizard. Thirty-something playboy with a Midas touch. He's one of our regular clients in Europe—uses the London office mostly, for forensic accounting work. At any rate, the guy returned home from dinner last night to find a dead body in his study and the place crawling with cops. The would-be thief was after a sixteenth-century manuscript written in a strange language, something Medina's workmen stumbled across during renovations a week or so ago. Medina wants to know exactly what was found and why someone wanted to steal it. That's where you come in. Those are hardly questions for the cops. Not that they're even interested, what with the perp already in their hands."

"Why didn't he just show it to an expert at a local museum? Or auction house?"

"He was planning to. But one of the guys in our London office mentioned your background to him. He decided that you make more sense. Another Renaissance scholar might be more experienced but won't have the investigative background to coordinate the historical effort with the police work. You're the perfect person to put all the pieces together. He had some other business in New York, so he flew over this morning."

"Got it. Well, I'm here. I'll check in soon."

The Pierre Hotel's intimate circular tearoom brimmed with quiet conversation. Kate admired its tasteful opulence—frescoes that combined classical scenes with images of New York society figures from the sixties, ornate golden sconces, two sweeping curved staircases, and an oversized vase with a bouquet that towered over her. Just nine tables were arranged around the room along the wall, with armchairs and loveseats upholstered in tapestry.

She realized that the elegant setting was a perfect place to begin her bookish mystery, a welcome change of pace after her last assignment. Not that she shied away from danger, but sometimes she missed her old life: a quiet nook in a well-stocked library, the comfort of immersion in another place and time, the excitement of peeling back the layers obscuring a subject that fascinated her with every turn of a page. At least to Kate it had been exciting; her college roommate had threatened to sic the nerd patrol on her with shocking regularity and would blast Norwegian thrash music if she tried to stay in and work on a weekend night.

Kate gave her name to the host, then followed his eyes to her client's table. *Oh, my.* Not that Medina was conventionally handsome, by any means. His nose was too prominent—hawkish, in fact—and his jaw and cheekbones were sharp enough to hurt someone. Lips, a touch too full. But it was an arresting face. Framed in unkempt short blond hair, it was a face that made you stop, stare, and wonder what was going on behind it.

Crossing the room, Kate glanced at the fresco painted on the wall behind him. A nude Venus stood on a scallop shell, with a half-man, half-serpent curled around her feet. *Now there's a chick who'd be cool with her first hot client—even if he could put a Versace model to shame.*

Turning back to him, Kate recognized a familiar expression, one she encountered just about every time she met a new male client. First, the eyebrows raise with pleased surprise that she's attractive, and then the mouth purses slightly as they mull over her unexpectedly young age.

Rising, he extended his hand. "Cidro Medina. A pleasure to meet you." His accent was public school English, seasoned with a sprinkle of Spanish.

"I'd like to shake your hand," Kate said, "but . . . I had a little accident yesterday."

Medina looked at her questioningly.

No way to avoid this. She showed him the back of her right hand. A big purple lump, the size of a large grape, covered her last two knuckles.

"Looks to me like your *accident* involved somebody's face," he observed with surprise. "I may look like a choirboy . . ."

Yeah, right.

" . . . but I do know what happens when you throw a bare-knuckle punch."

"Oh? Tell me more."

He laughed. "Impressive. Appeal to my ego and draw the attention away from yourself. Well, I won't press. But I'm still curious. I didn't realize you white-collar P.I.s were in the habit of scuffling like football fans."

"We're not," Kate said, which was true. The private investigation company she worked for—one of the world's top firms—was actually founded as a cover for an off-the-record U.S. intelligence unit. Her boss, Jeremy Slade, a former deputy director for operations at the CIA, had chosen the closest private sector equivalent to be the unit's front company, because he knew that the best lies are cloaked in as much truth as possible. Only a handful of his investigators were aware of the company's dual nature—those who participated in the covert government operations in addition to conducting their regular work. Kate was one of them. And it was the government assignments that tended to be dangerous, that sometimes got physical. As she'd quickly learned, the idea that P.I.s are always getting into scrapes is a myth of popular culture.

But Kate couldn't explain all of that to Medina, so instead she said,

"The fact is, we rarely scuffle. Almost never. But once in a while, if a client is really, really pushy . . ."

Medina grinned. "The London office faxed me your bio last night, but they didn't tell me you'd be such good company."

With a shrug, Kate slid into her chair.

Sitting down himself, Medina continued, "I'm impressed—two Harvard degrees. You know, I couldn't even manage one."

"I heard. It's a shame. Your career does seem to be suffering."

Flattered, he grinned again. "You were in the middle of a doctorate program in English Renaissance studies when you left university, right?"

Kate nodded.

"What exactly were you studying?"

"Curiosity . . . the pursuit of secrets and forbidden knowledge."

"Oh?"

She continued. "I found it interesting that England's first official state-funded espionage organization was formed around the same time that Englishmen were searching in new ways for the answers to cosmic mysteries—you know, God's secrets—exploring the farthest reaches of the globe and turning the first telescopes on the heavens. And that all the while, curiosity wasn't exactly the virtue it is today. I—"

"What do you mean?" Medina interrupted.

"Mmm, theologians in the Middle Ages tended to condemn excessive curiosity as a vice—if you probed heavenly mysteries, it was heresy. Black magic. That attitude lingered among hardcore churchmen in Elizabethan times, so certain lines of inquiry could get you in trouble with the government, like wondering if hell existed, or whether the earth was really the center of the universe. Anyway, I wanted to compare the two. Think about which type of knowledge was most dangerous to pursue—state secrets or God's secrets."

"Brilliant. Why the move to the Slade Group?" he asked. "Seems an unusual choice for a budding scholar."

Kate looked away for a moment. It *had* been an unusual choice, but two years into her graduate program she'd been faced with an unusual personal circumstance. An event that had broken her heart and turned her life upside down. But it was nothing Medina needed to know about.

"It's pretty simple," she answered. "I decided I wanted to have an impact in the real world—help people get answers to important questions, get them out of trouble, recover something they'd lost. Slade's does do a fair amount of corporate work, as you know, but it's not my area. I mostly handle personal matters for people—crimes the police never solved, that type of thing."

She smiled. "Now, I know I should make more idle chitchat, but what happened in your home last night—the dead body, the mysterious manuscript? I'm impatient to hear more."

"I'm having a new property restored. In the City, near Leadenhall Market," Medina began, referring to London's financial district.

"New office space?"

Nodding as he clicked open his briefcase, Medina leafed through some materials. "During structural reinforcement work, the men came across a hidden compartment beneath the building's foundation."

He handed Kate a rectangular object encased in a thick velvet sack. "This was found sealed in an airtight metal box. Presumably that's why it's so remarkably well preserved." He snapped the briefcase shut and moved it to the floor.

Easing the manuscript from the sack, Kate stared at the plain, gilt-edged black cover, then turned to the ridged spine, checking for a title. Seeing none, she lowered the manuscript to the table and gently, as if caressing the cheek of a newborn, ran a fingertip across the cover. "The leather's barely cracked," she marveled. "Hard to believe this is from the sixteenth century."

She lifted the cover, turned past the blank first page, and for a moment was transfixed as odd arcane symbols resembling hieroglyphics glared back up at her.

"I looked up a tutor I knew well at Oxford," Medina said. "An historian called Andrew Rutherford. Showed it to him last week. Though he was able to roughly date some of the paper, he couldn't make sense of that writing—consulted a specialist in ancient alphabets, but apparently those symbols are nothing of the kind."

"Could be nullities," Kate said softly, lifting the page.

"Pardon?"

"Come closer."

He leaned toward her across the small table, and after a split second, the right corner of his mouth curled up a bit. Not quite a smile, just the hint of one.

"Closer to the book," she admonished. "What do you smell?"

He assumed a crestfallen expression, then asked, "Do I want to smell anything? It's hundreds of years old."

"Have a little faith in that airtight seal you mentioned. You'll be fine."

"Okay. Leather and, uh, some type of old paper."

"Right. What else?" Kate asked, gently waving the page back and forth.

"Ink, I suppose?"

"And?"

"And . . . something else," he murmured, inhaling again. "Lemon."

Kate reached down and pulled a slender but powerful flashlight from her bag. Turning the manuscript sideways, she trained the light onto the page they'd been examining. Translucent letters appeared between the lines of inked symbols.

"Bloody hell," Medina whispered. Reading the translucent letters aloud, he said, "*The Anatomy of Secrets* by Thomas . . . what does that say? Philip . . . Phel . . ."

"Phelippes," Kate said, stunned. "The two letters at the end—that backward *e*, and the backward *s* with a closed loop at the bottom? This is an Elizabethan style of handwriting."

Eyes wide with amazement, she lowered the page. "Do you know who Phelippes was?"

Medina shook his head.

"You might have heard of Francis Walsingham, Queen Elizabeth's legendary spymaster? He's considered the founder of England's first official secret service, and Phelippes was his right-hand man, his covert op director—was called 'the Decipherer' for his expertise in code breaking. Today, Phelippes is mostly remembered for helping Walsingham with the entrapment of Mary Stuart, Queen of Scots."

"His name looks French."

"Yeah. He was born Phillips. Changed it, probably to add some panache," Kate said quickly.

She then pointed to the hieroglyphic-like symbols. "These characters written in ink were known in the Renaissance as nullities. They're decoys—meaningless symbols intended to throw you off. Codes and ciphers were a crucial part of covert communications at the time, but so was penning information in lemon juice, milk, onion . . . anything organic.

Someone shuffling through Phelippes's papers might look at a sheet like this and give up, perplexed. But if he held it to a candle . . ."

Kate turned to the second page and shined her flashlight toward it. This time, however, no translucent letters appeared. She looked at the page more closely. It was slightly smaller than the previous one, a darker shade of yellow at the edges, creased as if once folded several times, and appeared to be in a different person's handwriting. Focusing on the characters themselves, she saw that they were simpler than the nullities—the decoy symbols—inked on the title page. There was one that resembled a tadpole, another that looked like the planet Saturn encircled by its ring, a number three with an extra loop, and another that resembled an eight with a pig's curling tail on top.

"I wonder if . . ." Kate's voice trailed off as she examined the next few pages. They, too, were more battered than the first page, with simpler characters, varying styles of handwriting, and no hidden lemon-juice text.

Scanning the fifth page, she nodded. "Yeah. I'm pretty sure these are real Elizabethan ciphers. Some of the characters are familiar to me. This one," she said, pointing to an *o* with a cross jutting out of it, "I've seen used to represent France. And this one, Spain," she continued, pointing to what looked like a number four standing on a short line. "And this upward-pointing arrow, England."

Looking up, Kate noticed two teenagers across the room peering at her over their teacups, and an older woman at the next table glancing over in between bites of scone. Reluctantly she closed the manuscript and said softly, "This looks like a collection of sixteenth-century intelligence reports."

"Odd that my tutor didn't . . ."

"Espionage isn't a common or particularly prestigious academic specialty."

"Hmm. Even so, I still don't see why someone would try to steal this when so many things in my home have got to be worth far more. My car keys were out on the hall table . . . next to some diamond cufflinks. The thief didn't touch them. Seems a bit daft."

Unless . . . Intent on maintaining her composure, Kate took a deep breath. "These might not be just any old intel reports. After Walsingham died in 1590, his secret files disappeared, and both Elizabethans and modern-day scholars consider Phelippes a possible suspect. The files were certainly valuable. Walsingham's network of snoops would have put J. Edgar Hoover's henchmen to shame. Secrets, scandals, anything suspicious—you name it, they sniffed it out. For decades. And the thing is, those files have never been found. Maybe—"

"Hold on. Can you back up a second? Why so much spying back then?"

"How's your English history?"

"Piss poor," Medina admitted. "I *am* half English but grew up in Spain . . . and was never really one for books."

"Well, Elizabeth I's Protestant government was threatened by scheming Catholics from all sides, not to mention from within. Catholic conspiracies were constantly in the works, usually involving both domestic and foreign players. The Spanish in particular. Also the pope—he issued a bull commanding his flock to do whatever it took to get rid of Elizabeth."

"So a lot of people were trying to kill her."

"Exactly. And by the 1580s, Walsingham finally convinced her to spend money on espionage. So for the first time in English history, the Royal Treasury footed a big chunk of the intelligence bill, and Walsingham was able to really expand his operation. With Phelippes at his side, he built a vast network of informants and spies—or intelligencers, as they were known at the time. Sometimes his people used threats and intimidation for their recruitment, but mostly just the promise of money. And as a result, Walsingham was able to ferret out traitors so thoroughly it would have made Joe McCarthy's head spin. His people had so much dirt on people, they could threaten to bury almost anyone at any time."

"Sounds like a charming place to be," Medina said dryly.

"I know. When it comes to Elizabethan England, most people think of Shakespeare and royal pageantry. But beneath the glitter, it was an ugly police state. No concept of innocent until proven guilty. If the queen's security was at stake, suspicion was what mattered. And so the words of spies—the brokers of secrets and sins—could send you to the torture chamber like . . . that," Kate finished, snapping her fingers.

"You said Walsingham's files have been missing since his death?"

Kate nodded. "More than four centuries."

"And you think . . ."

"I think this manuscript may prove that Phelippes is the one who took them. That he sifted through decades of voluminous paperwork, selected the juiciest spy reports, had them bound, and—*presto!*—*The Anatomy of Secrets.* A collection of information as threatening to the Elizabethan aristocracy as the Hoover files were to U.S. politicos. As an historical artifact, it might not've been the most valuable thing in your home, but I'd guess the thief wasn't concerned with its sale price."

"What do you mean?"

"Well, any Renaissance scholar would love to get his hands on this. Publish an explosive paper and get famous—though most academics are pretty mild mannered and not exactly known for breaking and entering or hiring a pro . . ."

Kate looked off into space for a moment. "Maybe something in here would still be threatening to someone today. Like, say, evidence that some duke's ancestor was really a bastard, and he'd lose his family seat if that information came to light."

"That'd be something."

"You're telling me. And since hardly anyone knows you even found this, it shouldn't be too hard to—"

At that moment, their waiter set down a three-tiered silver tray laden with pastries and triangular sandwiches, along with small pots of tea and china cups.

Kate thanked him, then turned back to Medina. "Can you tell me more about last night's break-in?"

"It was early evening," he said, reaching for a cream-filled pastry swan. "Police think he came in through a rear window. I'd left a few open . . . at my new house in Belgravia."

Kate knew his neighborhood well—had once spent a week there on surveillance. A stone's throw from Buckingham Palace, the area was developed by the rich for the rich in the early nineteenth century. It remained an ultrachic locale where old and new money intermingled.

"You moved in recently?" she asked, pouring herself some tea.

Chewing, Medina nodded. "Until a proper security system is installed, I've had a guard on the premises when I leave. He rang the police soon as he heard the noise. It didn't matter that they took their time—after cracking my safe, the thief made himself comfortable. Poured a glass of cognac, if you can believe it."

"How did he end up dead?"

"He was armed. When my guard opened the door and saw a pistol trained on him, he fired. Aiming to disable the fellow's gun arm, of course, but with the angle . . ."

"Have the police identified him?"

"Not yet."

"They've run his prints?"

"This morning. No match." Medina turned to his briefcase and retrieved a sheaf of Polaroids. "Crime scene photos, if you . . ."

Kate took a look. In the first shot, the thief was slumped in an armchair, his head resting on his shoulder, his face obscured by blood and shadows. "*Nice* suit. Hand tailored. Looks English. Could be a way to trace him."

"Good idea."

Continuing to leaf through the photographs, Kate marveled, "Your safe . . . wow, this guy was good. He did this in a couple of minutes?"

"If that."

Seeing that the hardwood slats to the right of Medina's safe were barely charred, she added, "He must've used a shaped charge. Not easy to get your hands on one of those."

"One of what?"

"A piece of metal-lined plastique—allows for a controlled, directed explosion. Looks like he used one to melt through the steel bolts holding the door in place. Remember Pan Am flight 103? The CIA was able to trace the Libyans who blew it up from a similarly rare, high-end device—the bomb's timer—some Swiss expert only made twelve of them. Yeah, identifying him shouldn't be too hard."

"How about motive? The detective didn't seem too fussed. Got a little grumpy with me, as a matter of fact."

"I imagine I can find that in here," Kate said, gesturing to *The Anatomy of Secrets*. "The thing is, as much as it pains me to say it, a manuscript like this—sixteenth-century, one-of-a-kind—it really belongs in a museum, with proper climate control, lighting. . . . There might also be a law in Britain about turning such discoveries over to a particular cultural institution. I'm not sure how you want to—"

"While I'm loath to offend the scholar in you," Medina cut in, "I was hoping you wouldn't mind letting the bureaucrats wait a few days. I've got the airtight box upstairs in my room, and as it's been preserved in there for four hundred years . . ."

"Sold!" Kate said, laughing. "If I scan all the pages tonight, then seal it away, my conscience will survive. Tell me, though, why do you, uh . . ."

"Care?"

"Yeah. From what you've said about your interests . . ."

"This is the most exciting thing that's happened to me in quite a while. Not that it takes much to beat playing around with numbers." He paused for a moment, then continued with his crooked smile, "Besides, who could resist the chance to play amateur sleuth with a gorgeous girl like you?"

To Medina's delight, Kate shrugged, palms in the air. Mentally, however, she rolled her eyes. *Gorgeous* was not a word she'd ever use to describe herself. In Kate's opinion, her looks were good enough to be useful now and then but not so good that they were ever a liability; she could blend into a crowd if need be, easily.

Getting back to business, she pulled a notepad from her bag. "Your professor, Dr. Andrew Rutherford—I need to call him." She checked her watch. In England, it was after ten o'clock. "First thing in the morning, I guess. I'd like to find out who he showed the manuscript to—start to generate a list of everyone who knows about your discovery. Can you give me his number? And can I hold on to these?" she asked, holding up the photographs.

"Yes, and yes." Copying the number from his cell phone, he added, "You know, I was impressed with you before we met. And now, well, even more so. It's clear to me you're very capable. But I have a concern, and it's a grave one."

"What?"

"I can't help but wonder if I should trust you. Let's face it. Wily female spy types can be dangerous. I mean, if I think about some of your more illustrious predecessors—Delilah, Mata Hari . . ."

Picking up her spoon, Kate pretended it was a microphone. "Memo to self: Client is well versed in history of double-dealing trollops. Has promptly mistaken me for same."

Medina raised his teacup with a twinkle in his eye. "Here's hoping your fate is not quite so grim."

Delilah, Kate knew, had been crushed alive in a collapsing temple, but Mata Hari? *Oh, that's right. Firing squad.*

Leaning back in her chair, Kate folded her arms across her chest. "And this from a man who claims his command of history is slim."

"Oh, I know my trollops."

"Cidro, I'm sure you do."

Heading back down Fifth Avenue, on her way to catch the E train to visit the shop of a rare-book dealer she knew, Kate tried to stifle the smile that stubbornly refused to leave her face. As soon as she'd said good-bye to Medina, it seemed to have taken on a life of its own.

If her theory was correct, Thomas Phelippes—a man she felt she almost knew—had actually created a bound version of Walsingham's most delicious secrets. And it could have been buried since the Renaissance, she thought with excitement. Phelippes had lived near Leadenhall Market, the area in the City where Medina's new office was being restored. Secret compartments were more than commonplace back then. Some, known as "priests' holes," were constructed to hide the illicit black-garbed men wealthy Catholics couldn't bear to do without. When most of London burned to the ground in the Great Fire of 1666, the compartment could have been lost in the rubble and ash. Until now.

Kate clutched her bag closer. She felt like a conspiracy buff who'd just stumbled across Lee Harvey Oswald's diary. The keys to dozens of mysteries could be concealed in the ciphered pages: Did Queen Elizabeth's first love really toss his wife down the stairs? Did she take as many lovers as everyone thought? Was Mary, Queen of Scots behind the murder of her first husband and the plotting of Elizabeth's assassination? What about proof that Shakespeare did, in fact, write the plays attributed to him?

As a grad student, Kate had never dreamed of being the one to decipher something like Phelippes's *Anatomy of Secrets*, or that such a thing would ever be discovered. And she'd certainly never expected her love for Renaissance history and literature to play a role in her career. She could not have been more thrilled. So why had a vague nervousness just killed her mood?

A sharp knock threw her right shoulder forward. Holding her bag with both hands, she stared at the person who was shoving past, then relaxed.

It was a typical midtown blonde in a hurry, with an immaculate pedicure, a self-important expression no actress could fake, and irritated thoughts as predictable as the color of her roots. A moment later, the woman's rapid strides were reduced to an impatient shuffle—she was trapped behind a pair of stooped old ladies meandering along arm in arm. Kate listened to the blonde's muffled curses with amusement; no doubt she was one of the many New Yorkers who considered slow walking at rush hour to be a cardinal sin.

But Kate's heart was still racing, and it wasn't from thoughts of the manuscript. She paused to talk to Blake, the dashing young security guard standing outside of Harry Winston. Though usually surrounded by fawning female tourists, he was alone.

"See anyone I should worry about?"

He let his eyes wander for a moment, looking over her shoulder, then answered, "Mmm, middle-aged, salt-and-pepper hair—at least what's left of it—hovering over a newspaper bin across the street. He just glanced up. And, well, a guy who walked by looked you up and down, as did his girlfriend, but I don't think that means much. Coupla folks just ducked into stores."

Kate had not seen anyone herself but sensed that someone was following her. She'd been trained to spot watchers, but if they were good, more often than not she just felt them.

Pretending to peruse the Winston display case, she listened as Blake finished, "My money's on Salt 'n' Pepper. You want to walk through?" There was a hidden exit off one of Harry Winston's storage rooms that led to an abandoned network of construction tunnels. On a prior case, Kate and one of her colleagues had exposed a Winston employee's string of embezzlements, and the grateful store manager had given her carte blanche to pass through at any time. It was a kind of a midtown trapdoor for her.

"Thanks, but not today. I'd like to know what he wants."

"You've got a little glow about you. Meet someone new?"

"Nah, just a client. Really easy on the eyes, but he's so not my type—bored rich guy with that I-know-everyone-wants-me look in his eye."

"That look gets me every time," Blake sighed. "He plays for *your* team, huh?"

"I think I saw our jersey in his locker, but I'll keep you posted."

Continuing to walk south, Kate paused here and there, allowing her pursuer to keep her in sight. Looking up at the lighted trees on the sloping tiers of the Trump Tower, she wondered if she were merely being paranoid. *Well, there's an easy way to find that out.* A blue and white Manhattan bus had just come to a stop beside her, and Kate took a step toward it, as if she were about to board, then threw a quick glance behind her. The man Blake had described was trying to hail a cab.

So he *was* following her. *Hmm.* Kate checked her watch as she began walking again, pretending to have changed plans. A few blocks down, she turned into the Banana Republic in Rockefeller Center. Eyeing the reflective storefront for a moment confirmed that her shadower was right where she wanted him.

In the dressing room Kate took off her suit, rolled it up, and put it in her bag, then took out a wig and a short Lycra skirt. She rarely left home without the makings of a simple disguise. The chin-length wig was straight and blond. Her own father had once failed to recognize her in it. She tucked her hair beneath it, then slid into the skimpy skirt—a far cry from the conservative knee-length pinstripe she'd been wearing earlier.

After replacing her dark lipstick with a shade of frosty pink, Kate went up to a customer at the cashier's desk and told him she'd give him a twenty if he escorted her out. With his arm around her shoulders, they left the store and melted into the rush-hour crowd. He refused the cash.

The man with the salt-and-pepper hair and the beginnings of a beer gut stood watching the entrance to Banana Republic from across the street, partially concealed by the tourists hovering outside St. Patrick's Cathedral. *If that girl's anything like my wife, she'll be in there for hours.* He looked at his watch. Only twenty minutes had gone by. All the same, he should get ready for her exit. This was the perfect place to make his move—the most densely crowded spot around.

With his eyes still trained on the clothing store, he reached into his jacket pocket to get hold of his razor blade, then panicked. The blade was gone. And so was his wallet. He'd spent twenty-five years in New York, fifteen in the PD, ten as a gumshoe. Caught hundreds of thieves but hadn't ever been robbed himself. *Damn.*

Someone tapped his shoulder. "Excuse me, sir," a timid voice said. "Could you tell me where is the . . . the . . . ?"

What's that accent, Italian? He turned around. Ah, some hot tourist lost in the city—map in hand, an imploring look on her face. Oh, he could show her a thing or two. But he was working. "Sorry, miss. Can't help you right now."

"Actually, I think you can."

He took a step back, confused. Her features were suddenly hard, words commanding and smooth, the accent gone. She handed him his missing wallet. He bit his lip in alarm. In spite of the new hair, clothes, and makeup, he recognized her: his target.

"Bill Mazur," Kate said, having glanced at his driver's license minutes before. "Thrown off the force because you got a little too friendly with the local dealers." Before confronting him, she'd phoned his name into her office for a few quick background details. "Who hired you?"

He turned to hail a cab, but Kate stepped forward, grabbed his arm, and twisted it, and him, back around. "You didn't answer my question."

Mazur scowled, struggling to shake free of her grip.

"Oh, I almost forgot," Kate said with feigned sincerity, slipping his razor blade into the limp hand she was still holding hostage. "Men like you need things like this to get the job done."

Embarrassment flickered across his face as the blade fell to the ground. Kate was pinching a nerve in his wrist and his fingers were useless.

"Answer my question, and your friends on the force will never know you got made by a girl half your age."

With a jerk, Mazur wrenched his arm away and stepped back angrily. "Bitch, I don't know who the hell you are or what you're talking about . . ."

But Kate had a final trick up her sleeve—another detail her colleague had relayed moments before via cell phone. "How's your son doing at home on Carroll Street? I could send someone to check on him if you like."

Having no idea she would never harm a child, Mazur capitulated. "I don't know who it was. Guy didn't give me his name—just emailed the assignment a couple of hours ago. Named a drop for your bag, which I was supposed to take. He paid up front in cash. When I left my office, there was an unmarked envelope outside my door."

"Did he say what he wanted, specifically?"

"Something about a book."

"His email address?" Kate asked, handing Mazur her notepad and a pen.

He complied, then turned once more to find a taxi.

"I'll just let you know if I have any more questions," Kate said to the back of his head.

Then, reading what he'd written, she murmured to herself, "Guy calls himself Jade Dragon?"

Opening her cell phone, Kate dialed Medina to let him know that someone was still after his manuscript, that the dead thief was, in all likelihood, a hired hand. She also warned him to be careful and offered him a bodyguard; it was probably an unnecessary precaution but a good idea all the same.

Kate still considered her new case to be a low-risk mystery. Sure, there had been a couple of attempted thefts, but there couldn't be any real danger involved. Not on account of some antique gossip and double-dealing.

Two days would pass before she'd learn that her assumption was wrong.

OXFORD, ENGLAND — 11:02 P.M.

Rucksack slung over her shoulder, Vera Carstairs stepped out of the nearly empty Christ Church library. It was closing time, and as usual, she was among the last students to leave. Leaning against one of the massive Corinthian columns, she paused for a moment to press her sore eyes shut and enjoy the evening's warm breeze.

Then she gasped in alarm.

Two boys carrying unidentifiable pink objects burst past her, kicking up dust as they raced across Peckwater Quad. Watching them weave and stumble, Vera decided it was safe to assume *they* were not coming from a long, frustrating night of studying. They disappeared into Killcanon Passage, and Vera, heading in the same direction, heard drunken shouts echoing along the stone corridor. "Come on then, idiots! Get to your places!"

"Good Lord, what is it this time?" she mumbled.

Emerging from the passage, Vera entered Tom Quad and stopped short, squinting at the bizarre antics unfolding before her. Students stood facing each other with hands clasped above their heads, forming arches, through which other students, dressed in brown, were somersaulting, after having been swatted on the backside by . . . *what are those?* Vera put her glasses on. *Plastic flamingos?*

With that, Vera realized she was watching a reenactment of a scene from *Alice in Wonderland*. The queen's croquet match. Though in the book the balls were hedgehogs, the mallets live flamingos, and the players the Queen of Hearts and her entourage. So where is she? Vera wondered. Where's the queen? The answer was quickly apparent. A fat blond boy with a giant red heart lipsticked on his bare chest started jumping up and down, shouting, "Off with his head! Off with his head!" and the offender, in turn, dutifully tipped back his head, allowing another player to pour something from a plastic cup down his throat.

Remembering that Lewis Carroll had been a math tutor at Christ Church, Vera figured it was some kind of tribute. *Well, that's what they'd call it, anyway.*

It was Vera's first year at Oxford, but she'd figured out straightaway that her fellow students were particularly adept at inventing seemingly noble reasons to drink themselves silly and cavort like jackasses. Two hedgehogs, she noticed, were snogging in the far corner, and another had just crashed into one of the wickets, which teetered back and forth, ultimately collapsing in a heap of flailing limbs.

At that moment, the king—a tall skinny boy named Will wearing a paper crown—approached her.

Vera's stomach fluttered. She'd been mad about him all term.

"Wanna play?" he asked. "I need a ball." Gesturing toward a boy in brown chasing a girl in a white swimsuit, he added, "My hedgehog is trying to shag the White Rabbit."

Vera nodded to a lit window atop a stone arch on the far side of the quad. "Actually, since he's in, I was going to go see—"

"Dr. Rutherford. I should have guessed." Will rolled his eyes. "You know, all work and no play . . ."

"Well, I still haven't come up with the right hook for my essay," Vera explained, "but this weekend, maybe . . ." She paused, hoping he'd ask her to do something.

"Hi, Will," another girl interrupted. She was wearing a black leotard and had whiskers painted on her face and velvet ears on her headband. "Feel like cheating on the queen tonight?"

Vera tried not to scowl. Isabel Conrad was gorgeous, with breasts out to tomorrow, and whoever you liked, inevitably Isabel would steal him away, or rather distract him just enough that he lost interest in you. For some reason, Isabel needed to have every last boy in Christ Church panting after her.

Ignoring Isabel's question, Will turned back to Vera. " 'I don't like the look of it at all . . . however, it may kiss my hand if it likes.' "

Vera burst out laughing. The line was one of her favorites from *Alice in Wonderland*. Then her smile faded. In the book, the Cheshire Cat declined the king's invitation, but this one grabbed his hand, yanked him to the ground, and—to his delight—climbed on top of him.

Sighing, Vera continued walking toward her tutor's office. She was anxious to write an essay that would really impress him this week. Maybe even intrigue him, at least a little bit. He had taught her so much. Her sense of gratitude was sometimes overwhelming. She hoped he'd invite her in, and maybe, like last time, they'd chat over port, sipping late into the night from his two chipped black goblets.

Climbing the spiral staircase to the third floor, Vera heard from the courtyard, "Out o' vino? Bollocks! Leigh, Conrad, form a rear guard. To the pub! Troops, forward, march!"

The croquet players' shouts and laughter faded quickly as she neared her tutor's door. She knocked softly. No answer. *Must be on the telephone.*

She turned, but then her nose twitched. There was a funny smell. "Dr. Rutherford?" she called out timidly. "Dr. Rutherford?"

Still no answer. He wouldn't ignore her like this, Vera knew—not even if he were concentrating deeply on his new book. He was too kind. So had he gone home? *Perhaps . . . but he never forgets to shut off his light when he leaves.*

The door was unlocked. Cautiously entering the room, she turned toward his desk. For a few seconds, her vision blurred and the scene before her went gray, as if obscured by dry-ice smoke—the kind that billows up from the stage in productions of *Macbeth*. Disoriented, she shook her head and blinked.

Finally her vision cleared. And once again she saw Dr. Rutherford slumped over his desk. On the back of his head, shaggy white hair was matted into clumps with a dark brownish substance, and that same substance had pooled on the floor and splattered across the far wall. Realizing it was blood, Vera screamed.

4

Alas, I am a scholar, how should I have gold?

—Ramus, in Marlowe's *The Massacre at Paris*

Southwark—dusk, May 1593

*P*ushing his way through the noisy, bustling crowds on the south bank of the Thames, Marlowe paused at London Bridge. More than a dozen severed heads impaled on pikes crowned the archway. He recognized the faces, had been seeing them up there for months. Some for nearly a year. Parboiled in salt water, they'd been fairly well preserved.

"Good evening, gentlemen," he said with a slight bow. "Anyone for a game of dice?"

A young prostitute with exposed breasts tugged Marlowe's sleeve. He started to shake her dirty fingers loose, then frowned, noticing a crimson droplet perched upon her bare shoulder. Checking for a wound, he lifted her hair from her neck, but she appeared to be uninjured.

Mistaking his gesture for the scrutiny of a potential customer, she closed her eyes and puckered her lips awkwardly.

Marlowe touched the drop and brought his finger to her nose.

"Your lips smell of copper," she told him, her soft voice muffled by the cries of produce vendors, fishmongers, and two urchins cursing a foreign couple.

"I'm impressed."

"My father was a blacksmith," she announced, opening her eyes. "What was that?"

"Blood." He showed her the ruby smudge on his fingertip.

Seeing her alarm, he added with a smile, "Don't worry, miss, it's not yours. Either an angel in the sky has scraped his knee or the city decorator is at work again."

She followed his eyes to the top of the archway. A freshly severed head was just being set in place. "Poor man," she said, seeming genuinely sad. "I'll pray for you."

Marlowe realized she must be new to the city. Most residents were immune to the grisly sight. As she walked off, he wondered how long it would take the streets of London to deaden her capacity for pity.

Swatting aside the furtive hand of a pickpocket, he returned his gaze to the new head, the only one that still had its eyes. Some condemned traitors were merely beheaded. More often than not, those faces were calm, resigned. Others were not so lucky. This one had probably been castrated alive before the ax crashed down on his neck, Marlowe thought. The features were twisted in anguish, filling the air with silent screams.

"Did you hide a priest beneath your floorboards, my friend?" he asked softly. "You look too smart to have plotted to kill the queen." Someone bumped into him, and a gravelly voice cursed. Marlowe glanced at the water seller trudging past with a barrel yoked to his back, then looked up again. "But where are you now?"

Passing beneath the arch, he stepped onto London Bridge. It was lined on each side with tall half-timbered houses owned by wealthy merchants who maintained upscale shops on the bridge's ground level and lived in the floors above. Though the setting sun still shone, the narrow rutted passage was gloomy; the upper floors of each house jutted outward, almost merging overhead, and the laundry strung between blocked all but a few flickers of sky.

Halfway across, he turned down a set of stairs leading to the water, stepped into a wooden boat headed east, and handed over three pennies. "Greenwich Palace," he said, sinking into a cushion. The oarsman began slicing through the layer of brown sludge on the river's surface. Elbows resting on the gunwale, Marlowe watched the spikes of London's church steeples shrink in the distance.

The tall buildings that had crammed the shore gave way to scattered wharves, trees, and fields as they left the filthy, plague-ridden city behind. A new assignment, he mused. Once again the world would become his secret theater—a stage upon which the drama was real, the danger palpable, the final scene unwritten. *Act 1. Scene 1. Enter Marlowe.*

At Greenwich, the slight figure of Thomas Phelippes stood waiting upon the dock's edge, watching Marlowe from behind small wire-rimmed spectacles. Phelippes's dark yellow hair was tucked behind his ears, and his thin beard did little to hide the pronounced pockmarks covering his face.

The oarsman looked questioningly at Phelippes, then at the sentry upon the shore. Both nodded. Thus authorized, Marlowe disembarked and followed Phelippes past the palace. The queen's roving court was in residence, and the elegant turreted building overflowed with music, laughter, and raucous chatter. After being cleared by another sentry station, they were shadowed briefly by a mounted guard as they headed deep into the well-tended grounds, the sounds of the court's evening revels fading behind.

Marlowe trailed Phelippes quietly. He'd long since learned that the little man was not one for small talk. They'd met in 1585, when Marlowe was a student at Cambridge writing *Tamburlaine the Great*, the wildly successful play that had ravished the London theater scene two years later. Phelippes had approached him one day that winter, asking if he'd heard of Sir Francis Walsingham, the secretary of state. Marlowe nodded. The university was rife with awed whispers about the infamous spymaster, a man whose clever machinations saved the queen from assassination time and time again.

Introducing himself as Walsingham's deputy, Phelippes informed Marlowe that he could make a good deal of money if he were willing to spy for Walsingham's newly created secret service. Was he interested? *Oh, yes.*

England's Catholic enemies had an invisible presence at Cambridge, Phelippes explained. An invisible menace, he added with a hiss. There was a priest masquerading as a well-to-do Protestant student who was recruiting fellow students to defect to the Catholic seminary across the Channel in Rheims, France. And it was there at Rheims, the headquarters of English Catholic exiles, that the Duke of Guise was hatching a plot to assassinate Elizabeth, in order to allow his niece, Mary, Queen of Scots, to assume the English throne. English spies were already in place at the seminary in Rheims attempting to gather the details of the duke's strategy. Walsingham wanted a student to infiltrate and expose the network of covert Catholics at Cambridge. Did Marlowe think he could do it?

Does London reek in warm weather? Not only could he do it, Marlowe knew, it would be no effort at all. Growing up in Canterbury, he'd acted in a number of plays at the King's School, but this task would require few of the skills he'd sharpened upon the stage. To play a rebellious malcontent, a Catholic sympathizer in an environment where defying the repressive government was fashionable—it was as though Phelippes were offering him money to wear his own shoes.

Nodding thoughtfully, Marlowe said it was an exciting prospect but for one little thing. "My true, utter, and unflagging devotion to the Holy Father in Rome."

Having been warned that his new recruit had a penchant for telling jokes at the most inappropriate of moments, Phelippes smiled.

Marlowe didn't.

There was silence, and Phelippes's face darkened. At which point Marlowe broke into a grin and offered his hand. Phelippes shook it, and Marlowe's secret life as an intelligencer began.

Of course the money involved was tempting enough, as Marlowe, a cobbler's son, was a poor scholarship student who'd given little thought to any profession other than writing poetry. And though confident in his ability, he knew that a mind full of well-turned verses did not tend to fill one's pockets.

He was also charmed by the prospect of fancying himself a secret knight, gallantly protecting his royal lady. He'd had a cynical outlook on the government for years—had seen half a dozen innocent men hang before he could spell—but he chose to indulge in the idealistic notion anyway. After all, what good was life without romantic dreams, in spite of their foolishness?

Phelippes's investment proved to be a sound one. Marlowe was able to infiltrate the university's network of covert Catholics with ease, something a dozen other spies had failed to do. Word of his success quickly reached Walsingham's ears, and to Marlowe's unexpected delight, the old spymaster requested a meeting with his promising new recruit. In his

London home overlooking the Thames, Walsingham praised Marlowe for his excellent service to their queen and country. Did he wish to continue while he completed his degree?

Marlowe nodded.

"A wise choice," Walsingham said. "Books, you see, are but dead letters. It is travel and experience—ferreting out the double-dealings of men here and abroad—that shall give *them* life and *you* true knowledge."

"As well as good plays," Marlowe replied. "I've begun my second."

"Oh, yes, a Bankside poet . . ." Walsingham recalled, pouring them each a mug of fine Madeira. "That could prove useful."

Marlowe sipped with pleasure. It wasn't every day that he was flattered and encouraged by one of England's most powerful men.

"To spend one's life unearthing hidden secrets is a most noble pursuit," Walsingham finished. "For such a searcher will always have power."

Inspired by those words, Marlowe's commitment to his intelligence work deepened and ultimately almost cost him his master's degree. His pose as a covert Catholic was so convincing that the university administration, suspecting Marlowe to be a traitor, prepared to expel him. The Privy Council quickly intervened, however, and he left Cambridge in 1587 with his degree, as well as his finished *Tamburlaine*.

Phelippes stopped at a cluster of benches far enough from the palace to avoid drunken wanderers or couples in search of a spot for a breezy tryst. Taking a seat, Marlowe noticed that they were but a few feet from the so-called Queen's Oak, the tree with a deep hollow in which Queen Elizabeth was said to have hidden as a child.

"I've arranged for you to have a bed here tonight in the lodging house nearest the river," Phelippes began. "And to get you started . . ." Reaching into a leather pouch, he withdrew several coins.

Marlowe pocketed the pleasantly heavy handful, money he knew no longer came from Francis Walsingham. Walsingham had died three years before, and the queen had kept the position of secretary of state open ever since, a position that was tantamount to possessing a set of keys to the kingdom. England's clever monarch loved to incite competition among her courtiers, and it was an effective strategy. Two arch rivals were jousting fiercely for the coveted title, and as a result, the parsimonious queen got first-rate intelligence from two competing networks with little financial investment on her part.

One of those courtiers—Phelippes's new employer—was Robert Devereux, the dashing and tremendously popular Earl of Essex. A man as beloved by London's commoners as by the ladies of the court. Each time Marlowe had seen Essex enter the Rose, the playhouse had erupted with cheers. Queen Elizabeth was said to be equally as captivated by him. At twenty-seven, he was more than thirty years her junior, but she'd granted him the rooms adjoining her own in Greenwich Palace, and everyone knew what *that* meant. Essex had entered the espionage game quite recently, after learning that providing the queen with valuable intelligence was one of the best ways to maintain her favor, perhaps even better than warming her bed, a feat Marlowe was certain the amorous earl performed admirably. The young nobleman's string of sexual exploits was the talk of the town. Apparently he was very generous—and adept— with his affections.

Essex's rival for the position of secretary of state was Sir Robert Cecil, son of the queen's most trusted adviser. A small, dour-looking hunchback with years of experience in the intelligence world, Cecil was Essex's polar opposite in every way. Whereas Essex was impetuous and loose-tongued, Cecil was shrewd, patient, and quiet. Essex was emotional, and often quite warmhearted, but Cecil, always utterly ruthless. Marlowe had been playing both sides of the fence since Walsingham's death, taking assignments from each network. He knew it was dangerous, but other spies did it, and more important, having a front row seat to the courtiers' bitter rivalry was irresistible.

"Well, what have you for me this time . . . Tom?" Marlowe asked, knowing that Phelippes despised it when employees used his first name.

Pressing his lips together, Phelippes visibly bit back a reprimand.

Good. You still need me.

"A delicate matter has arisen, and I thought you might be particularly suited to it. There's been talk about a certain new publication of yours . . ."

Marlowe assumed a look of mock innocence. "I've no idea what you mean."

"You damned well do. That book of vile smut," Phelippes exclaimed with distaste. Marlowe had translated a collection of erotic elegies from the Roman poet, Ovid. As such erotica was banned in England, he'd had the poems printed at a secret press in the Netherlands.

"I *could* report you to the proper authorities . . ." Phelippes continued.

"If you could trace it to me."

" . . . but since you obviously had the lewd thing smuggled into this country illegally, it occurs to me that you must have the unsavory sort of connections that could help us with a matter of the utmost consequence."

"And if I choose to help you?"

"If you are successful, I will pay you more than I ever have. At least twice what you receive for your silly little dramas."

Marlowe raised his eyebrows. Phelippes was talking about more than twenty pounds. "What about my so-called unsavory connections? How can I be certain you aren't using me to hunt them down?"

"This matter is of far greater import than catching a ring of book smugglers."

"Even so . . ."

"I am not interested in having your misbegotten friends arrested—they could be useful to me on this assignment and others to come. You will have to take my word on that. And once again, your reward will be considerable. Have we a deal?"

"Yes." *For now.*

Leaning in closely, Phelippes said softly, "You've heard of the Muscovy Company?"

"Very little," Marlowe lied.

"Named for its monopoly on trade with Russia, it was founded forty years ago by a group of wealthy merchants and royal courtiers determined to find a Northeast Passage to the Orient—a sea route that no one in Europe had yet found, that could be dominated and controlled by Englishmen. A route that would give us direct access to the riches of the East, free from the threats of the Barbary pirates in the Mediterranean Sea."

Phelippes toyed with his sparse beard for a moment. "Obviously the Muscovy merchants didn't succeed in that quest, but they established a lucrative relationship with the czar, trading English goods for Russian furs, cable, and oil. And for a share of the profits, the czar allowed them to travel from Moscow to Persia by land many times—along the Volga to

Astrakhan, over the Caspian, and on to Bukhara—to exchange English wool for precious gems, silks, and spices. Then, twenty years ago, Turkish conquests left that route impassable, and such exotic goods have not passed through Muscovy hands since."

Phelippes paused to glance around once more, then added softly, "But on two recent occasions, gems from the Far East *have* appeared in London at the Royal Exchange, not long after a Muscovy ship docked downriver in Deptford. Rubies, diamonds, pearls . . . only they do not appear in the company's books, and shareholders, among them our queen, have not seen any profits."

"Trading under the queen's flag while stealing from under her nose—how very bold. I assume the old Muscovy trading route from Moscow to Persia is now open? That land route you spoke of?"

Phelippes shook his head. "No. Still blocked by the Turks."

Then how had Muscovy merchants gotten access to the gems? Wasn't it more likely that English privateers had stolen them from Portuguese ships, then neglected to inform local customs officials? Or that England's Levant Company—with its monopoly on trade along the eastern shores of the Mediterranean—was responsible?

Marlowe noticed an unusual gleam in Phelippes's eyes. The man always discussed matters of espionage with intensity, but his gaze at the moment was positively aflame. *What might he be . . . ah!* "You suspect certain Muscovy merchants have finally discovered a Northeast Passage, that they're keeping it secret and trading on the sly?"

"It's one among several possibilities, but one that bears looking into, as you might imagine."

Marlowe could imagine. Such a discovery would have enormous consequences for England, in terms of international prestige as well as financial gain. The Spanish and Portuguese had been far more successful at exploring and colonizing the New World, and England's national pride was wounded. But Marlowe knew that the good of their country was not Phelippes's primary concern.

"Is Essex a shareholder?"

"Yes."

"So he stands to profit handsomely should this smuggling be exposed."

"Naturally," Phelippes answered calmly.

"And should he take credit for exposing the smugglers and alert the queen to the existence of a secret sea route to the Orient . . ."

Phelippes smiled like a cat with a mouse in its paws.

I see. If Phelippes's suspicions were true and the mission was successful, Essex's power at court would soar; perhaps the position of secretary of state would finally be his. And Phelippes, of course, would be right there at his side.

"Your informant at the Royal Exchange, did he see who was selling the goods?" Marlowe asked.

"A representative of an unknown Dutch trading company. Legerdemain, I suspect. A cleverly fashioned shield to hide the true source, which I expect you to find."

Marlowe nodded.

"Now, Kit," Phelippes said gravely. "Discretion."

"Of course."

Phelippes rose to his feet. "I hope to hear from you shortly."

"And you shall," Marlowe responded, slouching lower on the bench. Watching the little man slink through the trees, he finished, ". . . hear what I see fit to tell you."

5

The dove-gray townhouse in the East Seventies had a narrow stone façade and a charcoal gabled roof. It was a sedate, old-fashioned exterior. Most people would never guess that electronic jamming signals crisscrossed each of the windowpanes, preventing voice-stimulated vibrations from being picked up by directional microphones.

Kate entered the lobby and walked toward the brass elevators in the far left corner. The shy, heavyset doorman looked up and nodded at her briefly, then continued reading his book. As always, his paperback was missing its cover.

"*Hearts Aflame? The Knight's Embrace?* Which one you got this time?"

He blushed. "You just can't give a harmless old guy his space, can you?" He'd managed to hide his addiction to romance novels from everyone but Kate.

"Lemme see some cash, Jerry, or the whole building's gonna know about the shirtless Fabios on those missing covers."

Twin gilt-framed portraits of a Victorian couple who once lived in the building hung on the interior sidewalls of the first elevator car. Kate's office was on the fifth floor, but she wasn't headed there at the moment. Her boss had sent a page. There was a meeting.

She pressed the button for the second floor and the elevator began to move. Then, while looking at the eyes of the painted Victorian woman, Kate pushed a button hidden in the ornate gold frame. From the lady's right eye, a blue laser beamed forth to analyze the distinctive pattern of interlacing blood vessels on Kate's retina while a closed-circuit camera behind the woman's left eye cross-checked her face against a small set of stored images. The button Kate was pressing scanned and transmitted her fingerprint to the security system's database. A moment later, the elevator stopped, but the sliding front door remained closed. Instead the mirrored back wall of the elevator swung back, revealing a narrow corridor.

The rear wall of the Slade Group's headquarters was a dummy, hiding twenty feet on each of five floors that were unaccounted for in city blueprints. Because the building was enclosed on three sides by its neighbors, the spatial inconsistency was impossible to detect from street level. Kate's boss, Jeremy Slade, used the hidden enclave as a command center for the covert operations he quietly managed for the government.

Passing a small kitchen on her way to the main conference room, she heard a telltale hissing sound and glanced inside to see Slade standing over the cappuccino machine frothing some milk. He'd just mastered that particular culinary art. He was so good, in fact, that Kate had circulated a confidential interoffice memorandum recommending his immediate demotion from head spook to chief office barista.

Intent on his task, Slade's deep-set eyes were cast in shadow. In his mid-forties, he was just shy of six feet tall with dark hair and brown eyes that looked black under his prominent brows. The genes of a grandmother from India and ten years of Middle Eastern sun had given him dark, burnished skin. He was in exceptional physical shape; only his generous crow's-feet hinted at his age.

Slade had spent a dozen years as a CIA case officer collecting intelligence and planning missions in dangerous and often war-torn locales around the globe, but only recently had he dared to enter a kitchen. Since then he'd become obsessed with gourmet cooking, which delighted his employees because whatever Slade chose to do, he did with perfection. A Princeton graduate with a degree in Classics, he had risen to the position of deputy director for operations—the highest position in the Agency's clandestine service—before his departure. Stylishly dressed even when casual, he had a humorous nonchalance that would give way to cold efficiency when the moment required. For Kate, the sight of a classic gentleman spy wearing an apron to fuss in the kitchen was priceless.

She'd met him three years earlier when her father had reluctantly introduced them. It was the second year of her doctorate program, just after the unexpected death of her fiancé. A fellow grad student, he'd been on a hiking expedition in the Himalayas, and while sitting at a campfire one night had been killed in a grenade attack by Pakistani militants. The two German tourists beside him had died as well. Devastated, Kate had sunk into a depression that lasted for months. Slowly, however, she recognized that only part of her life was over, the part involving the man she loved and the prospect of marriage and a family someday.

She told her father, a U.S. senator who served on the Senate's Select Committee on Intelligence, that she was going to apply to the CIA's Directorate of Operations. Not out of a desire for revenge—she simply wanted to spend her life trying to keep other people's lives from turning into hers. Though her father was sympathetic, he made every effort to stop her. Having lost Kate's mother years before, he couldn't bear the thought of anything happening to his only child. But her mind was made up, and Senator Morgan eventually gave in, setting up a meeting with Slade in New York. If Kate was determined to leave the academic world for fieldwork in the intelligence community, he figured, better it be with a man he knew and trusted than a sprawling bureaucracy where mistakes were made and leaks inevitable.

Slade had left the CIA because he'd tired of catering to the whims of politicians whose motives he often found questionable. His recent move into the private sector, however, was a ruse. Slade still reported to the director of central intelligence (the head of the U.S. intelligence community and director of the CIA), and the small and secret team of operatives he managed acted under their exclusive guidance. It was a mutually beneficial arrangement; the DCI had a way of bypassing the gauntlet of approvals necessary to launch certain covert actions by the book, and Slade could focus on the business of saving lives, free of political pressures.

When Kate entered Slade's office that first time, she was starstruck. While growing up, she'd immersed herself in spy fiction, filled with the murky bogeymen in dark suits and Bond-like über-spies that pop culture continually recycles. But Slade was real. A flesh-and-blood cloak-and-dagger man. Someone she'd imagined many times but had never gotten the chance to meet.

They connected immediately. After a two-hour interview and review of her background materials, Slade offered her a job as a private investigator, explaining that his new company was opening offices in several major cities around the world. There were already ten investigators in the New York office, he said, most of whom came from careers in journalism or law enforcement. She could begin by working alongside one of them on a case that was already under way. Slade added that he'd start training her for intelligence work as well, and in time, depending on her progress, she'd get her first government assignment. He said that Kate's credentials were as strong, if not stronger, than any CIA trainee he'd come across, and he also had a good feeling about her, which to him was what mattered most.

Kate accepted right then, grateful to Slade for giving her a reason to wake up in the morning and keeping her so busy she barely had a moment to be sad. The Slade Group's back rooms might not officially exist, but they'd been home to Kate since she'd first walked in the door.

Continuing along the narrow corridor, she entered the second-floor conference room. With the exception of computer equipment, the place looked more like J. P. Morgan's library than a typical intelligence op-center. The walls were lined with hand-carved built-in bookshelves, and two wrought-iron spiral staircases hidden behind them led to the floors above. An antique Turkish rug covered the floor, and several chocolate-colored leather couches and armchairs were positioned near the walls.

At a circular table in the center of the room, Max Lewis, Slade's top computer guru, was hovering over a laptop. Against the muted colors of the room, he stood out sharply; his T-shirt was bright red, small gold hoops glittered from his ears, and his short dreads had recently been bleached a bold peroxide blond, a color Kate thought looked cool against his mahogany-colored skin.

Max had joined the Slade Group around the same time as Kate. Then a senior at NYU, he'd decided to apply for his first-choice job in a slightly unorthodox manner. After hacking into the CIA's most secure database, he copied a dozen files and sent them as attachments, along with his résumé, directly to the DCI's internal email address. Impressed with his nerve as well as his skill, the director had mentioned him to Slade that same day.

"So how'd it go with Bill Mazur?" he asked. "Did you figure out if he was after the old book?"

"Yeah, he was. Thanks again for the quick background."

Max nodded.

"Turns out someone hired Mazur by emailing the assignment to him, using the screen name Jade Dragon," Kate said, reaching into her bag for the exact address. "Could you see if this leads to anyone? And can you blow these up a bit?" she added, handing him Medina's crime scene photos.

"Sure thing." Max slipped them into his shirt pocket. "Now that Medina. Gemma calls him 'dishy,' " he said, referring to the receptionist in their London office. "Says he's hot and heavy with some runway string-bean."

Kate smiled. Max liked short plump women. She'd walked in on him surfing porn sites featuring plus-size actresses on more than one occasion.

"Well?" he demanded. "You saw him—what did you think?"

"I wasn't thinking. I was praying I wouldn't trip while he watched me cross the room."

Max laughed.

"I was on my way to see a book dealer I know to help me authenticate the manuscript, but I got Slade's page. What's up?" Kate asked, sitting down next to him.

"Director Cruz called. The assignment involves the art world."

Alexis Cruz, the DCI, referred matters to Slade if they were extremely urgent and of the utmost secrecy or when Slade simply had someone more suited to a particular assignment than she did, which in this instance was the case.

"It's nothing serious," Max explained. "Just a low-level threat for you to handle in Europe." Grabbing the back of Kate's chair, he slid it closer to his own. "Time to meet your new friend."

A video clip began playing on his computer screen. Two middle-aged men were dining together. One was Middle Eastern, the other Caucasian.

"I may have seen the guy on the left before," Kate said, looking closely at the slim Persian man's familiar features—short receding dark hair, a smoothly shaven fine-boned face, and large wide-set brown eyes.

"That's Hamid Azadi. Very senior guy at VEVAK," Max said, referring to Iran's Ministry of Intelligence and Security, the Vezarat-e Ettela'at va Amniat-e Keshvar. "Believed to be their counterintelligence chief."

Gesturing to the video, Kate asked, "Agency footage?"

"Yup. Taped two weeks ago in Dubai. No audio, though. The restaurant was loud and they were too far from the window."

"And the other guy?"

"Luca de Tolomei. Billionaire art dealer. Heard of him?"

"Yeah," Kate said, staring at de Tolomei's profile—a long straight nose, sharp jaw, and steel-gray shoulder-length hair. "Rumor has it he deals on the black market now and then."

"Right. So as far as we're concerned, he's been considered harmless."

"Until . . ."

"This afternoon, when an eleven-million-dollar wire transfer from de Tolomei was traced to Azadi's Liechtenstein account. It set off a red flag at the Agency."

"Eleven million," Kate repeated.

"I took a look at the route myself," Max said. "I've never seen money washed so many times. The cash toured the islands like a cruise ship. Cyprus, Antigua, the Isle of Man . . ."

"So, the question is, what exactly did de Tolomei buy from Azadi, and why?"

"Bingo. If Azadi wanted to get something nasty to terrorists, a guy like de Tolomei would make a great cutout. A rich Catholic art dealer? He'd be perfect."

"But Iran *gives* weapons to Hezbollah and Hamas all the time, along with hundreds of millions of dollars a year—they don't *charge* those guys."

"Unless it's a rogue thing and Azadi's in business for himself, making a sale to a group Iran doesn't sponsor. He could easily have squirreled away some nerve gas, and what government employee wouldn't like a little extra cash?"

"Maybe, but I have a hard time picturing the bad boy of the Sotheby's set rubbing shoulders with terrorist thugs," Kate said. "My guess is de Tolomei's buying Persian antiquities on the black market. Those deals can run into the tens of millions. Someone almost laid out more than forty for the first Persian mummy ever found."

"Almost?"

"It was fake. Persians didn't mummify. Maybe Azadi's connected to an antiquity smuggling ring—or better yet, some counterfeiters. You know, to dupe collectors from the Great Satan."

"That could be it," Slade said, walking into the conference room. "But we have to be sure."

He set a tray of cappuccinos on the table. Perfectly swirled foam peaks—lightly dusted with cinnamon—rose impressively from each mug.

Kate reached for one and took a sip.

Slade raised an eyebrow.

She clutched her stomach for a moment, pretending to be queasy, then smiled. "Boss, you've outdone yourself."

Taking a seat, he leaned back with a deeply dimpled grin.

Kate turned to Max's computer screen once more. "What do we have on de Tolomei, other than his friendship with Azadi?"

"Why do you put it that way?" Slade asked. "These two have never been spotted together before."

Kate reached over to Max's keyboard, struck a key, and the dinner scene began to replay. A moment later, she pointed to the first telltale gesture. "Right there," she said. "De Tolomei pushes the ashtray toward Azadi before he pulls out his cigarettes." She paused for a minute as the video continued. "And check that out—de Tolomei stops eating, looks around, and Azadi asks the waiter for something before de Tolomei says anything." Another pause. "See? The waiter just brought pepper. Azadi didn't ask for salt—he knew what de Tolomei wanted. They know each other's habits too well to be strangers."

Slade turned to Max. "Tell her what you've found in the past hour."

"It's not much," Max said, as a few images of de Tolomei popped up on the computer screen. "It's slower going than usual because—well, he's kinda like that Persian mummy. A fake. I did some digging, and a Luca de Tolomei died in a private loony bin almost two decades ago. His parents never admitted he was there—they pretended he was out of the country—and now they're dead, too. It looks like our dude assumed that identity around 1991."

Looking at Kate, Max added, "Good choice for a legend."

She nodded. The best fake identities, or legends, were taken from real people who died quietly or disappeared from home, leaving little trace.

Max went on. "The guy's got a palazzo in Rome and a refurbished medieval castle on Capri."

"You're kidding me—a villain living on Capri?" Kate marveled. "Talk about a cliché."

"What do you mean?" Max asked.

Slade cleared his throat.

Kate recognized the sound. It meant her boss was in the mood to uncork something from his classical arsenal.

"Tacitus," Slade began, referring to a second-century Roman historian, "described Capri as the place where the emperor Tiberius spent his time in secret orgies or idle malevolent thoughts. It was said that bevies of girls and young men, adept in unnatural practices, were culled from all over the empire to perform before him in glades and grottoes."

"Like Hef," Max said. "I'm impressed."

"He also forced himself on infants. Made them try to, uh . . . nurse him."

Max wrinkled his nose. "Now that's some nasty shit."

"And had traitors tossed from a cliff, and if they weren't crushed on the rocks below, he had them thrashed to death with boat hooks."

"Definitely time to reshuffle," Max said thoughtfully. "That one debuts at . . . number four."

He kept a running list of the worst ways people have died. The number one spot, Kate knew, had been untouched for months. Over a Bloody-Mary brunch one Sunday, she'd told him how during the reign of the drink's namesake—the queen of England before Elizabeth I—Protestant "heretics" were burned at the stake so slowly sometimes, on account of inept executioners using green wood and wet rushes, that one woman gave birth and watched her baby die in the flames before succumbing herself.

"The past few centuries," Slade finished, "the lovely isle has remained notorious for behavior that would make the residents of Sodom and Gomorrah blush."

"So," Kate said, getting back to business, "we've got a billionaire buying contraband from one of the world's biggest troublemakers, and we have no idea who he really is?"

"Nary a clue," Slade replied. "Which has to change. Max will be working his magic, of course, looking into de Tolomei's associates, and with you in Europe anyway—"

"What about our people in Rome?" Kate cut in. "They could break into his palazzo, plant some bugs . . ."

"Kate, a billionaire who keeps company with the likes of Azadi will have the best security on the planet," Slade responded. "Break-ins like that take weeks of surveillance and planning. Who knows if we have that much time. Not to mention the fact that strong-arm tactics may not do the trick here. This is the kind of guy who doesn't keep all his secrets in little metal boxes."

"Oh, I see where this is going," she said wryly.

Max's eyes twinkled. "You don't use guys in black jumpsuits and night-vision goggles to break into a man's head. You use a hot chick in heels."

Slade flashed one of his trademark split-second grins, then his features dropped back into seriousness. "In the meantime, our people in Rome will use directional mikes on him and make inquiries, but they won't approach him directly. As good as they are, to a man like de Tolomei they could seem a little obvious. You, on the other hand . . ."

TEHRAN, IRAN — 3:05 A.M.

At that moment, Hamid Azadi, chief of counterintelligence for VEVAK, was at home alone in north Tehran's posh Gheitarieh district, humming softly in his calfskin desk chair. It was Azadi's favorite time of the week, the few minutes he savored with pure, uncut satisfaction. Never on the same day, never at the same hour, but once a week, without fail, he indulged. And during those treasured minutes, he felt like Sisyphus relaxing at the top of his hill, leaning against his rock, enjoying a thirty-year-old single malt Glenmorangie on ice.

Azadi unlocked the bottom right drawer of his black wooden desk and pulled it open. It was a file drawer, about two-thirds full. He pushed the files to the far end of the drawer and slipped his letter opener into the crack where the drawer's face met its false bottom. Made of half-inch-thick black rubber, the panel was flexible, and prying up the edge closest to him, Azadi slipped his hand beneath. From the thin pocket of hidden space, he withdrew a satellite phone. A phone he reserved solely for this special indulgence.

The power on, the encryption functioning, Azadi dialed.

A familiar voice answered, and Azadi recited the thirteen digits he knew as well as his own name. His password. The voice asked him a series of questions and Azadi provided the necessary answers, answers that varied with each day of the week.

"Good. Now, how may I help you this evening, monsieur?"

"I'd like to check my balance, please," Azadi said softly.

"Thirteen million, two hundred thousand U.S. dollars. Will there be anything else?"

"Not today."

The money at the discreet private bank in Liechtenstein was Azadi's parachute to paradise, to a new life free of the limitations and constant fear of his current one. Decades before, during his final year of university, Azadi had chosen his path into the upper echelons of Iran's Ministry of Intelligence and Security because there were few other options open to an intellectual, ambitious Iranian. Plus, he had to concede, he'd been swept up in a romance with national pride, having watched his countrymen yank the rug from beneath the corrupt Shah and his brutal secret police, along with their bloodsucking imperialist backers. War was raging with Iraq at the time, and when he got his first taste of intelligence work, of striving to outwit that camel's ass Saddam, he was sure he'd found his calling.

As the years passed, however, he'd slowly come to loathe the mullahs who ruled his country with steel-tipped whips. They had proven to be far more brutal than the Shah had been, with their constant use of torture, steady stream of assassinations, and plotting of mass murder around the globe. Ultimately Azadi had decided to leave. In truth, he had no choice. For him, time was running out.

Money was his first requirement. Heaps of it. So when he met Luca de Tolomei years ago and heard the man's initial proposition, Azadi did not require extensive persuasion. They quickly entered into a highly profitable business relationship, and Azadi's secret account had grown steadily. Their most recent transaction had been the real coup. A tremendous and unexpected bonanza. He knew the item was valuable but had not anticipated that de Tolomei would offer quite so much—eleven million dollars. Praise Allah for the peculiar art dealer and his bottomless bank accounts.

At last, Azadi had enough to make his move, and conveniently de Tolomei—now a trusted friend—had sweetened their deal with two perks: several sets of expertly made fake papers with different identities and an appointment with a discreet and top-notch plastic surgeon, from whom he would get not only a new face but a new ethnicity.

Azadi's defection had to be undertaken very carefully. The Committee for Secret Operations would send an elite team of assassins for him, and Azadi did not want to spend the rest of his life looking over his shoulder and beneath his car.

He was going to move to a small island off the coast of America called Key West, because there, he'd been told, men could kiss in the street and not fear a lashing. And if the mood was right, they could go home with their lover and not risk death by stoning.

THE MEDITERRANEAN SEA—1:16 A.M.

The ship was Russian. Her name was *Nadezhda*, and she was one of 240 oil-laden vessels slicing through Mediterranean waters that night. The *Nadezhda*, however, was no ordinary carrier of oil. The 138-meter river-sea tanker was owned by a member of the Russian *mafiya*, and her oil was a cover for the smuggling of contraband.

During the 1990s, oil itself had been her contraband. Operating primarily in the Persian Gulf, carrying barrels of crude from the Iraqi port of Umm Qasr to the United Arab Emirates, she'd repeatedly violated the U.N. embargo imposed after Iraq's invasion of Kuwait. With the international Maritime Interception Force patrolling the Gulf to enforce that embargo, the *Nadezhda*'s master had done what all clever smugglers of Iraqi oil did: bribe the Iranian Navy for false documents of origin for the oil. It had been enormously profitable, because Russian-flagged ships were almost never stopped. But then, in early 2000, the MIF boarded another Russian ship doing the exact same thing and delivered samples of her oil to a special lab where biomarkers and gas chromatography tests proved it had come from an Iraqi well. When the MIF decided to confiscate not only the oil but the ship itself, the *Nadezhda*'s owner had opted out of the business.

Now she really did carry Iranian oil. Nearly five thousand tons of it. But in two special compartments built into the lowest point of her hull—accessible only to divers—Afghan heroin and Stingers for Hezbollah lay hidden.

After leaving the Iranian port of Bandar Abbas ten days before, the *Nadezhda* had passed through the Strait of Hormuz and cruised north through the Red Sea to the Suez Canal. From there she had slipped into the Mediterranean the previous evening.

Upon her foredeck, the young navigation officer paced, unable to sleep. He had never felt so nervous in his life. A storm had hit when they were in the Red Sea, and he'd retched until the very last raindrop had fallen. After loading their barrels of crude in Bandar Abbas, he and three other crewmen had been instructed to carry a mysterious wooden crate to the master's cabin. The master told them to carry it with extreme caution, as if it contained priceless porcelain . . . or a nuclear bomb. Then the master had winked. What did that wink mean? Were they really transporting a bomb, or did the master simply enjoy making his crewmen sweat, perhaps to impress his new girlfriend?

Staring into the night sky, the navigation officer prayed for the moment when they would unload the menacing crate. It would happen soon, he'd been told, long before they reached their destination. There would be an open-sea transfer, and finally he would be able to rest.

As he continued to gaze up at the stars, the *Nadezhda*'s navigation officer had no way of knowing that he was looking right into the electronic eyes of a fifty-foot-long billion-dollar bird—an American spy satellite flying 120 miles overhead. Called a KH-12, it was a member of the keyhole class of satellites, whose high-resolution electro-optical cameras collected pictures of a swath of the earth's surface several hundred miles wide, detecting objects as small as four inches in size.

Nor did the navigation officer have a way of knowing that the KH-12, cruising along its sun-synchronous orbit, would pass over the very same spot the following night and collect images of his ship off-loading its mysterious crate. For no matter how fast she traveled over the course of the next day, no matter what the weather conditions or time of day, the *Nadezhda*'s open-sea transfer would not escape the satellite's prying eyes.

6

Admir'd I am of those that hate me most.

—MACHIAVEL, in Marlowe's *The Jew of Malta*

LONDON—NIGHT, MAY 1593

*T*he twenty-foot canopied barge glided silently along the Thames. The river was quiet. Most of London was sleeping.

Just ahead, the Tower. Thick, crenellated stone walls. Smooth but for the arrow slits hewn in. How many eyes, the master wondered, were peering out from those ominous black fissures? And could any of them see his face? He lowered his hat.

Turning abruptly to the left, the barge slid into a narrow waterway in the middle of Tower Wharf, heading for a set of latticed wooden doors. The feared archway known far and wide as Traitors' Gate.

The stench was overwhelming. Garbage and sewage floating downriver tended to collect in the moat and remain to rot. Holding his ornately carved silver pomander to his nose, the master breathed in deeply, filling his nostrils with the rich scent of cloves.

In the murky darkness beneath St. Thomas's Tower, the barge pulled up to a paved road running parallel to the moat. A stout white-haired man was standing on its edge, with six large wooden crates stacked beside him. The old man nodded at the barge's master, and the master nodded back. While two of the oarsmen used their paddles and lengths of rope to hold their craft steady, the others labored to transfer the heavy crates, arranging them in a single row beneath the barge's overhead canopy.

His arms folded across his chest, the master watched with approval. The whole operation—though effectively illuminated by moonlight—was concealed beneath St. Thomas's Tower. Even if someone wished to report the arrival and departure of his vessel, he would not find it an easy task; it bore no name, and the oarsmen wore no distinctive livery.

When the transfer was complete, he began to inspect each crate. Prying open the first, he saw a triple-barreled cannon from the time of Henry VIII. A *beauty*. He ran a finger along the smooth, cold bronze.

The second crate contained two swivel guns—the kind typically mounted on warships—the third held gunpowder, and the fourth, bullets of lead. Then finally, in the last two, his favorite products from the White Tower's Royal Armory: wheel-lock pistols made of walnut, brass, and staghorn. The old guns had undoubtedly been imported from Germany years ago; he could make out town marks for Dresden and Nuremberg on the barrels. He picked one up and with a swift pivot pointed it straight into the face of one of his men. The poor bastard nearly lost his dinner.

Laughing, the master replaced the gun and reached up to shake hands with the white-haired man. "Until next time."

At their master's nod, the oarsmen backed their vessel out into the river, came about, and continued east on their way to Deptford.

Leaning back in his cushioned seat, the master toyed with the ends of his mustache. He had just successfully raided the queen's armory on behalf of his employer. Which meant that his employer, however indirectly, was stealing from the queen. Well, he would steal from his employer. When his men were offloading the first few crates, he would conceal a dozen pistols beneath the cushions of his seat. Lie to the liars, cheat the cheaters. *That* was how the game was played.

Back on Tower Wharf, the white-haired man stood watching the barge melt into the night. His hands, clenched into fists, were trembling. He did not know who owned the nameless barge, or where it was headed with its deadly cargo. All he knew was that no matter how much he wanted to, he could not stop it.

Ned Smyth was Her Majesty's Master of the Ordnance, keeper of the Royal Armory in the White Tower. The mysterious barge master had approached him six months earlier, explaining that he worked for one of the queen's battle commanders in the Netherlands. The man had then produced a written request for a shipment of weapons. The letter appeared to be legitimate, and by the time Smyth realized he'd been duped—that the letter was forged and that the battle commander it named did not exist—the unauthorized shipment had already been delivered.

At that point Smyth was trapped. He could not tell his queen what had happened because he had no way of proving that he had behaved with the best of intentions; the wily barge master had kept his forged letter. To make matters worse, the villainous dog had said that if Smyth refused to cooperate and hand over additional armaments upon demand, he would go straight to the queen and accuse Smyth of selling items from the Royal Armory for personal profit, and how could Smyth prove otherwise? The inventory *was* missing.

Smyth strode angrily along the wharf. Part of him yearned to confess and pray for forgiveness, but he knew it was too late. He had just committed his third act of treachery. Besides, he might be afraid of his disloyalty coming to light, but he was far more afraid of the barge master. No doubt that man would kill anyone who stood in his way.

With that unpleasant thought, the queen's trusted servant passed through the Tower's west gate and continued on his way home. No one stopped him. No one asked to see his identification. All the guards had known Smyth for years and, believing him to be a man of integrity, never questioned him. Not even in the middle of the night.

The barge master had chosen his reluctant accomplice well.

GREENWICH—NIGHT

Long after Thomas Phelippes had disappeared from sight, Marlowe remained on the wooden bench near Greenwich Palace. If Phelippes's suspicions were true, and certain merchants with the Muscovy Company had discovered a secret sea route to the Orient, what were they trading in exchange for the gems? Definitely not English silver. There was little use for that in the Far East. They must be embezzling the company's exports, he figured. Woolen cloth, in all likelihood. Or perhaps not—perhaps they were using another commodity, from a different source.

Our weaponry remains far more advanced than what they have in the

Orient, Marlowe thought to himself. Were Muscovy men facilitating massacres in remote corners of the world again?

Marlowe was one of the few people in London who knew that several of the company's directors had orchestrated the smuggling of surplus English armaments aboard their ships years before. Unbeknownst to Phelippes, Marlowe's distant cousin Anthony was the general manager of the company's London warehouse—had been for nearly two decades. A loyal functionary paid handsomely to keep his mouth shut, Anthony had once made the mistake of bragging about the fact that he was privy to a shocking company secret, a secret he swore he'd never reveal. Anthony's mistake was a grave one, because Marlowe was never able to leave such a stone unturned, even if no payment was involved. From the moment he heard Anthony's boast, that so-called secret was about as safe as a rabbit cornered by a hungry dog.

Wanting to give his cousin time to forget their conversation, Marlowe had waited more than a month to do battle with Anthony's steadfast, determined silence. Then, courtesy of a simple but elegant plan, it had only required one night, one clever whore, and a small armada of ale cups to loosen his smug cousin's lips.

That night was seven years ago, when Marlowe was still a student at Cambridge. He'd traveled to London for a weekend and had met Anthony at a popular Southwark tavern, asking questions about everything *but* the Muscovy Company. On that subject he feigned a lack of interest. Then, as soon as Anthony was drunk to the point of slurring, Marlowe pretended to leave but hid behind a thick wooden beam instead. He had paid a beautiful, quick-witted whore to sidle up to his cousin and seductively murmur a few carefully memorized lines, then follow them up with any questions she could think of.

"I hear you do *very* important work," she had begun, batting her eyelashes.

"Oh, I shouldn't . . ." Anthony had stammered, blushing.

"They say you work with *powerful* men. Men who have the queen's ear. Is it true?"

"Well, I, uh . . ."

She put her hand on his knee.

"Yes. I . . . I do."

"Oh, how that fires my fancy! Is it dangerous?" she asked, sliding her hand up Anthony's leg.

"Truly. You would not . . . oh, my."

She caressed his inner thigh. "Hmm?"

"You would not believe what I'm involved in."

"Oh, how I should love to know." Leaning in closely to suck on Anthony's earlobe, the whore glanced at Marlowe, who nodded, pleased.

Anthony—now with a hand unfastening the front of his breeches—seemed pleased, too. "You could say that, well, that . . ." He paused for a moment, searching for the right words. Looking down, they came to him. "You could say I have held the fates of entire cities in *my* hands."

The whore gasped dramatically, then whispered, "I wonder if you're as good with them as I?" She tugged at the seeming deadweight of one of his arms, placing his hand on her breasts.

He groped clumsily, trying to pinch her.

"Mmm . . . tell me," she sighed, feigning near ecstatic pleasure. "Tell me everything."

Belching, Anthony shook his head. "I would like to, but I cannot. You see, I—"

"Oh, but you must! Powerful men, men who face danger—oh, how they make my heart pound! My knees tremble!" With a purr, she climbed onto Anthony's lap, wrapped her legs around his waist, and demonstrated exactly how she might tremble.

"Forgive me, but—"

"If I thought you were a man like that, a fearless, dangerous man, why, I wouldn't charge you a penny to . . ."

Ah, the coup de grâce. In addition to being tight-lipped, Anthony was incredibly tightfisted. *No doubt that will push him over the edge.*

Marlowe's hunch proved correct. Anthony told the whore everything he knew about the Muscovy Company's secret operation that night, and she, delighted to earn silver with her clothes on for once, repeated it all back to Marlowe as soon as Anthony fell to snoring.

For decades, she reported, the company had secretly supplied Ivan, then czar of Russia, with the weapons he had used for his terrible massacres.

"Who was involved?" Marlowe had asked.

She mentioned a wealthy merchant and a prominent government official, both of whom had been dead for years. Marlowe did not blink. But when she named the third man, a man who was still alive, his mouth fell open. It was Francis Walsingham, his admired mentor. Having read eye-witness accounts of Ivan's atrocities, said to have been unprecedented in their scope and brutality, Marlowe shook his head with disgust.

According to Anthony's drunken ramblings, supplying Ivan with weapons was the only way to secure the company's monopoly on trade with Russia, a monopoly that was considered too valuable to lose. And England had a vast supply of surplus armaments, so why not? Under-standably the leaders of the Baltic States had been furious with Queen Elizabeth for arming their bloodthirsty neighbor. She denied the accusa-tion, but to mollify her allies had issued a specific proclamation forbidding the trade. The shipments had continued without interruption, however, and in spite of a few well-placed questions, Anthony had never determined whether the queen had been secretly authorizing them all along.

Marlowe had cursed loudly as he walked back to his inn that night. Vi-cious murders and the mass slaughtering of innocents might draw crowds to the stage, but he did not wish to help create them in real life. Disillu-sioned, he'd considered leaving Walsingham's employ. Ultimately, though, he'd resolved to stay, planning to carry out assignments in his own way, doing what he thought was right. It was a delicate balance to maintain—satisfying his handlers while operating according to his own set of principles—but somehow, he was managing it. All for a queen and a country he consciously romanticized. It was senseless, he knew, and dangerous. Doomed to an unpleasant end. But so was life.

Now today, certain Muscovy men might have yet another illicit scheme under way. But who? There were dozens of possibilities, Mar-lowe realized. It was likely that most, if not all, of the wealthiest and most powerful men in London were involved with the company, either as shareholders or directors. If a select few had, indeed, revived the illicit weapons trade to acquire Oriental goods, how to identify them? All the players in the old scheme were dead.

Marlowe knew he had no hope of tricking information out of his cousin again. Seven years had passed, but Anthony still scowled every time he saw Marlowe's face, sometimes even grabbed the hilt of his sword. *Perhaps if I hadn't taunted him the next morning, reminding him in exquisite detail precisely how he'd been so thoroughly bested . . .*

It then occurred to Marlowe that Essex, a company shareholder himself, could be involved. That Phelippes might have hired him to see how effectively Essex and his fellow conspirators were concealing their scheme.

He was mulling over that possibility when several faint shouts cut through the quiet evening air. Curious, he stood and headed toward the noise, moving quickly but quietly beneath the thick tree cover.

It was coming from the uppermost floor of the palace's south wall. The stables would give him a perfect line of sight into the room in question, but how to scale the tall smooth walls? He noticed one small window just beneath the stable's rooftop. After entering the building, he slipped past the sleeping stable boy and positioned a ladder beneath the window. Then he climbed up, shimmied out the window, and hoisted himself onto the roof.

Immediately his eyes shot upward to see two figures silhouetted in a window nestled in a tower at the peak of the south wall. A man and a woman. Both appeared to be quite tall—the man was broad and impressively built, the woman thin and bent, her skirts voluminous. Her thick, snakelike ringlets whirled about as she slapped the man's face and pummeled his chest. He stormed out. "Robert! Robert, come back here at once!" she cried.

With a start, Marlowe realized who they were. Elizabeth and Essex. The queen and her handsome young paramour. She disappeared from Marlowe's line of sight for a moment, but he remained riveted to the window. Suddenly there was a flash of silver, and then another. The muslin curtain floated to the ground in tatters, and Marlowe saw the queen standing before the window clutching a sword, her jewel-encrusted collar glittering in the moonlight.

Elizabeth's pale face was twisted with rage. Her dark red wig was slightly askew, revealing some of the thin gray hair beneath. Marlowe retrieved his trick coin for the second time that day and held its face to the light. "You're more stately on your money than you are in your bedchamber, aren't you, my queen?"

Turning his gaze to the window once more, he saw that her features had settled. The queen appeared calm. Only the dark streaks in her thick alabaster makeup revealed the previous moment's anguish. She disappeared again, and a moment later, sweet musical strains floated out from her rooms.

A cluster of musicians must be standing just out of sight, Marlowe thought, watching a figure sashay to the delicate lute music. The movements alternated between a pleasing fluidity and an almost violent sharpness. The figure's face flashed by the window. It was the queen, and she was dancing alone.

Marlowe looked down at his feet and surveyed the gently sloping roof of the stables. He was standing on its peak. Extending his arms, puffing out his chest, and cocking his head slightly, he began to move. Navigating the awkward surface with deft footwork, he was managing a precarious, though still graceful, pavane in time with his sovereign.

Suddenly Essex burst back into the room, grabbed the queen by her shoulders, and kissed her roughly.

"Excuse me, but you may not cut in," Marlowe said softly, with mock severity.

Elizabeth pushed Essex away and pointed her finger at the door. After her crestfallen courtier slunk out, she stood stock-still. The musicians had paused.

Down below on the stable roof, Marlowe held out his arm and bowed. "Shall we?" he asked.

Up above, the queen began to move briskly as the music started up again, unknowingly joining Marlowe in a lively galliard.

Pushing through Greenwich Palace's heavy front doors, Robert Devereux, the second Earl of Essex, dashed down the water steps to his barge and shook his men awake.

Well aware of their employer's mercurial nature and volatile relationship with the queen, they had wisely chosen to sleep on the boat instead of in the palace. Groggily they stumbled to their feet, took their positions, and began to row.

Too upset to sit, Essex paced the length of his barge. "Damn her false promises!" he muttered. "A plague on Cecil, a plague on that pathetic creature!"

Passing the sleeping town of Deptford, Essex saw another barge— roughly the same size as his own—pulling up to a small abandoned dock.

A number of large wooden crates were stacked on board. Was it a wealthy Londoner fleeing the recent outbreak of plague? Essex wondered. Transporting his most valuable possessions to a country home for the summer? Noticing that the barge was unnamed, he also saw that the oarsmen were not dressed in the livery of anyone he knew. In fact, they were not in livery at all. Their clothing was ordinary and mismatched. Essex narrowed his eyes. Didn't everyone capable of purchasing such a vessel wish the world to know? *How very odd.*

With Deptford out of sight, Essex's thoughts returned to the queen and to the praise she'd showered upon his enemy that evening. Once again she had refused to name him secretary of state, suggesting he had yet to prove himself more capable than Robert Cecil. Why couldn't she see that a man of action—a man who'd fought the enemy on the battlefield—was far more suited to the position than a faint-hearted penman?

Essex resumed his pacing and cursing.

Twenty minutes later, he was standing in the great hall of his London mansion, facing a wooden board with a painting tacked upon it. Gripping the tip of a knife, he drew it over his shoulder and threw. Hard. The handle smacked up against the battered image, then clattered to the floor.

Crookbacked whoreson! May God rot his soul!

Breathing deeply, he tried again. The second knife skimmed Robert Cecil's ear, quivering slightly after embedding itself in the board.

Not good enough. For several minutes, Essex stared at those hateful eyes, at the dark half-moons etched beneath.

Then he threw the third knife. Perfect. *Soon.*

7

Kate was aiming for his head. He drew closer. She blocked his two quick jabs, pivoted on the ball of her left foot, and with her right knee up in the air, snapped her foot forward.

Just before contact, Slade grabbed her ankle and, in spite of the sweaty slickness, held it firmly in the air. "Eyes, Kate. What do I always tell you?"

"Peripheral vision, disguise my intent. I remember, boss, it's just that I'm about to collapse."

"Excuses like that won't save your life."

"Right. May I have my leg back please?"

"Until next time."

Back on two feet, Kate threw off her gloves and smoothed back her hair, pulling it into a ponytail. "You know, if you weren't my revered elder, the legend of the spook world, and, yes, my personal hero . . ." She took a step toward him. "Well, if all that weren't the case, I'd tell you that one of these days, I'm gonna kick your ass."

Slade flashed a grin. "I'm waiting." Turning and moving to the edge of the sparring ring, he slid into his Nike flip-flops, bent to retrieve his gym bag, and added, "I've been waiting for a while."

Kate had been studying martial arts since she was a teenager and had spent years teaching kickboxing to make extra money during college and grad school, but her ability was still no match for Slade's. Glaring at the well-muscled V-shaped back outlined by his formfitting blue T-shirt, she said, "Well, the truth is, I've been holding back, you know, to spare your ego for a while, but—"

"You're too kind." Slade reached into his gym bag, withdrew a bottle of water, and handed it over. Kate took a drink and grabbed her things, and they strolled from the gym into the cool evening air.

"You fly to London for Medina's case . . . tomorrow?"

"Yeah, probably the last flight out," Kate said. "In the morning I'm meeting a source to plan my encounter with de Tolomei, then—"

"That Sotheby's guy?"

"Right. Later in the afternoon, I'm briefing Medina on the progress I've made up to that point."

"You feel okay with this juggling? If you weren't so well matched for both assignments . . ."

"Hey, it ain't juggling if you only got two balls in the air."

Slade smiled, then looked pointedly at the injury on Kate's neck. "Stay in better touch this time, all right? You shouldn't have gone in alone last night. If I'd known—"

"Yes, sir. Will do, sir," she responded playfully.

Slade stopped to face her. "I'm serious, Kate. You were almost killed."

"I know. I'll be careful."

"You say that every time."

"If it weren't true, there wouldn't be an every time," Kate teased.

Slade sighed.

"Oh, come on. You know I do whatever you say. You're talking to someone who's literally followed you over a cliff."

"Good point."

Throwing a light punch to his shoulder, she added, "And I'll do it again, whenever you ask."

"That won't be necessary any time soon," Slade said gently. "But I've got a heap of dirty laundry the size of Texas and a pair of shoes that could use a good pol—"

"See you tomorrow, boss."

Forty minutes and a quick shower later, Kate was in Greenwich Village, sitting in the musty, dimly lit basement shop of a rare-book dealer she'd been friendly with for years. The old dealer, Hannah Rosenberg, had a messy gray bun and was twirling an errant tendril while examining the binding of Medina's manuscript through a pair of crooked gold-framed glasses.

"Oh, this was beautifully stitched . . . black morocco leather, very expensive at the time. This type of gold tooling was a new, fashionable technique in Tudor England . . ."

Kate reminded herself to breathe. "What do you make of the paper?"

Opening the volume, Hannah began to leaf through it, pausing now and then to study certain pages against the light of a low-watt lamp. "Hmm." She reached for her fiber-optic light pen, put on a pair of tinted goggles, and continued her examination.

Knowing the process could take a while, Kate stood to peruse the glass-fronted cabinets of antique books lining the shop walls.

"Mind getting me a glass of wine?" Hannah asked. She lived in the floors above her shop.

"Not at all." Kate slid out the door, her heart pounding.

"Good news, dear," Hannah said, when Kate returned with two glasses of Merlot. "I'd say your theory fits."

"What do you mean?"

"Well, to start with, the binding, the paper, and the ink—they're each right for the time period. This is definitely a collection of pages written on different kinds of sixteenth-century paper by what appear to be many different people. The paper itself is from all over Europe. Hardly any of these pages come from the same batch as the ones next to them, and that's highly unusual for any bound manuscript, even a collection of personal letters. The title page is a thick spongy Florentine linen, with a watermark that was used in the 1590s. The next is a far cheaper English rag paper, and I'd say it's much older, maybe by a few decades. The third is Venetian parchment. Also appears much older than the title page."

Taking a seat on the stool across from Hannah, Kate leaned in eagerly. "They get progressively newer, right?"

Hannah nodded. "Very roughly speaking, it appears chronological. I'd need a few days to date each page more precisely."

"Hmm. I need to take this with me, but . . ."

"I think it would make more sense to decipher the content first anyway. If you've got yourself a bunch of soup recipes . . ."

Kate smiled. "True enough."

"In the meantime, we can pretty safely rule out a modern forgery. People forge for profit, and something like this, with so many different authors and different kinds of paper . . . oh, trying to forge this would be an incredibly expensive, time-consuming nightmare."

Hannah reached into one of the pockets of her rumpled black linen dress, took out a pack of nicotine gum, and popped a piece in her mouth. "If you could convince a buyer this really was a collection of Walsingham's missing spy reports," she continued, "it would still be worth it, I suppose. A handwritten, one-of-a-kind object of major historical interest? Mmm . . . would probably fetch a couple million. But if your client was after money, he'd have taken it to an auction house or someone like me. Not you."

Kate nodded. "He doesn't need the money anyway. He's just curious why someone's after this. Speaking of which, let's see if Phelippes really wrote that first page."

Kate slipped a folder from her backpack and withdrew several sheets of paper. In grad school, she'd received a travel grant to research Elizabethan espionage in Britain and had microfilmed dozens of documents from different archives and libraries, some of which were penned by Thomas Phelippes. Handing them to Hannah, she said, "Can you compare the handwriting?"

"You're sure Phelippes wouldn't have used a scrivener?"

"Definitely," Kate said. "If these reports are what I think they are, this collection would have been his prized possession, something he would've guarded jealously, never shown to anyone."

Hannah placed the four sheets before her, arranging them around the manuscript, which she opened to the title page. Peering through her magnifying glass, she moved back and forth between the various samples. "It's a perfect match. And you know Elizabethan secretary hand is nearly impossible to forge."

Looking up, Hannah continued, "I can't say with a hundred percent certainty—no one in this business can—but I think Phelippes did write this. That he gathered this collection of coded, uh, somethings and had them bound somewhere in London. But to determine whether the rest of the pages are from Walsingham's missing files? That's up to you."

Closing the manuscript, Hannah handed it over.

As Kate started to put it back in its pewter box, Hannah said quickly, "Wait a minute. Let me see that again."

Kate complied, and Hannah squinted at the manuscript's back cover, a smile slowly forming on her face.

"What is it?"

"Looks like the binder's work was interrupted," Hannah said, laying the manuscript between them with the back cover facing up. She positioned a lamp directly over it. "See those faint impressions?" she asked, pointing to the bottom two corners. "Three in one corner, two in another?"

"Oh, yeah, how did I miss those?" Kate murmured. Five small rosettes, resembling profiles of blooming roses, had been lightly stamped into the black leather, leaving shallow, barely discernable impressions.

"In that period, a skilled binder, an artist like this, usually made far more ornate decorations. I'd guess he was beginning an elaborate design—three rosettes in every corner, probably a large design in the center, more thin stripes, all to be filled with gold leaf . . . but that never happened."

"Because Phelippes was in a rush to hide this!" Kate exclaimed. "As soon as it was discovered that Walsingham's files were missing, Phelippes would've been high on the list of suspects. I bet he put this collection together and hid it immediately, knowing people would search his place. Or maybe . . ."

Kate bit her lip, her mind racing over the possibilities. "Maybe he didn't have it bound right away. Maybe he held on to the whole file collection, to threaten certain people or blackmail them, but got worried one day that someone was coming after the evidence he had against them, *then* ran off to the binder."

"Both sound plausible," Hannah said, nodding.

"You know, I wonder if . . . no, it couldn't be."

"What?"

"Oh, I was just getting carried away, wondering whether the reason Phelippes rushed to hide this back then could be connected to the reason someone wants it now. But that's not possible . . . is it?"

Three blocks from her subway stop in east midtown, Kate turned onto her street and walked quickly toward her apartment building, an ivy-covered brownstone a block in from the East River. She was impatient to decipher as much as she could of *The Anatomy of Secrets* that night. As she climbed the marble steps, her cell phone chirped. It was Max.

"I've been looking into that Jade Dragon email address you gave me," he told her. "I haven't been able to trace it to anyone yet—a series of anonymous remailers were used—but I hacked into Bill Mazur's system and took a look at Jade Dragon's emails. He sent the first one this morning, offering Mazur two thousand dollars to block out the whole day for an unnamed assignment. Mazur replied that he was up for it. Then, while you and Medina were at the Pierre, Jade Dragon sent Mazur a second email naming the location and the task. Mazur was supposed to steal your bag and leave it in a locker at Penn Station."

"So, he must've had someone following Medina, looking for the best time to grab the manuscript, and when we met at the Pierre and were obviously discussing it, he and his associate must've assumed I'd leave with it," Kate speculated. "Probably viewed me as an easy mark."

"Yeah, and they used Mazur as a cutout in case something went wrong. You have any idea who this Jade Dragon dude might be?"

"The same guy who sent a thief to break into Medina's home," Kate said. "Beyond that, I'm not sure, but I'd guess it's a wealthy Brit with something to hide . . . or lose."

"Like what? A title?"

"Maybe. If it came with a valuable estate. Titles are losing their cachet pretty fast over there. But that reminds me, a little while ago I read about a Scottish landowner who was selling a mountain range on the Isle of Skye for more than fifteen million bucks. There was a local uproar for trying to sell what most Scots viewed as a national treasure, but the court ruled he owned it, based on some fifteenth- and seventeenth-century documents. If this manuscript contains some kind of evidence invalidating property ownership on that scale, someone would definitely go to the trouble of trying to steal it."

"I'll say. Hey, what about something to do with the government or the church?"

"Anything directly connected with Elizabeth would be irrelevant since the Tudor line died with her," Kate replied. "But a religious matter—that's an interesting idea."

Max's tone took on a dark, conspiratorial edge. "Maybe there's a report about a saint who was into little boys, and some Vatican thug is desperate to keep it under wraps."

"As if anyone would even raise an eyebrow at this point," Kate said wryly. "But I'll let you know."

"Cracked any of those reports yet?"

"I'm just about to start," she said, unlocking her front door.

"Cool. See you in the morning. And watch your back, Kate. Whoever's after that manuscript? I doubt he's ready to give up."

After saying good night to Max, Kate pulled a small bottle of diet Dr Pepper from her fridge and headed into her living room. With the exception of two walls of built-in bookshelves, the room had the feel of a Moorish harem or an opium den. The walls and ceiling were red, the windows were draped with gauzy gold curtains, mismatched Turkish cushions surrounded her dark wooden coffee table, and the carpet was an old Kilim from her grandmother's house. The end tables were African with carved cobra legs, and the lamps resting upon them had shades an old Florentine craftsman had fashioned from medieval maps, with unusual creatures—dragons with pretty human faces and blond hair—lurking at the edges. It was an eclectic blend of stuff Kate had picked up on her travels, but it worked. At least for her it did—a guest had once asked if her decorator was a crackhead.

Settling onto one of her couches, Kate unzipped her black backpack. It looked ordinary enough but was actually a reinforced computer bag with a built-in alarm. Sliding out Phelippes's box and opening it, she turned to the manuscript's fifth page, the one with the ciphered characters she'd recognized earlier that day in the Pierre.

By today's hi-tech standards, most Elizabethan ciphers and codes would be considered remarkably simple. They typically involved the substitution of invented characters, numbers, or words for various letters and proper names. Robert Cecil's father, for example, Elizabeth's chief adviser, used the signs of the zodiac to represent the different European monarchs and other leading political figures. Another courtier favored the days of the week.

The writing Kate was examining consisted solely of invented symbols. As she'd told Medina in the Pierre, she recognized three of them, characters that had been used to represent England, France, and Spain. But where had she seen them? Racking her brain for a minute, the answer suddenly came to her—the characters were from a cipher key she'd seen at the Public Record Office in London.

Sifting through one of her file cabinets, she found the right folder and, looking at her microfilmed version, located meanings for two additional characters on the page—a sliver moon with a line drawn through it referred to King Philip II of Spain, and two letter *c*'s drawn back to back with a line between them represented the pope.

All five of the symbols she now understood were positioned alone, Kate realized. The others were grouped together. Looking at the characters within each group, she decided that they must stand for letters, that the groups had to be words, with each symbol signifying an English letter. Knowing her computer's decryption software could help her translate the rest of the message, Kate scanned the page into her laptop.

Deciphering the next dozen pages of the manuscript was not so easy. In fact, it was a slow and tedious process. But Kate didn't mind. In a few hours, she was knee-deep in salacious accounts of Renaissance mayhem and murder. She was in heaven.

Her father, on the other hand, was in hell.

WASHINGTON, D.C.—1:24 A.M.

In upper Georgetown, moonlight illuminated a simple yet stately white home. On the fourth floor, Senator Donovan Morgan sat alone in his study in the dark. He was staring, riveted to the poorly made black-and-white video playing on his laptop for the seventh time. It had appeared in his inbox fifteen minutes earlier.

The heavily bruised, emaciated young man on the screen sat on the floor of a filthy prison cell with his head slumped forward. The soles of his feet were crusted with blood, and oozing white stripes zigzagged across them. Track marks on his arms suggested he'd been injected with sodium pentothal or a similar substance, over and over again. A guard came into view, opened the cell door, and began to shout. The prisoner looked up. His open eye was glazed, the other sealed shut by dark swollen flesh. With a shaking hand, Morgan adjusted his mouse. He clicked the STOP button and the scene froze.

It's definitely his face, Morgan thought, studying the features of the spy he had known quite well. But was the video real, he wondered, or had the facial image been lifted from an old photograph? They said he died during the operation. Were they wrong?

The spy had been sent on a mission that Morgan, then the chairman of the Senate's Select Committee on Intelligence, was aware of. Somehow the mission had been compromised and their man had disappeared, his fate unknown until the report of his death came in. Could he still be alive?

Morgan's brief bloom of hope withered quickly. Even if their spy had survived his capture, surely he'd have been executed, shortly after suffering forms of torture far worse than death. Morgan felt responsible; the guilt was overwhelming. Clicking the PLAY button again, he watched the guard grab the young man's bony arm, jerk him to a standing position, and drag him, stumbling, from his cell.

The video over, Morgan leaned back in his chair and turned to gaze out the window. The moon was unusually bright, and it shimmered on the dewdrops clinging to the leaves of his elm tree. But Morgan did not notice. The disturbing images shuffling through his mind had temporarily stolen his sight. A recovering alcoholic, he had not tasted liquor in more than five years, but damn, how he wanted to now.

Picking up the phone, he dialed Jeremy Slade. "We need to meet. It's about Acheron."

8

Your Machiavellian Merchant spoils the state,
Your usury doth leave us all for dead,
Your artifex & craftsman works our fate,
And like the Jews you eat us up as bread.

Since words nor threats nor any other thing
Can make you to avoid this certain ill,
We'll cut your throats, in your temples praying,
Not Paris massacre so much blood did spill.

—signed "Tamburlaine," author unknown

LONDON—NIGHT, MAY 1593

For a moment, the spy lingered in a shadow, scanning the street for passersby. No one. Good. He drew closer.

His destination soon came into view—a small church attended by the neighborhood's Dutch immigrants, the thieving dogs who stole jobs from good Englishmen. Leaning around the corner of the adjacent building, he squinted into the churchyard. It was empty. He moved in.

From beneath his doublet, he withdrew a parchment scroll that felt as heavy as iron. If he were caught with it, his employer would look the other way and he'd find himself in shackles. Fingers trembling, he unfurled the fifty-three-line poem and nailed it to the church wall.

Threatening London's immigrants with murder, his clever rhymes would strike great fear in Dutch hearts. They would also, the spy knew, throw Kit Marlowe into a deep cauldron of trouble. For the hateful poem, signed "Tamburlaine," made other references to Marlowe's plays, and the authorities would no doubt conclude that the popular playmaker was a pernicious influence on society, a miscreant who inspired the masses to violence and murder.

Immediately the spy's eyes jumped to his favorite lines. Unable to resist reading them one last time, he whispered softly, " 'We'll cut your throats, in your temples praying, / Not Paris massacre so much blood did spill.' " Perfect, he thought with pride. Marlowe's most recent play, *The Massacre at Paris*—about the slaughter of French Protestants on St. Bartholomew's Day in 1572—had debuted at the Rose that very winter, just before an outbreak of plague had forced the playhouses to shut their doors. No one could miss his reference to Marlowe's title. *Massacre* had been the most heavily attended play of the year. And it was, the spy had to admit, a truly marvelous one—a series of murderous spectacles that set your blood afire.

The spy did not know why his employer was so eager to bring about Marlowe's doom, but this poem would very likely do it. Similar anti-immigrant writings had been appearing around town for more than a month—all anonymous—and the Privy Council had appointed a special five-man commission to track down the culprits. The last thing the government wanted was more rioting in London's streets. Beyond that, the queen was said to be personally outraged, as she considered the immigrants—fellow Protestants who'd fled their war-torn homelands—to be her friends. And so, to root out those who'd offended her, wrists would be shackled, joints would be snapped, and bones would be crushed.

Slipping from the churchyard, he resisted his impulse to break into a run. It would not do to attract attention, but he desperately wanted to be at home in bed, far from this neighborhood, come sunup.

GREENWICH — MORNING

The cloud-capped towers of Greenwich Palace receded behind as Marlowe strolled west along the Thames to Deptford, the port town where soldiers, traders, explorers, and pirates converged. A brief but intense storm had just passed, and glistening raindrops clung to the new green buds of spring. With stray gusts of wind, slender tree branches shivered. Marlowe watched the lingering droplets plummet and merge with the puddles in the carriage ruts along the road.

Crossing the wooden bridge over Deptford Creek, he headed past the green on his way to a familiar tavern. The normally rowdy town felt crammed beyond capacity. Greenwich overflow, Marlowe figured, along with Londoners fleeing the spring's furious bout of plague. As he rounded a bend, the bawdily decorated sign for the Cardinal's Hat appeared. On his way inside, a few French and Italian phrases drifted past Marlowe's ears—probably voices of the foreign dancers and musicians who walked the Deptford streets by day and performed before the queen at Greenwich by night.

In the back corner of the tavern, Marlowe spotted the friend he was looking for at his usual table. Not that he could see his friend's face. On the contrary, the man's head was obscured from view by a curvaceous woman with long flame-colored hair and a low-cut bodice. What Marlowe did recognize was the fleshy hand squeezing the woman's bottom.

Sixty-year-old Oliver Fitzwilliam was known to his friends as Fitz Fat because his father, William, had been enormous, too. The nickname literally meant "son of fat." He was one of Her Majesty's customs officials, though not her most loyal; he took more bribes than trips to the chamberpot and ran a book-smuggling operation on the side.

The woman swatted his arm away from her, slammed a tankard down onto the table—so forcefully that amber liquid sloshed over the edges—then stormed off with a curse.

"Kit! Come join me!" Fitzwilliam exclaimed before turning to catch another eyeful of the comely tavern hostess. "She's new. Calls herself Ambrosia. Rightly so—by God, I'd sell my soul to the devil for a night with her."

"I think a few coins might do the trick," Marlowe replied, sliding onto the opposite bench.

Eyes mournful, Fitzwilliam sighed. "She said she wouldn't climb this huge hill of flesh for all the silver in England."

Marlowe struggled to keep a straight face. "Could be a spell of madness. Perhaps the moon has taken possession of her wits."

Still despondent, Fitzwilliam nodded slowly. A moment later, however, he broke into a grin and bellowed out an order for another ale.

Marlowe was not surprised. His friend's moods shifted faster than England's weather in springtime.

"Great big trunk of vile beastliness, that one is," Ambrosia declared, setting down Marlowe's drink.

Unfazed, Fitzwilliam took hold of his tankard and lowered his voice to an excited whisper. "To your dirty little ditties and their spectacular success!"

"To Ovid," Marlowe replied, raising his as well. "God praise his filthy mind. And you, for the safe journey." Fitzwilliam had arranged the shipping for Marlowe's newly printed translations of Ovid's *Amores* as well as their passage through customs.

The two tankards clinked.

" 'What arms and shoulders did I touch and see? / How apt her breasts were to be pressed by me! / How smooth a belly under her waist saw I? / How large a leg, and what a . . . what a . . . ' Uh, 'nice fat thigh'? No, what is it Kit? 'Nice plump thigh'?"

"Well, it's 'lusty' thigh, but if you prefer 'nice and plump,' by all means . . ."

"No, lusty. I like it. I'd advise you to keep it."

"Done. Now tell me, Fitz," Marlowe said, leaning in. "What's new? Come across any smugglers these two weeks past?"

Fitzwilliam ran a finger along the soft flesh of his second chin. "Let's see . . . a spy with messages from the Spanish court sewn into his doublet buttons."

"How'd you catch him?"

"He was masquerading as a lute player. Claimed the Dutch sent him as a gift for the queen's entertainment, but the rascal had a nervous look about him, so I asked him to play a tune, and . . ." Putting his hands over his ears, Fitzwilliam winced.

Marlowe laughed.

"Nothing else out of the ordinary. Several priests tried to sneak in, of course, Latin Bibles strapped beneath their clothes."

"Keeping Bibles out and bringing erotic verses in . . . Fitz, you're a national treasure."

The fat man blushed. "Now, Kit, is this mere curiosity, or are you here on some of your *special* business?"

Fitzwilliam was one of the few people who knew about Marlowe's secret government work and the unusual way in which he carried out his assignments. They'd met years before when Francis Walsingham—who suspected that there was a book-smuggling network operating out of Deptford—sent Marlowe to crack it. Marlowe quickly identified Fitzwilliam as the network's ringleader, but instead of his informing Walsingham, they reached a private agreement. Marlowe wouldn't turn him in; on the contrary, he'd pacify Walsingham by confiscating several crates of banned books and claim that the chief smuggler had fled England for a life of piracy. Fitzwilliam, in turn, would allow Marlowe to use his smuggling network whenever he wanted, though it would, of course, have to operate far more discreetly.

"As a matter of fact," Marlowe said, "I've a few questions for you."

"Have that wanton wench fetch me a cup of Canary, and whatever it is, I'll spill my guts."

"Figuratively, I hope?"

After ordering the wine Fitzwilliam had requested, Marlowe began, "You've mentioned that your father once owned shares in the Muscovy Company. What can you tell me about it?"

"Satan's minions, the lot of them," the fat man said, as if the words tasted like river sludge. "Should all be hanged."

"Mere merchants?"

"They swindled my father out of his fortune. Ruined his reputation."

"How so?"

"He was one of the original investors, helped finance that first doomed voyage to Moscow so many years ago. Three ships set out, but only one reached the Russian court. The others got trapped in the ice. Everyone aboard froze to death." Fitzwilliam shivered. "The northern journey was too difficult for real profits, but my father kept investing anyway. Then one disaster after another—fires in the warehouses, more ships lost, bloody Turks cutting off the land route to Persia—but the merchants shared a dream."

"Of a Northeast Passage?"

"What else? Imagine it, a secret route to the Orient! But a number of years ago, the directors decided to have done with their debt and reissue the company's stock, leaving the original shareholders with no chance of recovering their silver. My father took the matter to court, but the solicitor general was a Muscovy man himself, so . . ." He slammed his fist on the table. "Then they accused him of embezzlement."

"Bastards."

"No hole in hell is hot enough for them. Good thing I could feed the family myself by then. Got my start smuggling English Bibles in by the crateload when Bloody Mary was on the throne. Her people kept burning them, so . . ." Fitzwilliam shook his head sadly. "My poor father never took to my business, though. Always wanted to play by the rules. Being branded a cheat broke his heart. He was as sad as Orpheus's lute till the day he died."

They were quiet for a moment, then Marlowe asked, "What about rumors of Muscovy merchants, or anyone else, smuggling in goods from the Orient?"

"Nothing of note. But if those rogues are sneaking something in without giving me a share of the profits . . ."

"When do Muscovy ships next leave Deptford?"

"Month's end a few sail for Russia."

"Just before, if you could check them for anything suspicious—weaponry, perhaps . . ."

"Gladly. Now, Kit, I don't know if this will help, but a young Muscovy sailor passed through customs yesterday. Stepped off one of their ships just in from Rouen. *Said* he was coming ashore to visit his family . . ."

"Rouen?"

"The company exchanges English cloth for paper in France, then ships the paper to Russia."

"You remember his name? His looks?"

"Lee Anderson. A memorable one, he was. Had the face of an angel, looked too young for a sailor. Short marigold hair, thin mustache, leather doublet, I think . . . black, no, tobacco-colored hose, and . . . small gold loops hanging from each ear.

"I found nothing illicit on him," Fitzwilliam continued, "but something about that sailor did not sit right with me. Not that he was fidgety—in fact, that was the problem. Too calm."

"So . . ."

"He had half a dozen gold pieces. I let him in—I just made sure he can't get very far." Fitzwilliam's bland expression shifted into a wolfish grin. "You see, I confiscated his papers. Yes, sir, that little fellow is stuck here like a mouse in a trap."

A few minutes later, Marlowe walked back across the green to Deptford Strand, the riverfront area jammed with warehouses, shipyards, and docks. A buzzing hub of exploration, trade, piracy, and war. Across the river lay the nadir of the Elizabethan underworld, the murky Isle of Dogs, swampy forested terrain with criminals lurking in its shadows and London's sewage lazily licking its shores. The treacherous isle was a stark contrast to the royal luxury of Greenwich Palace twinkling to Marlowe's right, less than a mile downriver.

Standing near the base of the commercial dock, he watched sailors in tassled Monmouth caps unloading bolts of shiny cloth—satin, velvet, gold, and silver lace—and heading toward the clusters of warehouses. Others moved in the opposite direction, hauling crates of what smelled like wool and coal.

Then, a sudden sharp movement. Two young sailors grappling with each other.

The common sight was ignored by everyone else in the vicinity, but it was exactly what Marlowe had been hoping for. He approached them. Standing a few feet away, he cleared his throat loudly.

Surprised, they paused.

"Lads, I have a proposition for you."

They looked at him with confusion.

"I'm guessing it is money you're fighting over, and I will give each of you the offending amount if you will give me a few minutes of your time."

Their eyes narrowed suspiciously.

"You will exchange ten, maybe twenty words with a man up the road, then walk on."

"In truth?"

"Have we an understanding?"

They nodded.

"Tell me, then, you've heard of the *Madre de Dios?*"

They shook their heads.

"About a year ago, English privateers captured a Portuguese carrack, the *Madre de Dios*, as it was returning from the East Indies. Heaped with riches said to be worth three hundred thousand pounds. As the ship docked, everyone who got word went to Dartmouth harbor and pinched what they could. Clouds of pepper, cloves, nutmeg, and Java cinnamon filled the streets. Perfumed people's hair for weeks. And that, my friends, has given me an idea."

Thirty minutes and a dozen rehearsals later, the two formerly belligerent sailors ran toward the Muscovy Company's warehouse and rapped loudly upon the door.

No answer.

They rapped again. A heavyset man appeared, his upper lip curled in a half-snarl.

A napping guard, Marlowe thought to himself. *Perfect . . . appears he is the only one inside.* Marlowe was standing just out of sight, silently coaching his makeshift players.

"Mate, have you a spare bag, an empty box, or—"

"You bloody pains in the backside! Be off!" the guard spat.

Marlowe bit his lip as the guard began to push the door shut. *Stay strong, lads, stay strong.*

One of the sailors grabbed the door and held it open. "Haven't you heard? Jesu, a half-mile downriver—it's like a second *Madre de Dios!* Guarded by a mere two men. If we don't hurry, all its riches will be gone!"

The guard's eyes were sparkling, but he had yet to budge.

It was Marlowe's cue. He raced up wearing a touch of a costume—a sprinkle of pepper in his hair—and asked with urgency, "Did you get the boxes?"

The sailors appeared frantic. "Sir, we were—"

At that moment the guard's nose twitched. He sneezed, then grinned. Flinging the door open, he raced back inside. "We're crammed with inventory, but . . ."

Breathing heavily, the guard reappeared moments later. With a sly smile, he pulled the door shut, then raced off with the lone canvas sack, leaving Marlowe and the sailors to struggle with two heavy wooden boxes.

Or so he thought. Marlowe had something else in mind.

While the sailors departed with their coins, he unlocked the warehouse door with a pair of wooden picks. Twenty minutes until the buffoon of a guard would return, he figured. Stepping into the small office, he knelt before a bookshelf and leafed through a few dozen ledgers. Nothing.

Rummaging through the desk drawers, he found seven scrolls, all sealed. After lighting the office's lone candle, he took a strand of wire from his pocket, held it in the flame, then brought it to the edge of each seal and slipped it through.

Damn. Sloppily written letters from someone—the guard, he supposed—to a woman named Moll. Using the candle flame once more, he warmed both sides of each seal and pressed them back together. No need to leave a trace.

Out amidst the inventory shelves, Marlowe could smell most of the goods destined for Russia—woolen cloth, wine, and currants—while others he could see. Salt and sugar granules dusted the floor, and a few sheets of French paper lay crumpled in the corners. Remembering Fitz Fat's words that a Muscovy ship bearing paper had come into Deptford recently, he began untying the boxes. Each contained two stacks of smooth gleaming paper, positioned side by side. For Marlowe it was a mouth-watering sight. The quality was unlike any he'd ever used.

Halfway through the task, he had yet to find something unusual. One more, perhaps. Again only paper. Intent on making the morning worth his trouble, he reached in and took a sheaf, then stared in surprise at what he had uncovered. A rectangular hole about seven inches deep, the length and width of two men's feet, had been cut into the stack. It was empty, but . . . *just big enough.*

Leaving the warehouse, Marlowe headed for the nearby stables to hire a horse. He was going to Scadbury House, his closest friend's estate, about ten miles away in the lush Kentish countryside.

WESTMINSTER, ENGLAND—LATE MORNING

Around a table in a stuffy windowless room adjacent to the Star Chamber, five frustrated men sat reading the most recent anti-immigrant threat. It was the sixth they had seen that month and the most malicious by far. The Privy Council had given them the task of apprehending the unknown authors. Quickly.

"Every tradesman and apprentice in town is a suspect," one member of the commission grumbled. "They all despise the foreigners."

"I say we offer a reward for information. One hundred crowns," another said.

His colleagues nodded.

"Perhaps it would be wise to probe the Marlowe connection," a third man suggested. "Search his lodgings, those of his associates . . ."

Another agreed, "We should dispatch constables to find him and bring him in for questioning at once."

At that moment, a young messenger walked in with an official-looking document. He handed it to the head of the commission.

"Gentlemen," the man said, looking up. "This is to be easier than we thought. Should any suspect refuse to share with us what he knows, the Privy Council has granted us free rein to change his mind using any means we see fit."

9

*K*ate stood just inside the entrance of Doma in the West Village, scanning the café for a familiar face. A flamboyantly dressed silver-haired man in the far corner, seated alone with an espresso and a sugared brioche, was staring at the backside of a teenage boy on his way out the door.

Noticing Kate, he smiled shamelessly. "How'd ya find me, darlin'?"

"Slipped a tracking device in your briefcase last month," Kate said, sliding into the chair across from him. She ordered a mochaccino, then added, "Well, not really. You've just gotten a little, uh . . ."

"Predictable? Oh, how *boring*," he lamented in a lazy Georgia drawl. "On the other hand, it did bring me an *enchanting* surprise."

Edward Cherry, a top executive at Sotheby's and a self-proclaimed southern belle, was a charmer. Also sleazy and unethical, but Kate found him useful from time to time, so she had built a relationship with him. She'd gained his trust through flattery, friendliness, and the false impression that her ethics were as elastic as his.

"So, to what do I owe this pleasure?" he asked, dabbing his napkin at the corners of his mouth.

"There's a favor I could use, if you have the time." Leaning in, Kate lowered her voice. "A client of mine has a few pieces in his collection he'd like to sell, but discreetly, if you know what I mean. The items are not exactly suitable for public auction."

"I see," Edward said, a conspiratorial smile lighting up his face.

Continuing with her fabricated story, Kate's eyes darted to either side. "My client wants to approach a Rome-based dealer named Luca de Tolomei and asked me to check him out. De Tolomei's rumored to specialize in this sort of situation. My client wants to make sure of that and also get a sense of his taste. What can you tell me about him?"

"Not much beyond the rumors, but I'll make some inquiries for you. I can check our sales logs in Europe to see what he likes. Maybe even call one of those impish little bastards over at Christie's."

"My client is especially interested to know if he deals in ancient artifacts from the Middle East. Persia, in particular."

"I'll see what I can do."

"One more thing. Is he going to one of your auctions this week?" Kate asked. It was auction season, the week in May when Sotheby's and Christie's held invitation-only evening sales of Impressionist and modern art. "I'd like to meet him."

"Mmm, not New York, but I believe he's a regular presence at the London auction, which is tomorrow night. Is that—"

"Perfect! I'll be there anyway on other business."

"I'll check the list to make sure and let you know later today."

Kate batted her eyelashes.

Edward laughed. "Yes, precious, I'll make sure you're on the list, too."

"Thanks. Now, is there anyone *you* need some dirt on today?"

"Not right now," he said softly, taking her hand, "but, honey, let's take our conversation into the gutter anyway. Who's up to what? Who's doing who? Anything I should know about?"

"Oh, I've got something good, something truly Grade A. But it might be a little out of your league." Playfully, she looked off into space. "Hmm, let's see, what else could I—"

"Spill it, or I'll scream."

ROME — 2:34 P.M.

Half a world away, in a cobbled alley behind a family-run restaurant on the edge of the old city, a long-haired Pakistani businessman was pacing with mounting fury. Two associates hovered nearby, waiting for their instructions.

"This is too much," Khadar Khan spat, stopping abruptly to smash his fist through the window of one of the garages lining the alley.

Shaking his bloody hand, he looked each of his associates in the eye. "Go in there and politely inform Mr. de Tolomei that I've reconsidered and the deal's off. Then, please ventilate his head."

The two gunmen disappeared into the wooden-beamed trattoria, making their way to the private back room where, moments before, their boss had been sharing grilled octopus and a carafe of table wine with the man whose life they were about to end. As they approached the narrow archway leading to the stone-lined back room, they heard the clink of silverware.

Taking positions on either side of the arch, they looked at each other and nodded, then slipped around the corner into the windowless room, silenced Berettas poised at the ready.

Only they didn't fire. No one was there. But forming a neat triangle on the antique damask-covered table were three glass plates, each featuring a mouth-watering chocolate confection.

A sudden voice from behind made the two men jump. A dapper waiter in white tie and tails was holding a third chair. "The gentleman thought you and your employer might like some cake."

As the confused gunmen glanced nervously around the empty stone room, ten yards away and five yards below, in a stretch of forgotten Christian catacomb, a lone figure slipped away in the darkness, whistling.

New York City — 9:37 a.m.

"Our boy de Tolomei hangs with some seriously shady motherfuckers," Max said as Kate walked into their office.

She handed him coffee and a couple of pastries from Doma, then took a seat by him at the center table.

"Damn, sabotaging my diet yet again," Max moaned, patting his soft Buddha belly.

"Sorry . . . didn't realize it was back on."

"Well, thanks to you, it isn't," Max said, his mouth full of croissant. "I've been searching for de Tolomei's face. No agency here has focused a major investigation on him, but courtesy of his bad-guy friends, his mug pops up all over the place. A number of times he's with Hamid Azadi, as you thought, but he's also been spotted with drug dealers, arms dealers, mafia hotshots, corrupt politicians—no known terrorists yet but still a dirty fuckin' bunch."

"Show me some?"

Max clicked his mouse a few times, and an image of de Tolomei with a heavyset balding man appeared on the screen. Kate recognized the location. They were sitting in a café in Positano, on the Amalfi coast.

"Taddeo Croce. He's high up in the Camorra, the Neapolitan mafia. Primary business is drugs," Max said. He then displayed two more images. "These two are dealers. Jean-Paul Bruyère on the left, Wolfgang Kessler on the right. Word is, they sold things they shouldn't to Iraq throughout the nineties. And this charmer," he continued, blowing up another image, "he's Russian *mafiya*."

"Damn. Who's *that*?" Kate asked, looking at a photo of a shockingly handsome South Asian man with long black hair.

"Khadar Khan. Runs a textile business in Pakistan. Apparently he controls nearly half of the heroin production in Afghanistan. The DEA's been trying to nail him for years."

Finishing his coffee, Max swiveled his chair to face Kate. "I've looked into possible cash connections between dozens of these guys and de Tolomei, and guess what? Over the course of the past thirteen years, he's done business with all of them."

"Well, he's definitely not your average fine-art dealer."

"No shit."

"What do you think?"

"That the art's a cover for the smuggling of everything deadly."

"You still think he could be a middleman for a WMD sale?" she asked, using the shorthand for weapons of mass destruction.

"We can't rule it out. And until we do . . ."

"I know. I'm on it. It's just that I read some press about him this morning, and he seems like someone who really enjoys the world, or parts of it, at least. He's refined, well educated, and, from what I can tell about his taste in art, well, it's extraordinary. Arming terrorists requires so much more than coldness, you know? It takes real malice toward humanity. De Tolomei doesn't strike me as the type."

"Kate, just because he likes pretty pictures doesn't mean his soul isn't rotten." Max's tone wasn't patronizing, it was curious. Kate was far from naïve, but every once in a while Max noticed a strange idealism at an unexpected moment—an unfortunate chink in her armor, in his opinion.

"Any news from our people in Rome?"

"They're checking out his every move."

"Have they overheard anything interesting?"

"Not yet. His windows are resistant to directional mikes, and tapping his landlines won't be easy either—he uses buried fiber-optic cable."

"Well, I'm meeting him tomorrow, I think."

"That was fast."

"It turns out that de Tolomei's a Sotheby's regular and there's an invite-only auction at their London house tomorrow night. Eddie Cherry is pretty sure he's going and is going to hook me up with an invitation."

"Okay, lemme print this stuff out for you real quick," Max said. "I'll give Slade an update when I get the chance."

"He's not here?"

"He's upstairs doing something we're not cleared to know about, and he isn't answering his phone."

"I wonder what's going on?"

Max shrugged. "No idea. When he came in this morning, he was radiating a neon 'Do Not Disturb' sign. He's in one of those moods where his facial muscles barely move when he speaks. Dimples flat as . . ." He threw a glance at her not-so-generous chest size.

"Flat as your face is about to be?"

Max flashed a smile, then his expression shifted back to one of concern. "I've seen him angry before. But never like this. It's different. You know how when something bad happens, that look of calm control washes over him, and you know he's gonna fix it, whatever it is?"

Kate nodded. "I like that look."

"I know, me, too. But he doesn't have it right now. It makes me kinda edgy."

"No kidding," Kate said. Then, checking her watch, she added, "I guess I should run. I'm meeting Medina for an update this afternoon, but I'll call you before I leave."

"I have a better idea. How about I give you a ride to the airport?"

"The chopper's free?"

"Anything for you."

Kate laughed. "What's the catch?"

Max waved a scrap of paper in the air. "Duty-free, baby. I've got a list."

"You're on." Kate stood to leave. "I'm on one of the last flights out of JFK."

"I'll call you later to coordinate timing."

"Great. Ciao."

Max heard a soft creak. One of the conference room's bookshelves swung outward. Slade emerged and headed for the elevator. Considering his boss's mood, Max decided to leave him alone.

Then, thinking of Kate's upcoming trip, Max changed his mind. "So, Kate's probably meeting de Tolomei tomorrow night."

"Good," Slade said, with barely a glance. "Keep it up."

What? Slade failing to process operational details? It was unheard of. Max tried again. "You know, he does business with some of the world's more dangerous dudes, Slade. Arms dealers, drug dealers . . . I think he's—"

Slade paused to face Max. "Brief me this afternoon, okay? I've got something else on my mind right now."

"Sure thing, boss."

As Slade disappeared into corridor, Max called out. "Hey, it's raining out. Don't you want an umbrella?"

But Slade—who forgot such an item once a decade—didn't even respond.

Damn, Max thought. *What is up with him?*

The heavy rain that poured down onto Kate's umbrella as she neared her home was pelting Jeremy Slade's head as he approached the Victorian dairy in Central Park. Taking a seat on one of the benches beneath the dairy's freestanding Gothic roof, he stared at the stone wall before him.

"What do you think?" Donovan Morgan asked when he reached Slade.

"That I finally know why he went quiet and why none of my sources—on the ground or defectors abroad—ever heard about his detention."

"*Finally* know? Three years ago, you said he was dead, that a source saw him take six bullets to the chest. How—"

Slade's face said it all.

"You've been lying to me all this time?" Morgan was stunned. "For God's sake, why?"

"To spare you. The truth was maddening. Simply put, a month into the operation, he vanished. I collected intel on every single Iraqi prison. Nothing about him. No arrest for a petty crime with his cover intact, no arrest for espionage. Not a word, not a whisper, not a twitch."

"So you assumed he'd been killed."

"Yes, and as time wore on—with defectors scrambling out of Iraq like rats off a sinking ship and *none of them* mentioning him—I was sure of it. And don't forget, for that entire decade, every time Saddam's people thwarted one of our attempts at a coup, they mocked us. Remember the package from '96? The hand of that Republican Guard who'd been working with us? The snide calls we received, on the cells we'd provided our people? I *knew* the Iraqis didn't have him. But I also knew that if he was alive and hadn't been captured, he'd have gotten word to me . . . eventually."

Not hiding the pain in his eyes, Slade turned to face Morgan. "Don, surely you know I'd have done anything for him. He was like a kid brother to me."

Morgan nodded. "And now . . ."

"The parameters have changed. I know how wrong—and how limited—my analysis was. That video? It's authentic. The thing is, it wasn't shot in Iraq. The guard, he was wearing an *Iranian* prison uniform. His name is Reza Mansour Nasseri, and he works at Evin, Tehran's Bastille."

Morgan's breath caught in his throat. Evin was a notorious lockup for dissidents, a fortress with Iran's most brutal record of torture. "So somehow Tehran got wind of the operation back then and sent a team across the border to . . . *abduct* him?"

"They wouldn't have had to travel far. He was using an archaeological site near Basra as a dead drop," Slade said, referring to a region in southeastern Iraq—close to the Iranian border—where the Tigris and Euphrates converge and the Garden of Eden is said to have been.

Puzzled, Morgan frowned. "But that would mean Tehran deliberately chose to delay Saddam's fall, to *rescue* him, which seems . . ."

"A brilliant gamble, in a way," Slade cut in. "It's possible Tehran just wanted information on us, but my guess is they were betting that if the

Agency failed to topple Saddam covertly, eventually our military would go in, and their longtime rival could be dealt a far harsher blow—the whole country severely weakened, far more susceptible to the promotion of a Shia theocracy. Hell, for all we know—particularly if Tehran's got a source in the Agency—they could've been undermining our efforts in Iraq all along."

Pensive, Morgan stared at the ground. "The theory's plausible. Seems probable, in fact. But if he's alive, why clue us in with the video?"

Slade's expression was bleak. "Hard to say. It could be Tehran's way of telling us he's served his purpose . . . they've extracted everything they can from him, and now, they're through. Zooming in on those track marks like that? Then showing him being led out of his cell? They're telling us he was being taken somewhere. For torture? We already know about that. I think they're suggesting he was being led to his death."

"Well," Morgan said, "either he's already dead and this was just a means of taunting us—perhaps to inspire a doomed rescue attempt—or it's an opening gambit for a demand of some kind."

Slade nodded.

"My God," Morgan continued, "to have been in the hands of those sadistic bastards for years . . ." Voice breaking, he stopped speaking.

"If he's alive, Don, we'll get him back. Whatever it takes."

NEW YORK CITY—2:40 P.M.

"Now, *he* was one sadistic bastard," Kate said to herself.

She was in her living room deciphering an entry in *The Anatomy of Secrets* about the royal rack-master, a man named Richard Topcliffe, who worked in the Tower, the Marshalsea, and Bridewell, Elizabethan England's main prisons for Catholics and other dissidents. At the time, he was widely thought to be mad for the great relish and amusement with which he inflicted pain.

Her cell phone shrilled, interrupting her concentration.

"Precious."

"Edward, I knew you'd come through for me. What've you got?"

"You're going to owe me, love. Huge."

"I'm holding my breath."

"I spoke with a pretty young thing at our London house. He's heard a few whispers about de Tolomei."

"Yeah?" Kate asked, as Edward sucked on a cigarette.

"Like you, he's heard the rumors that de Tolomei deals on the black market, that a number of highly publicized stolen items have passed through his hands. Now, your client wanted to get a sense of de Tolomei's taste. He deals in paintings and sculpture from all periods. High-end stuff, mostly. He collects, too, but doesn't seem to favor a particular region or period. The only pattern I can see is that he's a fan of Artemisia Gentileschi—has acquired several of her paintings for his personal collection and is currently involved in a private trade with a dealer I know for one of her sketches."

"What's the subject?"

"Judith. It's one of the more detailed sketches for Artemisia's *Judith Beheading Holofernes.*"

Kate pictured the grisly oil painting. Numerous Renaissance and Baroque artists had painted scenes from the biblical story of Judith, a beautiful Jewish widow who murdered an Assyrian general preparing to invade her town. But Artemisia's was arguably the bloodiest and most violent, which certain art historians attributed to the fact that she painted it shortly after being raped. They suggested she was expressing pent-up rage and a desire for revenge.

"Interesting choice," Kate said.

"My therapist would suggest that de Tolomei has some anger."

Kate nodded to herself. She'd been thinking the same thing.

"Now, about tomorrow's auction," Edward continued. "Guess whose name is on the list?"

"De Tolomei's, right?"

"Wrong. He declined. But there's another name on the list that might interest you."

"Damn, you're coy. Whose?"

"Yours."

"What?"

"Courtesy of a Miss Adriana Vandis. You're listed as her guest. And she is?"

"My college roommate," Kate answered, remembering that she'd left a voice mail for Adriana that morning, asking if she was free to get together the following evening. "That'll be great, but how am I going to meet—"

"Patience, darling. You're not doubting me, are you?"

"Never."

"Good. There's a private art event in Rome in a couple of days, and I've gotten word that de Tolomei will attend."

"What is it?"

"Well, it's very exclusive . . ."

"A new gallery opening?"

"No. As I said, *very* exclusive."

"A star-studded charity event?"

"Ex-clu-sive."

Giving up, Kate groaned and muttered sarcastically, "Bucket-o'-beer night at the local disco?"

"*Very* funny." Then, speaking slowly and dramatically, Edward asked, "Tell me, what's the one invitation in the Eternal City that *no one* will turn down, not even a busy billionaire?"

"An invitation from the pope."

"Precisely. And thanks to me, now you've got one, too."

"You're a godsend. How ever do you do it?"

"Please. You should know better. A lady never reveals her innermost secrets."

THE MEDITERRANEAN SEA—8:45 P.M.

Twenty kilometers east of Malta, the *Nadezhda* was cruising gently, having slowed her speed from thirteen to seven knots. In spite of the evening darkness, she was about to unload her mysterious cargo.

The plain four-cubic-meter wooden crate was on the foredeck, resting on rubber pads. The ship's navigation officer approached it slowly. His master's joke about the crate's fragile contents—that they could be anything from porcelain to a nuclear bomb—continued to haunt him. In his mind the sinister possibility had crystallized into terrifying reality long before.

The arm of the ship's crane was positioned directly above the crate, and the navigation officer reached for the cable dangling down. He took hold of the heavy steel carabiner at the end of the crane's cable, silently cursing the ship's master for giving him this terrifying assignment.

His hands were not serving him well. They trembled and glistened with perspiration. *Concentrate. Almost over.* Still clutching the crane's carabiner in his left hand, he gathered the four smaller carabiners connected to ropes crisscrossing the crate with his right and, careful not to jar the crate, clipped them all together.

He took a few steps back and looked up. Over the starboard side of the ship, he saw a sleek yacht coming up alongside the *Nadezhda*. The yacht was running dark, all deck lights off. Only the phosphorescent blue bulbs lining her hull just above sea level cut into the surrounding blackness.

Within minutes, the two vessels were moving side by side at the same speed, only a few meters apart. The navigation officer turned his attention back to the crate. The ship's engineer was operating the crane, rotating a lever to retract the cable and hoist the crate into the air. Slowly it began to rise.

A metal creak tore through the quiet night. The crane's cable hit a snag, and the crate jerked to a halt.

The navigation officer gulped for air. Dizziness washed over him. But nothing happened. There was no thunderous crack, no fiery boom. They were safe.

The engineer continued his work, and the navigation officer exhaled with relief as the crate he so despised swung away from him toward the yacht's bow. Four deckhands were waiting to ease the crate down to the foredeck. Watching them unhook the crane's cable, the navigation officer studied their faces. They didn't appear to be nervous. Clearly no one had warned them about the crate's menacing contents, he thought to himself, not sure whether to pity or envy their ignorance.

The yacht veered away and vanished into the night. Overwhelmed with relief, the navigation officer breathed deeply and for a moment closed his eyes.

Another set of eyes remained wide open. Eyes that never closed. The American spy satellite passing overhead on its way to the Persian Gulf had snapped dozens of digital photographs of the crate's transfer. Almost instantaneously the photos had been encrypted into electronic pulses and beamed upward to a relay satellite hovering farther out in space. Within seconds the relay satellite had beamed them down to a set of bland buildings in southeast Washington, D.C., a brick and concrete complex with tinted windows and a barbed-wire fence known by intelligence insiders to be part of NIMA, the National Imagery and Mapping Agency. And it was there, at the headquarters of NIMA's Directorate of Analysis and Production, that the encrypted images of the crate joined the day's enormous collection of geospatial intelligence—a collection so vast that only a fraction of it would ever be analyzed by the directorate's thousands of employees.

Oblivious to what had taken place more than a hundred miles above him, the *Nadezhda's* navigation officer descended the aft stairs and headed to his cabin. Climbing into bed, he sighed with contentment and, for the first time in nearly two weeks, fell into a deep, unbroken sleep.

ROME—9:12 P.M.

Standing beneath a sequoia on the edge of the Tiber, Luca de Tolomei gazed at the sluggish green water inching past. He was savoring a cigarette and the moment.

The captain of de Tolomei's yacht had just rung his cell phone. "The shipment was successfully received, sir," the man told him. "I can assure you it is being handled with the greatest of care."

"Good," de Tolomei replied, exhaling a cloud of smoke.

"It will arrive in Capri on schedule."

"By way of the southern entrance?" de Tolomei said, referring to a grotto in the cliffs beneath his Capri home. Uncomfortable in enclosed spaces that didn't have hidden escape routes, he'd had an elevator shaft drilled, connecting his basement with the grotto below.

"Yes, sir. Of course," the captain said.

"Have a good night, then."

"You, too, sir."

Oh, I will. I certainly will.

NEW YORK CITY—3:15 P.M.

Kate was in her kitchen popping crisp red grapes into her mouth, waiting for her kettle to whistle. She squeezed some honey from a plastic honey-filled bear into her favorite oversized mug, then dropped in an Earl Grey tea bag.

Minutes before, she'd been thrilled to come across two of the first intelligence reports written by Robert Poley, the most notorious agent provocateur in Elizabeth's secret service. As a graduate student, Kate had read almost everything available on him, but the historical records were thin. So much about that fascinating spy remained a mystery, and now she was deciphering messages of his that had been buried for centuries. It didn't feel real.

As she stirred soy milk into her tea, her buzzer sounded. Picking up a remote control, she flipped on the television set in her living room. Instead of an afternoon soap opera, the screen showed a delivery man standing in the building's foyer. Unbeknownst to her landlord, Max had fiddled with the building's wiring one day, allowing Kate to pirate the security footage.

The overweight delivery man wore a tight T-shirt and equally snug knee-length denim shorts. No weapons hiding beneath those clothes, Kate thought. She answered her intercom.

"Hey, Miss K," her doorman said. "Flowers here. Shall I send 'em up?"

"Sure, thanks."

After Kate signed his form and gave him a tip, the delivery man handed over a cylindrical glass vase full of fragrant Casablanca lilies. "What's the occasion?"

"I don't know," she said, feeling as if she'd just dropped several floors in an elevator too quickly. "But thanks. They're gorgeous."

Shutting the door behind him, Kate reached for the card as she headed back into her kitchen.

Only she didn't make it that far.

She froze in her hallway, staring at the card's message in disbelief, barely noticing the sound of the vase crashing to the floor.

10

... I stand as Jove's huge tree,
And others are but shrubs compar'd to me.
All tremble at my name, and I fear none ...
—MORTIMER, in Marlowe's *Edward II*

LONDON—AFTERNOON, MAY 1593

While city constables ransacked Kit Marlowe's lodgings, as well as those of his former chamber fellow, Robert Poley was walking briskly to Whitehall for a meeting with his employer, Sir Robert Cecil.

The forty-year-old spy was tall and lithe, in spite of his dissolute lifestyle. Poley had thick, short black hair, harsh features, and snakelike eyes that missed nothing and mesmerized whomever he chose. It had been said that he could beguile a man of his wife or his life. The assessment was correct.

Poley had just returned from Flushing, a Dutch seaport currently occupied by England. Spain had invaded the Netherlands eight years earlier, and English forces were helping their Protestant allies fight to drive the Spanish from Dutch soil. Poley had delivered the queen's correspondence to government officials and military commanders, collected their responses, and met with local spies both on and off the battlefields.

Turning onto a narrow street, he coughed with disgust. *What in God's name is that vile stench?* Then he saw the red wooden crosses nailed to several doors. *Ah, plague homes.* The neighbors were burning old shoes and leaving rotten onions about to ward off the disease. It made it harder to breathe, but at least the overpopulation problem was being addressed, Poley thought to himself. Holding his sleeve over his nose, he picked up his pace.

At Charing Cross, a group of rowdy apprentices passed by on his right, all clad in their characteristic dark blue doublets. Poley eyed them curiously. The boys in blue were a major cause of the recent rioting. Returning from a country at war, he had been shocked to learn that London had become something of a battlefield itself in the brief period he had been away. With the soaring unemployment rate and influx of Protestant refugees from the Netherlands, France, and Belgium, London's workers had long been grumbling, but the outbreaks of violence were a more recent phenomenon. Many locals—apprentices, in particular—were consumed with rage that the government allowed the immigrants to stay.

The city was going to hell, Poley mused. The thought added a spring to his step. Chaos was always good for business.

Poley had been directing Robert Cecil's espionage operations in the Low Countries for the past couple of years. He liked the power of the position but missed his early days as a projector. Posing as a Catholic in the mid-1580s, he'd infiltrated several antigovernment conspiracies, slipping into clandestine masses and secretly marrying a Catholic woman to fine-tune his cover. When Walsingham grew impatient to make arrests, Poley would urge the plotters to act swiftly and decisively, collecting evidence against them all the while.

One such young plotter was Anthony Babington, who considered Poley a trusted friend even as the hangman's noose tightened about his neck. Babington had given Poley a gift, a diamond that now dangled from Poley's left ear. The glittering teardrop was an enduring reminder of his most spectacular betrayal.

Poley had come far since his early days sweeping other students' floors and making their beds at Cambridge. He had loathed performing menial tasks while the wealthy, fashionably dressed sort idled about. But now, in addition to being the most feared and admired man in the service, he had the lifestyle he'd always wanted: new clothes, lavish dinners, and plenty of mistresses. All of whom were married, of course. He loved to seduce other men's wives.

Stepping into his employer's office, Poley saw Robert Cecil sitting behind his desk, a white parrot fidgeting in a silver cage near his head. The exotic bird from the East was much more than a beloved pet, Poley knew. Possessing such a creature proved that its owner had well-placed connections and a good deal of money. It was a subtle but effective display of power.

Gravely ill as a child, thirty-year-old Cecil was left a stunted crookback. He was near colorless, with a weak, effeminate chin barely hidden by his neatly clipped beard. The queen referred to him as her "elf," sometimes as her "pygmy."

Although he appeared insignificant, Cecil wielded tremendous power. The son of the queen's treasurer and top adviser, he'd been knighted two years before and granted a seat on the Privy Council. Cecil was also expected to be named secretary of state sometime soon, Poley knew, though apparently the queen was still considering her young favorite, the Earl of Essex, for the post.

"You've heard of the latest threatening placard?" Cecil asked.

Sitting down, Poley shook his head.

"Anonymous letters and poems have been appearing around town this month past, promising death to all foreign workers who do not quit the city at once. Last night the most violent yet was tacked upon the wall of the Dutch church on Broad Street. Threatened to slit their throats while they were at prayer."

"And the queen is—"

"Incensed," Cecil cut in, impatient. "What troubles me is that last night's threat was signed 'Tamburlaine.' "

"Ah, the poor shepherd turned world conqueror who wanted to march against God in heaven. I always fancied him," Poley mused.

Cecil ignored the comment. "The doggerel filth makes other allusions to Marlowe's plays. You're better acquainted with him than I. Think he wrote it?"

"Last I heard, he has been in the countryside for weeks, working on a new play or some such thing," Poley replied. "I'd say he has an admirer who despises the immigrants or an enemy who wants him in trouble. Marlowe might enjoy shocking people, but he would never do something that overt, that stupid."

"The Council has set up a commission to investigate the placards, calling them dangerous incitements to anarchy. I'm sure they're looking for him."

Leaning back in his chair, Poley studied his employer. "It's not like you to be concerned about someone else, even if it is an innocent man. A man who has served you well over the years, I might add."

"Marlowe has information," Cecil said tightly. "Something . . . compromising."

Poley's eyes lit up. "Ah, and if he's tortured, he might reveal it. Well, what is it?"

Cecil was silent.

The bones in Cecil's hands were sharply outlined, Poley noticed, enjoying the rare display of nerves. *It's quite a dilemma for you, isn't it? I'm the most capable man in your network—in the entire service, in fact—but you don't entirely trust me.*

Poley tried again. "Sir, I cannot help if you do not tell me the problem."

Tugging on his small pointed beard, Cecil watched his parrot peck at its food for a minute. "You recall the coining operation from last year?"

Poley nodded. They'd sent Marlowe to the Netherlands to infiltrate a group of exiled English Catholics plotting against Queen Elizabeth. Marlowe and a highly skilled goldsmith had begun counterfeiting coins. Coining was considered to be treason under English law, so simply committing the crime enhanced Marlowe's antigovernment pose. But in addition, Marlowe was going to offer the conspirators a collection of counterfeit shillings as proof of his loyalty. They would have been easily tempted; the plotters were desperately short of money.

The plan would surely have worked if a meddling spy from Essex's network, a man named Richard Baines, hadn't discovered the illicit coining and gotten Marlowe arrested.

Ever discreet, Marlowe told the local governor that he had coined out of curiosity, that he wanted to see what the goldsmith could do, nothing more. Luckily the governor chose to deport Marlowe and his partner instead of incarcerating them, sending them straight into the hands of England's treasurer, who was Robert Cecil's father. Marlowe was quietly released without his cover being compromised, and the bungled operation was never exposed.

So Poley did not understand why Cecil was worried. "He might admit that the coining was part of an operation we had planned, an operation that failed miserably—it would be a minor embarrassment, but hardly a cause for major concern."

Cecil pressed his lips together. "There's more to it than you think. I was quite low on funds at the time, and . . ." His voice trailed off.

"Ah, well done, sir!" Poley exclaimed. "You told Marlowe to quietly fashion a set of coins for *yourself*. Now that just crosses the line, doesn't it? England's next secretary of state dabbling in treason. How exciting! I'm impressed."

"You do realize this puts us in a sticky position," Cecil said, his teeth clenched.

"*Us?*" Poley loved to goad the little crookback, to throw verbal darts at his legendary self-control.

"Of course *us*," Cecil hissed.

A further jibe tickled his lips, but Poley bit it back. There was no need to alienate his employer too much. Though without question, if Cecil did start to sink at court, Poley would be the first to jump ship.

"Sir, our charming playmaker will never divulge your secret," Poley said with exaggerated nonchalance. "He could have sold the information to Essex for a fortune, if he were so inclined. But he never would. You see, Marlowe has got something you would not recognize. It might be a touch warped, but the man's got a sense of honor."

"That and a penny might get me to London Bridge," Cecil said, his calm demeanor intact once more. "But do you really think some lowly spy's honor code is going to help me sleep at night?"

"What do you wish me to do?"

Cecil cleared his throat and narrowed his eyes.

"You're not asking me to kill him, are you?" Poley shook his head slowly. "I despise killing. Makes me feel like a cheat, as if I have to sneak a piece off the board in order to win."

"Murder is messy. Could lead back to us. So, on the contrary, I want you to watch out for him. Let us hope the commission will show some sense and leave Marlowe alone, but if not, you will protect him at all costs, and so will I. If he ends up on the rack, we—and I do mean *we*—will have trouble."

"Guardian angel is not a role I ever envisioned for myself," Poley mused, then shrugged. "Will there be anything else?"

"Yes." Cecil's tone sharpened to a hard, authoritative edge. "If you fail, I will take away everything you enjoy."

Poley's expression remained nonchalant.

Cecil wasn't finished. "And when you beg me to reconsider, I will toss you in the Tower and tell Topcliffe you seduced his wife."

RICHMOND, ENGLAND — DUSK

A pair of shiny black geldings trotted along a country lane, drawing a sleek lavender coach. On a thick velvet cushion inside, Her Majesty's rackmaster, Richard Topcliffe, sat alone, sipping his best Scotch from a silver flask.

Forty minutes earlier, a messenger had appeared on the doorstep of his country home with a letter from the Privy Council summoning him back to London. A major investigation was under way. Apparently the first arrest had just been made.

Topcliffe ordered his coachman to pick up the pace.

11

Kate reached for her dirty martini.

Medina watched her hand with dismay. "Is something wrong? You're shaking."

"Oh, I lifted too much weight at the gym earlier," Kate lied. Plastering on a smile, she added, "Clearly *you* know how that is."

"I'm glad you noticed."

Good thing you're so easy to distract. Kate surreptitiously tucked her shaking hand beneath her thigh. The chilling message she'd received hours earlier and the confused, fragmented thoughts spinning off from it were hurtling through her brain, bouncing off the edges like bumper cars.

She and Medina were sitting on plush armchairs in the living room of his suite at the Pierre, having a brief meeting over cocktails before he left the city to catch his flight back to London. While Medina examined the hors d'oeuvres on the coffee table between them, Kate slipped her right hand from under her leg, flexed it a few times, then held it still. Good, she thought. The shaking had stopped.

"How was your day?" Medina asked, looking back up at her. "Anything interesting happen?"

Kate took a tiny pastry shell stuffed with smoked trout and caviar, put it in her mouth, and chewed thoughtfully. "Mmm. Wow, this is really, *really* good."

"All right, Miss Secrecy," Medina said playfully. "I get it. If you tell me what you've been up to, you'd have to kill me, but if we spend this idle pleasantry exchange time talking about *my* day, I wouldn't have to kill you, but there's a pretty good chance you'd die of boredom."

"Try me." *Boring sounds pretty good to me right now.*

"Just a couple meetings. I manage a hedge fund, do a lot of short selling, some venture capital here and there . . ."

"What's been your biggest coup?"

"Spotting that your country's top companies were not as upstanding as they pretended to be. I shorted Enron and WorldCom at the right time. But enough about me—"

Uh-oh, so not in the mood to talk about myself. "You're right," Kate cut in. "I've got major news for you."

Medina raised his eyebrows.

"I consulted a rare-book dealer, then got started myself last night, and I'm virtually certain your manuscript is exactly what the title page suggests—a collection of secret information compiled by Thomas Phelippes."

"With pages taken from Walsingham's files?"

Kate nodded. "Many were addressed to Walsingham, and the rough dating I got for the paper correlates with the timing of the events mentioned in the reports I've deciphered so far. Also, where possible, I've compared the handwriting with samples I have from various Elizabethan spies. They've all matched."

"My goodness."

"Wait. It gets better. Looks like Phelippes only included really juicy stuff. I haven't come across any humdrum intelligence. No tedious reports about the status of the Spanish naval fleet, for example. Nothing like that."

Kate took a sip of her drink. "I haven't found anything yet that would affect someone today—in a serious way—but I bet I will soon."

"My money's on you, too."

Kate smiled, and for the first time since she'd entered his suite, it was genuine. Finally her nerves were settling down. "By the way," she said, "I called your professor but got his voice mail. I haven't heard back yet."

"Neither have I," Medina said thoughtfully. "I'll try him again tomorrow morning. But in the meantime, I'd love to hear more about what you read last night."

Kate's eyes lit up. "Well, I wasn't surprised to read about the so-called

Virgin Queen's racy sex life—who, when, where—that type of thing. But it *was* cool to come across evidence that her first lover might not have pushed his wife down the stairs, as almost everyone thought."

"Was he arrested?"

"No. Just mired in suspicion. People believed the rumors because they knew he desperately wanted to marry Elizabeth and become king. The report was written by a young maid who claimed to have seen his wife trip and tumble down the steps accidentally. There's no historical record of this witness's claims, so I'm guessing that Walsingham suppressed it."

"Why?"

"Keeping Elizabeth single and available for courtship by Europe's many princes was better for foreign policy."

"Makes sense. What else did you find?"

"Intel from a classic sleeper spy."

"Oh?"

"His name was Richard Baines. He was one of Walsingham's earliest spies at Rheims, the seminary for English Catholics across the channel in France. Major hotbed of plotting against the English government. Baines enrolled in 1578 like your average wanna-be priest. His mission was to pick up information about Catholic military strategy and learn the identities of covert Catholics back in England, which he did and wrote up in this report. He was also in Rheims to promote unrest among the budding priests, so he sang the praises of sex and rich food to anyone who would listen."

"Good strategy."

"Yeah. Ultimately, though, he screwed up. Told a fellow student he was going to poison the seminary well, and the student turned him in. He ended up in the town jail for a year."

"What about the codes? How are you figuring them out?"

"Tricks of the trade, my friend. Sorry." Taking a notebook from her bag, Kate's mock stern expression softened into a smile. She turned to a particular page and handed it to Medina. "This was originally in cipher. It was one of the easier reports to translate, but it's senseless drivel, right?"

"Appears that way."

Kate then gave him a sheet of paper with holes cut into it. "I made this for you."

"Um . . . thanks?"

"It's a Cardan Grille. Invented in the 1550s by a Milanese natural philosopher, Girolamo Cardano. Most were thicker than this, usually made of stiff board. Both a sender and recipient would have the same one."

Leaning toward Medina, she placed the grille across the notebook page. About twenty words and fifty individual letters were visible through the holes. "Sound familiar?"

" 'The Earl of Northumberland,' " Medina read, " 'has built a secret chamber in Petworth, from which a priest conducts mass . . . on Whitsun Eve, he met with one Francis Throckmorton to discuss letters from their French and Spanish contacts . . . ' "

Medina looked up at her. "This is that report you just described—of covert Catholics plotting in England."

Nodding, Kate reached for her notebook and flipped to a page covered with columns of letters and symbols. "This is a key to another one of the reports," she said, handing it over.

Each vowel had five different ciphers, each consonant two. The letter *b*, for example, could be represented either by a cross made of two squiggly lines or a letter *z* positioned diagonally. The letter *m* could be represented by a pair of bird wings or by what looked like an upside-down tadpole.

"My computer helped me with that one," Kate said, watching Medina peruse the ciphered letters. "It was also common back then to convey hidden meaning in a seemingly bland letter," she added. "To disguise information about troop movements, for example, as a merchant's report about a shipment of inventory. You know: 'The wine will be reaching Lisbon in a fortnight.' Something like that."

"Hmm."

"Now, want to hear about the most infamous sadist of the time?"

"Who wouldn't?"

"Richard Topcliffe. Numero uno state torturer. He had a passion for his job, loved taunting prisoners while he crippled them. He also had a passion for the queen. One of Walsingham's prison informants reported hearing Topcliffe screaming her name while raping a female prisoner in the next cell."

"Sounds about as pleasant as jails do today."

"Yeah. Trust me, you don't want to mess with the law."

"I wish you'd told me that sooner," Medina said, slapping his palm against his forehead. "Just this morning, I was—"

Kate laughed. "Actually, the spy who wrote the Topcliffe report was an interesting character, too. Robert Poley. Got his start posing as a Catholic jailbird and snitching to Walsingham. Not so glamorous a beginning, you might think, but word was he had a grand time. Made some *serious* use of the conjugal visit . . . with other men's wives. Eventually he became the most effective spy in the secret service. Has been called the very genius of the Elizabethan underworld. His bosses never trusted him, but he was too good not to use."

"What was *his* biggest coup?"

"Playing a big part in the downfall of Walsingham's nemesis, Mary, Queen of Scots. Poley infiltrated a circle of conspirators plotting her rescue, nudged them along . . ."

"Wait a minute," Medina said. "The government spy, Poley, *encouraged* a plot against Elizabeth?"

"Until Walsingham had enough evidence to execute everyone, including Mary. Today he's also remembered for his role in—"

A knock sounded. Someone was rapping on Medina's door.

Checking his watch, Medina said, "Good. I've been expecting something essential. Absolutely essential."

"Our food's here, the porter's taken your luggage—what now?" Kate asked. She then noticed that he was stifling a smile. He was up to something.

Medina stood and headed toward the suite's hallway. "If you'll *excuse* me . . ."

Puzzled but mildly intrigued, Kate craned her neck, watching him.

He turned back. "*Please*. Can a man have his privacy?"

Medina returned with a large rectangular box wrapped in bright red paper and handed it to Kate. A gift? No, that would be strange, although he was a flirt. Chocolates? Did he know she had a weakness for them? No, the box was too big, and it rattled. It couldn't be, but it sounded like . . .

Still not convinced, she quickly unwrapped the box, and there it was. A board game. *Clue.*

"I know your credentials are impeccable, and I'd love to continue working with you, but I have very exacting standards," he explained. "You see, if you can't best me at this . . ."

"You'll clobber me over the head with the candlestick?"

"No. I'd have the colonel do it," Medina said, his eyes sparkling wickedly. "He's in the conservatory as we speak, plotting the perfect murder."

ROME — 12:09 A.M.

Just off the Tiber in the heart of old Rome, a wide straight street slices through a thicket of crooked medieval alleys. Designed by Donato Bramante for Pope Julius II, the cobbled Via Giulia is lined with Renaissance palazzos, one of which—a russet-colored structure with elaborate carvings on the façade—was owned by Luca de Tolomei.

In his bedroom on the top floor, de Tolomei was sitting in a leather armchair speaking on the telephone. "Anything from the Kate Morgan tap?" he asked his assistant.

"One call, sir. About an hour ago, she spoke with a friend, a young woman in London, about attending the Sotheby's auction there tomorrow night."

"Is that it?"

"Ah, yes it is, sir." De Tolomei's assistant hesitated, then added, "It would seem she uses her mobile primarily."

"Indeed," de Tolomei murmured, his irritation evident. "Any progress in that regard?"

"Not exactly. The mobile's encryption system is unlike anything we've seen before. The algorithms are—"

"Just let me know when you hear anything new."

"Right, sir. Will there be anything else?"

"Have the Gulfstream ready for a short flight tomorrow morning."

"Certainly. Good night."

Hanging up, de Tolomei stood and retrieved a small black suitcase from his closet. Laying it on his bed, he began collecting the few items he would need for a brief trip to London.

NEW YORK CITY—7:34 P.M.

Kate's flight to Heathrow was taking off in a few hours. Holding an open toiletry bag, she was scanning the shelves in her bathroom, searching for anything she might have forgotten. "You're not exactly going into the jungle," she mumbled to herself. "They do sell this stuff over there."

Zipping the bag shut, she hurried back to her bedroom to double-check the contents of the suitcase lying on her bed. She was meeting Max at the Upper East Side helipad in less than an hour, and there was someone she needed to see beforehand. Picking up the phone by her bed, she dialed a very familiar number.

Five rings later, her best friend, Jack O'Mara, answered with a scratchy croak. "Yeah?"

"Hey, I'm sorry," Kate said, realizing he'd been sleeping. He was a writer and kept unusual hours. "Go back to sleep, honey."

His response was somewhere between a groan and a purr.

"Bye, Jack. I'll call you later."

"No, no," he said, more lucid. "You sound funny—something's wrong. Wanna come over?"

"Um, yeah. If that's okay."

"I'll meet you. I have to be up soon anyway. Bring me a double latte, will you?"

"Sure . . . thanks, Jack."

Since elementary school, Jack had been like family to her—the sibling she never had, the only person she leaned on emotionally. Like Kate, he was an only child who lost a parent at a young age and grew up quiet and serious, with a vague sense of guilt and sadness that was rarely out of reach. Fear, too—Jack's father, a police officer, was killed on the job, and as Kate's father rose through the ranks of the U.S. Attorney's office, prosecuting increasingly dangerous felons, death threats and bodyguards were not uncommon. Both she and Jack had been vaguely uncomfortable in social situations as children and had gravitated to each other shortly after meeting.

Ten minutes later, with Jack's coffee in hand, she headed up Second Avenue rolling her suitcase behind her. The wind was strong. Tree branches shook angrily, and Kate's hair flew before her face, obscuring her vision. The sky was an odd grayish lilac color with an orange glow, and dark clouds were jockeying for position overhead. Another spring shower was on its way.

On Kate's left, a quaint brownstone restaurant row—backed by neck-strain-high skycrapers—gave way to a number of bars, popular during the week with the midtown working crowd. Black-clad yuppies on cell phones hovered out front, concentrating deeply as they solved the world's problems.

"She was wearing *what?*" one heavily made-up Prada drone shouted into her phone.

Kate tried not to roll her eyes as she continued up the avenue.

Crossing Fifty-ninth Street, she climbed the awning-covered stairs to the Roosevelt Island tram, passed through the turnstile, and entered the small red cable car. Staring out the windows at the Queensboro Bridge, which runs parallel to the tram's cable system, she watched the hundreds of red taillights moving away from her. Rain began coming down. Large droplets pelted the roof. The last passengers dashed aboard, and within moments the tram operator shuffled in and her short ride over the East River began.

The car passed over Second, First, and York Avenues as it headed to the river. Kate gripped the railing tightly, mesmerized by the city lights gleaming through the pouring rain.

The brightly lit swordfish snout of the Chrysler building whipped out of sight, and then they were over the river. Turning around, Kate looked out the opposite set of windows to search for Jack, who lived in an apartment building on the northern end of the island. The boardwalk skirting the western shore was empty, but the tree-lined path connecting it to the tram station was not; she saw a lone silhouette walking its course. The car swooped along the cable down to its home, and Kate waited impatiently for the doors to open.

Jack's worn navy sweater and jeans were plastered to him, and rain dripped from his nose. With plain features set in a hard pale face, dark hair as closely clipped as the stubble on his chin, and the solid body of a triathlete, he was unremarkable-looking, but his blue eyes shone brightly—beautifully—against the evening's drab backdrop. Kate went up to him. He hugged her tightly, and melting into the comfort of his familiar—if not soft—embrace, she burst into tears.

Entering a well-tended park, they walked toward the boardwalk hand in hand and stood at the railing facing the Upper East Side, the swiftly moving river sparkling before them, the warm spring rain drenching them. With Jack's arm around her, Kate rested her head in the crook of his shoulder.

"What happened?" he asked softly. "I haven't seen you like this in ages."

She pulled a small card from her pocket. "This came today. With a bouquet of lilies. Casablanca lilies, the same ones Rhys used to send me."

Angling the card toward a street lamp, Jack read softly, " 'Tick, tock, tick, tock, boom. Limbs fly, love dies, doom. Tell me, how does it feel to hold a melted hand?' "

Stunned, he turned to face her. "Holy shit."

The memory of what Kate had found in Rhys's casket, an image she was able to block from her conscious mind, had haunted her every night for more than a year after his death. Following the funeral, a closed-casket ceremony, Kate had remained in the room alone. Against the warnings of Rhys's brother—who'd been nearby when the grenade that had killed Rhys exploded—she'd opened the casket, desperate to say good-bye, no matter what state he was in. It was a mistake. What she saw was far worse than she'd ever imagined. There was nothing but a burned arm, with bone protruding where his shoulder should have been. The blue fabric of his shirtsleeve had melted into his split, blackened flesh, and the gold ring she'd designed for him dangled from the bones of a shriveled finger.

Jack put his hands on her shoulders. "Who the hell—"

"I have no idea who could hate me so much and know those . . . details."

"Your company wasn't able to trace it?"

Kate shook her head.

"Could it involve something you're working on now, someone who might want to unbalance you, get you off your game?"

"I've got two new cases, but one of the targets doesn't even know I exist yet," Kate said, thinking of de Tolomei. "And the other case involves a guy who wants something I've got—an old manuscript—but I don't see why he'd get this personal with me. Send a gumshoe to jump me in the street and steal my bag, yes, but play mind games? I'm just a random obstacle for him to bypass. That note seems too vindictive, too personal for someone like him." Kate shook her head, puzzled.

"You must have made some enemies in the past few years," said Jack, "someone who could want to get back at you."

"I guess so, I . . ." Kate paused to check the number on her ringing cell phone. "It's my father. You mind?"

"Of course not," Jack said, smoothing her hair back from her face while she took the call.

"Hi, Dad."

"I'm in town. Had an unexpected meeting earlier, and I thought, if you were free, that we might get together."

"I'm actually on my way to the airport in a few minutes."

"Where to?"

"London. A couple new cases came up."

"Oh, that sounds great. You'll be seeing, ah . . ."

"Adriana, my old roommate? Yeah. Is everything all right?"

"Of course. I—well, we haven't seen each other in a while, angel. That's all."

"I'll call you soon?"

"Great. And Kate?"

"Mmm-hmm?"

"Be careful, okay? I—" Her father's voice broke, and he cleared his throat. "Well, it's just that I miss you."

"Me, too, Dad."

As Kate hung up, she bit her lip, curious why her father sounded so uncharacteristically emotional and, more so, why he seemed relieved to hear that she was leaving town. She looked at her watch, then up at Jack. "I have to run. But thanks for coming out here like this."

"Anytime," he said with a smile. "So, when these cases are done, how about taking a trip with me? Somewhere new . . . go hiking to Incan ruins or something."

"Yeah, I'd like that."

Kissing his cheek, Kate thanked him once more, then headed back to the tram station.

Jack remained on the shore of Roosevelt Island watching the cable car cruise back to Manhattan. Its interior was well lit, and he could see Kate standing near the window. He was worried about her. Sipping the coffee she'd given him, he wondered who had sent her the malicious note, what kind of vendetta the person could have, and whether he or she was finished or had something else in store for her.

While Kate disappeared onto the opposite shore, Jack also wondered how she would react if he ever told her that he'd been in love with her for as long as he could remember.

Just off Sixtieth Street, at the helipad overlooking the East River and Roosevelt Island, Kate walked toward the Slade Group helicopter. She saw Max in the pilot seat, as she'd expected, but was surprised to see two other men in back.

Climbing inside, she could tell instantly that they were a couple of Slade's former Special Forces or CIA paramilitary operatives. They were dressed like ordinary civilians, but the way they sat, the way their eyes moved, what Kate could sense of the bodies beneath their clothing, the absolute confidence they exuded—it was unmistakable.

"Hi," she said, wondering where they were headed, what kind of operation Slade was orchestrating overseas.

Both nodded at her.

"Have a seat," Max said, handing her a headset. "We're late."

She turned to the men in the backseat. "I thought I'd have to make conversation with this fool the whole time," she joked, nodding her head toward Max. "What a pleasant surprise."

"Sure is," one of them said, grinning as Max tugged on a fistful of her hair. "I'm Jason, and this is . . ."

"Connor," the taller one said. "And you're . . ."

"Kate," she responded, shaking their hands.

Flicking switches, Max started the chopper. The engine hummed, the lights came on, and the rotor blades whipped around, getting faster and louder by the second.

Glancing into the night sky as they rose from the ground, Kate was grateful she'd remembered to scan the pages of *The Anatomy of Secrets* into her laptop. She knew she'd need an absorbing distraction as soon as she was alone. Peaceful sleep was not in the cards for her that night.

12

As for myself, I walk abroad a-nights,
And kill sick people groaning under walls.
Sometimes I go about and poison wells . . .
But tell me now, how hast thou spent thy time?

—BARABAS, in Marlowe's *The Jew of Malta*

. . . I have done a thousand dreadful things
As willingly as one would kill a fly,
And nothing grieves me heartily indeed
But that I cannot do ten thousand more.

—AARON, in Shakespeare's *Titus Andronicus*

CHISLEHURST, KENT—EARLY MORNING, MAY 1593

*K*it."

No response.

Thomas Walsingham, the thirty-year-old cousin of the deceased spy-master Sir Francis, approached the four-poster oak bed in his guest room and pulled back the red curtain.

"Kit."

The large shape under the linen sheet failed to stir.

Tom leaned in to nudge what looked like a shoulder. The shoulder gave way, then slowly returned to its former position. "The queen is really a man in disguise."

Gripped tightly by two sets of fingers, the sheet flew down.

Marlowe stared up at his old friend in shock, momentarily gullible as he sailed the last few yards out of dreamland. Seeing Tom's smug grin, Marlowe's wide eyes narrowed into a scowl. "Damn, that would've been good."

"Join me for breakfast?"

"Yes, sir," Marlowe said resolutely, scampering from his bed like an eager schoolboy. The two friends had met at Cambridge and remained close during Tom's brief run in the service, and now Tom was one of Marlowe's literary patrons. Marlowe frequently addressed him with mock subservience. In his mind, the joke had yet to wear thin.

Following him from the timber and stone house, Marlowe breathed deeply, relishing the pleasant fragrance—clean, country air scented with primroses. A refreshing contrast to the rancid odors of London. Crossing the drawbridge that spanned the swan-filled moat, they headed toward a table beneath an old willow at the edge of a pear orchard.

Gesturing to the pewter pitcher and mugs on the table, Tom said, "Perry from last year's crop . . . truly exquisite. Perhaps it might get you in the mood."

"God's nightgown, I've been trying," Marlowe muttered, drinking some of the pear-based liquor.

"How about resurrecting Barabas? He deserves another run."

"I know. A shame someone else has done it for me."

"Someone else? Oh, you mean . . . what's his name? That rustic upstart writing sugared sonnets to the Earl of Southampton?"

"Mmm-hmm. Will Shakespeare. If you ask me, his *Richard III* should be called *Barabas II*."

"Is it any good?" Tom asked. "Perhaps I should meet him."

Marlowe scowled.

"A joke, Kit. So do you know him?"

"Will was writing for Lord Strange's Men last year, too. I gave him a few pointers with his *Henry VI* plays." With a wry smile, Marlowe added, "I'd no idea he would go on accepting my help long after I had finished giving it."

"You mind?"

Marlowe shrugged. "Not much. No one forgets an original. But imitations?"

"Forgotten faster than a drunken roll in the hay," Tom agreed.

"I hear he's got yet another new play along the same lines. *Titus Andronicus*. Claims it has a villain to top Barabas, that audiences will be breathless, cup-shotten with delight."

Tom raised his eyebrows. "Imagine that. Boasting he can best the cleverest quill in town."

"You've got to be impressed, though. I can't help but admire a man who will take on a challenge of such *tremendous* magnitude."

Tom grinned.

"As it happens, it's a poem I should like to write this time."

"Any ideas?" Tom asked.

Marlowe slumped in his chair. "Still nothing." Then, tilting his face to the sky, he lamented, "Where are you when I need you?"

"Perhaps she needed a nap."

"My muse?"

Tom nodded.

Marlowe picked up their empty metal cups and clanged them together three times. Then he set them back on the table and covered his eyes with his hands.

After a moment Tom asked, "Any luck?"

"No. Seems she's a heavy sleeper."

DEPTFORD — MIDMORNING

For several hours, Marlowe had been poking his nose around the inns and taverns lining Deptford Strand. He was looking for Lee Anderson, the Muscovy sailor Fitz Fat had mentioned the day before. Anderson was in trouble. Without papers he could be arrested and jailed for vagrancy at any time. But Marlowe was just the person to help . . . for a price.

After the sixteenth establishment, he lost his patience and headed back to the Cardinal's Hat. Ambrosia came over and took his order.

Hearing footsteps approach moments later, Marlowe looked up, expecting to see Ambrosia with his drink. Instead he saw the familiar face of Nicholas Skeres, a fellow spy from Francis Walsingham's old network, also currently working for the Earl of Essex. Thin and blond, Skeres was Marlowe's age but had the receding hairline of a man twice their years.

"What brings you downriver, Nick?" Marlowe asked. A Londoner, Skeres had an expensive home in Blackfriars near London Bridge.

"Business. A big deal."

Marlowe rolled his eyes. He knew that Skeres meant some kind of dirty trick. The man was a known cony-catcher. He duped the naïve out of dozens of pounds whenever he had the chance. "What is it this time?"

"Commodity brokering."

"I should have guessed." By law, moneylenders could charge no more than ten percent in interest, so commodity brokering was a favored way for swindlers to double their money. Such a broker would find someone in need of a loan, promise money, and extract a signed bond for the amount in question. Then the broker would claim not to have any money and offer a commodity instead, a commodity worth far less than the amount written on the bond he had just received.

"I'm meeting my partner soon," Skeres said, sitting down. "But perhaps you have time for a game?"

"Always," Marlowe responded. He slipped a pair of dice from his bag, shook the wooden cubes, and tossed them on the table. A three and a five. He threw again. Two sixes. "Well, Nick?"

Most people played dice for money, but with Marlowe and Skeres, whoever threw a matched pair within three attempts won gossip instead of coins.

"I was at Essex House yesterday, and the earl was in one of his states. You know, sullen, morose, stalking about glaring at people. I don't know what in hell bit him, but—"

"He had a nasty row with the queen."

"How do you know?"

"She whispered it in my ear the other night as we were dancing."

"What!" Skeres' shock quickly gave way to skepticism. Apparently it had not taken long for it to occur to him that a commoner like Marlowe would never be so intimate with their sovereign.

Marlowe dismissed the question with a wave of his hand. "Please. You know you must wait your turn. Carry on."

Grudgingly Skeres continued. "A servant went up to him, whispered something, and Essex's quiet sulking turned into a rage, the likes of which I've never seen. He smashed his fist through one of his windows and ordered me from the room."

Marlowe raised his eyebrows. Glass cost a fortune.

Skeres smiled slyly. "After I left the house, I stood beneath the broken window."

"And?"

"It seems Lopez got drunk and let something slip."

"This does sound promising," Marlowe said. Roderigo Lopez was the royal physician.

"He told the entire court about Essex's latest bout of clap."

Marlowe leaned forward with enthusiasm. "Has the queen heard?"

"Not yet, but God help Essex if she does. And God help the man who tells her. I suspect he'll be boxed about the ears."

Skeres took a sip from Marlowe's tankard, then added, "I'm to follow loudmouthed Lopez around in hopes of catching him at secret Jewish rites. If Essex can prove the conversion was a sham, he knows the queen will have the good doctor deported."

Reaching for the dice, Skeres concluded, "I'd say that closes this round. Let us see what I can get from you." He threw. A two and a five. He threw again. A two and a four. Then he threw his final roll. A three and a six. "Damn!"

Marlowe grinned. He'd won again, with dice that weren't rigged. *Imagine that.*

"Hmm." Skeres stared at the wall for a moment, scratching his head. "Ah, I do have another one," he said. "Walter Ralegh's in town."

Marlowe sipped his drink to conceal his smile. Ralegh was a close friend he'd not seen in months.

"He's come into a fortune recently," Skeres said. "Fifty thousand pounds. Where from? No one knows."

"But . . ." Fifty thousand pounds was a veritable king's ransom, and Ralegh had been deeply in debt for years. He had lost tens of thousands attempting to colonize Virginia, his Irish lands weren't profitable, and his privateering vessels hadn't taken a valuable cargo since the *Madre de Dios.* And even then, Marlowe remembered, the queen had claimed the lion's share of the profits. Was Ralegh the one? Marlowe wondered. Had he grown so weary of turning his maritime coups over to the Royal Treasury that he'd turned to smuggling?

Skeres was still speaking. "Apparently Ralegh's using the money for another of his clay-brained schemes. The damned fool failed miserably with his colonies in the New World, but it seems he is plotting another voyage all the same. Thinks he's to discover gold."

Irritated, Marlowe defended his friend. "At least *he* goes after it like a man. Braving high seas and venturing into unknown lands."

"Least I *get* the gold *I* go after," Skeres retorted.

Glancing up, Marlowe saw Ambrosia grinning at them. "Care for another?"

Skeres shook his head. "I was just leaving."

"I'll take one," Marlowe said. Then, watching Skeres stride off, Marlowe noticed a face across the room. It was extraordinary. He would go so far as to say magnificent, but there was something else that caught his attention. Did he know the boy?

Then it hit him. The lad's short hair was the color of marigolds, he had gold loops in his ears, a thin mustache, tobacco hose, and a leather doublet. Lee Anderson. *At last.*

"Fifty, maybe," Ambrosia declared, setting down his drink.

Marlowe looked at her quizzically. His bill should have been under four pence.

"What?"

"Fifty ships, I think. But not a dinghy more."

"What are you talking about?"

"That face. I'd say it could launch about fifty ships."

Marlowe grinned as he caught on. She was alluding to a line from his *Doctor Faustus*, when the magician, gazing at a specter of Helen of Troy, wonders if he was, indeed, beholding the face that launched a thousand ships. "Why so few?"

"Fifty's more than it took to crush the Spanish Armada," Ambrosia answered with a patronizing grimace. "Didn't you know?"

For once Marlowe was speechless and delighted to be so. A tavern whore had confused him by playing with his most famous lines, then had flung a history lesson in his face.

"A theatergoer, are you?" he asked.

"It's marvelous for business. If not for the plague, I'd be at the Rose right now."

"You liked my, uh, you liked Marlowe's *Faustus*?"

Ambrosia sneezed loudly. "I've never paid much attention, actually. Usually have my hands full, if you know what I mean. But I've heard the playmaker is a handsome sight."

"Really?" Marlowe turned his head to give her another angle.

"But apparently he's past his prime."

"What?"

"I hear some new fellow is about to steal his thunder."

Marlowe's face fell. "Will Shakespeare?"

"That's him. He's got these marvelous villains. Everyone raves about them."

"His villains?"

"Oh, yes."

"They rave about *his* villains?"

"For a few pennies, I'll tell you something *really* interesting."

In shock, Marlowe handed over the coin. Ambrosia threw a glance in the direction of the Muscovy sailor. "You're in luck, master. That pretty youth? He's a she."

In spite of his brief flash of disappointment, Marlowe remained intrigued. A girl in sailor's clothing was extremely unusual. Dangerous, as well.

"Business was slow. I thought I'd get things moving with a well-placed grope, but my hand came up empty."

Marlowe smiled.

"I thought you'd be pleased."

And he was, though not for the reason she thought. With yet more damaging information on the Muscovy sailor, he'd definitely get her to talk. He resisted his impulse to kiss Ambrosia's forehead—not a gesture someone in her line of work would particularly appreciate. Searching for a good compliment, he touched her cheek, then exclaimed with exaggerated ardor, "Who ever loved, that loved not at first sight?"

Ambrosia rolled her eyes, but Marlowe was oblivious, momentarily captivated by his phrase. "Oh, that's good!" he murmured, rummaging in the satchel at his belt for ink and a quill. He wrote the line onto a cloth napkin and handed it over. A keepsake she could treasure, perhaps sew onto a pillow.

"Many thanks!"

Marlowe inclined his head.

Unleashing a full-bodied sneeze, she used it to wipe her nose. "Why are you staring at me like that?"

"You're heartless, madam."

Crossing the room, he approached the young sailor. "Mind if I join you?"

Swallowing a mouthful of seafood stew, she shrugged.

"So you're a sailor."

"Something like that."

"A privateer plundering Spanish ships laden with New World riches?"

"What's it to you?"

"Rethinking my choices. Tell me—"

"If you're trying to distract me in order to rob me, you can forget it. I'll cut off your hand before you can blink."

"Perhaps you work for one of our illustrious trading compan—"

"How about I buy you a drink and give you something else to do with your mouth?" she interrupted. "At another table."

"I'm not thirsty."

Bringing a large chunk of cod to her lips, she chewed it slowly, looking away.

"You work for the Muscovy Company," Marlowe pressed. "You just came in from France aboard one of their ships."

"And you just came into territory you shouldn't have."

Persisting, Marlowe improvised, "I have a friend who's a shareholder, and he's worried there's something amiss. I'd just like to ask you a few questions."

"I'm sorry. I can't help you."

"I think you can."

"You're wrong."

Marlowe knew she was lying. Fitz Fat was never off when it came to such details. "No, I'm not wrong. You call yourself Lee Anderson, but you're really a girl in disguise."

"And what are you going to do about it? Turn me in? Are you some kind of government snitch?" She turned her nose in disgust.

"On the contrary, miss, I'd like to help you."

"Because you want something from me."

"Of course." He smiled shamelessly.

"Least you're honest about it."

Satisfied that he had convinced her to talk, Marlowe sat back calmly, waiting.

But all did not go according to plan. She slipped from her seat, whirled around, and raced off.

The girl was through the door before Marlowe had even digested the unexpected turn of events.

Making his way out of the crowded Cardinal's Hat, Marlowe brushed past a very pale, well-dressed man with a pearl-encrusted sword. After a moment, he realized it was Ingram Frizer, whom he loathed. Frizer, Marlowe figured, must be Nick Skeres' partner on the commodities deal. Like Skeres, Frizer was an extortionist, but one with even fewer scruples. Frizer would swindle food from a starving orphan.

Frizer also made no secret of the fact that he scorned the theater. He'd told Marlowe on more than one occasion that such bastions of idleness and lewd criminal behavior had brought the plague down upon them all. Frizer did business deals for Tom Walsingham from time to time, and whenever he and Marlowe crossed paths at Scadbury House, he would mumble some comment to that effect.

Glancing back, Marlowe saw Frizer sliding onto a bench across from Skeres. They were not looking in his direction, but he threw a scowl at them nonetheless.

"I did as you asked," Nick Skeres began, speaking softly. "Found the perfect gull . . . a young gentleman from the country. Desperately short of money. He asked me for assistance this very morning."

"Then we're ready," Ingram Frizer replied. "For our commodity is stored but a stone's throw from here."

"What is it?"

"A dozen German wheel-lock pistols."

Skeres was impressed. "How did you . . . ?"

"They were given to me, as a matter of fact."

Standing atop a set of water steps on the south shore of the Thames, Marlowe was watching Lee Anderson being ferried over to the Isle of Dogs. She had hopped in the only available boat, and he was stranded. Looking down at his expensive doublet—black silk with silver buttons down the front and along the sleeves—he grimaced, then raced down the steps and dove in. He swam awkwardly, using one arm to hold his satchel above the surface.

After reaching the opposite shore and wiping the fetid water from his face, he dashed after the girl into the woods. Seconds later, he grabbed her arm.

"Rot in hell! Let me go!"

Abruptly he did, murmuring, "Lee Anderson . . . Leander . . ."

Lee narrowed her eyes at his dumbfounded smile.

"She's awake!" he marveled. "How can I ever thank you?"

"Who?"

"My muse." Phrases about the classical lovers Hero and Leander were tumbling through his head.

"What?"

"Does anything that just happened strike you as oddly familiar?"

"A sodden fool who reeks of the Thames?"

"No, my dear. A dashing swain braving treacherous waters to reach a fiery beauty."

Playing along, she looked around, as if searching for something. "Dashing swain?"

He laughed. "Although the roles are reversed here," Marlowe said. "Leander, you see, is the man in the story, whereas you're . . ."

Hands pressed to his forehead, he looked at the ground, mumbling to himself. "A maid in man's clothes . . . in man's clothing . . . no, man's attire . . ."

Looking back up, he said slowly, with pride, "Some swore he was a maid in man's attire, for in his looks were all that men desire."

Lee nodded. "Catchy."

Marlowe rummaged through his bag, eager to put it to paper. But before he could find his quill, his breath caught in his throat. He felt something cold against his neck, something sharp. A knife.

"If you turn around and leave right now," she hissed in his ear, "I just might let you live."

Marlowe's tone remained light. "But if I leave, how will you get what you need?"

"What?" She pressed the knife harder.

"You're hiding out in this den of derelicts because you don't have papers, am I right?" The Isle of Dogs was a notorious haven for fugitives.

"A fat bastard with three chins took them from me."

Thank you, Fitz Fat. "Did I forget to mention that I've a friend who's a forger?"

"Keep talking."

"I don't know who you are or what you're afraid of, but I know we can help each other."

She withdrew her blade.

Facing her, Marlowe gently set his hands on her shoulders. "My name's Kit. I'm going to take you to the city and get you a set of papers. If you don't want to trust me, trust the fact that I want information from you."

Her bluster melting away, she nodded reluctantly. Slipping her knife back into her boot, she grabbed her things from a nook in a hollow tree. Marlowe took her hand and led her back to the river.

Moments later, they settled into a boat bound for London.

13

Stepping off a British Airways jetliner, Kate entered Heathrow airport, cleared passport control, and headed for the baggage claim area. The carousel was not yet moving. She checked her voice mail and listened to a message from Jack telling her to call him as soon as she landed.

"How are you?" he asked.

"Tired."

"Couldn't sleep, huh?"

"No."

"I'm worried about you."

"Actually, this case is exactly what I need. Absorbing. Light."

"Anything I can do?"

"I'll be fine. I'm working all day and seeing Adriana tonight."

"Well, if there's anyone who can get your mind off your troubles, it's her," Jack said wryly. It was true. Adriana was very different from Kate — a superficial party girl, in Jack's opinion — but he could not deny that her infectious energy and perpetual dramatics made for a fun evening.

"I'll let you get back to sleep," Kate said, grabbing her suitcase. "But thanks for calling."

She passed through the international arrivals gate and scanned the line of drivers for a sign with her name on it. Medina had said he would send a car for her.

"Kate."

Recognizing Medina's voice, she turned toward the sound, preparing to tease him for being overly eager to see her. His troubled expression startled her.

"The professor we spoke about?" Medina began. "He's dead."

For a moment Kate thought he might be playing games, might have finished their round of *Clue* without her, but the look on his face said otherwise. As much as she would have preferred it to be the case, Medina was definitely not referring to an imaginary wrench attack in a ballroom.

OXFORD — 11:12 A.M.

"Shot in the head while bent over his desk," the stout gray-haired policeman said grimly. "Probably never knew what hit him."

Kate looked at Medina. His jaw was tightly clenched, and a tiny muscle beneath his brow twitched. They were standing in the late Andrew Rutherford's office, a cozy L-shaped affair overflowing with books. The policeman, Hugh Sinclair, had called because he'd heard their messages on Rutherford's answering machine.

Though all three windows were wide open, the stench of death lingered. Kate followed Medina's gaze out to the Christ Church meadows — large swaths of close-cropped grass stretching to clusters of dark trees lining the Isis River. This place must bring back a lot of memories for him, she thought, glancing at the patched dark green velvet couch nestled at the foot of the L's smaller leg. Having studied briefly at Oxford herself, she knew how the system worked. Medina would have sat on that couch once a week, reading his essay aloud to launch a discussion with his tutor.

"No gunshots reported," Inspector Sinclair continued. "So the killer had to've used a silencer."

"Who found him?" Kate asked.

"A student. The night before last."

"Did anyone report him missing?"

Sinclair shook his head.

"He's a widower," Medina offered by way of explanation. "No children either . . . his daughter overdosed on heroin as a teenager."

God, how sad, Kate thought. "What about the time of death, Inspector?"

"M.E. said three days ago."

Kate looked at Medina. "So if they're related—this shooting and the break-in at your place—both could have happened on the same day."

Medina nodded.

"After you met with Rutherford," she continued, "whoever learned of your discovery and decided to steal the manuscript probably didn't know whether you took it with you or left it here. Maybe he dispatched the thief to your place and a second man here at the same time in order to avoid alerting either of you before he got what he wanted."

"Sounds likely," Medina said.

"Or maybe it was the same person. Maybe the thief came here first, realized Rutherford didn't have it, then headed for your house."

As she spoke, something about Rutherford's desk caught Kate's attention. With the exception of a laptop on the far left corner, the wooden surface was bare. Near pristine, in fact, but . . . "Has this room been cleaned?" she asked, her eyes traveling to the bullet holes and the droplets of blood splattered across the wall.

Sinclair shook his head.

"So the killer must have taken the papers or books Rutherford was using when he was shot."

Seeing Medina's curious expression, she explained, "The blood on the wall is mostly lower than Rutherford's head would have been, so the shots must have been fired at a downward angle. At least a little blood should be on the desk, but there's barely a drop."

Fishing in his pocket, Sinclair withdrew a sheet of paper and handed it to them. "A scene-of-crime bloke sketched a diagram of what the splatter pattern should have been, figuring the type of slug and all. Should've been a fair amount of blood, actually."

Rocking back on his heels, he added, "All day yesterday I was wondering what on earth a tutor could be working on that anyone would want to steal—other than the failing exam book of some spoiled little sod."

Kate smiled grimly.

"You think he had notes about that manuscript you mentioned on his desk?" Sinclair asked. "Copies of the pages?"

"Yeah," she said slowly, "the timing seems too . . . much to be coincidence, but to *kill* him? An old man? It would've been just as easy to hit him over the head and take what he wanted."

"Bloody heartless," Sinclair agreed. "He didn't care either way."

"Any leads from ballistics?" Kate asked.

"We've got the gun, I think. I expect a match. Not many silenced pistols pass through town. Unfortunately, though, it's unregistered."

"How did you . . . ?"

"Some pissed punters were rowing on the Cherwell yesterday," Sinclair explained, "in a shallow section by the Magdalen Bridge. They tipped over, and a girl stepped on it with her bare foot." Evidently not a fan of drunken Oxford undergraduates, he rolled his eyes.

"An unregistered Hämmerli 280," he then told them. "Worth a fair whack, apparently."

"More than a thousand pounds," Kate said, nodding. The Swiss-made pistol with its custom-fitted walnut grip and adjustable trigger—a discontinued model—was one she'd practiced with on several occasions. "Did anyone you interviewed have any insights, Inspector? See any strangers around, hear anything unusual?"

"Nothing much. A few students remembered noticing his light on quite late three nights ago but didn't see anyone enter the building. Vera Carstairs, the girl who found his body—it seems they were pretty close, but she hadn't seen him in days."

"Can I speak with her?"

"I'll phone her just now," Sinclair said, flipping through his notepad for the number. After making the call, he added, "She'll be over in a bit."

"Would you mind if I look around till then?" Kate asked.

"Not at all. I'd like to see what you find."

"Thank you." Relieved, Kate smiled. When their work overlapped, police officers were not generally receptive to her input. Sinclair's willingness to involve her was refreshing.

"I'll take you to his rooms, too, if you like."

"That would be helpful," Kate said. "By the way, did you find a Rolodex? Address book?"

"A diary, in his bedroom. Near blank this past week, though. Just a few tutorials marked in."

"Do you mind if I borrow his university directory?"

"Go right ahead, but what do you . . ."

"Shortly before he was killed, Rutherford suggested to Cidro that he showed the manuscript to an ancient language specialist. I'd like to identify any in the area and see if my company can trace a call from Rutherford to one of them this past week. That scholar is the only person we know Rutherford contacted about it."

Synclair nodded. "Just give me a shout when you're finished here."

Medina turned to leave as well. "I've got some calls to make, Kate. I'll wait for you outside."

"Okay. See you soon."

Alone, Kate looked around the office. Where to start? Maybe Rutherford kept his contact information on his laptop. She lifted the screen and booted it up. Opening his address book program, she was disappointed to find that he didn't seem to have used it at all, unless the killer had deleted its contents. Kate checked to see if it had been modified anytime in the past week.

It hadn't.

Biting her lower lip, she skimmed through hundreds of documents, searching for personal notes of some kind—anything that might relate to the manuscript. Nothing.

No loose papers remained near the desk, she noticed, shutting down the computer. A stack of academic journals lay by her feet. She knelt on the floor and flipped through them, looking for any stray papers the killer might have overlooked—a name, a phone number, the time set for a meeting. Again nothing.

"Guess I'll have to rely on phone records," she mumbled, rising to her feet. Turning, she decided she might as well check Rutherford's file cabinet. Most people left their schedule and contact information in more accessible places, but maybe Rutherford's habits weren't the norm, she thought. The top two drawers held photocopies of journal articles and other research materials related to his writing projects. Nothing relevant.

Opening the third and fourth drawers, she saw that each folder had a person's name. Flipping through, she realized that all the names belonged to students. The folders were filled with fact sheets, plans of study, and copies of their essays.

As she pushed the bottom drawer shut, one of the names jumped out at her: Moor. *It's probably just a coincidence, but . . .* Kate pulled out the folder and flipped it open. "Moor" had been Queen Elizabeth's nickname for Francis Walsingham.

"Oh, my God," she murmured, shocked to see translations of the *Anatomy's* first few reports along with microfilmed versions of the corresponding originals. So Rutherford *had* been able to identify them as coming from Walsingham's files, she realized. But had he recognized them immediately—and lied to Medina—or had he studied the copies for a few days, *then* made his breakthrough? Was he the kind of person who would have hired a professional thief to steal something from a former student? He definitely was not the man calling himself Jade Dragon, because Jade Dragon had hired Bill Mazur to grab her purse two days after Rutherford's death. Maybe Rutherford had colluded with Jade Dragon to orchestrate the theft at Medina's home, then been double-crossed?

Hearing footsteps approach, Kate replaced the folder and turned around. A small pale girl with short pixieish black hair and big bloodshot eyes stood in the doorway, a solemn expression on her face.

"Vera?"

The girl nodded. "Inspector Sinclair said you're a private investigator? That you're . . . helping him?"

"Yeah. Thanks for coming. I'm Kate."

"Dr. Rutherford just asked me to be his new research assistant. We were going to talk about it today . . . during my tutorial," Vera said numbly. "I was so excited, I . . . I still can't believe someone would hurt him."

"It must have been awful to find him like that. I'm so sorry you had to face that."

"Do you know why it happened?"

"I think whoever killed him stole the papers he was working on that night—"

"But he was just writing another history," Vera interrupted, confused. "Why would . . . I mean, to me it would've been really interesting—a few hundred other people, too—but he only got started a month ago. There couldn't have been much to nick—an outline, maybe—and it's not as if selling that would fetch any money. Most people find history tedious, you know?"

"I do," Kate said. "But I don't think he was working on his book that night, Vera. He started in on another project this past week. He didn't mention anything to you in your last session? Anything that sounded unusual? A discovery he'd made, a surprise he'd gotten?"

"I don't think so. Let's see . . . I read him my essay, we talked about it for a while—a couple of hours, actually. Then, as I was leaving, he mentioned the assistant job. I think that's it."

"Do you know who his friends were? Which other tutors he was close to?"

"I've seen him with the president of Christ Church a few times . . . a physics tutor called Mildred Archer, um . . . I can't think of anyone else just now," Vera said.

"All his students think he's lovely, though," she added, her lower lip quivering, eyes welling. "He'd never turn you away. If you had a few questions or just needed to talk about something. He made you feel . . . like what you had to say really mattered."

"He sounds like a wonderful man."

Wiping away her tears, Vera nodded. "Do you think you can, um . . ."

Kate reached into her bag for a Kleenex. "Yes. I'll find whoever did this."

OXFORD — 12:37 P.M.

Medina pulled out of Christ Church's visitor parking area.

"So *that's* what Andrew wanted to tell me," he said, after listening to Kate's description of the file labeled Moor. "He left me a phone message a few days ago, and I'd been trying to reach him, but . . ."

"A colleague of mine is getting hold of his emails and recent phone records. They might show us who he did tell and who's responsible for his death." After speaking with Vera, Kate had abandoned the idea that Rutherford might have been dishonest with Medina. Someone so adored by his students did not strike her as capable of what she'd initially suspected.

"I'm sick about drawing him into this," Medina said softly, his voice uneven. "When I was here last week, we had dinner together, catching up. I didn't tell him to keep quiet about the manuscript, or anything. I—"

"You had no way of knowing, Cidro," Kate said, touching his arm.

"You really think you'll find the guy? This Jade Dragon?"

"Yes. Not many people could have learned of your discovery. And if I can't trace him through your tutor, there's still the thief. As soon as I find out who he is, I can look to see who contacted him in the past week. And then, of course, there's the manuscript. If the crime scene details don't get us there first, I believe one of Phelippes's pages will."

"Have you found anything in it since yesterday?"

"Yeah, but definitely nothing someone would kill for," Kate answered.

"Tell me?"

"I came across evidence that the conviction of Mary Stuart went way beyond entrapment. It was rigged."

"Oh, that Scottish queen. Walsingham's bête noire, right?"

"Yeah," Kate said, sliding her laptop from her backpack and powering it on. "As a Catholic and the great-granddaughter of Henry VII, she was the legitimate queen of England in the eyes of Catholic Europe. A serious threat. Even so, Elizabeth kept refusing to have her cousin executed, in spite of Walsingham's urging. She thought imprisoning Mary was enough."

"So what'd he do?"

"Set up a scheme to intercept Mary's mail without her knowledge. Used double agents to convince her that a supposedly secret post—a waterproof pouch in her beer keg deliveries—was really secure. That way, as a plot to rescue her gathered steam, Phelippes was able to read all of her correspondence. Eventually, with enough coaxing from Walsingham's double agents, the conspirators decided to assassinate Elizabeth. Phelippes waited eagerly for Mary to authorize that plan, but she never did. So he forged the incriminating letter himself. Which has long been suspected but never proven."

"What's the proof?" Medina asked.

"Mary's real letter to one of the conspirators," Kate said, clicking open a document. "The letter Phelippes and Walsingham suppressed. Until now all we've had is a copy, so no one could agree as to whether it was simply rewritten or heavily embellished."

Kate reached into her bag and took a pair of dark red cat-eye glasses from their case. Slipping them on, she told Medina, "Dated July 17, 1586, it's from Mary to Anthony Babington, a young Catholic who'd served as a page in the household of her earliest English captor, years before. He was definitely smitten with her—she's supposed to have been bewitchingly beautiful—and he yearned to rescue her. Anyway, he'd written to Mary about the plan, which included assassination, and asked for her blessing. In response—in the letter Phelippes included in his *Anatomy*—Mary authorized Babington to free her, but she begged him not to murder her cousin."

Pushing her glasses firmly up to the bridge of her nose, Kate read, "Elizabeth may have held me prisoner these long years, but I cannot take her life. She shares my blood, my royal blood. I cannot do it. I am afraid of hell."

"So Phelippes and Walsingham convinced everyone she was a would-be murderess?" Medina asked.

"Not just would-be. They also suppressed evidence proving she wasn't behind the murder of her first husband."

"Poor woman."

"I know. A lot of historians would love to get their hands on these pages. Her descendants might be interested, too, might like the idea of exonerating their royal ancestor. One of them's a big shot in the Knights of Malta, you know, one of those Catholic secret societies, but—"

"I agree," Medina cut in. "Doesn't strike me as a motive for murder."

Kate scanned the document titles of the other reports she'd deciphered on her flight the night before. "There was one other good scandal," she said. "About an English spy named Anthony Bacon."

"Any relation to Francis?"

"His brother. Both dabbled in espionage. Anthony ultimately rose quite high in the Earl of Essex's intelligence network. But long before that, he ran afoul of French law."

"Caught spying?"

"No. He was pretty discreet in his *professional* life."

"A dalliance with an angel-faced French boy?" Medina guessed.

"Right, an illicit affair. Literally. The French king shared Anthony's fondness for young boys, but French law was not as sympathetic. Sex between men was a capital crime at that time, punishable by burning at the stake."

"What happened?"

"Oh, Anthony had good connections. Hushed it up pretty well. Word of the incident reached very few English ears. It seems that Phelippes was one of the ones protecting him."

Closing the document, Kate looked up and saw that they'd left the town of Oxford. Medina was turning onto the motorway back toward London. She craned her neck around for a moment to watch Oxford's famous "dreaming spires" recede in the distance.

"I've been meaning to look more closely at those photos you gave me," she said, opening a set of images Max had emailed her the day before. "You know, of the thief. My colleague digitized them."

The first few were of the blown safe. Looking for anything she might have missed in the Pierre, Kate made a mental note to ask the Scotland Yard detective on the case for details about the explosive supplies.

Perusing the next several images, she saw the dead thief sitting in an armchair by a window, blood oozing from his forehead. He wore only one glove, on his right hand, and a small hole in the fabric—as well as a fair amount of blood—suggested he had been shot through the wrist. That hand had fallen, along with his pistol, to the small round table before him. His left hand lay on his left thigh. Glass shards were scattered, a few across the table, most of them on the floor by his feet.

Looks like one of the bullets tore through his glass, Kate thought to herself. Then the thief's ring caught her attention. She clicked on it, and courtesy of Max's programming efforts, the section of the thief's left hand tripled in size.

"That's strange," she murmured aloud.

"What?"

"I think the gemstone on his ring is dislodged."

"Maybe he damaged it while cracking my safe."

After a moment, Kate replied, "You know, I think I might recognize it." Opening her cell phone, she asked Medina, "Will you excuse me for a minute?"

"Sure."

She dialed Max's home number. "You awake?"

"Drinking coffee and skimming the *Times*'s website."

"Oh, good. I'm in a car for another hour—mind doing a quick search for me?"

"No sweat."

"Okay, for key words use *Portofino, cat, cocaine,* and *ruby ring.*"

"Gotcha. Here we go: *Cat Strikes Again, Cat Pounces in Portofino, A Ruby in the Cat's Paws . . .* "

"Can you find a photo of the stolen ring?" Kate asked. "Or scan the articles for a description of it?"

"Uh, let's see . . . no, no, no . . . okay, got a picture. Pretty thick gold band with a pattern carved into it. The ruby's damn big . . ."

"Square-cut?"

"Yeah. Gimme a minute . . . okay, nine years ago there was a heist at the Splendido . . ."

Kate recognized the hotel's name. It was the priciest one in Portofino.

"The thief broke into the suite of Peregrine James, Marchioness of Halifax," Max continued. "He stole a ruby ring with a hidden cavity, where, an unnamed source says, Lady Halifax kept an emergency stash of coke."

"Thanks, man."

"Sure thing."

Hanging up, Kate turned to Medina. "Well, I think I know who your thief was. Or his nickname, at least."

Medina glanced at her. "Then why do you sound so disappointed?"

"There's a man the press call 'the Cat.' He's the most notorious burglar in Europe since Cary Grant in *To Catch a Thief.*"

"Good movie. There's really a living counterpart?"

"Yeah, and I think this is him. You saw the ring your thief was wearing, right?"

Eyes back on the road, Medina nodded. "If real, it's one hell of a ruby."

"I'm pretty sure it's the same ring the Cat's thought to have stolen a while back. Plus I know his M.O., and everything fits. Your safe, for example. If he can't manipulate a lock, the Cat always uses a shaped charge, just as your thief did. Places it with expert precision. He's not the kind of guy to tolerate the racket of a drill or the blinding light of a cutting torch. He's neat, and he's quiet. Elegant, you might say. Not many out there like him."

"You got all that in a three-minute phone call?"

"No, I've been reading about him for years. I was an armchair crime and espionage buff before I set foot in the P.I. world, and he's particularly interesting. Only steals from the very rich and, rumor has it, donates the bulk of his proceeds to charity."

Kate didn't add that she admired him and wished she were wrong about his death. She kept a file in her bedroom crammed with newspaper clippings about the Cat's exploits and eagerly awaited the next installment.

Turning back to her computer screen, Kate looked at the shattered remains of the glass. Resting on Medina's table, it would have been at least a foot beneath and away from the thief's raised gun arm, she realized. *That's strange. The other shots showed far better aim—the bullet to the wrist was right on target, and the two to the head and chest were just an inch or two off.*

Wanting to take a closer look at the thief's pistol, she clicked on it. From what she could see—it was partially covered by his right hand—the pistol was made of wood, steel, and mother-of-pearl and was unusually small, with a very slender barrel. But still fairly heavy, which meant that it should probably have . . . "Did you notice any nicks on the surface of your table?" she asked Medina.

"Ah, I don't think so. Why?"

"If that gun crashed down to your table when the thief was shot, it would probably have done a little damage—some chips in the wood or something. I wonder if he was raising the glass of cognac and not the gun, when your guard found him, which would explain why the glass was hit. You know, in a dark room, it would have been easy to mistake one for the other."

"Sounds possible," Medina said slowly. "I hope it didn't happen that way."

But was he lifting the glass to his lips or making some kind of toast? Kate wondered. *A toast would make more sense. The arm position would more closely resemble a raised gun, and if that were the case* . . . "Actually, he might already have been dead when the bullets hit him."

"What?"

"Well, if the ring is the same one the Cat stole, it has a hidden cavity, and since the gem was dislodged, I would think—"

"You're not suggesting he had poison in his ring."

"I am. In case he ever got caught. You know, to avoid the dishonor of failure, of jail."

"But that's so . . . old-fashioned."

"Exactly," Kate said. "Perfectly appropriate for a gentleman thief."

Medina seemed intrigued but still doubtful. "The detective didn't mention any of this."

"Well, he didn't know about your manuscript's enormous value. To him your break-in was just an ordinary B and E. No reason to link it to the Cat."

Medina remained skeptical.

"Why don't you ask him to check into the ring and have the body tested for poison?" Kate asked. "And how about asking for the composition of the plastique? We can see if it matches the kind the Cat always uses."

"You're on," he said, reaching for his phone.

"Oh, and while you're at it, can you ask him for some morgue photographs? Can we send a messenger to pick them up and drop them at my hotel? And the label inside the thief's suit jacket. Let's see what that says, too."

Listening to Medina ask for Detective Sergeant Colin Davies, Kate closed her eyes.

"I'm holding," he told her.

"I'm sorry, but I couldn't sleep on the plane. I think I'm about to pass out," she sighed, fumbling for the lever to crank back her seat.

"First time in a Ferrari, huh?"

"What makes you say that?"

"The seats don't recline."

"Useless bucket o' bolts," Kate grumbled. "Pretty sad how much cash you wasted on it."

"I know. You don't seem impressed."

Mayfair, London — 1:55 p.m.

The Connaught Hotel is nestled on a quiet, triangular intersection in the heart of Mayfair, a perennially fashionable neighborhood in central London filled with smart shops, luxury hotels, and expensive offices and homes. A redbrick Georgian mansion with pale stone trim, it has a pillared entrance and miniature ivy hanging from the wrought-iron balcony above. The same ivy, along with yellow pansies, filled boxes resting on the three-foot-high outer wall.

"Here we are," Kate heard Medina say after she felt his car come to a stop. Opening her eyes, she turned to her right and saw a man dressed in a gray jacket and black top hat leaning toward Medina's open window. *Must be the doorman.* "The lady will be checking in," Medina said.

As a bellman took her suitcase from the trunk, Kate unfastened her seat belt with surprise. "Not exactly the Holiday Inn, is it?"

Medina shrugged. "Since it's across the street from your office, I thought it made the most sense."

Stepping from his car, Kate slipped on her backpack and followed him inside. Passing through a stone arch festooned with carved Grecian women, they headed to the concierge desk. Medina helped her check in, then turned to leave.

"Cidro?" Kate asked. "Will you be reachable this afternoon?"

He nodded. "I'll be in the City for the next few hours, but home after that. By five, I'd say. Then I've got another meeting at seven, but you can ring and interrupt if you like."

"Oh, no, I'll call or stop by when you're free. I think I'll have an interesting update for you."

Turning to the mahogany-paneled stairwell, Kate climbed the red-carpeted steps to the second floor. Wearily she stepped into her suite, turned to the right, and found herself in the living room. Her eyes widened. It was a luxurious space with ivory damask walls, golden sconces, an ornate gilt mirror hanging over a large fireplace, a glass chandelier, and a plush sofa and chairs upholstered in turquoise and yellow silk.

Spotting a manila envelope on the desk across the room, she walked over and took a seat. Positioned before a window, the desk offered a view of the turrets and chimneys of the buildings across the way. Looking down at the street below, Kate watched a man in head-to-toe black and red leather climb aboard a matching Ducati and roar off.

She then reached into one of her backpack's outer pockets, withdrew a small transmitter, and pressed the power button. It remained silent—to her, at least. Designed to ward off electronic surveillance, the transmitter was actually emitting a high-frequency white noise inaudible to human ears. Confident that she could make a secure call even if her room were bugged, Kate used her cell phone to dial Max at their office.

"Hi, I'm on my way out, but since Slade asked me to give regular updates, and I was with Medina earlier . . ."

"Yeah, what've you got?"

"Well, to find Medina's thief, I was going to show the coroner's photographs to his tailor," Kate said, opening the envelope in front of her, which had come from Scotland Yard. "Unfortunately, I don't know who that tailor is. His jacket didn't have a label. But since I'm convinced he's the Cat, I've got another idea. A better one, actually. Saves me from having to freak anyone out with pictures of a dead body," she added, staring at the dead thief's pale, slightly blue face.

Slipping the images back inside the folder, she finished, "Also, the professor Medina showed the manuscript to—he was murdered a few days ago by someone relatively sophisticated . . . using a silenced Hämmerli."

"The Cat? Before he broke into Medina's place?"

"No. Had to be someone else. The Cat never hurts anyone."

"So Jade Dragon hired Europe's top thief and a professional hit man? Shit, this is more serious than we thought. What are you carrying?"

"My usual," Kate said, referring to a tube of red lipstick she always had with her that concealed a single 4.5-millimeter bullet. A tiny pistol known as the Kiss of Death, its prototype had been invented in the sixties by the KGB. She also had one with two tranquilizer darts instead of a bullet, made by the CIA's Office of Technical Service, per her request. She called that one her Good Night Kiss. Kate liked them because anyone looking through her things would think she was unarmed.

"Okay, but it wouldn't hurt to pick up a regular gun at the office."

"Maybe. You know, I'm right across the street. Medina got me a suite at the Connaught."

"Damn. And here I was feeling sorry for you—out there risking your life and all."

"There *are* perks," Kate said. "Hey, I almost forgot. How was your date last night?"

"Mmm, not enough going on upstairs."

"What, she was quiet? Couldn't keep up with your jokes?"

"Sweetheart, I wasn't referring to the attic."

Kate burst out laughing.

"You're still meeting de Tolomei tomorrow night, right?" Max asked.

"Yeah, the Vatican thing is at eight. I've got an afternoon flight. Got anything new on him?"

"Mmm, I might be on to something. I'll let you know."

"Talk to you soon."

Four blocks away on Park Lane, a stretched black Mercedes just in from a private airstrip in West London was speeding south on its way to the Ritz. From the backseat, Luca de Tolomei gazed out the window, smiling as he pondered the evening ahead.

NEW YORK CITY—9:28 A.M.

Sitting alone in the Slade Group conference room, Max continued examining his latest research on Luca de Tolomei's financial transactions. Since the evening before, he'd had the vague feeling that there was some kind of pattern to the mess of people, dates, and numbers on the printouts before him, but whatever it was, it kept hovering just outside his consciousness.

Oh, maybe Slade can help, Max thought, hearing his boss's familiar footsteps. "Morning, Slade. Can I run something by you? I'm thinking that—"

"Can it wait a few minutes? I've got an urgent call to make."

From the privacy of his office three floors above, Jeremy Slade dialed Donovan Morgan.

"Don. Can you talk?"

"Of course. What have you found?"

"He's alive," Slade said. "A tip came in. We'll find him soon."

Hanging up, Slade put his elbows on his desk and lowered his head to his hands. He was so disgusted with himself for thinking inside the box three years ago—for not considering the possibility their spy had been imprisoned somewhere outside of Iraq—he didn't know how he would live with it. Barring nuclear detonation, letting someone down like this, failing to protect one of his own, was his worst nightmare.

With accounts of the torture inflicted in Iranian prisons flooding his mind, Slade pressed his palms over his eyes, hard, until a kaleidoscope of dark colors blocked the horrifying images, if only for a moment.

14

Birds of the air will tell of murders past?
I am asham'd to hear such fooleries.
Many will talk of title to a crown:
What right had Caesar to the empire?
Might first made kings, and laws were then most sure
When like the Draco's they were writ in blood.

—MACHIAVEL, in Marlowe's *The Jew of Malta*

LONDON—AFTERNOON, MAY 1593

Does he deny Christ's divinity?"

No response.

"Does he mean to incite rebellion?"

No response.

"You lived with him, did you not?"

As before, only the distant clanking of fetters broke the silence.

Richard Topcliffe turned to the men standing at either end of the rack. "Taut, then just beyond."

Very slowly, they pushed their oak levers toward the ground, a hair's width at a time. The ropes tied round the prisoner's wrists and ankles stretched him tighter, and the stones placed beneath his back dug deeper into his flesh. Wood squeaked steadily. Then there was another sound few would recognize—the faint ripping of skin.

"Shall we chat?"

Blood staining his bonds, the prisoner nodded.

"Well?"

Coughing, the prisoner struggled to clear his throat. "Fancy the theater, do you?"

Topcliffe moistened his lips. Softly he gave the order: "To the floor."

A popping sound. Then another. And finally, screams.

Bearing paper and ink, a scrivener entered the room.

Defeated, the broken man spat out anything that might interest them. Again and again. He slandered Kit Marlowe until his tear ducts were dry and his voice was hoarse. And then the playwright Thomas Kyd, a gifted and popular wordsmith, did not have any words left.

"Am I to learn your real name?" Marlowe asked, leading the young sailor north along Gracechurch Street.

"Why the devil—"

"I could guarantee you'll never be troubled at customs again."

Stopping midstride, she sank into an elaborate curtsy. "Helen, sir. So very pleased to meet you."

"I should have guessed," Marlowe said wryly, thinking of Helen of Troy. In spite of her false mustache, the beauty of this Helen's face was unmistakable. "Why did you leave England?"

"I was accused of witchcraft. Two children in my village fell ill."

"Common story," Marlowe replied with a nod. "Even royalty like someone to blame for their misfortunes. There was a tempest when James of Scotland was at sea, bringing his new bride home from Denmark. He accused dozens of his countrymen of raising it. Had them burned at the stake."

They turned onto Lombard Street. "You fled to the Continent?"

She shook her head. "I snuck into a brothel, nicked a sailor's clothes, and found work on a privateering vessel bound for the Mediterranean. A few days into the voyage, we were attacked by Barbary pirates. The aged captain took me aside and yanked off my mustache. I thought I was done for. Turned out he was amused and impressed with my charade. I've been with his crew ever since."

"But your golden hair . . ."

"Many Christians sail under Barbary flags. We sail for ourselves, unlike our English counterparts."

"Why have you returned?"

"I was to give money to my family, but that cursed fat man took it all."

"So the Muscovy Company bit . . . a ruse to pass through customs?"

"Exactly."

"Well, then, technically one could say you've wasted my time."

"On the contrary . . ."

Marlowe raised his eyebrows.

Helen shook her head. "Papers first."

"Fair enough."

He paused before the arched doorway of an enormous brick building. Its single tower stretched up behind him, a metal grasshopper decorating its peak. "Welcome to the Royal Exchange. Home to just about everything money can buy."

"You're taking me shopping? You do realize I could be arrested at any moment, perhaps tied to the Dock," she said. Pirates and smugglers were strung to Executioner's Dock at low tide and left to drown.

"Imagination, Miss Helen. Black market goods are sold in more places than dark alleys."

The building's lively courtyard, decorated with statues of former kings of England, was teeming with merchants and shoppers. Passing glass sellers, candlemakers, and goldsmiths, they moved slowly toward the far end of the courtyard, elbowing their way through the dense crowd. Near a cluster of booksellers, Marlowe stopped before a freckled redhead leaning against a thick marble pillar. The man was a forger named Kit Miller.

"Ah. My *other* favorite Kit," the redhead said, grinning. "I sold every last copy of your elegies before ten minutes had passed. Even after I trebled the price. Whatever you need, I'm your man."

"Identity papers for the lady."

"Lady?"

Helen discreetly peeled back part of her mustache.

"I see," Miller said, leading them beneath the flap of his tent. "You've come to the right place." Reaching for a box beneath his table, he withdrew a set of parchment pages and other equipment. "Is there a particular name you would like?"

"Lee Anderson," Helen said. "I've grown used to it."

Using three different inks, Miller filled in the appropriate blank spaces and applied the necessary seals. "All right," he announced with pride, "we're ready for the magic touch." With that he placed the pages on the ground, jumped upon them several times, and handed them over.

As they left the building, Helen reached for her new papers, but Marlowe held them over his head.

"Feed me well," she said, "and I shall tell you everything I know."

WESTMINSTER — DUSK

Wearing sharp spurs, two red-crowned roosters circled each other, glaring intently. Seconds later they were in the air, wings flapping, taloned claws scratching, dirt and feathers flying.

Leaning against a nearby tree, Robert Poley watched hundreds of coins changing hands. His eyes flicked across the faces illuminated by torchlight, gathered round the ring's wooden fence. Shaking their fists and yelling, the spectators cheered their favored bird.

Turning, he saw his employer approach. The wooded grounds just south of St. James's Palace, site of daily cockfights, were one of Cecil's preferred meeting spots. Anonymous and convenient to his office in Whitehall.

"Did you speak with him? Tell him to quit England?"

"Not yet. When I got to Scadbury House earlier today, he had already left. Walsingham wasn't about either."

"The commission dispatched four constables. You must get to him first."

"Torture?"

Cecil nodded. "Topcliffe is back. Last night he started on Thomas Kyd."

"Kyd?" Poley repeated, surprised. "That quiet lily-livered playmaker? He's not the type to promote violence."

"Constables searched his lodgings. Seems they found a document containing heretical statements. Kyd denied ever seeing it, said it must have belonged to Marlowe — they lived together not too long ago. He also made reference to Marlowe's monstrous opinions, said that Marlowe has a tendency to jest at Scripture and slander holy men. Claiming, for instance, that Christ and St. John . . ."

"Yes?"

"Shared an unusual sort of love."

Poley grinned at Cecil's discomfiture.

"Another informant reported that Marlowe promotes atheism. Said he is able to show more sound reasons for it than any minister in England can give to prove divinity. The informant said that he himself was persuaded to atheism on account of Marlowe's words." Cecil paused for a moment. "Any truth to it?"

Poley frowned. "Perhaps. Marlowe has always had a penchant for irreverence."

"In any case, I believe that particular document was planted, that someone is plotting against him—setting him up for a fall," Cecil said grimly. "Alert him. Make sure he's gone for several months, at least."

"It's too bad about Kyd," Poley said, gazing off into space. "An innocent pawn . . . good writer, too. I loved his *Spanish Tragedy.*" He paused for a moment, then turned back to Cecil. "If I were a different sort of man, I think I'd feel sorry for him."

LONDON—DUSK

Helen swallowed her last bite of venison stew. "My captain has an alliance with an Englishman of the Muscovy Company."

Marlowe nearly choked on his wine.

"These six months, he's been providing the Englishman with riches from the East, goods my captain confiscated from Portuguese traders. In return, the Englishman has offered us weaponry."

No Northeast Passage, Marlowe realized. Someone was simply using Muscovy ships for his own smuggling operation, ensuring the deaths of many of his own countrymen in the process. Aboard pirate ships, those weapons would be aimed at English sailors before long. In fact, they probably had been already. "The smuggler was definitely with the Muscovy Company?"

Helen nodded. "Claimed to be. As a favor to my captain, he ordered one of the company's ship captains to take me here as one of his own."

"His name?"

Helen shook her head.

"You've seen him?"

"When boarding our ship, he insisted the crew remain below deck."

"Damn."

"But I heard his voice. I know it well."

"That might do. There's a disguising at Greenwich Palace the day after tomorrow. Care to join me?"

"For a few shillings," Helen said, then frowned. "But why should you care who it is? I fail to see how your friend the shareholder would be affected by this."

"Well, you see . . ."

"God's teeth, you *are* a spy!"

Unruffled, Marlowe quietly finished his wine.

Then, watching her slip her knife from her boot and draw it overhead with dizzying speed, he said, "Whoever I might be, I told you I'd never turn you in, and I won't. Besides, you do stand to profit—"

"A spy who keeps his promises?" Helen interrupted. "I'd never have thought it possible."

Marlowe shrugged. "I'm used to amazing people."

Helen lowered her knife. "I don't know why, but I think I believe you. Perhaps I won't kill you just yet."

"Of course you won't."

"Excuse me?"

"You like me too much."

Helen dipped two fingers in her wine and flicked them at Marlowe's face.

"You wish to start something?" he asked, cocking a spoonful of stew.

"When I do, you'll know. Now, Kit. Another thing. The Englishman? He was especially pleased with one particular item my captain gave him. Declared it to be his new favorite possession."

"What was it?"

"A small statue with rubies for eyes."

"A human figure?"

"No. It was a dragon, carved from jade."

15

A ny luck?" Kate asked Max. She was just stepping out of the Victoria tube station on her way to Medina's. Having discovered the dead thief's identity a half hour before, she had asked Max to trace any recent additions to his bank accounts, on the chance he'd been paid in advance.

"No money's come in during the past month, not to any of his offshore accounts," Max said. "I checked his email, too. No messages from that Jade Dragon address."

"He might use some kind of agent. Can you send me the names of everyone who's emailed or called him since the discovery of the manuscript?"

"Sure thing."

Pausing in Belgrave Square, Kate took another look at the year-old photo she had found of Medina's thief. Having assumed that he was the Cat, and that the Cat was a jet-setting society type — since every expert believed he'd already seen the interiors of the wealthy homes he'd robbed — Kate had gone to a public library and leafed through stacks of old society magazines. Before long she had found a shot of Medina's thief in Monaco, vacationing with friends.

A thirty-five-year-old named Simon Trevor-Jones, the thief was, in fact, a globe-trotting aristocrat. A baron. When it came to his appearance, however, Kate's preconception turned out to be wrong. She had expected him to be dashingly handsome — James Bondish, even — which she hadn't been able to prove or disprove from the bloody, shadowy crime scene photos or the bluish, distorted morgue shots. Trevor-Jones, she discovered, did not resemble James Bond, not in the least. He'd inherited the very worst that British noble blood had to offer—the pasty inbred look and the skinny but soft build. Even so, there was something deliciously sexy about him, Kate thought. His smile exuded a blasé devil-may-care attitude along with a palpable, almost predatory, sexual energy.

He was a legend, and Kate thought it sad that his mythic status would die along with him. She had considered keeping her theory from the police—in the hopes that they would never connect Trevor-Jones with the Cat—but she knew it would be futile. The body would be identified eventually, and as soon as any of Scotland Yard's top brass heard the words *baron* and *thief* in the same breath, they'd put the pieces together themselves.

Slipping the photograph back into her shoulder bag, Kate resumed walking across the square. Medina's neighborhood was refreshingly clean and white with pretty gated gardens, but the wide streets and opulent columns struck her as sterile and too self-consciously grand.

Better, she thought, turning onto Wilton Crescent. The curving row of smaller, attached stone townhouses didn't have columns or elaborate façades of any kind. After scanning the street for Medina's car, she figured he was running late.

Nearing his front door, she was pleased to spot two camera lenses. After her first meeting with Medina a couple of days before, she'd asked one of her colleagues at Slade's London office to put a rush on his new security system. She'd also tried to convince Medina to accept a temporary bodyguard, but he seemed to think he could take care of himself, had joked that her suggestion was overkill.

After Kate knocked and gave her name over the intercom, a cherubic-faced middle-aged woman answered the door. "I'm Charlotte," she said with a big smile. "Come in. Mr. Medina will be here shortly."

Kate followed Charlotte into the living room. It was minimalist, with a lot of white and chrome—formal but comfortable. Settling onto a soft white sofa, she pulled her laptop from her backpack and started in on the page of the manuscript where she'd left off when her plane landed that morning.

• • •

Detective Sergeant Colin Davies was fuming. There had been a double murder on his street corner the night before, but his chief refused to assign him to the case. Said he wasn't senior enough. Instead, there he was in the most pompous neighborhood in London, dealing with a bloody robbery-gone-awry at some rich bloke's home, who, to add insult to injury, was good-looking, too. *Bollocks.*

Davies was always suspicious of very attractive people. He felt they had it too easy, skating through life across other people's backs. Their looks distracted you, he believed, and if you weren't on your toes, you'd miss the true mischief they were invariably up to. Excessively pretty girls were bad enough—felt they were too good for just about anyone—but good-looking men, rich men, forget about it. The smug bastards should all be shot, in his humble opinion.

Davies had loathed Cidro Medina on sight, but he'd tried not to show it. His chief would not be happy if he ruffled the man's feathers. But whatever his chief might say, there was one thing Davies was sure of—this was the last unnecessary house call he would make to Medina or to anyone else in this neighborhood. Special treatment for the rich was not, as they'd say, his cup of tea.

A girl answered the door. She wasn't dressed like a maid, Davies noticed, but she definitely wasn't the girlfriend. He pictured that Medina fellow with some haughty-looking glamorous type. Not someone like this, wearing glasses, a T-shirt, and—he looked down—blue and white Nike trainers.

She extended her hand. "Hi, Sergeant Davies. I'm Kate Morgan, Cidro's private investigator."

Is she kidding? Davies wasn't sure what exactly he'd been expecting when he heard Medina refer to his P.I. Probably something closer to a middle-aged man in a fedora. Definitely not a cheeky girl, smiling innocently while she played policeman.

"Did your coroner get a chance to look at the body yet?" she asked.

Davies shook his head. "No, but as none of the bullet wounds appear to have been fatal, your poison theory is plausible. Probable." Reluctantly he added, "You were right about the ring, too—it was stolen nine years ago from a hotel suite in Portofino, a crime long suspected to've been committed by the thief known as the Cat."

"How about the plastique?"

"Uh, tests showed the presence of . . ." Davies pulled a notepad from his pocket. Flipping through, he shook his head slowly. *For fuck's sake!* "The techs mentioned something, but . . ."

"Does PETN ring a bell?" the girl asked. "Penta-erythritol tetra-nitrate? Traces of it have been found on each safe the Cat's blown."

Oh, sod off, Miss Know-It-All! Making little effort to conceal his scowl, Davies nodded.

"If you could give me a second . . ." she murmured.

Davies watched her reach into her purse. *What, does she need to pow-der her nose?* The girl seemed to find what she was looking for, slid a piece of paper out, and handed it to him. Davies frowned. It was a Xeroxed page from a society rag. He hated that nonsense.

"Look in the lower right corner," she suggested. "At the man on the left."

Fuckin' hell, it's him. " 'Simon Trevor-Jones, Lord Astley,' " he read from the caption beneath. "The thief was a baron?"

The girl nodded with what appeared to be . . . *what is that? Wistful-ness?*

"If you analyze Trevor-Jones's offshore accounts, I bet you'll find large amounts coming in right after the Cat's known heists and anonymous do-nations to charities going out soon after. That's probably as close to cer-tainty as we're going to get."

"I'll look into it," Davies said tightly.

"I'm sorry if you think I'm stepping on your toes, Sergeant," the girl said. "But a man has been murdered on account of the manuscript the thief was after. I'm just trying to figure out why and to make sure no one else dies."

"Murdered?" he asked skeptically.

"In Oxford," she said. "A few days ago."

Then Davies noticed that Medina had arrived. In a Ferrari, naturally.

"Good afternoon, Sergeant."

Bollocks to you.

"Want a drink?" Medina asked, ushering Davies into his foyer.

"No thanks."

"What'd I miss?"

"Your thief was a baron named Simon Trevor-Jones," the girl said, "and we're close to confirming he was the Cat."

"It's only been a few hours. How—"

"Well, the police are doing the tough stuff," she said. "I just flipped through *Hello!* magazines till I saw his face."

Reaching over to hand Medina the photograph, Davies noticed the man flinch at the mention of *Hello!*. Davies smiled. *He must hate that crap as much as I do. Maybe he does deserve to live . . . a little longer, at least.*

"Oh, that's your copy," the girl told Davies, handing Medina another. Then, as Medina walked over to a lamp for a better view of the Xerox, she added softly, "If you tell the super you identified the Cat today, I bet you he'll choke on his fag."

Davies couldn't help but grin. The chief superintendent of the Metropolitan Police was known for always having a cigarette in his mouth. Always. Very few people had ever seen him take it out; the man breathed and spoke through the corners of his mouth. And the girl was going to let him claim all the credit? With a start, Davies realized he'd probably get his long-awaited promotion.

"Mind if I look around Trevor-Jones's house with you sometime?" she asked him.

"Shouldn't pose a problem," Davies said with a smile.

"Oh, and the marchioness, Lady Halifax; would it be all right if I'm the one who lets her know her ring's been found?"

His smile widening, Davies nodded. "Be my guest."

"There's something I've been meaning to ask you, Cidro," Kate said, after the detective had left.

Medina was sitting across from her in his living room with a dish of ice cream in his lap. "Yeah?"

"I was thinking about what I would do if I were desperate to get my hands on the manuscript, and I were, you know, an unscrupulous criminal."

"Mmm-hmm?"

"I'd take something that matters to you more and hold it hostage. Like someone you love. A sibling, a girlfriend, your parents. . . . I think my company should—"

"Actually, that's one prospect we don't have to worry about. I was an only child, I don't have a girlfriend, and my parents live in Spain."

"I'll have our Madrid office keep an eye on them," Kate said. "And I'll leave the manuscript here," she added, taking Phelippes's pewter box from her backpack. "Let's put it in your new safe."

Medina nodded. "That thief, though, Kate. The photo of him still alive—it struck me as familiar. He might belong to my club or something."

"I'm pretty sure he overlapped with you at Oxford. He graduated from Magdalen twelve years ago. That could also be where you've seen him."

"Maybe. You sure you don't want a bite?" he asked.

"Okay," she said, reaching for the spoon. As she swallowed the mouthful, she saw him open his briefcase and pull out a small white box wrapped in silver ribbon. Judging by his expression, it was for her.

"Oh, I know all about your *gifts*, mister. What's this, another test of my abilities? Another hoop you want me to jump through?"

Smiling, Medina shook his head, then stood and moved to sit on the sofa beside her. Facing her, with his elbow resting on the back of the couch, he said, "I stopped by the Yard on my way home and, well, told a bit of a fib. I said the thief got his gun from my desk, that it was mine. An unregistered antique. They hadn't any use for it, and I thought you might want it."

"I don't know what to say," Kate said, opening the box. "The Cat's pistol—I've never gotten something so thoughtful, so . . . thank you."

"I usually have to spring for diamonds to get a reaction like that," Medina said wryly. Lowering his hand to her shoulder, he added with concern, "That bloke came after you in New York, and I'm just worried something like that could happen here. I hope you don't need it, but just in case . . ."

What's that hand still doing on my shoulder?

Medina continued, "You do know how to use one, right?"

Buddy, I could hit an apple off your head from two hundred yards away. "Uh, Cidro, weren't you the one who compared me to history's most illustrious double-dealing trollops?"

"I believe so."

"Then you must know that when it comes to taking out the enemy, we're all highly, *highly* skilled."

"Oh, that's interesting," Medina said, pausing to stroke his chin with theatrical flair. "Because I seem to remember that Mata Hari was supposed to be a real bumbler of a spy, that her most notable skills were of the bedroom variety. I wonder if . . ."

"Oh, I can shoot in there, too. Music, dim lighting—they don't distract me."

Medina laughed. "I'll be right back," he said, standing up and leaving the room.

He returned a few minutes later with a plate of grilled cheese sandwiches. "Fancy one?"

"Grilled cheese after ice cream?" Kate shook her head, and as Medina sat down, she noticed that his eyes appeared darker than their usual pale blue. Looking closely, she realized that his pupils were almost fully dilated. *Ah-ha.* "You have another business meeting pretty soon, right?"

"Yeah."

"Do you always go to them, uh, altered?"

"Only when I know they'll be really, *really* boring. You want some? It's Northern Light. Won the Cannabis Cup not too long ago."

"Cannabis what?"

"In Amsterdam there's a contest every year. Though with sampling contender after contender, the judges perhaps lose their ability to make the most scientifically adept assessments. Not that a panel of stoners would ever be the most scientifically adept lot, but . . . anyway, you interested?"

"No thanks," Kate said, shaking her head with amused surprise. "I'm meeting a friend pretty soon, and I don't think she'd appreciate it if I showed up high."

"Oh," Medina said, visibly dismayed.

"What's with the hangdog look? Some kind of peer pressure?"

"No," he said, smiling once more. "It's just that I was hoping you'd be going out with me later tonight."

"Uh . . ."

"How about afterward?" Medina persisted.

"I won't have any new information at that point, so—"

"In case you haven't noticed, Kate, I'm trying to ask you for a date."

"Is that you talking, Cidro, or the gold-medal ganja?"

"Me. Most definitely."

"Oh. Well, I can't date a client. Office policy." It wasn't exactly true—

Slade had never said anything to her one way or another—but it sounded better than anything else she could come up with.

"How about I fire you now and rehire you in the morning?"

Laughing, Kate shook her head. "Okay, I lied. There's no policy. It's just a personal thing. You know, what if it's awful and I'm stuck interacting with you till I close your case?"

"Understood."

Checking her watch, Kate got ready to leave.

Medina wasn't finished. "Okay, no date. Yet. Just a drink to plot your next move . . . on the case. How's ten? Eleven?"

"If I'm free then," Kate said, walking toward his door, "and soul-crushingly bored, I *might* give you a call."

KNIGHTSBRIDGE, LONDON — 6:12 P.M.

A few blocks south of Hyde Park in Montpelier Square, Kate stepped from a black cab and walked over to a white brick townhouse. She pressed Adriana Vandis's buzzer, then headed up to her flat.

"Nice outfit," Kate said.

Adriana was wearing a gold lace strapless bra, a matching thong, and nothing else. "I'm sorry to be running so late," she said, kissing Kate's cheeks and welcoming her in.

"No problem."

"I just bought this bra at La Perla. Makes my breasts look divine, don't you think?" she asked, pivoting to give Kate a multiangled view.

"Seriously, Ana. If I weren't staunchly heterosexual . . ."

"If you're lucky, I'll restrain myself from caressing them lovingly in public."

"Not on my account, I hope," Kate said, grinning. "I'd love to see how those Sotheby's guards react."

Petite but curvy, with black hair to her shoulder blades and a sultry Mediterranean glow, Adriana Vandis did not remotely resemble a banker. No one would ever guess that she was one of the most highly paid traders in the City. She was also one of the least popular. Of course the women hated her for her looks; long stressful days in the City left most of them with drooping figures and faces as haggard as Edvard Munch's screamer. The men, on the other hand, who loved her looks but wished they belonged to a secretary, hated her for her talent and sky-high salary. And both sexes hated the fact that Adriana tended to roll in late and waltz out midafternoon, using her trademark combination of purposeful stride and sexy sashay.

The bank she worked for, Silverman Stone, exalted its team-player philosophy to the level of a religious mantra, which made Adriana a veritable Antichrist, but since she made the company four times the money any of her colleagues did and the CEO liked to look her up and down at least a dozen times a day, her position was more than secure. Which suited Adriana, because she intended to stay until she had enough money to drop it for good and open up her own art gallery in a hip part of town.

She and Kate had been freshman year roommates, and they'd continued living together throughout college.

"Do you need a dress or—"

"I've got one in my bag, but if I could borrow some shoes . . ."

"Of course. Want a shower?"

"That'd be great," Kate said. "So how was work today?"

Pulling a towel from her linen closet, Adriana shrugged. "Less awful than usual. I started trading exotic options a few weeks ago. It's kinda fun."

"You're dealing with strip club stocks now?" Kate joked, following Adriana to her bedroom.

"Ironically, *exotic* just means there's more math involved. Like, instead of buying the right to buy a specific stock—shares of Ralph Lauren, for example—for a certain price on a certain day, you're buying the right to buy, say, the third best performing fashion house stock for that price on that day, whichever one it might turn out to be."

Kate noticed a new painting hanging over the bed. "Oh, I love that one!" Adriana had taken up oil painting their senior year of college and had been doing it ever since.

"Notice the hat covering most of her face? I gave up. Still can't do faces."

"Well, you're partway there. I think that might be the perfect chin."

"After a whole weekend, it ought to be," Adriana laughed, shaking her head. "You know, there's a Cézanne watercolor for sale tonight, same blue and green in it. I'm hoping to hang *it* in here, too."

"Sounds good."

Adriana opened her closet and gestured to the full-length red halter dress hanging on the back of the door. "My new Valentino. What do you think?"

"Perfect. Totally you," Kate said enthusiastically, though she wasn't nearly as taken with designer clothes—or other trappings of material success—as Adriana was. Kate had always been far more interested in looking behind glittering façades than in creating them, but she was proud of her friend. Adriana had grown up poor on the Greek island of Santorini, helping her mother clean rooms at one of the seedier hotels. A widow, her mother had lived with an abusive boyfriend out of financial necessity. Adriana's earliest memory was of resolving to become rich enough to buy her mother a spacious apartment on the beach. Spending summers at Silverman Stone and starting to work there full-time right out of college, she'd been able to make that purchase by the time she was twenty-five.

"Try the body wash on the windowsill. Honey vanilla, smells amazing."

"Will do," Kate said, heading into the bathroom. She pinned her hair on top of her head, showered quickly, then slipped into her black strapless sheath and the shoes Adriana had left outside the bathroom door.

"I'm in the kitchen," Adriana called. "So what's this new case?" she asked when Kate entered the room.

"It involves a collection of sixteenth-century spy reports that someone is trying to steal from my client," Kate said, watching Adriana splash a little orange juice into two flutes of champagne. "Remember how I wrote my college thesis on Christopher Marlowe?"

"How could I forget?" Adriana moaned, playfully rolling her eyes. While she'd spent their senior year painting most days and going out every night, Kate had spent her time in remote corners of the library stacks.

"Well, this afternoon I came across what's got to be one of his first intelligence reports. He identified the assassin who murdered the eighth Earl of Northumberland in the Bloody Tower, along with the prominent

Catholic family who paid for the hit. You know, to keep their plot against Elizabeth from being exposed."

Noticing that Adriana's expression remained blasé, Kate added, "Until now, very little has been known about Marlowe's espionage career. This *is* thrilling."

"Let me get this straight. You're *still* reading about a guy who's been dead for centuries?" Adriana sighed. She preferred the here and now. "And here I was, telling everyone you were some kind of Charlie's Angel seductress battling villains in a white bikini."

"Not yet, but . . ." Clasping her hands together, Kate said dreamily, "If I'm lucky, maybe someday my bikini assignment will come."

They sat at a glass table by a bay of windows overlooking the garden behind Adriana's building.

"Have you heard of a guy named Cidro Medina?" Kate asked her.

"The hot blond fund manager who eats female hearts for lunch? Every woman in the City has. I met him at a party a year ago."

"Were you interested?"

"Well, to see him is to be interested," Adriana said, grinning. "But at the time I was too hung up on Mark to pay much attention."

"Which Mark?"

"The cokehead."

"Oh, right," Kate said, remembering. There had been a lot of phone calls and tears over that one. Though Adriana was the liveliest, most stunningly beautiful woman Kate had ever seen, her friend was in a state of perpetual heartbreak. Lost her marbles over one sleazy cad after another. "I'm glad he's out of the picture."

"Me, too. Anyway, Cidro. Why'd you bring him up?"

"He's my client."

"And he's hitting on you."

Kate nodded.

"Be careful. I once overheard him cooing to one girl on his mobile with *amazing* sincerity, while another girl was groping him and kissing his neck. If I hadn't seen it myself, I'd have had no idea he was full of shit."

"It's not like I'd ever fall for him."

"I know," Adriana said sympathetically, fully aware that Kate still mourned her dead fiancé. "But as soon as Medina senses that it'd be easier to doodle a nose ring on the Mona Lisa than get access to your heart, he'll be relentless."

"A minor inconvenience," Kate said with a shrug. "But I can't say I'd mind all *that* much."

MAYFAIR, LONDON — 7:20 P.M.

"I've got two-point-two million from the young gent on my right, paddle eight-twenty-two. On my right at two-point-two million. Who will say two-point-three? Two-point-three from a telephone bidder. At two-point-three million pounds. Back to you, sir. Will you say two-point-four?"

Giles Spencer lifted paddle 822 with a smile. Wearing his lucky pin-stripe suit, he knew he was looking particularly dapper, and now he was about to own another new painting, his second so far that evening. The familiar rush flowed through his veins. Once in a while it was better than coke.

"I've got two-point-five from the telephones. At two-point-five million. We have two-point-six on my right, at two-point-six from paddle eight-twenty-two. At two-point-six million pounds. Who will say two-point-seven? Anyone for two-point-seven? Fair warning then, at two-point-six million. Another warning at two-point-six million pounds. And it's yours, sir. Well done, then. Sold, at two-point-six million pounds."

Giles watched the auctioneer slam down his gavel, then scribble onto a notepad, peering through reading glasses that seemed to clutch the end of his nose for dear life. He wondered when they would fall. *Five, four, three, two . . . must be glued there.*

As he left his seat to fetch a drink, an unexpected sight stopped Giles in his tracks. Against the room's drab backdrop — navy walls with white trim, subdued gowns and dinner jackets, mostly gray hair and pale skin — a deeply tanned young woman in a bright red dress compelled him to blink, then pinch himself. The dress was tight, and it clung to her perfect breasts like cellophane.

Giles glanced away, not keen on getting caught staring. That was when he noticed that someone else was doing so as well. The man was tall and fit with a full head of dark gray hair tied back in a ponytail. His dark **V**-shaped brow was jarring against his pale skin and gave his face a decidedly sinister quality. Clearly the man was not afraid to stare, and he did so with a strange look on his face, an almost mesmerized, quiet smile to himself. As if he knew her but not quite. Was the dish in red some kind of celebrity?

Giles turned back to her. She was tiny—not more than an inch or two above five feet. He didn't recognize her, he realized, but the perfect name for her came to him: Robin Redbreasts. No one who spent more than a few moments in his consciousness escaped without a nickname. He watched as she spotted the bar, murmured a few words to her friend, then sauntered toward it. Giles admired her liquid movement, a tasty confection of grace and sexiness. Then he shifted his gaze to follow the eyes of her other admirer, perhaps to share a moment of lecherous complicity.

To Giles's surprise, the man with the **V**-shaped brow was looking at the friend, a taller, aloof-looking girl in a black cocktail dress. She was pretty, he supposed—fairly flawless, in fact—but with her standoffish body language, she was altogether uninteresting to him. A bit too muscular as well. Her arms looked as if they belonged to a teenage boy. Yeah, Giles thought, Redbreasts was the fox. No, Redbreasts was the hot chick, and *he* was the fox.

With the flush of excitement from his new purchase bolstering his confidence, Giles zeroed in on his quarry.

Kate watched the young dandy strutting toward Adriana with a self-satisfied smirk. His hair was slicked back, emphasizing his virtually nonexistent chin, and he was wearing a pinstripe suit that was a couple of inches too short for him—perhaps to show off the pink socks that matched his shirt. He murmured a few words—some kind of line, Kate assumed—then, after listening to Adriana's reply, dropped his drink as well as his jaw. I wonder what she used this time, Kate wondered. Her "I prefer transsexual blowup dolls" line?

With drinks in hand, Kate and Adriana took their seats. Sighing quietly, Kate settled in to enjoy the soothing sensory experience—the rhythmic timbre of the auctioneer's voice; the soft buzz of hushed tones murmuring into cell phones in different languages; the bright numbers of foreign currency equivalents flashing above the auctioneer with every new bid, each flash in sync with his words; the small men in navy smocks moving back and forth like pendulums, replacing every painting on the wooden easel with new inventory.

Kate was staring at a set of white hairs waving hello from behind a pale earlobe in front of her when Adriana nudged her out of her reverie.

"Lot one-thirty-five," the auctioneer announced. "*The Balcony.* Second in a series by Paul Cézanne, circa 1900. Graphite and watercolor on white paper. We'll start this at three hundred thousand pounds, please. At three hundred thousand. A new bidder, the lady in red near the back wall. Who will say three hundred and twenty? Three hundred twenty thousand from the telephones. At three hundred and twenty thousand. Who will say three hundred forty? Do we have three hundred and forty thousand? Ah, paddle seven-seventeen, the gentleman on my left. Three hundred and forty thousand pounds from paddle seven-seventeen. How about three hundred and sixty? Three hundred and sixty from the woman in red. Who will say three eighty? You, sir, paddle seven-seventeen. On my left at three hundred and eighty thousand pounds. Four hundred from our telephone bidder. At four hundred thousand. Four hundred and twenty. Four forty. Four hundred and sixty."

The auctioneer's head and his gesturing hand flicked in a triangular motion from bidder to bidder until the telephone caller dropped out. Then his head whipped back and forth between Adriana and the man with paddle 717, his voice getting faster and louder. In vain Kate craned her neck to catch a glimpse of her friend's competition. But then Adriana gave up.

"At five hundred and twenty thousand pounds. Do I hear five hundred forty? Who will say five hundred and forty? Are you sure, miss? This is your last chance. All right then. Fair warning at five hundred twenty thousand."

The auctioneer looked around. Nothing. "All done then, at five hundred and twenty thousand. Sold to the gentleman on my left. Well done, sir."

Adriana leaned over and spoke to Kate in an irritated whisper. "I think I might have to find that persistent little bugger and give him a piece of my mind. Maybe if I bat my eyelashes at him . . ."

During a short break, Adriana and Kate stood chatting beside a large panel of Monet's water lilies.

"So Kate, I had my first affair with a woman."

"Yeah?"

Adriana frowned. "Damn. I expected some shock."

"Come on, Ana, it takes a little more than that. The first chief of MI6 used to stab his prosthetic leg with a letter opener to freak people out. That's the kind of thing that would get me."

"Oh, well. Anyway, the whole thing started with a night of ménaging à trois. Afterward the guy wouldn't leave me alone, but whenever I saw the girl out, she gave me the cold shoulder."

"Which intrigued you."

"Well, that and the fact that satisfying a woman is like playing an instrument, and most men haven't had proper lessons."

"Was it everything you'd hoped for?"

"It was okay, I suppose," Adriana replied. Then, staring into space as if searching for an answer, she added, "It just felt like something was missing."

Kate laughed.

"I might have to try it again, though."

"Why's that?"

"Because I've got this fantasy where a spurned lesbian storms into my office and hurls something heavy at me. The expression on my stuffy colleagues' faces would be so priceless. My God, they'd—"

Suddenly Adriana's words faded as Kate caught a glimpse of a familiar profile. About eight yards farther along the wall, a man in an exquisitely tailored dinner jacket stood facing a painting. He had dark gray hair tied back, and a jaw line with an edge like a cleaver. As she looked at him, a number of images tumbled through her mind. Two men at dinner in Dubai. Two men on the Amalfi Coast. In Paris. In Berlin. Without question, the man before her was Luca de Tolomei. But he had declined the Sotheby's invitation, Kate thought with surprise. Of that Edward Cherry had been certain. De Tolomei must have changed his mind at the last minute. But why? Was it a coincidence? Of course, she told herself. It had to be.

"I've lost you, honey, what's going on?" Adriana asked.

"Mmm, an unexpected work thing. Can you do me a favor?"

"Sure."

"I'm going to carry on a conversation with you. It might sound strange, but just assume everything I say is true and ask 'Why?' and 'Tell me more' type questions. You know, allow me to keep talking without letting it sound like a monologue."

Taking Adriana's arm, Kate added, "Let's go look at the Fragonard, three paintings up."

Sipping a peppermint schnapps, Giles Spencer had been leaning against a wall watching the Ripper since the break began. He had nicknamed the man with the V-shaped brow after his country's most infamous serial killer. The man was probably harmless, but the way he was watching the girl in black so intently struck Giles as menacing. When she wasn't looking, the Ripper stared at her with a bizarre sense of ownership and periodic flashes of desire. Desire that, oddly enough, seemed somehow nonsexual. More carnivorous than lascivious.

But what should he call the girl, Giles asked himself, heading toward the bar for more schnapps. Next to Redbreasts, she was a plain Jane—but even so, she was a bit too pretty for that. Ice Queen? No, she wasn't imperious enough to be a queen, he decided. Or a princess. More like a commoner, he thought. The Ice Commoner. Too clunky, had a bad ring to it. Ice Pleb? No, still didn't suit her. Come on, Giles.

Got it! Glacier Girl, he thought with pride.

Returning to his vantage point across the room, Giles was intrigued to see that the two women were slowly moving toward the Ripper. *Hmm.* Then, looking more closely at Glacier Girl, he was startled to realize that he barely recognized her. Her large green eyes had taken on a near electric sparkle, she tossed her hair with flirtatious confidence, and she was holding her friend's arm and leaning in closely with an almost sensual affection. Wow, Giles thought, that smile of hers could corrupt a saint. She, too, was worth one of his trademark lines. How had he missed that when she first walked in?

Then Giles got another shock. He realized that Glacier Girl was stealing glances at the Ripper, that she was ushering her friend toward him deliberately. So there were two people, and each had recognized the other, yet pretended not to. What, exactly, was going on?

With his drink in hand, Giles leaned back against the wall, eager to watch the cracking little drama play out.

. . .

"Whoever buys this piece will wish he hadn't," Kate told Adriana. They were standing before an oil painting of a couple kissing in a garden by the eighteenth-century French artist Jean-Honoré Fragonard.

"What do you mean?" Adriana asked, seeming genuinely curious.

From the corner of her eye Kate saw that de Tolomei was holding a cell phone to his ear, but she could tell he was merely making it appear that he was carrying on a conversation. He was definitely listening to her. Satisfied, she continued. "It's a forgery. I'm sure of it."

"How?"

"Well, you know how in France during World War Two the Nazis had a task force confiscating art from wealthy Jewish families and dealers, cataloging everything, then shipping it off to Germany for Hitler's and Goering's collections?"

Adriana nodded.

"Before the war, a lot of those families, including the Rothschilds, transported the bulk of their collections out of Paris—not because they anticipated the looting at that point but because they assumed the Luftwaffe would be bombing the city. Anyway, before he fled to America, Robert de Rothschild sent his art to a number of places, one of which was his château, La Versine, in the countryside. Once the Nazis invaded France, it wasn't long before their art task force got to work, and they went after the world-famous Rothschild collections first. Before they reached La Versine, Robert's staff hid as much as they could. Including this painting."

Kate paused for a moment to take a sip of her wine.

"And when the Nazis arrived?" Adriana prompted.

"They found everything except for some antique clocks and furniture hidden in a storage shed, *as well as* two Fragonards and a Van Eyck hidden in the guest house of the neighboring château, La Faunier."

"But how does that make this a forgery?" Adriana asked, gesturing toward the Fragonard beside them.

Kate smiled. "Because when the Allies were bombing in 1944, Château La Faunier's guest house was completely destroyed."

"So those three paintings . . ."

"Ashes, baby," Kate said. "The forger must've used a photograph of the original to paint this, then probably had the Rothschild records at the various archives doctored."

"People can do that?"

Kate shrugged. "Pay off an archivist for access to the relevant documents after hours? It wouldn't be too hard."

"Are you gonna say something?"

"Eventually," Kate said, smiling mischievously. "But first I'd like to see how much someone pays for it."

Then, leaning in closely, Kate murmured her last words just inches from Adriana's ear. "Now get out of here, gorgeous. Go delight some of those poor souls who've been dreaming about you all evening." While speaking, Kate had also been pressing the bowl of her wineglass against her stomach and twisting it, using the fabric of her dress to remove any fingerprints and Adriana's body to conceal what she was doing from de Tolomei.

"I'm going to run to the loo," Adriana said, loudly enough for de Tolomei to overhear.

"Okay. I should check my voice mail anyway," Kate replied, careful to hold her wineglass only by its base as she transferred it to her left hand and retrieved her cell phone from her shoulder bag with her right.

As Adriana walked off, Kate turned to face the Fragonard and brought her phone to her ear, wondering whether de Tolomei would bite. If so, she would admit she'd tricked him, then introduce herself as the P.I. that she was, pretending to be interested in him for the sole purpose of signing a big client to impress her boss. By coyly tricking him once, she thought it likely he'd buy her act. People who were suspicious enough to look beneath surfaces—expecting the unexpected—tended to anticipate one 'Ah-ha!' Not two.

"Excuse me. I'm sorry to interrupt . . ."

Kate flipped her phone closed and turned to de Tolomei with a look of mild irritation. "Well, now that you have . . ."

"I couldn't help but overhear your conversation and was terribly curious about something."

Kate raised an eyebrow.

"I'm familiar with the Robert de Rothschild story—I've read about the items hidden in the storage shed at La Versine, as well as in the secret room Robert had constructed in his Paris home—but that Château La Faunier guest house? I've never heard that part of the story."

"That's because I made it up," Kate said with an impish smile. "Château La Faunier—the phony château? I just wanted to get your attention. Could you hold this for a second?" she asked, handing him her wine.

While de Tolomei did so, Kate reached into her shoulder bag for her wallet, pulled out one of her cards, then handed it over and reclaimed her glass. By its base.

" 'Kate Morgan, private investigator with the Slade Group,' " he read aloud, then looked back up and extended his hand. "Luca de Tolomei. Enchanted."

"Likewise. Your reputation precedes you. I've been wanting to meet you for a while now. One of my specialties is tracking down missing art. You may have read about the Veneziano I helped a client locate a few months back . . ."

"The one hidden beneath that ghastly Victorian fox hunt? How could I forget?" de Tolomei interrupted. "That was you?"

Kate nodded.

"Impressive."

She smiled. "Anyway, I thought my abilities—along with my company's other services—might be of use to you at some point. Our security team is the best in the business, I'd also imagine you might need background checks on people you deal with once in a while."

As she finished her pitch, Kate thought she saw a flicker of amusement in de Tolomei's eyes.

"My security system is, uh, adequate, I think . . ."

We'll see about that.

" . . . and I have an assistant who verifies the credentials of my clients, but there is something I'd like your help with. Something I've been after for more than a decade."

"A painting?"

De Tolomei shook his head. "Another form of art, actually . . ." Pausing, he looked around. Several people were standing nearby. "But I'd prefer not to discuss it in this milieu, if you understand."

"Of course," Kate said. "I remember reading that you're based in Rome. I'm headed there myself tomorrow. I've got business at the Vatican in the early evening, but perhaps we could meet afterward? Or the following morning?"

"Actually, I think we might be at the same gathering. The Apostolic Palace at eight?"

"The same."

"Serendipity graces us again. I'll look forward to it," de Tolomei said.

They shook hands, and as he turned away, Kate saw his auction paddle, number 717. *What?* De Tolomei was the man who'd outbid Adriana for the Cézanne, she realized with surprise. And in response, Adriana had vowed to find him and perhaps charm him into selling it to her.

Moments before, Kate remembered, de Tolomei had brought up the pleasantly coincidental nature of their upcoming meeting in Rome, an encounter she and Edward Cherry had deliberately engineered. Unlike this one. Tonight's encounter was the serendipitous one, the chance meeting neither of them had planned. Or was it? Who exactly had just fooled whom?

Shit, Giles Spencer thought to himself. He was disappointed that the evening's unexpected entertainment had been so damned anticlimactic. Instead of coming to blows or grabbing each other with unrestrainable passion, the Ripper and Glacier Girl had smiled over polite conversation and exchanged business cards.

Frowning, Giles left the main auction room and headed down the stairs. At least he had new paintings to cheer him up. As he passed the Sotheby's café on his way out, he noticed Glacier Girl—the wallflower-turned-center-of-the-room-bloom—just ahead. Should he make a play for her? It might be too late, he thought. She appeared to be in a hurry.

Giles paused when she veered off toward the ladies' room, wondering whether he should wait for her. Then, spotting what was in her right hand, he considered instead the odd fact that rather than dropping it off at the café, the girl had carried her empty wineglass into the restroom with her.

YESILKOY, TURKEY—11:05 P.M.

In the Cinar Hotel, leaning against the railing of his balcony overlooking the Marmara Sea, Hamid Azadi was holding a wineglass, too. But his was full, because he was drinking to celebrate the first day of his new life.

Azadi had escaped from Iran the previous evening. His plan had been simple but effective: pretend to be investigating rumors of an impending high-level defection and, in the process, defect himself. Aboard a truck driven by a heroin smuggler, he'd slipped across the border into Turkey, where a car had been waiting to take him to a hotel in Yesilkoy, a quiet suburb five minutes from Istanbul's Ataturk International Airport. During the ride, Azadi had used a wig, cheek implants, makeup, and false teeth to alter his appearance so he would resemble the first of his several new identities, an elderly Indian journalist. The following morning, Azadi would board a Turkish Airlines flight to Paris, and from Orly airport, he'd go by taxi to the clinic of a highly skilled plastic surgeon, a doctor whose services de Tolomei had once used himself.

Azadi owed his life to de Tolomei; the man had helped arrange every step of his escape. The thought didn't bother him in the least, however. De Tolomei might not have many friends, but to the few he did have, he was loyal to an extent Azadi had never imagined possible.

How fortunate it was that he, Azadi, had been in a position to provide the critical element for the revenge de Tolomei had so desired all these years. According to the master of the *Nadezhda*, the wooden crate Azadi had packed up himself had been transferred to de Tolomei's yacht the day before. Shortly thereafter, he'd learned, near Sidi Bou Said on the Tunisian coast, the package had been lowered to a speedboat and taken to a nearby villa, where it had arrived unscathed.

Earlier that day, de Tolomei had called and thanked Azadi for his help with an almost passionate intensity. Azadi had been thinking, "Luca, it's not as though I've just given you directions to the fountain of youth," but out of respect, he did not utter the words. He did not know what de Tolomei had in mind with his new acquisition, nor did he care. With his forty-third birthday looming around the corner and his colleagues now openly asking why he hadn't yet married, Azadi only had one emotion: elation at having escaped his predicament. To him, the idea of making love to a woman was about as appealing as drinking a barrel of crude, and getting married for show would never have worked. Without question, a wife would tell her friends that her marriage bed was cold.

Azadi also believed that in spite of its reformist president, his country was like a pot of hot stew on the verge of boiling over. The unemployment rate—so terribly high already—was rising, and young people everywhere were taking to the streets, protesting the lack of opportunities, rampant corruption, and repression of dissident journalists and intellectuals. Azadi was not the only Iranian who resented the all-powerful mullahs—not by a long shot. He was relieved he would not be around if and when the next revolution came. Angry mobs did not treat government officials kindly. The last time around, the chief of the Shah's secret police had been hanged, though not to death, then beaten and slashed until his bones were shattered and his lifeblood ran out.

Leafing through photos of the beach house de Tolomei had found for him in Key West, Azadi envisioned himself strolling along in the surf. Closing his eyes, he felt the warm but refreshing water lapping at his toes and the pressure of a strong arm wrapped around his shoulders.

MAYFAIR, LONDON — 9:11 P.M.

With her Sotheby's wineglass sealed in a plastic bag inside her purse, Kate was standing just outside the building's arched entrance, apologizing to Adriana for needing to cut their evening short. After making plans to go running together the following morning, they hugged good-bye, and as Adriana waited for her taxi, Kate walked north along Old Bond Street, then turned left onto Grosvenor, impatient to get to the local Slade Group office.

Passing galleries, law offices, and upscale hair salons, she dialed Max.

"I thought you were taking the night off," he said. "Didn't realize you'd miss me so much."

"Well, there's that and an unexpected development. Guess who decided to come to the auction after all?"

"De Tolomei?"

"Right," Kate said. "And I've got his prints on a glass. I'm about to scan them and send them over to you."

"Actually, Kate, the assignment's already over for us."

"What are you talking about?"

"Well, first of all, I was wrong about de Tolomei."

"What about all those criminals he does business with?"

"I'm pretty sure he's dealing in information, not weapons or drugs. That he's a big-time blackmailer."

"How on earth did you . . . ?"

"I was analyzing his financial transactions more closely—the dates, the amounts, which direction the money was flowing—and the first thing I realized was that all the people making payments to de Tolomei had major skeletons in their closets. Three of the guys I showed you yesterday, for example—the French and German arms dealers Bruyère and Kessler, and the Pakistani textile merchant Khadar Khan—they all have the trappings of legitimate businessmen. The illegal shit—selling chemicals and materials for making centrifuges to Iraq after Desert Storm or being a drug kingpin, in Khan's case—it's nothing but rumor."

Max took a sip of something, then continued. "And the people he's buying from—they're mostly intelligence officers, law enforcement types, and journalists. The kind of people who dig up rumors like that."

"Oh," Kate said, catching on. "So I bet you found payments to an Iraqi intelligence officer sometime in the nineties, just before de Tolomei started collecting money from Bruyère and Kessler."

"Exactly. And a payment to Hamid Azadi before the money started coming in from Khadar Khan. You see, Khan refines his heroin in western Afghanistan, then moves it through Iran to Turkey, which someone like Azadi would know."

"And that timing couldn't just be coincidental?"

"Not with dozens of people involved. But it's more than just timing, Kate. Think about who's paying whom. Take Khadar Khan. If de Tolomei were transporting heroin for him, he'd be paying Khan for the value of the drugs. But instead Khan's paying *him*. A lot."

"Khan couldn't be paying for the transportation service?"

"And trust that de Tolomei would really take the heroin to Khan's buyers, instead of unloading it elsewhere, keeping all the profits for himself? No way. Baby, that's one business that don't run on trust."

"Good point."

"The same logic applies to the arms dealers. De Tolomei bought something from an Iraqi intelligence officer a decade ago, then started receiving payments from Bruyère and Kessler right after. Iraq was rebuilding its arsenal at that time, not selling, so the money was moving in the wrong direction for an arms deal."

"And you're sure the money wasn't for art?"

"Yeah," Max said. "Check this, you'll be proud. I called Kessler's wife pretending to be a reporter for *Town and Country* wanting to feature her home. She was thrilled. Then I mentioned art, asked if she had an impressive collection, whose work she owned. She got all huffy, said, 'I'm an artist. Only my work hangs on our walls. And yes, it's more than impressive. It's *fabelhaft*,' whatever that means."

"Nice work. But if you're right, and de Tolomei's trading in secrets, not weapons, I still wanna know: What's the eleven-million-dollar doozy he just bought from Hamid Azadi?"

THE TUNISIAN COAST — 11:19 P.M.

Surina Khan squeezed half the tube of antibiotic salve into her palm and began to smooth it over the cuts on her patient's face, along his split lips, and into the scabbed patches at the tips of his fingers where the nails should have been. A local doctor had just checked in for the third time, and finally they were alone again. Though he had yet to open his eyes, Surina had been talking to him for nearly two weeks. She knew he could hear her in spite of his condition; when she held his hands, she could almost feel his thoughts.

The *Nadezhda* had picked her up in the Pakistani port of Karachi, where she'd pretended to be the shipmaster's new girlfriend. She'd slept on the sofa in his cabin, and after they'd loaded the crate containing her patient twelve days before, she'd been opening it up, changing his IV, and tending to his wounds. Then, when the crate had been transferred to Mr. de Tolomei's yacht, she'd been inside with him, terrified, but assuring him they'd be fine anyway. She could not understand why Mr. de Tolomei was so insistent about keeping him hidden, but she was happy to do anything he asked.

She loved being alone with her patient. She'd wanted to be a doctor for as long as she could remember—had been volunteering at a local hospital after school every day for years. But for some reason, this felt different.

Though his entire body was battered and emaciated, it was her patient's feet that made her shiver. The soles were covered with old scar tissue and more recent lacerations. What could he have done to deserve whippings like that? Nothing. It was impossible, she decided. No one deserved such punishment—not even the boy from her neighborhood in Islamabad who'd hurled acid at her face several years before, furious that she'd rejected his advances.

Hovering closely above, Surina circled her ointment-covered fingers over her patient's heels and along his arches, then paused for a moment to lean back and wipe away her tears. She didn't want the salty liquid to land on his wounds.

Who was he? she continued to wonder. His skin wasn't naturally pale; he had Arab in him, she was sure of it, but something else as well. Though his features were still blunted and disfigured by bruises and swelling, she thought he might be half European. But what had he been doing in a Middle Eastern prison? She couldn't imagine him as a common criminal. He must have crossed his government somehow—as an activist, perhaps, a dissident. Whoever he was, Surina thought to herself, she'd stay by his side day and night until he was better. No matter what her father thought.

Khadar Khan had been infuriated that she'd accepted this offer from his business associate. Surina did not know why, and she did not care. Since she had become disfigured, her father had never bothered to hide the fact that he could not stand the sight of her. But the few times they had met, Mr. de Tolomei had always treated her with kindness, and for this job, he had offered a salary so generous that Surina could finally leave home for good.

After screwing the cap back on the tube of ointment in her lap, Surina leaned over to place it back on the bedside table. As she did so, she glanced in the mirror above. It reflected the right side of her once breathtakingly beautiful face, the side with a cheek and ear burned and congealed into a web of ribbed scar tissue. A lone tear zigzagged jerkily as it made its way down the uneven path. Her patient cared for her now—she could feel it—but would he still when he opened his eyes?

MAYFAIR, LONDON — 9:26 P.M.

Crossing Berkeley Square, Kate was listening to Max recount his most recent conversation with their boss.

"While I was explaining my theory about de Tolomei, he cut me off. Didn't say anything for a minute, just stood there looking . . . I don't know, dumbfounded. Then he asked if de Tolomei's private jet had touched down recently in any of the countries bordering Iran or any other gulf states. It hadn't. He asked me to find out if de Tolomei's yacht had passed through the Suez in the past week. No to that as well. How about a port in Turkey? he asked. No. Then he had me scan satellite imagery of the Med for the past five days, using an aerial image of de Tolomei's yacht, and I got a few hits. Last night, just east of Malta, the yacht rendezvoused with a ship, and a wooden crate was transferred from the ship to de Tolomei's yacht. The yacht veered south, I traced it to Sidi Bou Said, and Slade had me search Tunisian property records. Turns out that de Tolomei, under a phony name, owns a villa on the coast. As soon as I said that, Slade pulled out his cell, dialed, and said, 'Black, get on the next flight to Tunis.' Remember those guys from the chopper the other night? Now we know—"

"Hold on. What was in the crate?" Kate interrupted.

"No idea," Max answered. "I asked Slade if he thought my blackmail theory was wrong—if de Tolomei was, as we'd initially suspected, acting as a middleman for a WMD sale to terrorists. I pointed out that the crate was definitely large enough for a nuke, and all he said was, 'No, de Tolomei bought something else.' Then, you know how he never swears or loses his cool? He goes, 'Fucking hell! Who the fuck is he?'"

"Well, we're about to find out," Kate said as she approached their London office. It was located on the upper floors of a highly ornate pink and maroon Georgian mansion across from the Connaught Hotel, property that had been a payment from a cash-strapped client. Made of brick and stone, the building's glass-fronted bottom floor housed several art galleries and antique shops. As Kate neared the entrance, drawings of birds caught her eye, then a Venus de Milo copy standing by a seated Buddha.

"Uh, Kate? Slade said you're off the assignment—that it's gotten too dangerous."

"But he wants to know who de Tolomei is, and I've got his prints," she said, climbing the stairwell. "Of course I'm gonna send them to you."

"I guess that can't hurt," Max said. "With that artful identity change, it's pretty likely de Tolomei's got a record on file somewhere . . . with prints. He must've had something pretty damn serious to hide to go to all that trouble."

"Let's hope," Kate said, entering the office and flicking on the lights. "Looks like everyone's gone home for the day," she added, making her way to the supply room.

"Hurry it up, girl. The anticipation's killing me," Max moaned.

"Almost there," Kate said. Holding the base of the wineglass with her left hand, she took a sable brush with her right, dipped it into a jar of black powder, and swept the soft bristles over the closest side of the glass, expecting the powder to catch on some swirling lines of fingerprint oil, but it didn't. There was nothing but a smudge. She twirled the glass and tried again. Still no prints.

"What's going on?" Max asked.

"Nothing. Just me being a complete idiot."

"He had his prints burned off with acid or something?"

"Must have. I mean, I saw him holding this glass, then I took it from him and slipped it in plastic immediately."

Putting away the equipment, Kate headed out of the office and added, "But I've still got tomorrow night."

"Rome?"

"Yeah. I'll figure out who he is there."

"No you won't. Slade meant what he said, Kate. You're dropping this assignment."

"Max, Slade clearly needs to know who de Tolomei is, and I've got a good chance of finding out. De Tolomei likes me. He wants to hire me to track down some piece of art for him. I'll get a voiceprint, a retinal scan . . . convince him to show me his personal collection, then drop some bugs in his house. . . . You *know* vampire entry is the only way we're gonna get in there any time soon."

"True," Max said. Their investigators in Rome weren't yet ready for a break-in; "vampire entry" meant getting an invitation inside. "But—"

"No *buts*. I'm going. Slade's just being overprotective because of promises he made to my father. Now, he needs the information, doesn't he?"

"He certainly seemed to. So what do I tell him?"

"Nothing. That I'm in London working Medina's case. If I get his answer, though . . ."

"You'll call him yourself. I ain't takin' the heat for this."

16

Tell me, where is the place that men call hell?

—Faustus, in Marlowe's *Dr. Faustus*

London—Evening, May 1593

*M*arlowe was in the rightmost section of the fourth pew, surreptitiously tucking a folded message into a crevice between the seat of the bench and its base. A hand settled upon his shoulder. He made an effort to appear calm. Turning slowly, he was startled to see the minister smiling at him sympathetically.

"Whatever troubles you, my son, God will forgive you."

"Thank you," Marlowe responded, realizing there were tears on his cheeks. He'd written with onion juice instead of ink minutes before and had forgotten to rinse his hands. Not exactly his most egregious sin, but a little grace, even if misdirected, might help him down the road.

Hearing the guttural cries of a Thames ferryman echo within the dark chapel, he stepped out onto London Bridge and descended to the waiting riverboat.

"You always bring all your earthly possessions with you?" he asked the boatman, looking at the heap of clothing and blankets in the back of the small barge.

"Wife threw me out."

"May I ask why?"

"She found me in bed with her sister."

"That'll do it."

"I'd have crawled in through a window, but my wife is . . . well, she's much bigger than me."

Feigning a cough, Marlowe covered his mouth.

"She had a copper pot and was threatening to bash my head in. I thought I'd leave for a few nights."

"Wise decision."

"Where to?"

"Durham House," Marlowe answered, his head turned away. Though struggling to assume an expression of concern, he couldn't help but grin at the image of the big and angry pot-wielding wife.

Seven feet away, beneath the thin layer of blankets and clothing in the back of the boat, a man lay hidden. He was reminding himself to pay the boatman extra. The fellow had been damned convincing.

Between Westminster and the City of London, Durham House was one of several prestigious properties overlooking the Thames from the north bank. Originally built for top churchmen, they'd long been co-opted for royal use. A little more than a decade before, Queen Elizabeth had given the lease for most of the sprawling mansion to her favorite courtier at the time, Sir Walter Ralegh.

Rising straight up from the riverbank, its bellicose facade dominated the skyline. Ralegh was sitting in one of the turrets. The little room was his study, and his sloped, wooden desk, delicately inlaid with pale wood, faced the curved window. With his crow's feather quill in the air, he was contemplating the next stanza in a new poem he was writing, an epic devoted to his lengthy relationship with the queen. He'd titled it *The Book of the Ocean to Cynthia*.

In the early 1580s, Ralegh, the son of a tenant farmer, had won Elizabeth's heart with his dramatic gestures, sparkling wit, and razorlike tongue. For a decade his jests amused her, his poetry pleased her, and he rarely left her side. The besotted queen gave him valuable monopolies, properties, and responsibilities, and his wealth and prestige grew rapidly. He was, perhaps, the most envied man in England. The previous year, however, everything had changed.

When his secret marriage to one of her maids of honor came to light, Elizabeth had him thrown in the Tower. At liberty now, Ralegh remained banished from her sight. Spending most of his time at his country estate in western Dorset, he slipped into London for only the most pressing of engagements. He was planning a voyage to the New World, a quest for the golden city of El Dorado, concealed deep within the jungles of Guiana. The ability to go on one of the ventures he planned was the saving grace of his exile; in the years preceding it, during the voyages to Virginia in the mid-1580s, Elizabeth had insisted that he not leave the British Isles.

Reaching for his enameled inkpot, Ralegh dipped his quill once more and penned his final lines for the day, the closing to the tenth book of his lengthy epic. Gazing down to the river below, he saw Kit step ashore from a riverboat. His peers might frown on him for mingling with a lowly play-maker, but the fellow was unbeatable company—had a restless intellect and spoke his mind as no one at court dared, which for Ralegh, was enormously refreshing. He'd had enough of the senseless chatter, lies, and false smiles bandied about Elizabeth's court.

Ralegh had met Marlowe years before during one of his visits to Henry Percy's country estate in Sussex. Percy, the ninth Earl of Northumberland, had one of the most well-stocked libraries in England, with more than two thousand volumes spilling forth from dozens of chests. Marlowe had been there for several weeks perusing Percy's extensive collection of occult literature, works by Europe's most famous magi—Cornelius Agrippa, Giovanni Battista della Porta, Giordano Bruno, John Dee, and others—research for what became his *Dr. Faustus*. Ralegh and Percy had spent the days hunting and hawking, Marlowe reading, and in the evenings, the budding playmaker had joined them for smoking and philosophical debates over games of cards or dice.

With a red ribbon, Ralegh tied his thick sheaf of pages together, stood, and carried the parcel toward the stairwell.

When he saw Ralegh approaching, Marlowe smiled. With his impressive height, flamboyant clothing, glittering jewels, and sword hanging by his side, his swarthy friend looked every bit the dashing explorer bound for exotic lands.

Marlowe had taken a liking to Ralegh long before they'd met, considering him something of a kindred spirit. The courtier's famous wit and penchant for defying convention were legendary during Marlowe's early years at Cambridge. But his affectionate regard was truly secured when Ralegh—who held a monopoly for the sale of wines—infuriated the university's puritanical administration by licensing a wine shop less than a mile away. For Marlowe, the convenience of nearby liquor was a boon in and of itself, but the sight of dusty dons shaking their fists at stumbling students was priceless.

They embraced.

"Ah, presents."

Ralegh laughed. "Not exactly. It's a new poem I'm working on. I thought you might have a look. I was planning to, uh . . ."

"Publish it?" Marlowe asked wryly. It was considered crass for gentlemen in Ralegh's circle to do something so *terribly* commercial. Aristocratic poets usually circulated their work quietly among friends for private amusement, not profit.

"At the moment I'm simply interested in your opinion, but when I've finished the last two sections . . ."

"An anonymous publication that could never be traced to you? It's possible." As they headed inside, Marlowe tucked the scroll into his satchel. "So, I hear you're preparing for another conquest, my friend. More virginal lands to enter, and, uh, plunder?"

"As ever, Kit, thy words are swords," Ralegh replied, leading Marlowe to his private apartment on the uppermost floor. "But you're hardly the first." Ever since he'd seduced one of the queen's ladies, Ralegh had been the butt of an endless series of similar jokes.

The dining room table was covered with a thick red cloth, and matching tassled cushions rested on the benches. Pewter dishware and utensils were neatly arranged, candles lit, wine poured, and a baked peacock—with its magnificent tail fanned out over the edge of the platter—awaited them.

Taking a seat, Ralegh tugged on a crispy leg. "I'm searching for El Dorado, city of gold nestled on the shores of Lake Manoa. Ruled by the descendants of an Incan prince." He leaned forward. "My sources say the kingdom has more riches than Peru. Temples filled with golden idols, sepulchres heaping with treasure . . ."

Listening to Ralegh's glittering descriptions, Marlowe wondered how reliable those sources actually were. Captured sailors, he imagined, would spin almost any tale when threatened with torture.

"I sent out reconnaissance fleets this month past," Ralegh added.

"Should hear their reports by summer. We will outshine the Spanish, my friend."

"I'll drink to that."

"Wait. I haven't yet told you my most exciting piece of news."

"You've secured the funding?" Seeing Ralegh's surprise, Marlowe explained, "Tavern gossip. How'd you do it?"

"Well, who wouldn't want the chance to multiply their money a thousandfold? I simply spoke of the golden city, presented the eyewitness accounts, and my benefactor opened his coffers with a willingness more in keeping with a baser sort of transaction."

"And this randy fairy godfather is . . . ?"

"Robert Cecil."

"But he's in debt!"

"Can't be. He's promised me fifty thousand pounds."

"I guess the rumor I heard was false," Marlowe murmured. But it hadn't been a rumor. Cecil was so desperate for money the previous year that he'd asked Marlowe to counterfeit coins. The man would definitely not have instigated a treasonous crime if he'd had tens of thousands of pounds to spare, so he must have come into the money recently. Was Cecil the Muscovy man dealing with Helen's pirate captain?

"When do you set off?" Marlowe asked.

"In the next year or two. We're still working out the navigational routes, preparing equipment lists . . ."

"A shame it's not as easy to travel . . ." Marlowe lifted his gaze to the ceiling.

Ralegh rose from his seat with an enigmatic grin. "Come with me."

Marlowe followed him down the hall to Tom Hariot's lodgings on the north side of the house.

Maps, atlases, and countless pages of numerical tables covered the desks in Hariot's study, as did the tools of his many ongoing experiments. A glass orb filled with water, suspended from the ceiling by a metal hook, drew Marlowe's attention first. A piece of stiff parchment with a hole in the center hung between the orb and the nearest window. *Hmm.*

An Oxford graduate, Hariot was an expert in mathematics, optics, astronomy, and cartography. As well as experimenting, he kept Ralegh's financial records, gave seminars on navigation to Ralegh's ship captains, and drew up maps of the shorelines Ralegh intended to explore.

Facing the opposite direction, Hariot seemed oblivious to their entrance. He was writing furiously. From his staccato arm movements, Marlowe guessed he was working with figures. Hariot was remarkably quick with them, so much so that he was a near priceless asset when it came to betting over rounds of triumph or piquet. But unfortunately for Marlowe, shortly after Hariot had mastered the art of counting playing cards and calculating odds, he'd tired of it and had yet to be coaxed back to a game. Such coaxing was a mission Marlowe typically pursued with vigor, but at the moment, he was curious about Hariot's newest discoveries. The man was brilliant.

"You're well, Tom?"

Hariot jumped. "Been better," he said, turning around.

"What vexes you?"

"Rainbows."

"Iris still outrunning you, is she?"

Harriot nodded, chagrined. "But I do know a few things," he said with quiet pride, gesturing to a glass basin. It was filled halfway with water, and a stick had been placed inside. About a foot long, the stick was only partially submerged. Hariot took a candle and brought it close to the basin. "The stick," he said. "What do you notice?"

Marlowe shrugged. "Looks ordinary enough."

"Its shape?"

"Bent."

Hariot lifted it out. It was perfectly straight.

Ralegh and Marlowe waited expectantly.

"Light bends when it enters liquid," Hariot explained.

"What has that to do with rainbows?"

"The sky is full of tiny droplets of water, and rays of sunlight bend as they enter. It's a process called refraction. Then, when the rays hit the back wall of the droplet, they reflect off it, bouncing back. The rainbow has something to do with those angles, of the sunlight's refraction and reflection. I've been studying the measurements, but . . ."

"If the sky is full of droplets, why a thin bow?" Marlowe asked. "In one particular place?"

"Has to do with the angle between the sun's rays behind you, the droplets of water in the sky, and your eyes, here on earth."

"And the colors?"

"I'm, uh . . ."

"I have faith in you," Marlowe said.

Ralegh caught Hariot's eye. "Is it a good night for . . ."

"Perfect. You wish to—"

Ralegh nodded.

Marlowe watched with interest. Hariot moved toward a rope hanging from the ceiling and pulled. With a loud creak, a door swung downward, a folded ladder attached to it. Hariot started climbing.

Close on his heels, Marlowe found himself in a dark chamber. Hariot pushed outward against one of its walls. Moonlight streamed in. One by one, they stepped from the dormer onto the gently sloping roof.

Hariot retrieved a long, odd-looking metal tube from a box sitting near the roof's edge. Sitting down, he leaned back, brought the tube to his eye, and pointed it at the sky. Bringing his hands closer together, he adjusted the two cylinders. The bottom half of the tube was thicker than the half near Hariot's face and seemed to slide right over it. "There she is," he whispered. "Kit, have a look."

Sitting next to him, Marlowe took the heavy tube and noticed a curved piece of glass just inside the opening. It was smooth, like that in a pair of spectacles. He peered through.

"Use your other eye to help you train it on the moon," Hariot said.

Marlowe did. "Good God! What . . . ?"

"It's a perspective trunk," Hariot said. "Makes the moon appear several times its size."

"It seems so close . . . the details, so sharp!"

"You've long spoken of exploring the heavens," Ralegh said, "and as none of my ships sail in that direction . . ."

Marlowe, Ralegh, and Hariot, high up on the roof of Durham House, assumed they were alone—free from prying eyes and suspicious ears. They were wrong.

Half a dozen yards away, a man was sitting on one of the upper branches of a nearby tree, watching as they lit up pipes and gazed at the sky. His name was Richard Baines, and it was he who'd followed Marlowe from London Bridge.

Probing God's mysteries is the devil's work, Baines was thinking to himself. No wonder people call Hariot a diabolical conjurer.

Baines's employer wanted proof of Marlowe's supposed atheism. Evidence could always be manufactured—it was done all the time—but Baines took his espionage work quite seriously. At the very least, he wanted there to be a few kernels of truth to his accusations.

As soon as Marlowe had announced his destination to the boatman, Baines had suspected that the evening's eavesdropping would prove a gold mine. Both Marlowe and Ralegh were notorious heretics.

And how right he had been. What he had just heard was enough to ensure that the only place Marlowe would be exploring was a prison cell.

You can sit on a tree branch only so long before your rear end goes numb. One of the knots digging into Baines's flesh felt like a torture device. Grimacing, he shifted with discomfort.

On the other side of the Thames in Southwark, a Dutch woman named Eva was shifting about as well. But rather than on a tree branch, she was sitting on her kitchen table. And instead of discomfort, she was squirming with pleasure. She had Robert Poley's head up her skirt and was praying that her husband wouldn't come home from the tavern early and find her in such an indelicate position.

To most people adultery is a form of cheating. But according to Robert Poley's unique personal code, when playing the romantic game, paying for sex was actually the lowest form of cheating, and seducing another man's wife was the most honorable form of success. The Dutch glassmaker's young blond wife was his latest triumph, though hardly his greatest.

Years before, when Francis Walsingham was still alive, Poley had taken the great spymaster's daughter to bed, who at the time was married to the beloved poet Sir Philip Sidney. Now the former Lady Sidney was married to the Earl of Essex, and to Poley's delight, she still had a weakness for him. He made a mental note to arrange a rendezvous with her soon. And perhaps this time he'd tell Cecil. No doubt his employer would be pleased that he was bedding the enemy's wife.

Poley's greatest romantic failure, on the other hand, had been with Mary, Queen of Scots. During the final years of her life, when she was imprisoned at Tutbury Castle, he had been sent to pose as a sympathizer, a covert Catholic who could help smuggle her correspondence. He would meet the queen as she rode through Tutbury's parks and soon learned that her reputation as a dangerous temptress could not have been further from the truth. The sad and devoted woman wrote dozens of love letters to the husband she would never see again. Once in a while, she cried with gratitude on Poley's shoulder as he assured her they would reach their destination. It was a lie but one worth telling. He'd been touched by the depth and endurance of her love and had quickly abandoned his original mission to become her last lover. The nemesis of Walsingham's secret service—inspiration to Catholic plotters throughout the Isles and across Europe—was just a lonely, aging woman longing for her husband. She would never be free, but with his false reassurances, Poley had hoped she would at least die in peace.

During those afternoons with Mary, Poley had learned something about himself. Betrayal might be his livelihood and greatest form of pleasure, but when it involved someone he respected, he lost interest. And beyond that, he wanted to help whoever was trapped in the tangle of government plotting. It didn't happen often, not once since Mary, but with the news of Kit Marlowe's predicament, the long-dormant part of his soul had awakened. He liked the charming playmaker, admired his reckless flouting of all that was foolish in their country.

Buttoning his linen shirt, he kissed Eva good-bye.

By the empty bear-baiting arena, Poley saw Teresa Ramires, a voluptuous raven-haired girl, standing in a shaft of moonlight. A maid in Essex's household, Teresa was one of Poley's most valuable informants.

"Hello Rob," she said, offering her hand palm up.

Poley reached into his pocket. "I assume this will be worth it?" he asked, holding up a shilling.

Teresa nodded. "I don't know exactly where Kit Marlowe is . . ."

Poley brought the coin back toward his pocket.

"But I do know that Phelippes is paying him to investigate one of the trading companies. The, uh . . ."

"Levant Company? Morocco? Muscovy?"

Teresa nodded. "Muscovy, that's the one. Phelippes suspects smuggling of some sort."

"By whom? Did he say?"

"No, but he's to Essex House tomorrow. I'll linger about."

"Good," Poley said, giving her the shilling. "Meet me here at noon."

As Teresa sauntered off, Poley stared at the Thames, mulling over her information. Apparently one or more of the merchants and courtiers in the Muscovy Company had something to hide, and Marlowe might be close to exposing it. Must be the reason for the "Tamburlaine" placard, Poley thought to himself. Marlowe's closing in on the truth, and this smuggler or smugglers mean to stop him. *Well, they won't. I shall see to that.*

17

Surina. How is he?" de Tolomei asked. He was lying on a floral sofa in his suite at the Ritz, his cell phone to his ear.

"Gaining a little weight, sir. His wounds are healing nicely, too. The doctor said he should wake up any day now, but . . ."

"What is it?"

"He's been having these . . . spasms. I, well, I was holding his hand earlier and it . . . it twitched. Several times."

"He was in a terrible prison for years, Surina. Among other things, he was tortured with electric shock."

"May I ask, uh . . ."

"He's not a criminal, Surina. He was betrayed by his country."

"Oh."

"How are *you* doing?"

"Very well, sir. I've never lived by the sea . . . it's so beautiful here. And I . . . I like him, too. I pray for him every night."

"Good. I'll be seeing you both very soon." De Tolomei paused, not quite sure how to phrase his next thought. "By the way, Surina . . ."

"Yes, sir?"

"If it's something you'd . . . like, I've made an appointment for you with a plastic surgeon in Paris. He's one of the best in the world."

She was quiet for a moment, barely breathing. "Oh . . . I don't know what to say, I—" Her voice broke, then she finished, "Yes, I—I am interested. Very much so."

"The doctor said your bandages would be off before your classes begin," de Tolomei said. Surina had told him that she'd used part of his payment to enroll at the Sorbonne.

"Thank you."

"Good-bye, then."

Turning off his phone, de Tolomei closed his eyes and sighed, marveling at how smoothly his scheme was unfolding. And to think he had a former enemy to thank for it all.

Three years before, a senior CIA officer on the payroll of multiple foreign intelligence agencies had alerted VEVAK's Hamid Azadi to a CIA operation under way on Iraqi soil. Tehran, the American traitor knew, wanted to see Saddam's regime pulverized by the full might of the U.S. military, not simply decapitated through a covert assassination. He'd therefore given Azadi enough information to locate the young man in charge of the operation and have him killed.

Azadi had indeed sent a team after the American spy. But he did not do so to further the geopolitical goals of his country. He had stopped caring about those long before. He wanted to use the spy for personal reasons—as a bargaining chip to facilitate his impending defection. And so he'd lied to the members of his kidnap squad, explaining that their quarry was simply a witness with valuable information about the Mujahedeen e-Khalq (MEK), the most militant of the Iranian opposition groups, which at the time had training bases and rendezvous sites all over southeastern Iraq. He'd then hidden the young spy under a false identity in Tehran's Evin prison.

Azadi hadn't intended to take three years to finalize his plans, nor had he wanted his prisoner to suffer at the hands of Evin's sadistic guards, but such is life. For the most part, Azadi had kept him drugged and isolated. The prisoner had been tortured, but with luck, would barely remember it. Knowing that Luca de Tolomei was more familiar with the inner workings of American intelligence agencies than he, Azadi had asked his friend for advice on how to use his bargaining chip.

Watching Azadi's video for the first time, de Tolomei had felt a jolt, as if he'd accidentally touched a live wire. After thirteen years of patiently biding his time until he could orchestrate a revenge befitting the man who'd ruined his life, the perfect tool had unexpectedly dropped in his lap. Immediately de Tolomei had offered to buy the prisoner from Azadi for personal reasons and use his extensive contacts to ensure the success of Azadi's defection to the U.S. He explained that American government officials could not be trusted to keep their end of any deal. If they didn't burn him intentionally after getting what they wanted, no doubt one of them would make a mistake regarding his relocation and get him killed. Azadi had readily accepted the offer.

Looking at his hands, de Tolomei watched them encircle an imaginary neck. When Donovan Morgan had destroyed his life thirteen years ago, he had wanted nothing more than to wring the life out of him. Over time, however, he had decided that death would be too easy.

McLean, Virginia — 4:44 p.m.

Alexis Cruz, the director of central intelligence, was relaxing in a spacious tub in the bathroom adjoining her office on the seventh floor of CIA headquarters. She had been in meetings for ten hours straight and had insisted that she not be disturbed for an hour, saying something to her executive assistant about an urgent call with a Southeast Asian head of state.

Alexis's predawn workout had been grueling. With a former D-boy (member of the army's elite Delta Force) as her new personal trainer, she was in excellent physical shape, but her muscles were now painfully sore just about all the time. Conducting her afternoon reading in the tub was quickly becoming a habit. One of her bodyguards—the only person who knew about it—liked to joke that she gave new meaning to the term "wet work."

She had just opened a thin file containing information that didn't exist anywhere in her agency's databases or tangible paper files. It was the personal history of an operations officer code-named Acheron, easily the Agency's best of the past decade. If Jeremy Slade could get him back with his cover intact, it would be a miracle; he was worth far more to his country than any missile shield ever could be. Even if the boys at Defense ever designed one that worked, Alexis thought to herself with a shake of her head.

One thing the file didn't contain was the spy's real name, which was known only to Slade and Donovan Morgan. Scanning the first page, Alexis saw that he was the son of an Egyptian father and American mother and had grown up in Cairo with dual citizenship. During the early nineties, when the Mubarak government was at war with Egypt's militant Islamic groups, several of their spy's friends had been killed in a terrorist attack at a coffee shop in Cairo's trendy Tahrir Square. Since most of Egypt's revenue came from tourism, the militants targeted tourist destinations in order to destroy the economy and thereby undermine the government.

Having heard rumors that Egyptian intelligence had been penetrated by members of the militant groups, their spy—then a student applying to Cairo University—had offered his services to Slade, the CIA's station chief in Cairo at the time. Despite his lack of standard training, under Slade's guidance, the spy had infiltrated Al Gama'a al Islamiyya, Egypt's most violent terrorist organization, gaining the militants' trust by participating in their favorite fund-raising activity: bank robbery.

A fan of classical Greek literature, Slade had decided to call his new recruit Acheron, after an ancient river said to have given Odysseus access to the underworld. It turned out to be a fitting name; with Acheron's information, Slade was able to help Egyptian law enforcement prevent nearly a dozen terrorist attacks on foreign tourists.

In 1995, Slade moved back to Washington to head the Agency's Middle East Division, and two years later Acheron joined him, having enrolled in a graduate program in archaeology in the United States. Using his archaeological fieldwork as a cover, he carried out assignments all over the Middle East for several years with extraordinary success until the Iraq operation of early 2001, code-named Hydra. So named because with his infamous doubles, Saddam Hussein was, in essence, a monster with multiple heads.

Their spy had had an incredible cover. Despite being a brutal, repressive dictator, Hussein had always been an enthusiastic champion of Iraq's cultural heritage, and after Desert Storm, welcomed foreign archaeologists—including British and American ones—to salvage and study his nation's archaeological sites. And as the cradle of civilization—land of the ancient Sumerian, Assyrian, and Babylonian empires—Iraq had thousands. Further endearing himself to the Hussein regime, their spy had been a member of a Boston-based organization that published a newsletter condemning the devastation inflicted on Iraqi heritage sites by American and British warplanes patrolling the no-fly zones; apparently their bombs had all but destroyed Ur, the birthplace of Abraham, among other sites.

In addition to being authorized to carry small laptops—for analyzing millennia-old cuneiform tablets—archaeologists in Iraq were encouraged to be armed in order to protect themselves from looters. On account of the chaos and poverty following Desert Storm, Alexis knew, the looting problem became so extreme that the few archaeologists working in Iraq were sometimes more heavily armed than soldiers. *Welcomed into the country, authorized to carry a laptop and a gun—it doesn't get better than that.*

In March 2001, there had been an international conference in Baghdad to celebrate five millennia since the invention of writing. Archaeologists and cuneiform experts from the U.S., Great Britain, and Europe had gathered to share the results of their recent research and debate new theories with their Iraqi colleagues. Thus Acheron had been one of dozens of Westerners traveling throughout the country to visit and resume work at old digging sites, during and after the conference. The coup he'd been so perfectly positioned to orchestrate would no doubt have been successful had he not been betrayed a month into the operation. Alexis had no proof, but she believed a senior CIA officer was responsible.

Alexis had not been at the Agency at the time. Though she had started her career as a case officer, she'd left in her late twenties to get a law degree, did a short stint as a federal prosecutor, and eventually became a congresswoman for the state of New York. Then, shortly after September 11, 2001, the president had asked her to take over the beleaguered Agency and, as he put it, clear out the cobwebs. Which was proving to be a painfully slow process. Among other things, she still had not identified this particular traitor, if he really existed.

As Alexis cursed, one of her secure telephone lines rang. "Cruz," she said, picking it up.

"Lexy? It's Jeremy."

"I'm just reading the file now. Have you found him?"

"Yes. After years in one of the world's most impenetrable prisons, he's in a lightly guarded villa on the Tunisian coast, if you can believe it. I've got a team preparing to move in as we speak."

"How did you . . . ?"

"He was taken from Evin by truck and loaded aboard a ship leaving the gulf for the Mediterranean. Last night the ship had a rendezvous with a yacht off the coast of Tunis. A KH-12 was in the right place at the right time to catch the transaction."

"So you think this de Tolomei, whoever he is, bought him from Azadi as a means of blackmailing us?"

"Appears to be his primary business," Slade said. "If it was Azadi, I'd guess he was trying to engineer some kind of prisoner swap, but with de Tolomei . . ."

"Right. Although, Don may be comfortable, but he certainly doesn't have money on the scale of de Tolomei's usual targets," Alexis said. "He could be after my discretionary funds, of course, unless . . ."

"He's after something other than money," Slade filled in.

"A pardon?" Alexis suggested. "Maybe he took a new identity because he's some kind of fugitive."

"That'd fit," Slade agreed. "Whatever the case, we'll get our man back, but we might have another problem. Remember those track marks on his arms? It's possible Azadi has a full confession on tape."

"Which could get everyone involved investigated by Congress, the Hague . . . possibly indicted," Alexis said. "My predecessor, you, Donovan, not to mention the president." Her mind raced over the murky territory of international law concerning the attempted assassination of a political figure in another state. "We couldn't argue there was a condition of war in early 2001," she continued, "so the charge would be . . . conspiracy to violate article one of the 1974 U.N. resolution on illegal acts of aggression. We couldn't go with anticipatory self-defense, of course. Yeah, it'd have to be humanitarian intervention."

"Would that work?" Slade asked.

"Legally? Sure. But a PR nightmare with the election around the corner? The president will have my head for breakfast."

"I won't let it come to that, Lexy."

"I know," she said softly, shifting her weight because her right leg was asleep. To her irritation, the movement generated a tiny splash.

"In the tub, huh?"

"Caught in the act."

"I'm sorry I'm not there with you."

In spite of the warm water engulfing her, Alexis shivered.

Sidi Bou Said, Tunisia — 11:56 p.m.

Moonlight and street lamps illuminated Sidi Bou Said, a picturesque blue and white town perched on a cliff overlooking the Gulf of Tunis. All of the whitewashed rectangular buildings had bright blue doors, trim, and intricate lattices dripping with bougainvillea. Tourists milled in the streets — mostly smartly dressed Europeans poking their noses down cobbled alleys, checking out the shops as well as each other.

Dressed in ivory linen, Connor Black and Jason Avera, two former CIA paramilitary operatives in Jeremy Slade's employ, were strolling toward their destination, a cliffside café with a view of the gulf below. They'd taken a flight from Istanbul to Tunis that afternoon. The café was half a kilometer northeast of the villa their four-man team had under surveillance.

"To think we were on our way to an Iranian prison. This is a fucking piece of cake," Jason said.

Connor nodded. Then, seeing a pair of women openly ogling them, he reached for Jason's hand. To avoid unwanted attention, they were posing as gay tourists.

Feigning a smile, Jason grumbled, "Bitch, your hands are clammy."

Connor grinned. "All the better to caress you with, my dear."

"Don't you think the pink and lavender shirts are enough to get the message across?"

"Apparently not," Connor said, letting go once the two women had passed with a predictable "the hot ones are *always* gay" lament.

Rounding a bend in the road, Connor and Jason entered a widened stretch lined with cafés and headed for the table they'd been sitting at earlier that day. Fortunately it was vacant. They ordered the house specialties — sweet mint tea in tiny glass mugs, baklava, and a hookah with apple tobacco — then gazed down at the curvaceous coastline below, pretending to admire the view.

The languid gulf waters sparkled, reflecting the moon and stars above. On the shore, about thirty yards from the villa in question, a man was meandering along on horseback. Wearing a Led Zeppelin shirt, he had a map spread across the horse's neck, a flashlight in hand, a compact disc player at his waist, and earphones on his head. Singing aloud periodically, with slurred words, he appeared to be a tipsy tourist.

Connor turned his attention to the villa. Nestled in a cluster of palm trees, it had a two-tiered balcony facing the sea and was Sidi Bou's requisite blue and white. When he began to speak, Jason nodded and chuckled, although Connor wasn't actually talking to him; there was a microphone hidden in his shirt collar.

"Mr. Revere, this is Lover One. What do you see?" Connor asked. They were using just enough coded words to conceal their identies and keep their target ambiguous, should anyone chance upon their radio frequency.

"Two cats on the first-floor balcony," the man on the horse reported, using their term for armed guards. "Don't know how, but it looks like they've got a couple of M4s," he added, referring to a model of assault rifle specifically made for the U.S. Special Forces. Lightweight and compact, M4 carbines had built-in night-vision scopes and grenade launchers.

"How about inside?"

Turning a barely detectable knob on his glasses to activate their thermal imaging feature, the horseman answered, "Same three bodies. Upstairs, Mr. Nightingale, prone. The missus still hunched beside him—touching his head, might be combing his hair. Another cat, a third one, downstairs near the front door."

"Lighting?"

"Probably extends about fifteen feet from the house."

"Overall assessment?"

"No cameras. No red lines, either," he added, speaking of laser trip wires. "An ordinary vacation home, I think."

"All right. See you soon," Connor said. Turning to face Jason, he leaned in closely. "Woodsman, what've you got?"

The man Connor was really speaking to was sitting on a comfortable mound of earth and leaves across the road from the entrance to the villa. Though concealed by dense trees and shrubbery, he had a good line of sight to the driveway and front door. He also had a directional microphone in his hands, and a pair of powerful binoculars in his lap.

"Hey, Lover One. A car came in and out today, twice, remaining for about twenty-five minutes each time. The plates have been identified as those of a local doctor."

"Anything bouncing off the glass?"

"Mrs. Nightingale got a call about fifteen minutes ago from whoever hired her. I'd guess he's paying her well—she sounded pretty grateful. Seems to like him a lot, too. Other than that, she's been talking to her old man. A continuous monologue about how she cares about him, wants him to come to Paris with her . . . asks him questions, then starts imagining what his answers might be."

"What did the doctor say?"

"That he's in a coma, that he could come out of it at any time. Gave Mrs. Nightingale more IV bags, antibiotic creams, stuff like that."

"Okay. Come in around two or three."

Looking once more at his colleague on horseback, Connor watched him trot past the villa and head toward the marina at the base of the cliff. Turning back to face Jason, Connor noticed that their dessert had arrived. He took a piece of baklava and, with a saccharine smile, brought it toward Jason's mouth, subtly nodding at a table of women gazing in their direction.

"Nice try," Jason said, leaning back with his tea.

Laughing, Connor fumbled for his ringing cell phone.

"Hey," he heard Jeremy Slade's voice say. "How's it look?"

"All clear."

"Feel comfortable going in tomorrow night?"

"Definitely. It's supposed to be completely overcast."

"Good."

"What about the guards?"

"Do they know who they're watching?"

"No. And apparently, his face is so battered his features are indiscernible."

"Trank them."

"And the girl? She's some kind of nurse, a teenager we think. She doesn't know who the hell she's taking care of, but she sure knows her boss."

"Then take her with you."

MAYFAIR, LONDON — 10:10 P.M.

Sitting at her computer, Kate heard a knock on her door and the familiar voice of one of the hotel's bellmen. He gave her a handwritten message. Glancing at it, she was surprised to see nothing but random garbled text.

"He thought you might need this," the bellman added, handing Kate a Cardan Grille, the Elizabethan code device she'd described to Medina the previous evening.

Thanking him, Kate walked back into her bedroom and placed the grille over the message. Letters forming six words were visible through the cutout boxes: I'M IN THE COCKTAIL BAR DOWNSTAIRS.

Kate hadn't decided whether or not she was going to call Medina that evening, but . . . *looks like he made up my mind for me.*

Still wearing her black strapless dress, she walked across the room toward the spiked Prada sandals she'd borrowed from Adriana earlier that evening. Sitting on the bed to fasten them, she changed her mind—*to hell with it*—opting to wear hotel slippers instead. Passing a mirror, Kate deliberated for a moment, then gave in, turning toward it to check her teeth for lipstick smudges.

Up on the third floor, the hotel's newest guest stood peering down into the stairwell.

"Had you a nice evening?" a German woman asked him.

"Perfect," he responded, using his best American accent. "I went to the theater. Wonderful comedy."

Reaching into his jacket pockets, he pretended to search for his room key until the old woman was gone, then returned his gaze to the stairwell. A few minutes later, he saw Kate Morgan's door open and watched until the top of her head disappeared from sight. She was carrying a backpack, but maybe . . .

Descending the steps two at a time, within seconds he was picking his way into her suite. Spotting a mobile phone on the desk, he strode toward it.

Medina was facing the opposite direction when Kate entered the dimly lit, wood-paneled cocktail bar. He was looking at either a stag's head or a painting of a horse. She used the opportunity to look at him. He was wearing black trousers and a charcoal gray button-down shirt, which, Kate had to admit, were very flattering. Not that he needed any assistance.

"Nice shoes," he said, noticing her.

"Thanks, I—"

"No need to explain. I know it's your way of saying you're not trying to impress me. But if you really didn't care, you'd have changed into a sweat-shirt."

Good point, um . . . "And get frowned at by the snoots around here? No thanks."

"Damn. I try to get you to miss a beat, just once, but—"

"Cidro, badinage is like tennis. It's easier to hit a winner off a good shot than a weak lob."

"A backhanded compliment, nice work. So what can I get you to drink?"

"Uh, I've already had a few tonight, so—"

"You're kidding, right? Come on."

Kate laughed. "Okay, I'll have amaretto with milk. But remember, I warned you. Any more booze and my internal censor hangs up her hat and goes home."

"Sounds like that's when things get interesting."

"Maybe. Just don't get mad if I . . . oh, I don't know . . . call you a pompous ass or something."

"I'm used to it." Medina headed over to the bar.

Kate settled into a leather armchair by a window adorned with thick red drapes.

"Tell me, how was your evening?" he asked, placing their drinks on the small table between them.

"Good. I went to a Sotheby's auction with my college roommate. And your meetings?"

"Good, too. Things are . . . moving. But what I really want to know is what you like to do when you're not working."

"I thought we agreed to talk business."

"Darling, I don't know what world you live in, but polite business peo-ple exchange more than two sentences' worth of pleasantries first."

"Forgive me," Kate said, lightly smacking her forehead. "But I have to say, getting me talking about what I like most? Cidro, that's textbook charm school. And you were so obvious."

"I may've been known to ask that question without meaning it," Med-ina admitted, "but in your case, I'd really like to know."

"Oh. Well, then . . . mmm, I like to travel. Go to a country I've never been to, start with some art and architecture, then switch to something physical—hiking or rock climbing or something. You?"

"Actually, you're not finished yet. How about day to day?"

Kate sighed.

"Last personal question. I promise."

"Okay. I like trendy pop music. Country, too, when I'm in the mood. Um, hip-hop dance classes . . . I love watching action movies a little drunk, preferably ones where the star takes his shirt off all the time, and I have a mild chocolate addiction. You know, once in a while, I need a fix. Not like a junkie, really—more like an accountant needs his calculator in early April. I have to have it, but I don't think, if thwarted, that I'd resort to violence. Is that enough for you?"

Smiling, Medina nodded.

"Ready for your case update?"

"Very."

"Okay. One of my colleagues looked into the last couple weeks' worth of calls and emails to and from the Cat—you know, Simon Trevor-Jones—since he had to have had some form of contact with the man we're looking for. Even if indirectly."

Kate paused for a moment to try her drink. "I've ruled out everyone we identified. There was one number my colleague hasn't been able to trace yet, but when he does track down the owner . . ."

"We may find our man."

"We hope. It's possible that Trevor-Jones and the Jade Dragon fellow only met face-to-face, or that Trevor-Jones used an agent whom he only met in person, which means I should probably get back to *The Anatomy of Secrets*. Are we through here?" she asked, feigning exasperation.

"Not yet. I have one more question." Seeing Kate's expression, he added, "It's related to the case."

"Yes?"

"The other day in the Pierre, you got me curious about something. I've been meaning to ask you about it. You described what you were working on when you left school, whether it was more dangerous to pursue state secrets or God's secrets in the Renaissance. I know you left before writing your dissertation, but did you have an answer by then?"

"More like a starting point." Kate said. "Some preliminary ideas."

"Which were?"

"It depended on how the secret knowledge was used — if it was desired for its own sake or for power, and if for power, who was threatened by it and how."

Seeing Medina's expectant expression, Kate asked, "You really want to hear more?"

"Yeah," he said, looking surprised she'd asked.

"Well, generally speaking, I was confining the state and God discussion to political and military secrets versus discoveries in natural philosophy, what we call science. The two overlapped of course, as they do today. Anyway, the military and political part is fairly simple. People have never really pursued those kinds of secrets for the hell of it; money and power are always involved. So same as now, a Renaissance spy who got his hands on sensitive war plan information could get himself killed. Or if he had damaging information on a political figure, in his own government or in another, same thing," Kate said, drawing a finger across her throat.

"The scientific discovery part is where it gets more complex," she continued.

Just then, a young waitress appeared at their table. Dressed in black and white, she had pearls in her ears, minimal makeup, and hair pulled back into a neat bun. "Another drink?"

Medina nodded. "I'll have another Sapphire and tonic, and the lady will have . . ."

"Bailey's with ice. Thanks."

Once the waitress had left, Medina turned back to Kate. "About science, you were saying . . ."

"That's the kind of knowledge that was sometimes pursued for its own sake, and when that was the case, you were safe. Take Copernicus. His theory that the sun was the center of the universe — people tend to think of it as really rocking the Catholic Church, something that got people killed. But the truth is, it wasn't. No one ever bothered him. Churchmen even sponsored his research."

"Really?"

"Yeah," Kate said, turning to thank the waitress as she set down their drinks. "See, Copernicus wasn't interested in challenging church authority of any kind, Catholic or Protestant. He was just in love with the idea of getting closer to the truth about the movement of what he called 'celestial spheres.' And he was good with numbers, and knew that with an Aristotelian earth-centered universe, the math just didn't work out. Which irritated him, you know, like a bee in his bonnet."

Medina smiled.

"He published his book about a sun-centered universe in 1543, and though it completely contradicted Scripture, religious figures barely blinked for the next fifty years," Kate said. "In fact, the pope really liked his ideas and wanted to use the math to reform the calender. And Protestant scholars—the few who understood astronomy, that is—they recognized that Copernicus kicked Aristotle to the curb, mathematically speaking, and were happy to use his theories, ignoring their theological implications. Strange as it sounds, they found a way to buy into the new astronomy without grafting it onto the physical world."

"But Galileo's *arrest*," Medina said, frowning. "And didn't someone get executed for talking about that stuff? There's this square in Rome . . ."

" . . . where Giordano Bruno was burned at the stake in 1600," Kate filled in. "You're right. But here's the thing. Galileo and Bruno didn't just enjoy the ideas, getting all rapturous about universal truth. They used Copernican astronomy to step on the toes of powerful people. And *that's* when the shit hit the fan."

"How so?"

"Well, when he started out, Galileo actually had top Catholics for patrons, even popes, but when he basically tried to tell them how to reinterpret Scripture—in the midst of their turf war with Protestants—they felt threatened, got steamed, and Galileo got arrested. And Bruno, the so-called mad priest of the sun—he considered Judaism and Christianity to be corruptions of ancient truths and used Copernican astronomy to symbolize his ideas for reform. He went to various heads of state to promote his new religious doctrine, telling them that, like the sun is to the universe, they were the center of the world, not the pope."

"So the pope called in the death squad."

"Exactly. People think that developments in astronomy caused a massive clash between science and religion in the early modern period, but the clash was never really about the astronomy. It was about politics and who was undermining whose power. Now, are you still awake?"

"Of course. And I've finally figured out why I couldn't make it through university."

She raised an eyebrow.

"I didn't have a pretty girl explaining everything to me."

Momentarily forgetting her rebuffing campaign, Kate blushed. *What is wrong with me? Oh, alcohol . . . right.*

"But don't let me interrupt you," Medina said. "Let's get back to the shark-infested waters of Renaissance curiosity. . . . You were talking about scientific discoveries."

"Yeah. Astronomy. I viewed that as a way of pursuing God's secrets in the vertical dimension," Kate said, moving her hand up and down. "Could be deadly if you used what you discovered to threaten kings or popes. But geographical discoveries—those made in the horizontal dimension," she continued, moving her hand from side to side, "that's a different story. You sure you want—"

"Yes, Kate."

"Okay. In a way, exploration was also a means of pursuing divine secrets—sailing to far-off lands once thought to be the haunts of monsters and demons and proving they weren't. Explorers were, of course, a bit more interested in money and glory than intellectual satisfaction, but travel was definitely a means of dispelling wonder, of sucking the enchantment out of mysterious places. The difference is your government never killed you over what you found. In fact, if you found a new trading route, or a place to start a new colony, or just pillaged and plundered, you were a national hero . . . perhaps knighted. And if you came back empty-handed, you were a broke loser but perfectly safe.

"Seeking knowledge in what I called the horizontal dimension wasn't any less dangerous than the other pursuits I've been talking about; the threats just came from different sources—storms, malnutrition, pirates, you name it. And sailors were sometimes captured and tortured for geographical information that had potential economic value, like tidbits about the location of the fabled city of El Dorado."

Kate smiled. "Now, optics, Cidro . . . sounds boring, but I've got a pretty juicy theory. Interested?"

"Very."

"Most people think that as soon as the telescope was discovered—by some Dutch eyeglass manufacturers in the early seventeenth century—the technology spread like wildfire, which meant that it never gave anyone a military advantage . . . say, to spot enemy ships before they spotted you. However, there's a passage in a sixteenth-century text written by a natural philosopher that's ambiguous, but it really sounds like the guy had used a telescope. I think it might've been discovered years before everyone thinks, and that the inventor just kept it quiet. It's definitely possible someone was killed to keep that secret safe."

"So, while you could get killed for both back then," Medina began, looking into his glass as he swirled the ice cubes around, "I'd guess you concluded that being a spy was far more dangerous than being a scientist, because you were *always* at risk? Not just some of the time?"

"More or less. The safest thing was definitely to be a humble scientist pursuing knowledge for its own sake, far removed from the power plays at court. I did have a catchy zinger in mind for the end, though," Kate said, smiling.

Medina raised an eyebrow.

"There were a lot of guys in Elizabethan England who were involved in the pursuit of both kinds of secrets. Like Francis Walsingham and Robert Cecil. They were both top spymasters and also helped finance several explorers, like Francis Drake and Walter Ralegh. And the top intellectual at Elizabeth's court—a man named John Dee—was suspected of being a spy and pursued God's secrets, too . . . claimed to be able to conjure angels and access heavenly truths. It was believed that he practiced black magic as well, and a frightened, angry mob once ransacked his library and destroyed his scientific instruments, but he lived to a ripe old age. However, there was one guy who pursued both, got murdered, and we still don't know for which. People speculate of course, but—"

"Who?" Medina asked, leaning forward with interest.

"Christopher Marlowe."

"Big playwright, yeah?"

Kate nodded. "He was also a spy . . . with dirt on some pretty dangerous political players. On the other hand, he pursued God's secrets pretty intensely, too. In fiction, at least, if not in practice."

"What do you mean?"

"His plays really pushed the religion envelope. His Faustus asks the devil's emissary where hell is located, then says he thinks hell's just a fable. Later Faustus sets off in a chariot drawn by dragons to explore the universe and, as he put it, 'To find the secrets of astronomy / Graven in the book of Jove's high firmament.' It was pretty subversive stuff at the time."

Kate took a sip of her drink. "During the last month of Marlowe's life, the government was investigating him. For sedition as well as atheism, you know, since undermining the church's authority meant undermining the state's. A few days before his death, an informant submitted a report suggesting his atheist propaganda was so dangerous his mouth ought to be forcibly shut."

"So he was arrested and executed?"

"No. He was interrogated, but released that same day. Soon after, though, he was murdered. We know the three men who were in the room with him at the time, but we still don't know which one did it or why."

"What do you think?"

"Well, first of all, I don't think Marlowe was an atheist. Definitely curious, full of doubts, and disgusted with the religious leadership of his day, which could not have been fun in an age when such skepticism was a crime. Whatever his views were, though, I don't think he died because of them. I think that a political figure had Marlowe framed, either to protect his own secrets or to get dirt on a rival."

"Who?"

Kate shook her head. "I couldn't say for sure."

Medina smiled. "You're right, though. The story's got zing. Packs punch."

"Thanks."

"Now, Kate. This Marlowe, you *really* like him, yeah?"

"Sure. For what I was studying, he was an interesting figure in a lot of ways," she responded casually.

The truth was that Marlowe was actually far more than just a subject of academic interest to Kate. When making the decision whether or not to leave school for the Slade Group, she'd thought about Marlowe strolling back and forth between the world of letters and the covert underworld and eventually chose to try following in his footsteps—up to a point, at least. She did not intend to die at age twenty-nine with a knife through her eye socket. But beyond relying on him for professional inspiration, Kate felt that Marlowe was something of a kindred spirit. Since Rhys's death, she'd known that she would live with painful desire for something she couldn't have for the rest of her life, and so she was drawn to Marlowe's tragic heroes, all of whom were doomed by an irrepressible desire for the unattainable.

Medina folded his arms across his chest and narrowed his eyes. "Anyone in *this* century put that look on your face?"

Kate sipped her drink quietly.

"Come on. What's his name?"

"Who?"

"The guy you're hung up on."

"What makes you think that?"

"I've been hitting on you from day one."

"And you never get turned down, huh?"

"Not really." Medina paused, then added, "I've been told that spending five minutes with me would turn an arthritic nun into an agile nympho."

Kate burst out laughing. "An ego the size of Texas and yet *somehow*, still charming. Impressive."

"I'm serious, Kate. We click, and yet . . . well, I can only conclude that someone else already owns your heart. So who is he? And when can we duel?"

"Not anytime soon. But he'd have kicked your ass. He won a Japanese fencing tournament once."

"Where is he?"

"I don't know . . . he's dead."

Medina's face fell. "God. I'm sorry."

"It's okay. It was a long time ago. But you're right. He still owns my heart, like it's a piece of real estate he bought and built a stone fortress on."

"How'd you meet?"

"It was the spring of my senior year of college. I'd been teaching a kickboxing class for a while but hadn't done any real martial arts in years, which is what he was teaching. After I finished my thesis, I started going to his informal sparring sessions, and . . ."

"It was love?"

"Within a few days," Kate said, finishing the drink she no longer tasted. She was remembering the salty taste of kissing Rhys's neck on their way out of the gym together back then.

"I can't imagine how tough that must have been. I've never lost anyone close to me. How did you . . ."

"Oh, for a while I fantasized about disappearing. Not committing suicide, just somehow vaporizing away. But I couldn't desert my father, so I just plodded along . . . eventually remembered how to find happiness in less obvious places."

"You really believe you'll never fall for anyone again?"

Kate nodded. "It's not just that Rhys was . . . irreplaceable. I think it's a physiological thing, that the brain chemicals that govern emotions like love get diluted after a heartbreak—maybe with age, too. Like coke cut with aspirin."

"So you're telling me that at my advanced age, if it hasn't happened yet, I'm doomed to a loveless existence?"

"No, but I'd say it's more likely that you'd really lose it, Romeo style, if you were still a teenager," Kate said, briefly placing her hand over his and shaking her head with phony consolation. "But wait a minute. I seem to remember hearing that you were pretty besotted with some fashion model these days."

"*Besotted* isn't the right word. Anyway, she's been dismissed," Medina said, waving a hand to the side. Then, reaching toward Kate, he brushed an errant tendril from her face.

"Cidro, I'm meeting a friend to go running pretty early tomorrow," Kate said, checking her watch, "and I'd like to get through as much as I can of the manuscript before tomorrow afternoon. I've got a short trip to take, so—"

"You're leaving me?"

"Briefly."

"Oh."

"It's just for half a day. You'll manage." Seeing his contemplative expression, she asked, "Trying to remember the last time a girl left your company voluntarily?"

Laughing, he nodded. "How'd you guess?"

"Reading minds is part of my job."

"By the way, Kate, with *The Anatomy*, I've got a suggestion—my usual technique for dealing with mysterious literature."

"I thought you didn't read."

"Well, I pick up mystery novels now and then. You know, if I'm stuck somewhere without . . ."

" . . . girls, drugs, or fast cars?"

"Exactly."

Guessing where he was headed, Kate smiled. "You start in but find yourself too impatient to wait for the answers, and you flip to the end."

"Every time."

Back in her room, Kate was following Medina's advice to skip to the end of *The Anatomy of Secrets*. As she'd told her book dealer friend, Hannah Rosenberg, a couple days before, Kate saw two possibilities for why Phelippes had rushed his binder. Immediately after stealing the deceased Walsingham's files, Phelippes might have decided to bind and hide his manuscript right away, before any government officials could find it in his possession. Alternatively, Phelippes could have held on to the files—using them to blackmail people, perhaps—then raced to the binder when someone threatened to track down his damning evidence. Neither of which suggested that the final report would be the proverbial smoking gun, but since she hadn't yet had any luck proceeding in chronological order, she thought it was worth a try.

Okay, backward it is. I wonder what the last few might be? Walsingham died in 1590, and if Phelippes included reports from that year . . . let's see. Not that either of them would've cared much about Shakespeare's plays, but what if they had some kind of solid evidence that could prove, once and for all, that he was the real author? He'd already written his lost version of Hamlet *and the first part of* Henry VI *at that point . . .*

Turning on her laptop, Kate opened up her electronic version of the manuscript's final page and saw only numbers, no letters. And the numbers were grouped together, as if they represented letters forming words. "Could it really be so easy?" she wondered aloud, looking for the right decryption commands.

Her thoughts drifting back to Christopher Marlowe, Kate said, "Damn. It's too bad this thing doesn't go through 1593."

18

Why, was there ever seen such villainy,
So neatly plotted, and so well perform'd?
—Ithamore, in Marlowe's *The Jew of Malta*

London — Morning, May 1593

Two hundred meters north of London Bridge, on the fifth floor of a half-timbered house adjacent to Leadenhall Market, Thomas Phelippes was kneeling on the floor of his study opening a cedar chest. It was full of clothing and loose papers, but he wasn't interested in any of them at the moment. He was after something else.

Phelippes's cedar chest didn't have a false bottom; anyone ransacking your lodgings would check for one of those. What the chest did have was a type of false top, a hollow space within its heavy lid about two inches thick. Using a knife, he pried up the thin velvet-covered panel on the underside of the lid, revealing a space about nine by twelve inches that had been carved into the otherwise solid wood. Nestled inside, surrounded by tufts of wool, lay a pewter box.

Phelippes carried it across the room to his desk. Fingers closing around the black silk cord that never left his neck, he drew a metal key from beneath his shirt. Leaning forward, he unlocked the box, lifted the lid, and gazed lovingly upon his most treasured possession: the stack of papers he'd culled from Francis Walsingham's files. His arsenal of secrets.

Just after Walsingham's death, Phelippes had sneaked the files home with him, hidden the reports he thought would prove useful, then burned the rest. After decades of faithful service, he'd certainly deserved them, but the Privy Council had officially declared the files to be stolen property, and Phelippes had no intention of being arrested for the theft.

He was planning to have the papers bound soon. Before autumn, in all likelihood. He'd been adding new reports now and then, and the stack would soon outgrow the special airtight box he'd designed for it. He had waited this long because he was holding out for the perfect final page—a report containing information that would elevate Essex to the position of secretary of state, either by impressing the queen with something of enormous consequence, or by ruining the competition: Robert Cecil. Phelippes had several irons in the fire to achieve those ends. He wondered which would come through for him first.

After returning the box to its hiding place, he stood to leave. Locking his door, he entered the building's stairwell and headed down to the street. He'd chosen to live in this particular building because it was located on the site of the old Roman court of justice, from the time when London was called Londinium. He found the parallel delicious; he might not be part of modern London's judicial system but possessing Walsingham's files gave him the power to mete out his own version of justice. At the moment, he had four blackmail schemes under way, which were funding several intelligence operations he was managing without his employer's awareness.

When Phelippes reached London Bridge, he retrieved Kit Marlowe's most recent message from their hiding place in St. Thomas's Chapel, then hailed a ferry.

"I'm to Essex House," he said. The enormous Gothic mansion on the north shore of the Thames was the earl's home as well as the nexus of his intelligence network.

Upon entering the great hall, Phelippes headed straight for the candles burning on the large dining table. He heated Marlowe's seemingly blank message with concentrated precision, and, within seconds, brown letters edged with yellow began to appear. It was a very simple cipher they'd each committed to memory. "God's blood!" Phelippes cried, learning that no one in the Muscovy Company had discovered a Northeast Passage. He then deciphered a sentence about the illicit alliance with a Barbary pirate captain and smiled. "Marlowe thinks he's to have this culprit unmasked before week's end?"

On his way up to his employer's personal chambers on the mansion's uppermost floor, Phelippes heard a faint mumbling and the rustling of papers coming from one of the first-floor studies. It was probably Anthony Bacon, who directed their network's gathering and analysis of foreign intelligence. A pale, gout-ridden man, Bacon sifted through papers while propped up in bed. Caressing the key dangling beneath his shirt, Phelippes snickered to himself. Bacon hadn't a clue about the report Phelippes had in his possession—the one detailing Bacon's sinful escapades in France.

Phelippes quietly worked his picks in the door to Essex's bedchamber. He liked to surprise people now and then, because you didn't really know someone if you saw him only the way he wanted to be seen. Slipping through the door, he crept down the hall, treading as lightly as possible on the scented rushes covering the floor. Clutching the fabric of a soft tapestry, he peered around the corner.

Oh, dear God!

Upon the room's enormous feather bed, Essex and a voluptuous naked woman were lying face to face with their legs intertwined, writhing about. A second woman, somehow even more buxom than the first, was kneeling at the foot of the bed sucking the earl's toes and touching herself in places people were simply not supposed to touch. Wiping a few tendrils of hair from his glistening face, Essex strained his neck to watch her.

"My lord," the toe sucker said, "I . . . I must have you soon."

Just then, the woman wrapped in Essex's embrace started to make unseemly noises, and Phelippes watched—disgusted but fascinated—as her legs quivered. When she quieted, Essex nudged her aside and sat up with his knees in the air, naked but for the ruby and emerald pendant suspended from his neck. The second woman crawled over, sat before him, and slid her feet over his legs. As Essex placed his large hands on her cherubic posterior and pulled her toward him, she murmured, "Oh, my lord!" with sickening excitement.

At that moment, the other woman began kissing the back of his neck.

When will these wanton wretches have enough?

As Phelippes began to edge away, Essex's voice stopped him in his tracks. "By the way, Thomas, I do know you're there."

Curse the saints! "My apologies for the interruption, but I've a matter of great urgency to discuss."

"Hmm, let us ponder that. Teresa, wouldn't you call *this* a matter of great urgency?"

"Oh, yes, my lord," the woman in his arms sighed, tossing her dark hair about.

"But I'm here on a matter of state!"

"Oh, but so am I," Essex replied. "Now, would you care to see what we do when we bathe, or would you prefer to wait downstairs? I could make things even more interesting by inviting the stable boy . . . it's up to you."

"Tell me, Thomas. Why do you think I hold the power that I do?"

Turning around, Phelippes couldn't help but admire the sight. Freshly scrubbed, Essex's cheeks were rosy, and his dark reddish locks, neatly pulled back. His doublet, stitched of chestnut silk slashed with gold, hugged his tall, well-muscled physique to perfection. His lace ruffs were elaborate and new.

"The intelligence we uncover has long impressed the queen, and—"

"True. Much good it all may do. But the bedchamber, Thomas. I also impress her in the bedchamber."

Essex gestured to the table. Teresa was laying out an array of dishes upon it.

"My lord, if you don't mind my asking, how do you go from that to, well, to . . ."

"Elizabeth?"

Phelippes nodded.

"When I first sought her favor at court, it was . . . out of necessity," Essex began.

That Phelippes well knew. Essex had been born the poorest earl in England. He could not survive financially without the queen's love.

"But now, even though she's long past her prime, when I look at her I simply see a woman I am desperate to possess, to dominate—and it's captivating. Even more so than . . ." He nodded to the doorway.

Phelippes watched Essex spear a piece of wrinkled green plant matter with what resembled a miniature devil's trident. *What, in God's name . . . ?*

"Lettuce. Good for digestion. Very fashionable. And the dessert comes from a secret recipe closely guarded by Catherine de Medici. I had to bribe the French royal chef for it. 'Italian ice,' he called it."

In an effort to avoid scowling, Phelippes pressed his lips together. "Remember what I told you about Kit Marlowe?"

"That you've got him seeking out smugglers in the Muscovy Company? Men who may have found a Northeast Passage?"

"No passage, unfortunately, but the investigation may still prove useful. Perhaps. I am not counting on it, however, as unmasking dishonest merchants is no monumental affair. And obtaining proof of such dishonesty is no easy task. It is my *other* plan that will most assuredly advance you over Cecil."

"What is it?" Essex asked, reaching for the pumpkin custard.

"As a member of the commission hunting for the author of the threatening placards, I can steer the investigation however I choose. And I'm steering it toward Marlowe. Very soon, he'll be on the rack, revealing the illicit dealings Cecil is rumored to engage in. Ralegh, as well. We'll be in a position to ruin them both."

"But I like Marlowe, Thomas. Did you see his *Massacre at Paris* this winter?"

"No," Phelippes replied stiffly. "I prefer dramas that unfold in real life."

"Oh, but it was spectacular! The Rose was packed. The queen and I slipped in hidden behind masks. And his elegies! I read one to Anne and Teresa earlier this morning, something about . . . what was it? A large leg, and . . . and . . ." Essex clapped his hand to his forehead and shut his eyes. "A lusty thigh!"

Phelippes sighed. It was ever disappointing to be working for someone so terribly unlike Walsingham. Why could Essex not appreciate the beauty of felling so many birds with one stone? At least he'd quit sulking, though. While some men assumed a melancholic pose for fashion's sake, Essex's bouts of gloom were genuine and terrible for business.

"You may cease your fretting about Ralegh," Essex said. "He ruined himself already with that secret marriage."

"The very mistake you made three years back, and now look where you are. The queen did not banish you for long."

"I didn't impregnate one of her ladies. What ever was Ralegh thinking?"

Phelippes bit his tongue to refrain from laughing out loud at the hypocrisy. Essex was capable of far more reckless actions than anyone, Ralegh included.

"Thomas, your treacherous scheme is not necessary. Ralegh is in exile, and Cecil, well, we shall best him soon enough. Perhaps with the fruits of Marlowe's investigation. I suspect that he'll surprise you."

"My lord, you've only been a Privy Councillor these three months! We need to prove your worth and entrench your power. And please keep in mind that an enemy is not harmless until he is fully destroyed. Cecil's favor with Elizabeth grows steadily, and Ralegh, I've been told, is planning another voyage to the New World. Should he find gold, as he thinks he will . . ."

Essex stood and moved to the door. "I prefer my way," he said, adjusting his new velvet hat.

Then I shall cease keeping you informed. "Where to?"

"Greenwich. The queen wishes to play cards."

"Cards, my lord?"

Laughing, Essex attached his jeweled sword to his belt and struck off for the Thames.

The queen's nickname for her temperamental lover was Wild Horse, and Phelippes was left wondering which of the young earl's attributes had earned him the name.

"I believe I've what you need, sir."

Confused, Phelippes squinted at the spy.

"Material for the report on Marlowe. I overheard him, Ralegh, and Tom Hariot seeking to discredit our Lord, the majesty of His creation. They were using an odd contraption. A long, kind of—"

"That's . . . interesting, Baines. But unnecessary. I've told you what I wish you to do. Echo the accusations I've shown you. Very simple."

"But I did not hear—"

"Oh, include a bit about Hariot if you must," Phelippes muttered. Then he remembered something, words from another of his informants. "Suggest that Marlowe considers Moses a mere con man and one . . . far less skilled than Hariot, at that."

Baines nodded.

Phelippes scowled. "This won't do. Let us write it now." Looking toward the doorway, he called, "Teresa!"

"Yes, sir?" she asked, appearing seconds later.

"Fetch us paper, ink, and a quill."

Phelippes then went up to a storage chamber on the second floor to locate a copy of Kyd's interrogation, along with the other informant reports he'd collected. Returning to the great hall, he said, "Make sure you include the vilest of these statements."

Baines pressed the fingertips of his right hand against his forehead. "Title, title . . ." Looking up, he said, "How about, 'A note containing the opinion of one Christopher Marlowe, concerning his judgment of religion and God's word'?"

Phelippes shook his head. "Too bland, Baines. Make it, uh . . . '*damnable* judgment of religion.' And . . . '*scorn* of God's word.' "

Dipping his quill, Baines did so. He then turned to examine Kyd's accusations. "Says that Marlowe scoffs at Scripture, lodges arguments to confute what has been said by prophets and holy men."

"Write that he considers the New Testament filthily written, that he could do far better himself. Then . . ."

Baines was writing furiously.

" . . . that he calls Christ a bastard and Mary a whore."

"But, sir! That's—"

"Do you wish to share his fate?"

Reluctantly Baines did as told, then looked up. "I seem to remember hearing him refer to Protestants as . . . damn, what was it?"

"Asses."

"Actually, sir, I think it was hypocrites."

"Hypocritical asses, then!"

Peering over Baines's shoulder, Phelippes added, "Definitely the bit about Christ and St. John the Evangelist but less delicate. Say he calls them . . . bedfellows."

"While on the subject, sir, there's been talk that he . . . that he admires, uh . . ."

"What?" Phelippes demanded, impatient.

"Boys, sir."

"Splendid. Seems you're not an utter waste after all, Baines," Phelippes replied. "Oh, and do make a strong denouement. Something that leaves no doubt but that Marlowe is a danger who must be stopped."

Quill in the air, Baines mouthed possibilities.

Phelippes stared out the windows. After a few minutes, he said,

"When you present it to the chief commissioner, do tell him that Marlowe is at Scadbury House, Tom Walsingham's estate in Kent."

"He's to be arrested so soon? I thought you were—"

Phelippes shrugged. "If he's not yet finished his investigation, Topcliffe will get the necessary details from him. Probably best for us to finish it ourselves anyway. Marlowe's always been a bit of a rogue. I don't entirely trust him."

Robert Poley was irritated.

Teresa Ramires was late.

He was pacing near the bear-baiting arena, waiting for her. Judging from the last time he had seen a clock, it was about half an hour beyond their noon rendezvous. *Damn her.*

When he saw the expression on her face as she approached, however, all was forgiven. Teresa smiled that way only when she'd overheard exactly what he wanted.

19

*O*pening a bottle of water, Kate looked over at Adriana. "Mind if I make a quick call?"

"Not at all," Adriana said, stepping onto Westminster Bridge and leaning against the stone railing to stretch her calves.

They had met in St. James's Park an hour before and had jogged along the Queen's Walk—a wooden pathway on the south bank of the Thames—to London Bridge. On their way back, they'd stopped to buy drinks at one of the many kiosks near Westminster Bridge.

"Good morning," Medina said.

"I have news," Kate told him, looking across the river at the fairy-tale spires atop Big Ben and the Houses of Parliament.

"Tell me."

"Well, I took your advice to skip to the end, and I realized that Phelippes kept adding reports after Walsingham's death, at least until 1593. I'm having trouble with the last page, but the second to last—it's from May of that year and appears to have been written by Christopher Marlowe."

"What's it about?"

"It looks like Phelippes asked Marlowe to investigate an Elizabethan trading company. The Muscovy Company, England's first joint-stock enterprise. Marlowe discovered that one of its top players was shipping arms to a Barbary pirate—illegally—in exchange for riches from the East.

He said he had a way to identify the man within a matter of days. But here's the thing. Marlowe died that month. I can't help but think—"

"That he was murdered over what he found?" Medina interrupted. "By the merchant, trying to keep his crimes a secret?"

"Yeah," Kate said. "And I think Marlowe wrote the last report, too. It's numerical, and I haven't been able to decode it yet, but I don't think Phelippes would have included the report about the smuggling if he wasn't going to include one that revealed the merchant's identity. No other entry in his *Anatomy* presents an incomplete picture, so . . ."

"That final page may answer the question you brought up last night—who killed Marlowe and why."

"Maybe. It's probably just wishful thinking on my part, but . . ."

"Sounds logical to me," Medina said. "Now, Kate, the final page—is that what someone is after today?"

"Unlikely. There are a lot of academics and Marlowe fans who would love to know what really happened, but I doubt any of them would kill a harmless Oxford professor to find out."

"I'll buy that. By the way, where are you?"

"On my way to see Lady Halifax. In fifteen minutes, actually," Kate said, checking her watch. "Remember the Cat's ruby ring? He stole it from her, and I'm going to ask her some questions about him. She's playing tennis in Eaton Square. Invited me over for a postgame lemonade. Will you be around later this morning?"

"Yes."

"Okay. I'll come by soon. I need to examine a few of the pages in the manuscript before I leave."

Less than a mile away, the man Kate referred to as Jade Dragon was running a fingertip along the three-inch black steel blade of his double-edged Gerber knife. From what he'd just heard, Kate Morgan had, as expected, come across Christopher Marlowe's final intelligence report, and since she'd also revealed the manuscript's exact location . . .

It was time to strike, and quickly.

Belgravia, London — 9:30 a.m.

"Lady Halifax?"

"Call me Perry," the petite silver-haired woman replied. She was standing in the doorway of her Eaton Square mansion, wearing a short magenta tennis dress, gold-framed sunglasses, and sneakers so white they sparkled. "Do you play?" she asked, handing Kate a racket.

"Not since high school," Kate said. "I—"

"Well, you'll do. Better than Ella, anyway . . . canceled at the last minute saying her knee was sore." Lady Halifax shook her head. "Blast, when you get to be my age, everyone's either sitting idly, whinging about pain, or dead."

"I'm sorry to hear that."

"Play a set with me, and I'll be happy to answer your questions."

"Deal."

"You look flushed, dear. Have some lemonade," Lady Halifax said, handing Kate a thermos. She then grabbed a second thermos and another tennis racket—with pink strings that matched her dress—and pulled her front door shut behind her.

They crossed the street and headed for the entrance to Eaton Square's gated park. Appreciating the pleasant fragrance of the park's pink and lilac flowering trees, Kate flipped up the thermos's mouthpiece and took a gulp, then coughed with surprise.

Lady Halifax chuckled. "It's got Pimms in it, dear. One should never drink lemonade without it. Now, about my ring . . ."

"It's at the Yard. Not yet ready for pickup, though. It needs to be . . . processed."

"How did you find it?"

"Actually—"

"Come now," Lady Halifax interrupted. "I know you wouldn't be the one delivering this news if that weren't the case."

Kate smiled. "I was hired to investigate a failed heist. An unidentified thief was found dead at the scene, wearing your ring. Turns out he was the Cat."

"Good Lord. After all these years . . . so who was he?"

"Simon Trevor—"

"Jones?" Lady Halifax finished, her eyes wide. "Lord Astley? Oh,

Christ on crutches, I should have guessed! He always seemed to be having a little too much fun at the stuffiest, most *ludicrous* gatherings. Oh, Peregrine, you blind woman! How bloody obvious it was!"

"You knew him well?" Kate asked.

Stepping onto the court, Lady Halifax shook her head. "No. I'm sorry he's dead, though. Certainly made things more interesting, wondering if there was really a thief in our midst."

"Did he have any close friends or regular business associates that you noticed?"

"I can't remember. But one of my friends will know. I could make some calls."

"Thank you."

"Now prepare yourself, dear," Lady Halifax said, taking a sip from her thermos. "I'm going to wipe you off the court."

Turning onto Wilton Crescent, Kate sighed. The old marchioness had not been kidding. Kate was exhausted. And she'd lost every game in the set.

Her phone rang. "Hello?"

"Hugh Synclair, here."

"Good morning, Inspector."

"Kate, I spoke with Rutherford's doctor. Turns out he had acute metastatic prostate cancer. Would have been dead within a few months. Probably experiencing a good deal of pain, too. Makes me wonder if he asked someone to, uh . . ."

"He was Catholic?"

"Yes."

"And with a suicide note, he wouldn't get a proper burial."

"Right. It's a possibility, wouldn't you say?"

"Yeah. How about the papers taken from his desk, though?"

"Polite shooter, perhaps . . . trying to tidy up."

"What's your gut say, Inspector?"

"Actually, I was hoping you had come across something on your end that'd clear this up."

"I'll let you know as soon as I do. Thanks for the information."

"Of course. Good day to you, now."

Pressing Medina's doorbell, Kate wondered if asking someone to kill you was really a loophole for the suicide-is-a-sin crowd. If so, maybe a kind, innocent man had not been killed over the manuscript after all. Maybe Mr. Jade Dragon was about teacups and polite parlor mysteries, as she'd initially thought.

Charlotte answered the door.

"What is it?" Kate asked. Charlotte's face was pale and her hands were shaking.

"I was out round the shops, and when I came back, I saw that Mr. Medina, that he'd been . . . that someone had . . ." She swallowed. "Stabbed him."

"What?"

"He's upstairs. Refusing to go to hospital, shooing me away . . ."

"In his bedroom?"

Charlotte nodded. "The fourth floor."

Stunned, Kate ran up the stairs. She found Medina in his bathroom unscrewing a bottle of antiseptic. He'd wrapped a dark towel around his waist, over his clothes. "Cidro, are you—"

"Yes. I'm fine. Nothing but a scratch . . . Charlotte just has a bit of trouble with blood. I'm sorry if she worried you."

"I feel terrible. I should've insisted on a bodyguard, I—"

"Actually, it was kind of exciting. I've never been in a knife fight before."

Kate tried to give him a look of stern disapproval but failed. "What happened?"

"My bell rang. Young fellow said he had a delivery from the Yard. A woman had actually phoned ahead, claiming to be the super's secretary . . ."

"Someone must've been watching us," Kate cut in. "Probably saw Sergeant Davies come by here yesterday. Oh, I'm so sorry, I—"

"Kate, it's not your fault. I'm the ass who's too cocky to tolerate guards hovering about."

"True," she agreed, opening his medicine cabinet and pulling out a bag of cotton wool. "So you answered the door, he forced his way in, and—"

"I think his plan was: knife through the kidney, grab the manuscript. But I grabbed his knife instead."

"And he . . ."

"Ran out. Couldn't face my—"

"Overwhelming tower of power?" Kate said dryly, slipping the towel from his waist.

"Oh, my God," she murmured, seeing the large bloodstain on the back of his blue shirt. After she tugged it free of his pants and lifted it, her eyes widened at the sight of the gash on his lower back. It stretched from his hipbone to his spine.

"Cidro, if he hadn't missed, you'd have been dead in less than a minute." She put a hand on his shoulder and turned him around to face her. "I know you're an adrenaline junkie, but could you just stick to drugs and bungee jumping please?"

Wetting a washcloth with warm water, she added, "I hate to sound like your mother, but if you continue being reckless like this, you're going to get yourself killed. I'm calling my office for a guard, and I need you to promise me you won't shoo him away while I'm gone."

"Yes, ma'am."

"When we're done here, I'll drop the knife and the tapes from your security cameras by the Yard. *You'll* be getting stitches."

"Actually, there are some things I—"

"Whoever comes from my office will be armed, and he will take you to get them himself. At gunpoint, if necessary."

"Can't argue with that."

"Good. Now take off your shirt."

THE TUNISIAN COAST — 1:42 P.M.

"The Parc Monceau is wonderful," Surina Khan said, submerging a large natural sponge into the bowl of sudsy water on the table beside her. "Full of flowers . . . has lovely waterfalls," she continued, wringing it out. "It's supposed to showcase different periods of history and places in the world, so there are these fake Roman ruins, an Egyptian pyramid, a Chinese pagoda. . . . My brother and I used to sneak around where people aren't allowed—across the grass, up on the hill with the waterfall, into the brook . . ."

Taking his left hand in hers, she lifted his arm and lightly circled the sponge across his skin. Seconds later, his hand twitched. For the fourth time that day. Was it a spasm from the electric shocks he'd been tortured with, she wondered, or was he squeezing her hand deliberately? Communicating with her the only way he could?

"Maybe you'd like to come to Paris and see it with me this summer? Have a picnic by the pond with the crumbling colonnade?"

Gently pressing her lips against his forehead, Surina let the soft lapping of waves upon the beach, the calls of seagulls, and the constant dripping of IV fluid lull her into a quiet daydream.

BELGRAVIA, LONDON — 10:50 A.M.

"Uh, Kate?" Medina said tightly, his teeth clenched.

"Cidro, are you a man or a *mouse?*" she teased, cleaning his wound with peroxide.

"Right. Stay strong, Cid," he said, wincing with every touch. "Find a distraction. Let's see, uhhh . . . ow! Fuck me! Okay, focus. Lord's cricket ground, a balmy Sunday afternoon . . . uh, hundred runs to win, eight wickets down . . ."

Kate was also trying to distract herself. Being inches from him, with his shirt off—well, it was a challenge. *Okay . . . bills. You're sitting down, opening your checkbook—that City Sports one is gonna kick your ass this month. Um, a dentist with bad breath, shots for Southeast Asia . . .*

"Ouch! Must you get medieval, woman?"

"Oh, Cid, I'm sorry," Kate said, having inadvertently banged Medina's wound while applying antibacterial cream. She began taping a large bandage over it.

"Thank you," he said when she was finished.

"No problem."

He turned to face her. "You sure? You look . . ."

"Fine. Relieved you're okay."

Not in the mood to meet his eyes, she concentrated on putting away the various cleaning supplies.

Then her thoughts stopped.

She felt one of his hands slide across the back of her neck, drawing her toward him. Their faces inches apart, he looked at her for a moment, then pressed his lips to hers. Softly. Twice. When he kissed her the third time, he opened his mouth a little, his tongue caressing her upper lip. He pulled it gently between his own for a moment, then released her and leaned back.

Medina was watching her intently. "I've wanted to do that since the first day we met."

"Oh."

"*Oh?* That's all I get?"

"Okay, I admit. I'm a little dizzy."

"Good. Lord knows I tried."

"The thing is, I went for a really long run this morning, played too much tennis . . . haven't gotten around to eating anything, and it's a pretty hot day, so . . . but I'm fine now. Thanks for asking."

"I see," Medina said, pulling her against him once more. Then, running a fingertip along her lower lip, he asked, "Still fine now, I suppose?"

"Still fine."

"How about now?" he asked, kissing her neck.

"Can't complain."

"Come on, Kate. Tell me something slushy."

"Slushy?"

"What you people call mushy."

"Well . . ."

"I'm waiting," Medina pressed, his hands caressing her back.

"All right! When you touch me like that, I can't think straight, I can't see straight, I'm sure I can't walk straight. Will that do?"

"For now."

An hour later, with the knife and Medina's security tapes in Sergeant Davies' capable hands, Kate was in her hotel room packing, listening to Medina over her phone.

"I was planning on taking you to Heathrow myself, but as your company's holding me hostage . . ."

"I'm hitching a ride in one of our choppers, actually," Kate said. "Some VIP client is heading over in twenty minutes."

"Oh. When are you back?"

"Mmm, tomorrow afternoon, I think. Maybe sooner. Depends on how things go."

"Should I be worried about you?"

218 ||| Leslie Silbert

"Not at all. It's just a humdrum identity assignment. A name-that-person kind of thing."

"Is that person dangerous?"

Kate didn't feel like lying. *How to put this* . . . "He's a friendly art dealer. I'll be fine."

"Ring me when you get there?"

"Okay."

They said good-bye, and Kate double-checked to make sure that her wallet and airline ticket were in her shoulder bag. *Good.*

"Oh, thank God I remembered," she said aloud, pulling out the small white box containing the Cat's pistol. *Heathrow security wouldn't find this too charming.*

Maybe it's a trank, she thought, her right hand settling around the wooden grip. That would make more sense for a man who was so careful to never hurt anyone. Curious to see what was in the chamber, she used her second and middle fingertips to feel behind the trigger for the magazine catch. There wasn't one. *Come to think of it, there isn't a visible safety or slide, either.* But there was a decorative mother-of-pearl fleur-de-lis within reach of her right thumb. *Hmm.* Pressing down, she heard a clicking sound and watched as a two-inch steel prong extended from the muzzle.

"A pick gun . . ." she murmured. "Of course." If the Cat had been carrying a gun with tranquilizer darts, no doubt he'd have subdued Medina's guard and escaped over the roof.

But why had the Cat not been armed? He might have been breaking into a home with light security, but if he had known that in advance, how come he had not known about the guard? According to Medina, his guard had been around almost every time he went out. The Cat would never have missed such a critical detail. Kate was confused. She was missing something.

He must not have scouted out the place himself before the theft, she decided. Then why had he done it? He was not Mr. Jade Dragon, he was not the one personally affected by something in the manuscript, so why had he relied upon shoddy secondhand surveillance information to steal it? He usually stole objects of far greater value with less risk. It made no sense.

Unless he was a friend of Jade Dragon, Kate thought. Maybe his pal J.D. had called him in a panic, requesting an urgent favor. Maybe J.D. had done the half-assed surveillance himself, then told the Cat it was more thorough than it was, because he was too eager to get his hands on *The Anatomy of Secrets* to care about the welfare of his friend. If that was the case, then in a sense, J.D. had killed the Cat. In addition to Andrew Rutherford. And the attempt on Medina.

Hiding the pick gun in a jacket she was leaving at the Connaught, Kate's hands shook with anger.

Sidi Bou Said — 2:48 p.m.

Connor Black's hands were perfectly steady. Standing in a winding, cobbled alley near the cliff's edge in Sidi Bou Said, he was holding what appeared to be a long-lensed camera and had it trained on the coastline below. Using the device's thermal imaging feature, he saw one guard sitting inside the villa, in his usual spot near the front door. The other two were playing some kind of board game on the first-floor balcony. Directly above them, the young girl — the nurse he and his colleagues were calling Mrs. Nightingale — was standing on the upper balcony, gazing out at the gulf's perpetually calm turquoise waters.

It was the first time Connor had seen her as more than a red shape within the house. "She's stunning," he murmured, magnifying the image of her profile. Tall and slim, she had dark South Asian skin, black hair to her waist, and the kind of face poets ran out of ink over.

Lowering the cameralike device, he glanced behind him. He was alone. "Revere, how's it coming?"

"Good," came the reply over his earpiece, from the man whose first name really was Paul. "Lover Two rented a sixteen-footer down in the marina. We're preparing the cooler as we speak . . ."

"I'm on my way."

"Me, too," Revere responded. He was going to their regular café to take over monitoring the coast.

Entering his and Jason Avera's hotel room, Connor saw that the gear they'd need later that night had been fully loaded into the cooler. "Let's go," he said, grabbing one of the handles. Hauling it through town during the day would appear perfectly natural. At night, eyebrows might rise and questions could be asked.

Wearing shorts and sunglasses, they headed to the marina. For the sake of appearances, they were going to take a brief trip up the coast.

"Lover One," Connor heard from his earpiece. It was the Woodsman, still sitting amidst the trees across from the villa's front door. "Something's happening."

"Yeah?"

"The bodies have been fading. I saw Mrs. Nightingale come back in, but now she and her man have all but disappeared. Couple of flickers. I still hear her, but . . ."

"Binocular problem, you think, or a security measure?" Connor asked. He knew that if the guards wanted to disguise their movements, they could shut off the villa's air conditioning. Given the intense North African heat, the interior would then be too close to body temperature for thermal imaging to function.

"Hard to say," the Woodsman replied. "Oh, wait a minute. Van pulled up. Majid's Cooling Services? Looks like the A.C. broke, accidentally."

"Stay on it. Make sure no one leaves. Revere's got the beach."

"Will do."

ROME — 6:35 P.M.

The palazzo was pale yellow, with heavy wooden doors, stone-lined arched windows, and pots of red begonias on its small second-floor balcony. Scooters were parked in the cobbled alley out front, along with a few cars that in America would resemble children's toys. Though the building had seen better days—the paint was fading in patches, and graffiti marred its façade at street level—to Kate, it was perfect.

"Giuseppe, ciao!" she said, hugging the hotel's elderly owner.

"You have a new boyfriend. I guess it's time for me to—how do you say—throw the towel?"

"Never. I don't even know who you're talking about."

"Katy." With a playfully stern look, he reached behind his desk and handed her a small bag. Its design was familiar. Her favorite local candy shop. "He knows your chocolates."

"Oh, my new client," she said, glancing at the card—Medina thanking her for that morning.

"Client . . . mmm." Shaking his head, Giuseppe gave her a key. "Before you leave tonight, we will have a drink on the roof?"

"Absolutely. Give me twenty minutes."

Four flights up, Kate pushed her door open, set down her bags, and turned on hot water for a shower. As she untied her sneakers, Medina called.

"Hi. Thank you. So what else did Max tell you?" she asked, knowing Medina had to have contacted Max to facilitate the delivery.

"That you can't stop thinking about me."

"Shit, how *could* he?"

"Kate, about tomorrow, I have a dinner meeting, but afterward . . ."

"You'll try to interrupt my work?"

"Well, I thought it likely I could convince you to go out with me, what with . . ."

"This morning's . . . ?"

"Mmm-hmm."

"But that was just a pity kiss. You'd been hurt. Didn't mean anything."

"Liar."

"Did you say something? My phone just cut out," Kate teased.

"Say what you like. As soon as you're back here—"

"I'll be able to tell you about that final Marlowe report I mentioned, maybe the rest of the pages, too. After my work thing tonight, I'm going to stay at it until—"

"Wait. You cracked the final page?"

"Not yet but soon. It's more complex than I thought, so I sent it to Max. He's better with numbers and decryption. He won't be long. Hey, what happened with Sergeant Davies? Any luck ID-ing your attacker?"

"Still working on it. He was wearing gloves and a baseball cap when he came in. Ducked his head, too. The cameras didn't get a full picture. Davies had me work with a sketch artist. May lead to a driver's license or something. The blighter was at least twenty."

"Yeah. Unfortunately he probably never met the man who hired him.

Also, I'd imagine Jade Dragon might have chosen someone who'd be hard to trace—in England illegally maybe."

"Hmm."

"Common knife, right?"

"Fairly. A Gerber Expedition IIB."

"Okay. I'll call you tomorrow? Hopefully with some answers."

"Sounds good."

Stepping out of the shower ten minutes later, Kate pulled a few items from her suitcase and shoulder bag. *Nothin' says nonthreatening like flowers and glasses,* she thought to herself, slipping into a floor-length black silk skirt with a blue and green floral print. The studious-looking black glasses she put on, however, hopefully *were* threatening . . . to de Tolomei, at least. She'd picked them up at the local Slade's office on her way in from the airport. They contained an iris scanner. Kate then fastened an underwire bra she reserved for occasions like this. It looked like an ordinary Victoria's Secret cleavage enhancer, but the original wiring had been removed and audio recording equipment built in. The tiny battery could provide only three minutes of power, but it was more than enough to get a traceable voiceprint.

Pulling on a fitted black sweater, she looked in the mirror. Hair down, definitely, she decided. Gold hoop earrings. *And you're there. Betsy Johnson goes to the library. No way he'll be suspicious of me.*

The Borgo, Rome — 7:53 p.m.

"Paolo!" a small boy shouted, racing across the cobbles. Seconds later, a soccer ball zoomed toward him. He faked right, then careened past an opponent, but a motor scooter roaring by interrupted his dash to the makeshift goal. *"Vaffanculo!"* he cried.

Turning around, he came face-to-face with Kate.

She laughed. The boy had ordered the scooter driver to go take it in his ass.

A blush colored his indignant expression.

"You play for Lazio?" she asked in Italian, attempting to flatter him. Lazio, she knew, was one of Italy's top teams.

"Mai! Manco morto!"

Not on his life?

"*Forza Roma!*" he exlaimed with a disgusted roll of his eyes.

Oops, wrong team. Damn, Kate. Dissed by a ten-year-old. Nice work.

Maneuvering between tables covered with rosaries and a group of nuns carrying bags of produce, Kate continued on her way through the Borgo, a lively neighborhood that had been catering to Catholic pilgrims and Vatican staffers for centuries. Catching a glimpse of St. Peter's Square—framed by laundry overhead and tacky hotel signs on either side—her thoughts returned to Luca de Tolomei. He wanted her help in finding a piece of art he'd been after for years, he'd said, and he was also up to something that had Slade more agitated than Max had ever seen him.

The first made sense to her; de Tolomei was a successful art dealer, someone who hired people like her to handle the frequently tedious detective work involved in tracking down lost or stolen art. But the second—the mysterious crate now in Tunisia—what was that about? According to Max, de Tolomei dealt in secrets as well as art, but what kind of secret was transported in a wooden crate? And what, other than a weapon, could Slade find so threatening?

Then Kate remembered the odd feeling she'd gotten at the Sotheby's auction, that de Tolomei had been playing along with her ploy, as if he'd already known who she was. That was impossible, wasn't it? She'd just gotten the assignment days before and had only discussed him in the secure environment of her office and in a discreet manner with Edward Cherry. Could de Tolomei know she was investigating him?

Nearing the office of the *Vigilanza*, Vatican City's police force, it occurred to Kate that a professional blackmailer like de Tolomei would be enormously interested in *The Anatomy of Secrets*. Had he somehow learned of Medina's discovery? Could that be why he had changed his plans, deciding to attend the Sotheby's auction at the last minute? He'd said that he'd like her help in tracking down not a painting but "another form of art." Was Phelippes's manuscript the item for which he'd been searching for more than a decade? No, her two cases could not possibly be converging like that, Kate decided. It would be too much of a coincidence.

"I'm here for the art tour, sir," she told the officer behind the desk, handing over her passport.

Turning its pages and scrutinizing her face, he checked a list in front of him, made a call, nodded, then handed her a form and a pen. After she filled it out, he wrote her a pass and pointed her toward the Apostolic Palace. "They're waiting by Bernini's doors, *signorina*."

With that, Kate entered the world's smallest state, which, as someone had once told her, was about an eighth of the size of Central Park. Passing a troupe of altar boys, she caught sight of the group. Cardinals in black cassocks and scarlet zucchettos were mingling with businessmen in expensive suits, while a cluster of more casually dressed men and women struck Kate as journalists and off-duty policemen.

According to Edward Cherry, this event was intended to celebrate an upcoming excavation being funded by a group of bankers—the suits, no doubt, Kate figured. But the evening was also a perk for certain people who did favors for Vatican higher-ups. De Tolomei could be their main art dealer, she thought. Vatican City possessed a collection so vast that only a fraction was ever on display, and rumor had it that a number of works in storage had been obtained improperly during World War II. A black marketer like de Tolomei could be arranging quiet sales here and there, helping the Holy See avoid further negative publicity. She scanned the crowd, but he had not yet shown up.

Glancing up at the statues lining Bernini's elaborate colonnade—backlit by the pope's private offices, glowing just beyond—Kate approached the Swiss Guard standing before the palace's main entrance. With his poofy pants, yellow and blue striped sleeves and boots, black cape, and beret, he resembled a court jester, but the sword at his side and six-foot halberd in hand—part pike, part battle axe—suggested he was not there to amuse. The tour would begin at the beginning, he told her, with the excavations beneath St. Peter's Basilica, move through selected rooms in two of the museums, then conclude with a reception in the palace.

Spotting an elderly nun standing alone, Kate introduced herself. The woman, she learned, oversaw tapestry restoration. Moments later, a curator welcomed everyone and the tour began.

Luca de Tolomei was choosing a tie. He flicked through a few, then settled on a red paisley Dolce & Gabbana. The pattern seemed appropriate: serpentine. Devilish. Turning to his full-length gilt mirror, he tightened it carefully.

Tonight would be the preview. An unexpected but most welcome pleasure.

What a curious twist that Morgan's daughter was trying to land him as a client, de Tolomei thought. He found her charming, he had to admit—felt a vague reluctance, even—but he would still destroy her. Too much was at stake.

Vatican City — 8:26 p.m.

The long cramped tunnel was dank. Electric candles glowing from sconces barely nudged the darkness. Step-by-step, Kate descended through layers of Roman history, the tapestry restorer clutching her right elbow.

At the bottom, a pale bluish light beckoned. Reverent, the group entered the ancient burial site in silence, passing tombstones and cremation urns set deep in hollowed-out niches. Mosaic tiles glittered from the ceiling, and fresco fragments lingered upon the walls, pagan and Christian symbols intermingling—a delirious Bacchus raised his cup, Latin inscriptions abounded, and an Apollo figure cruised overhead in a chariot, a crosslike pattern of rays gleaming behind his head.

Standing by a wall covered with illegible markings, the curator gestured toward a hole hacked into it, at an array of bones set behind glass, believed by some to be the remains of St. Peter. The curator began describing the excavation project, begun in 1939, that had led to the find.

Never having been to these depths, Kate was fascinated. Even so, her mind kept flitting back to de Tolomei. Slowly the curator's voice faded to a hazy drone. And then—perhaps on account of the musty air, eerie light, or proximity of the remains of people who'd died in terrible pain—Kate felt a surge of uneasiness ripple through her. She was facing a frescoed image of dancing satyrs, and for a split second they flashed to life before her eyes, taunting her with hateful grins.

The shroud concealing de Tolomei's identity was nearly within her grasp—she could almost feel it wisping beneath her fingertips—but why was she suddenly overcome with foreboding? Something she hadn't experienced since childhood?

Spikes of adrenaline, the prospect of imminent physical danger—they were not at all unusual for her, but *this*—this most certainly was.

Though night had fallen in Rome, midafternoon sun was still shining in New York City when Connor Black's call came in on Jeremy Slade's secure line.

"We're on our way," Connor said. "We'll stay dark until we hit the beach."

Returning the phone to its cradle, Slade found himself praying. To what or to whom, he didn't know. A very long thirty minutes had begun.

20

On Hellespont, guilty of true-love's blood,
In view and opposite, two cities stood,
Sea-borderers, disjoin'd by Neptune's might:
The one Abydos, the other Sestos hight.

—Marlowe's *Hero and Leander*

CHISLEHURST, KENT—AFTERNOON, MAY 1593

Marlowe stretched his arms over his head, then leaned back and reached for his clay pipe.

A fresh sheet of paper lay on the table before him. Looking over at Tom Walsingham's house, he saw a woman picking herbs from the kitchen garden and a butterfly flitting among the primroses.

He exhaled a few rings of smoke then penned the opening lines of his new poem.

The woods were thick. To Robert Poley's right, distant hills rolled above the treetops. To his left, the wet rushing sound of a waterfall.

One more mile to go.

With a gentle kick, he brought his exhausted horse to a canter. Any moment now, a warrant would be issued for Marlowe's arrest. In fact, it might have happened already. It was widely known that the playmaker had been at Scadbury House for the better part of the past month, and the Council's men would be coming for him shortly. Poley meant to get there first.

He had to admit he'd been stunned by Teresa's revelation. It had never occurred to him that Phelippes—Marlowe's current employer— was the man trying to bring about his demise.

If Phelippes was willing to sacrifice one of the most capable intelligencers at his disposal, he must be confident it would prove worthwhile. Had he gotten wind of the counterfeiting operation? It was possible, Poley knew, and if Marlowe were to confess to it . . .

Poley shook his head. No doubt it would be damaging, but an admission elicited under torture would not be enough to take down a man of Cecil's stature. Although if an investigation were launched and the queen's trust began to erode, even if ever so slightly . . .

No matter. It's my move, now.

LONDON—AFTERNOON

At Essex House, Thomas Phelippes stood staring down at the river, drumming his fingertips against the glass.

Shortly after reading Richard Baines's report, the chief commissioner had done exactly as Phelippes had intended—he'd called for Marlowe's immediate apprehension and had dispatched a constable within minutes. Baines was in the Star Chamber, awaiting Marlowe's arrival.

Phelippes knew it was not yet time, but he could not resist checking every boat coming from the direction of Westminster. Soon Baines would hasten up the water steps and relay every detail.

21

*I*t was a perfect night for an operation. With the thick cloud cover, there was no moon, and starlight was minimal. The wind was picking up, and the distant rumble of thunder had driven most people indoors.

Revere was operating a sixteen-foot speedboat. From the marina, he'd cruised northwest, away from the Gulf of Tunis. As a result, a headland — the cliffs of Sidi Bou Said, jutting into the sea — stood between him and the men guarding the coastal villa. This was a good thing. Earlier that evening, he'd noticed that one of the guards was wearing a pair of binoculars he recognized, Rigel's 2150 model, which not only amplified existing light but also contained an infrared illuminator. So in spite of the near total darkness, that guard would be able to spot any hot object in his field of vision.

Half a kilometer out, he cut the motor. In silence, Connor Black and Jason Avera emerged from beneath a tarp. Reaching into their oversized cooler, they pulled on wet suits, masks, and fins, then secured oxygen tanks to their backs and waterproof pouches to their waists. Sitting opposite each other — on the port and starboard gunwales — they nodded once, then simultaneously leaned back and slipped into the water.

Revere watched the two sets of bubbles moving swiftly toward the gulf. When they were sufficiently far away, he pushed the boat's starter button. The engine sputtered then rumbled to life, and he headed back to the marina.

Lashing the boat, he spoke softly: "They're in."

. . .

On the opposite side of the villa, the Woodsman was leaning against a tree finishing an energy bar when he heard Revere's words. Standing up, he pulled a white *dishdash*—a robelike cotton garment—from his worn leather knapsack and changed into it. Then came a salt-and-pepper beard, a checkered *keffiyeh* for his head, and a pair of faded leather sandals. Of Turkish descent, he had a dark complexion and, dressed in this manner, could easily pass for a local. With his equipment tucked into his knapsack, he began walking parallel to the road.

Fifty yards down from the villa, he stopped. Checking his watch, he guessed it would be about five minutes.

WASHINGTON, D.C. — 4:09 P.M.

In a conference room in the Senate Hart Building, Donovan Morgan was attempting to listen as a senior analyst from the Defense Intelligence Agency delivered a brief that forecasted the erosion of the U.S. military's technological advantages. Certain enemies, the analyst was saying, would soon gain the ability to jam the Global Positioning System (GPS) signals that guided American troops and bombs. The DIA man was an engaging speaker, but for Morgan, his words kept merging into an indistinguishable hum.

Morgan's pager was in his breast pocket, resting against his chest. Any minute now, Slade would be contacting him to relay the outcome of their rescue mission. Pain from the knots in his stomach was not registering in his brain, but the pager's faint weight—its stillness—most certainly was.

THE GULF OF TUNIS — 12:10 A.M.

It was so dark they could have been locked in a closet. Seven feet below the surface, Jason Avera was swimming directly behind Connor Black, but if his dive mask hadn't contained an IR illuminator, he wouldn't have been able to see him.

Connor paused. Every few minutes, they were stopping to check the compasses and GPS devices strapped to their wrists. With a quick calculation, Jason realized the villa's beachfront was now no more than twenty meters ahead.

They continued swimming. In less than a minute, they were within touching distance of the smooth, sandy bottom. Ten feet farther on, Connor stopped. Jason drew up alongside him and waited.

In a crouch, with his feet on the sea floor, Connor reached up, slowly rising until his fingers broke the surface. When they did, he was standing straight up. Not close enough. They swam a bit farther, and Connor tried again. Perfect. The water was roughly waist high.

He pressed a button on his watch, twice, then stared at the digits. In sixty seconds, they would move.

Hearing two beeps come through his earpiece, the Woodsman stepped onto the road. Revere was sitting behind the wheel of a parked van. He handed Revere his knapsack, and Revere gave him the van's keys.

Adopting the hunched, shuffling gait of an older man, the Woodsman headed toward the villa, tossing the keys from hand to hand.

"Excuse me," he began in Arabic, knocking on the door.

"What is it?" came the muffled reply.

"My car. Died just down the road. Would you be so kind as to lend me a phone?"

The door opened. "I suppose that would be—"

"Sleep well, my friend." Having grabbed a silenced tranquilizer gun from beneath one of his loose white sleeves, the Woodsman fired.

The guard never finished his sentence.

Though Connor and Jason were confident that their approach had gone undetected, there was another danger. If the guard with the night-vision binoculars happened to be monitoring the shore at the precise moment they broke the surface, it would take him roughly 1.5 seconds to react and reach for his M4. Grabbing hold of the rifle and aiming it could take as little as two additional seconds. That meant that Connor and Jason would have about three to obscure his aim. With luck, however, the guards would be too distracted by the commotion at the front door to notice a thing.

Feet planted in the sand, fingers gripping the zippers to the waterproof pouches at their waists, they began to rise. When the tops of their heads broke the surface, they shot up and hurled two grenadelike objects at the beach. Called "fade-to-blacks," the devices were the exact opposite of their more commonly known counterparts, "flash-bang" or "stun" grenades. Flash-bangs temporarily blinded anyone looking in their direction and blew out the eardrums of everyone in the vicinity. Fade-to-blacks, however—as invisible and silent as their name suggested—disoriented in a different manner.

On the beach, the inaudible explosions had two effects. Black smoke immediately filled the air, and a hot carbon mist was released. The resulting cloud—about thirty feet high—rendered Connor and Jason completely invisible to everyone in the villa. Though the guards had sophisticated night vision equipment, it was currently useless. The smoke made ambient light amplification impossible, and the mist—composed of fine particles warmer than body temperature—neutralized IR illumination.

Wet suits protecting their skin, Connor and Jason raced up the beach. Standing about fifteen feet from the villa, with silenced tranquilizer guns pointed at the balcony, they waited for the mist to cool. When it did, they fired.

Vatican City — 10:16 p.m.

"Whenever Hitler came to Rome to meet with Mussolini, the pope would order this room closed for repairs," the curator was saying. Looking up to the ceiling, he continued, "First Pius XI, then Pius XII. Since childhood, Hitler had dreamed of seeing it but never got the chance."

The tour group had just entered the Sistine Chapel when Luca de Tolomei joined them. He mouthed an apology to the curator, then began speaking with a stout cardinal.

Kate watched him for a moment, then returned her eyes to the ceiling. Though she'd visited this room once before, it had been during regular hours, when tourists were crammed in elbow-to-elbow and a voice was issuing instructions every few seconds over a loudspeaker—not exactly the best circumstances to take in one of the most awe-inspiring sights in the world.

Neck craned back, she was walking slowly, perusing each panel when she sensed de Tolomei's approach. Pretending to scratch her shoulder, she activated her audio recording device.

"Good evening, Kate."

"Better be careful," she said, gesturing to *The Last Judgment* on the altar wall. "Saint Peter is not happy with you, skipping out on him tonight like you did."

De Tolomei laughed. "Actually, I stopped believing a long time ago."

"Why?" Kate knew the question was intrusive, but she couldn't help herself.

"My daughter was raped and murdered. She was seven."

"Oh my God," Kate said softly, stunned by the frank admission.

"It was many years ago."

"Still, I . . . how rude of me. Can you . . . ?"

"Of course," de Tolomei cut in. Quickly he changed the subject. "Speaking of fathers and daughters, I once knew *your* father long ago. In another lifetime, you might say."

A maelstrom erupted in Kate's mind. Face calm, voice even, she asked, "How did you meet?"

"I used to live in Washington," he replied. "Certain circles, you know . . ."

And then it hit her. If what de Tolomei was saying were true, her father could probably recognize his voice. They might uncover de Tolomei's identity that very day.

"By the way, you may tell him that his secret is safe with me."

Hearing those words, Kate resisted her impulse to look up at Michelangelo's ceiling. She already knew they were standing directly below the panel depicting original sin, and she knew it was no accident. De Tolomei was tempting her, but with what?

The Tunisian Coast — 12:21 a.m.

When the Woodsman entered the room where Mr. and Mrs. Nightingale were sleeping, he stopped short. A pale and very blond Nordic couple lay on the bed.

Looking up—toward the sliding glass doors across the room—he met Connor Black's eyes. Their conversation from that afternoon replayed in his mind. Within seconds, comprehension dawned. *Must've been a divider in the van—A.C. up front, warm air in the back. Blonds in, Nightingales out.*

"Fuck."

Less than a hundred miles northeast of the cursing Woodsman, de Tolomei's yacht, the *Sabina*, had just rounded the western coast of Sicily. In the master suite, Surina Khan was holding her patient's hand, murmuring sweetly in his ear.

22

Since thou hast all the cards within thy hands,
To shuffle or cut, take this as surest thing,
That, right or wrong, thou deal thyself a king.

—GUISE, in Marlowe's *The Massacre at Paris*

CHISLEHURST, KENT—AFTERNOON, MAY 1593

*H*eavy gray clouds raced overhead, merging and darkening. Just a few determined rays beamed through, sparkling here and there on the wild flowers lining the road. Thunder cracked. Seconds later, the first raindrops fell.

Screeching cats!

Wrists shackled, Marlowe was astride his horse, following the dour constable back to London. Why the devil had he let that Tarot woman deal his cards? A wretched mistake it was. To be interrupted when the words were flowing like a torrent? Churning more fiercely than the Hellespont he depicted? He should never have visited her at all.

Robert Poley galloped down the familiar tree-lined avenue. Rain streamed from the brim of his velvet hat and drenched his doublet.

"Kit!" he called, tethering his horse to a fence.

Crossing Scadbury's drawbridge, he tried again. Louder. "Kit!"

When he entered the front hall, footfalls sounded on the stairs. Tall black boots appeared. Then russet hose, hugging a trim pair of legs. But to Poley's dismay, it wasn't Marlowe's face that came next.

"Where is he?" he asked Tom Walsingham.

They'd known each other for years. It was Tom who'd helped Poley initiate his employment with Sir Francis, the late secretary of state, and for that, Poley would always be grateful.

"He was taken by a city constable—Maunder, he was called—twenty minutes ago. Do you know—"

Poley interrupted with a nod. "He's under investigation for sowing discord. For spreading ideas of atheism."

Unfazed, Tom shrugged. "Well, then, as in every other instance, his employer—Essex, Cecil, whoever it may be—will step in and the men of the Star Chamber will be made to see through the lies. They will be made to see that Kit serves his queen and that any behavior to the contrary is but a pose."

"This time it goes beyond hearsay," Poley said. "It began the night of the fifth. A poem was tacked to the wall of a Dutch church—full of threats, promising murder, and signed 'Tamburlaine.' Made other allusions to Kit's plays. No one thought much of it until a document—heretical, they say—was found in Kit's old lodgings. Kyd said it must have belonged to Kit, along with some other nonsense. Then, two informants submitted reports attesting to Kit's blasphemy, swearing that he persuades men to atheism."

Tom paled. "Who would—"

"Phelippes," Poley spat with disdain. "He's a member of the commission investigating the anti-immigrant placards. He hired the hack who wrote the poem, then kept leading the investigation to Marlowe, and when the head commissioner didn't bite, he drummed up those informant reports. Literally stood over shoulders, telling his dogs what to write."

"But Kit works for him. Serves him well. I don't see why—"

"Phelippes views what Kit may or may not know about Cecil as worth far more than his abilities as a spy . . . or his life."

"You'll stop him?"

"Yes," Poley said, black eyes flashing. "Cecil has ordered it, and even if he hadn't, I—"

Shaking his head, Poley cut himself off. Time was short. "Kit was with you the evening of the fifth, yes?"

Tom nodded.

"Write a letter swearing to that."

"Of course."

"And have you a sample of his penmanship?"

"Yes."

"Good." Placing a hand on Tom's shoulder, Poley said, "We'll get him out of this."

Reassured, a smile flicked across Tom's face. Turning, he headed up to his study. Grabbing a sheet of paper, he took a seat at his desk.

Poley pulled up a chair. "What about me? I've a letter to write, too." Retrieving a ring from his pocket, he presented its carved face.

Tom's eyebrows shot up. "Cecil trusts you with his seal?"

"Of course not. I had a copy made."

Finishing his salutation, Poley added, "When we're done here, if you lend me a fresh horse, I just might beat them back to the city."

WESTMINSTER—DUSK

The storm had passed, and the sky was a fetching maiden's blush pink when Marlowe was brought into the Court of Star Chamber. The panel seated at the far end of the room—made up of Privy Councillors and judges from both the civil and criminal courts—was taking testimony. The witness was claiming to have seen a certain woman nip three purses and pick five pockets in less than one hour, near the southern entrance to London Bridge.

Craning his neck, Marlowe spotted the offender, a well-dressed young woman whose ankles were chained together. Maybe it was *her* hand I felt the other day, he thought to himself.

Two more witnesses stepped forward—victims, or so they said—to identify her. The panel conferred. "A week in the pillory," the speaker declared, and the girl was led away.

Marlowe turned to the back of the room. The Star Chamber was a public place and tended to attract an audience, particularly when the theaters were closed. Good, he thought. The seats were filled. If he were arrested, word would travel quickly, and with any luck, Phelippes would intercede before nightfall.

Scanning the crowd, Marlowe recognized a couple of regulars—an old woman with grime on her face and oatcakes in her hands and a sour-faced Puritan preacher who was always dressed in the same fraying black cloak. Then Marlowe spotted Richard Topcliffe. The royal rack-master was engaged in private conversation with a man whose face was hidden behind the brim of a dove-gray felt hat. As if sensing Marlowe's gaze, Top-cliffe raised his eyes. *He looks on me as if I'm his dinner. Surely he doesn't think—*

Feeling Maunder nudge his elbow, Marlowe allowed himself to be led toward the panel.

"Christopher Marlowe. You've been informed that you face the charges of atheism and sedition?"

"Upon what evidence, my lord?"

"We have received three testimonials regarding your legion of vile, blasphemous statements. Upon oaths, these men relayed that you heap scorn on God's word, that you persuade men to atheism. Everywhere you go."

"Lies, my lord."

"You heard me say *three*, did you not? Three reports, all of which corroborate each other."

"In that case, my lord, I regret to inform you that there are at least three men in England whose sworn word is for sale."

The onlookers erupted. A chorus of guffaws rang out.

"Silence!" the speaker bellowed.

Marlowe glanced up at the gold stars painted on the domed ceiling. *What are you doing to me?*

Putting on his spectacles, the speaker looked down at a sheaf of papers before him. "It says here that you believe religion was invented to keep the common man in awe? That if you were to write a new one, it would be more excellent and admirable because the New Testament is filthily written? That if there be any God or good religion, it must be Catholicism, because they have better ceremonies? But you would prefer it if the sacrament were administered in a tobacco pipe?"

By the end, the speaker's voice had risen to an angry shout. Every muscle in Marlowe's face was tense. He was both fighting the urge to laugh and struggling—manfully—to appear aghast.

Turning to another page, the speaker grimaced in horror. "You've stated that the angel Gabriel was but a bawd for our Lord because he brought the salutation to Mary?"

Behind him, Marlowe heard titters. "My lord, I solemnly swear I have said no such things."

"Tell me, then, how do you explain *these?*" the irate speaker asked, handing several sheets of paper to a clerk.

On the first, Marlowe saw a poem. Skimming the clumsy verses, he shook his head. "The rhythm is all wrong. You can't possibly think I wrote this."

None of the men on the panel appeared impressed with Marlowe's logic.

"And the other?" the speaker demanded. "The document found in your former lodgings? Denying the divinity of Christ? Thomas Kyd confessed that it's yours."

"Then he's . . . mistaken, my lord. I've never seen it before, and it's most definitely not my handwriting."

A new voice called out. "Your lordships, I have proof of what Marlowe says."

The crowd buzzed with surprise. Marlowe turned. *Poley?*

"Approach!" the speaker ordered.

Robert Poley did so. He was carrying two sealed scrolls, Marlowe noticed, and a worn piece of paper twice folded over.

After a few minutes of review, the speaker pronounced, "Neither the poem nor the heretical document appear to be in your hand. And Thomas Walsingham swears you were at his country manor the evening of fifth May . . ."

Marlowe wondered if Tom's letter would help. Tom was no longer involved in government, but he was a well-monied property owner whose last name carried some weight.

A moment later, however, the question became irrelevant. Unfurling the second scroll, the speaker's expression utterly changed. "I see," he said, passing it to other men at the panel.

Their silent consternation could only mean one thing. Someone truly powerful had intervened. Marlowe had expected Essex—given the recent spate of assignments he'd undertaken for the earl's network—but with Poley as the bearer, the letter had to have come from Cecil.

The speaker beckoned Marlowe forward.

Studying the man's face, Marlowe saw that disgust had given way to reluctant admiration.

"You will not be placed under arrest, young man. But due to the gravity of the charges, until this matter is fully resolved, you will be required to report daily to the Privy Council, which tomorrow will be lodging at Greenwich."

Marlowe nodded solemnly. Inside he was marveling at his good fortune. It seemed his luck hadn't turned after all. Rather than relying on a risky scheme to gain entry to Greenwich's heavily guarded royal grounds the following day—a scheme he had yet to concoct—he was now *required* to enter. It might not be an invitation to the disguising, but it was good enough.

"I imagine you're here to slice out my tongue?"

Poley laughed. "Kit, it's been too long. Tell me, did you know your smile now hangs in the French court? I thought it was unique, but—"

"Excuse me?"

"Very popular Italian painter. Leonardo something."

"He's tremendously handsome, I take it?"

"Leonardo?"

"The subject of the portrait."

"It's a woman. Comely dark-haired one, as a matter of fact."

Marlowe was formulating a retort when he felt someone grab his arm. Turning, he saw the Puritan preacher in the fraying cloak. The man had followed them out into the hall and was thrusting a pamphlet into his hands. On its cover, Marlowe saw a woodcut of a winged man plummeting to the sea. Icarus. Squinting, he struggled to make out the faded Latin inscriptions: "Do not become proud, but stand in awe," followed by, "What is above us, pertains not to us."

"Harken to me!" the Puritan urged. "The devil has led you astray, my son, but you may still save your soul. Repent! Recant your dark words!"

"Tomorrow, perhaps."

"Save your soul before it's too late! The Lord shall smite you unless—"

"Later," Marlowe said, returning the pamphlet and shaking free of the man's grip. "Now, please, be off!"

Heading up a stairwell, Poley laughed. "Kit, I can't believe I'm to say this, but I agree with him. Not about your soul, mind you, but your person."

Finding an empty room on the second floor, Poley ushered Marlowe inside. "I urge you to leave town."

"Because of a bit of slander? Rob, you know I've been—"

"This is different. Phelippes is behind it."

"Have you forgotten, Rob? Your tricks don't work on me."

"This is no trick. Phelippes has decided that having you tortured is the surest way to discredit Cecil. I don't think he'll give up. I've worked out a way for you to leave England in secret. I'll send word as soon as—"

Marlowe rolled his eyes. "It is all too obvious what you're doing. I—"

"Cecil *is*, indeed, quite afraid you might confess to the coining operation, but that is not why I'm—"

"For God's sake, will you just admit you wish to keep me from unmasking the Muscovy smuggler?"

"Why should I give a fig about that?"

"Because Cecil is my primary suspect, and proof of his guilt is almost within my grasp."

Poley started with surprise.

"You do know he's just promised Ralegh fifty thousand pounds for a voyage in search of El Dorado?"

"Fifty thousand? Impossible! He doesn't . . . oh."

His shock appears genuine. Holy Mary, that means . . . "What you said about Phelippes . . ."

"On my life, Kit. I swear it's true."

Shutting his eyes for a moment, Marlowe sighed.

"Cecil has a cousin in Deptford. Eleanor Bull. She runs a lodging house and is very discreet. Starting tonight, no one else will be there. She's expecting you. Go, and I'll meet you with everything you may need—new identity papers, clothing. . . . Ralegh has a privateering vessel in port leaving for the Mediterranean the day after tomorrow. The captain has agreed to take you and drop you . . . wherever."

"You ask me to trust the most distrusted man in England? Everyone else who's done so has found himself swinging from a gallows."

Poley smiled. "You've never shrunk from risk before, Kit." Then his expression turned serious. "And I can't say that you've many alternatives."

"What's in this for you?"

"I loathe Phelippes," Poley replied. "I despise him for what he did to Mary Stuart. I warned her myself. I warned her not to put anything of assassination in writing, and she never did. The evidence that led to her execution was false. He fabricated it.

"He won that one," Poley finished. "This time I intend to win."

Marlowe took a deep breath. "All right. But not tonight. I need one more day."

"Kit, I don't think—"

"I'll keep out of sight, in disguise. Tomorrow night I'll meet you. Widow Bull's. I know where it is."

Reluctantly Poley nodded.

"Can you secure Kyd's release?" Marlowe asked.

"I'll try."

"Until tomorrow night, then."

As Marlowe and Poley turned to leave the room, the man in the gray felt hat took his ear from the door and hurried out of the palace. Pushing through the exit nearest the river, Richard Baines dashed to Westminster Bridge.

LONDON — DUSK

When Baines finished recounting the recent events at Westminster, Phelippes dismissed him. Pacing the great hall of Essex House, he considered his next move.

Marlowe had escaped the trap Phelippes had set for him, but oddly enough, that was a good thing. To Phelippes's great surprise, the Muscovy investigation was exceeding his fondest hopes. Apparently the man profiting from an illicit alliance with a Barbary pirate was none other than his and Essex's enemy, Robert Cecil. And for some reason, Marlowe was determined to finish what he'd started in spite of his near arrest—was actually on the verge of uncovering evidence attesting to Cecil's guilt. What luck! Without question, Cecil would be disgraced, perhaps executed. Essex might be secretary of state come summer.

But there was one problem. Having been utterly determined to destroy Cecil that spring, Phelippes had launched the campaign against

Marlowe before the Muscovy investigation was complete. It was the investigation he'd considered to be a long shot and Marlowe's torture the far more promising option. How wrong he had been. And now, unfortunately, Marlowe had learned of his betrayal at precisely the wrong moment. Who knew *what* the stubborn bugger would do with his evidence against Cecil? Well, Phelippes thought, he'd just have to take it from Marlowe by force.

Baines, Phelippes believed, was not to be trusted with a matter of such delicacy. Who was, though? It had to be someone who worked exclusively for Essex's network, which ruled out almost every spy he'd used lately, except . . . ah, yes. Nick Skeres. He and Marlowe were friendly, Phelippes recalled, but that would not pose a problem. Skeres could be bought. And he was good with a sword to boot.

Summoning a messenger from an upper floor, Phelippes dispatched the boy to Skeres' home in nearby Blackfriars. He then turned to the battered portrait of Cecil tacked to the hall's north wall. Torn in several places, it was now nearly unrecognizable. Essex had said something about replacing it, but . . . *looks as though that won't be necessary.*

23

*H*urrying along the Borgo Santo Spirito, Kate dialed Slade. She'd been impatient to leave Vatican City from the moment de Tolomei had mentioned knowing her father, but she had waited. Wanting her departure to appear natural, she had opted to stay for a cocktail at the reception following the tour. Then, after a decent interval, she'd ducked out.

When Slade didn't answer, she tried her father, then Max.

"Can't talk right now," Max said. "Slade's got me tracking down the *Sabina.*"

"The what?"

"De Tolomei's yacht. It left Sidi Bou Said earlier today."

"Oh. Okay, I'll let you go. But tell Slade that I was just with de Tolomei, and he said, 'Your father's secret is safe with me.' I'm guessing my dad will know what that means—apparently they once knew each other. I have a recording of his voice, and I'll get it to you all in a few minutes. My dad's in a conference, but pretty soon, Slade should know who he's dealing with."

"Got it."

"Call me when you're done?"

"Will do."

Taking the Ponte Vittorio Emanuele II across the Tiber, Kate mulled over her encounter with de Tolomei. It had the air of a choreographed stage entrance, complete with a carefully chosen set design. She believed he'd deliberately approached her as soon as she'd reached the Sistine ceiling's sixth panel, the one that showed Satan—painted as a woman with a snake's body—wrapped around the Tree of Knowledge, offering the forbidden fruit to Adam and Eve, and their expulsion from Paradise. By choosing to mention her father's so-called secret in that exact spot, Kate had gotten the impression that de Tolomei was suggesting he possessed information that would disillusion her.

According to de Tolomei, he and her father had known each other "long ago, in another lifetime," which undoubtedly meant at least thirteen years ago, before he changed his identity. Her father was still in Washington's U.S. Attorney's office at that time. Had he prosecuted de Tolomei for something back then? Kate wondered. If so—if de Tolomei had fled the States a fugitive—that would explain why he'd changed his identity. Or did it have something to do with de Tolomei's daughter? Could something have gone wrong with the prosecution of her murderer, for which de Tolomei blamed her father?

Kate had left the reception before he had a chance to tell her about the "other form of art" he was after. It wasn't a painting, he'd said, so . . . a sculpture? The manuscript? Or maybe it was an *intangible* form of art. Maybe revenge was what he'd been after for more than a decade. Revenge that would, perhaps, be made possible by an entry in *The Anatomy of Secrets?* Could de Tolomei be Jade Dragon?

For the second time that evening, Kate dismissed the speculation for seeming overly coincidental. Two separate investigations becoming one? Not plausible. Whatever was going on, though, she suddenly understood why Slade had been so adamant about ordering her off the assignment the previous evening. De Tolomei had a personal interest in her and her father, and it did not seem to be a friendly one.

Back in her hotel room, Kate had just emailed the digitized recording of de Tolomei's voice when she noticed a message from Max waiting for her. He'd sent it earlier that day, around the time her flight had touched down in Rome.

"Shit," she said, skimming it quickly. Max had been unable to make heads or tails of the numerical code on the *Anatomy*'s final page—the page Kate thought had been written by Christopher Marlowe shortly before his death.

"Bad news," Max had written. "The number crunching is a no-go.

The code's got to involve words or phrases in a book. Or a one-time pad type of thing."

Kate had suspected as much, but she'd been hoping Max's superior decryption skills would prove her wrong. She sighed. Unfortunately, she now knew, it would be extraordinarily time consuming to get at the meaning of Marlowe's numbers, if it was even possible at all. He could have chosen any piece of written material to use as a basis for his code. Since he had access to thousands of books and countless pamphlets and poems, the possibilities were endless. And even if he'd based it on one of his own plays, she still wouldn't be able to crack it, Kate thought. The surviving texts had undergone too many changes since Marlowe had written them, on account of transcription mistakes, printing errors, and revisions by other playwrights. Matching numbers with particular words in a scene would not be feasible.

By no means was Kate ready to give up. Eventually, when she had time on her hands, she'd compile a list of every book Marlowe was thought to have read and see which, if any, would allow her to read his perhaps final intelligence report. In the meantime, she had a murderer to catch. Jade Dragon was still out there, had almost succeeded in having Medina killed that morning. And somewhere in *The Anatomy of Secrets*—somewhere in the pages she *could* decipher—was the clue to his identity. Slipping her laptop into her backpack, she set off for a café near the Pantheon that served coffee past midnight. Tonight, no matter how long it took, she would finish.

Two hours into it, Kate was down to the last forty reports and still hadn't found what she was looking for. Frustrated, she ordered a third coffee. Then, holding the jar of sugar aloft, she was about to sprinkle a bit into her cup when a conversation at the next table made her dump most of it in.

Collecting herself a few seconds later, she apologized to the barista, gave him a huge tip, and hurried out.

The two teenage girls had been discussing movies. Their favorites. It was a comment about *Titanic* that resulted in Kate's accident with the sugar.

"I never saw the end," one of them had said.

"Why?" the other had asked, astounded.

"It was *so* wonderful, I loved it *so* much, I couldn't bear to watch him die. So I just shut off the machine and made up my own ending."

Listening to them, Kate had been reminded of a conversation she'd had with one of her Renaissance drama professors years before. They'd been discussing Marlowe's *Hero and Leander*. Specifically the reason it appeared to be unfinished, with Hero and Leander still alive at the end. Many scholars believed that Marlowe had been working on the poem in May of 1593 and suggested he never finished it because he was killed before having the chance to do so. Kate had accepted that as a likely scenario. Her professor had an alternative theory: that the poem was not an incomplete fragment at all. That Marlowe had kept his Hero and Leander alive deliberately because he wanted to take a story and a form in which the overwhelming expectation was punitive and end it without the punishment. Portray doomed lovers, but leave out their tragic demise.

Jack and Rose still dancing on the ship, Kate thought to herself as she ran up the stairs to her room. Leander never drowning, Hero never diving after his corpse. The poignancy of tragedy without the heartbreak at the end.

Connecting her laptop to the Internet, Kate hoped fervently that someone had put Marlowe's *Hero and Leander* online. Rome's bookstores were long closed, and she didn't want to wait another minute. She ran a quick search and—*thank you, whomever!*—brought one of the many copies onto her screen.

Whatever the reason for its unusual ending, the poem was not published until five years after Marlowe's death, which in Kate's opinion made it the perfect key for the coded message he was writing in May 1593. If he were still working on it and kept it with him, it would have been a convenient choice, and in addition to that, no one would have been able to decipher his message without a handwritten copy of his poem. For Kate, that was the clincher. If Marlowe considered the outcome of his final assignment particularly significant, he might not have trusted Thomas Phelippes with the information.

Scrolling through the poem, she felt pretty sure she was right. Each numerical "word" in Marlowe's report contained between two and five digits, and began with a number between "1" and "8." Marlowe's *Hero and Leander* was made up of 818 lines. No single line appeared to have more than ten words.

Here we go. The first number in the report was 3006. Looking at the poem, Kate clicked down to line 300, then read the line's sixth word:

most. The second number was 2164. *Hero and Leander* line 216, fourth word: *beloved*.

Then 23 . . . second line, third word: *and*.

Then 6044 . . . line 604, fourth word: *mighty*.

He's writing to Elizabeth!

"Most beloved and mighty Queen," she began reading aloud, slowly making her way through the letter. "I must tell Your Majesty of a treachery . . ."

After finishing a few minutes later, she dialed Medina.

"You awake?"

"Mmm-hmm."

"Cidro, I found it! The motive! And it's not at all what we thought. Where will you be tomorrow—say, around noon?"

"The City."

"Can you skip out for a bit?"

"For you? Of course."

"We're gonna take a cruise down the river and plot a little break-in. That cool with you?"

He laughed. "Absolutely. But as to the actual, um . . ."

"Breaking in? We'll discuss it tomorrow. How about meeting me in St. Katharine's Marina? There's a pub called the Dickens Inn."

"I'll be there."

"And do you by any chance have a picnic basket?"

"Yes."

"Can you bring it?" Kate asked.

"Sure. But what exactly—"

"Tomorrow, noon. I'll tell you," Kate interrupted.

"You're really going to keep me guessing *all night?*"

"You said you needed more excitement in your life," she teased. "I'm just trying to help."

After hanging up, she started to undress. Unaware that a listening device had been placed in her phone the previous evening, she assumed her call to Medina had been secure. She was wrong.

Twenty minutes later, Kate was staring at the ceiling wondering whether or not she'd be able to sleep that night, when Max called her.

"You still in Rome?"

"Yeah."

"Where?"

"My regular hotel. Near the Campo de' Fiori."

"Two guys from the Rome office will be there in less than twenty minutes. They'll take you to the airport, wait with you, and escort you to the first flight out. Slade wants you back in New York ASAP."

"Okay. I'll leave now," she said, flipping on the light. "But I've got to go back to London."

"Slade was dead serious, Kate. He didn't explain why, exactly, but you're in danger. Something to do with de Tolomei having a vendetta against your father. He wants you back here now."

"It *is* a vendetta . . . what did Slade say about it?"

"That he's handling it. Nothing else."

"Okay. I'll come home, but I need one more day in London. I made a breakthrough on Medina's case, and I . . . I have to do this. I can't tell you how much this means to me."

"Maybe it's payback for his daughter, I don't know, but Slade thinks de Tolomei will come after you. That the song and dance in the Sistine Chapel was merely an opening act."

"You know who he is?"

"Yeah. Slade didn't tell me, but after I read your email, I started looking for someone your dad prosecuted around the time de Tolomei took his new identity, someone who'd skipped town while out on bail. There was one possible candidate: a former FBI agent named Nick Fontana. He was in counterterrorism before he got married, then the Art Theft Squad. Kinda explains how he had the connections to start his new life. Anyway, like de Tolomei, Fontana's daughter was raped and murdered. Name was Sabina, incidentally. Then somehow—a Fourth Amendment thing, apparently—the perp got off, and . . ."

"Fontana killed him."

"Yeah. But not just that. We're talking brutal torture. For about three days—the same length of time the girl was held."

"And my dad prosecuted him?"

"Yeah."

"Okay, but while some might find his actions understandable, de

Tolomei—Fontana—had to've known he couldn't have gotten away with it. Not as a government agent, inflicting three days' worth of torture on someone. In what I'm sure was a case with intensive national coverage. Letting him off the hook would have been tantamount to telling the public that vigilante justice is okay. Whoever was prosecuting homicides at the time would have done exactly what my dad did."

"Yeah, but here's the thing. Fontana covered his tracks well. Left no evidence. Then somehow your father got Fontana's wife to testify against him. None of the articles say how."

"Max, I think that's it! In the Sistine Chapel, I got the sense de Tolomei was planning to tell me something that would make me think less of my father. Show me some kind of dark side. Maybe that's what his payback is going to be. My dad turned de Tolomei's wife against him, the only family he had left, and he must think he can turn me against my father."

"Either that or he plans to kill you, to teach your dad what losing a daughter feels like."

"Oh. I didn't think of that."

"You still want to traipse around London with this guy after you?"

"I just need twenty-four hours. Is Slade around, or—"

"He's on his way to the airport. The Tunis op didn't go as planned."

"Will you cover for me for a day?"

"You're asking me to let you get yourself killed? No way."

"What if I use an alias and disguise? De Tolomei won't be able to track me. I can wrap up the Medina case and be home before Slade finds out. What do you think?"

"This case, it's really that important to you?"

"Yeah."

"I guess I can't stop you," Max said reluctantly. "But check in, like, every other hour, okay?"

"Sure. Oh, one thing. Mind doing a little genealogical research for me?"

"Not at all."

"Thanks. I've got four guys—I'll email their names right now—and I'd love to track down any living descendants."

"Tomorrow all right? I'm on my way home."

"Of course. And thanks."

• • •

The man calling himself Jade Dragon was enjoying a homemade tiramisu when he heard the news that Kate Morgan had decoded the critical page.

Tomorrow, he realized, he'd be able to right the wrong done his ancestor so many years ago. What a lucky thing Kate Morgan was so clever. He was impressed. In mere days she'd cracked a code Thomas "the Decipherer" Phelippes had wrestled with for years. How unfortunate for her that she would never have the chance to appreciate the results of her efforts.

24

I hold the Fates bound fast in iron chains
And with my hand turn Fortune's wheel about . . .

— TAMBURLAINE, in Marlowe's *Tamburlaine*, Part 1

GREENWICH — EVENING, MAY 1593

In a riverboat fast approaching the palace, Robert Poley caught a glimpse of his employer's crooked silhouette in an upper-floor window. Pacing, Cecil appeared vexed. Poley was not surprised. Earlier in the day he'd sent Cecil a message regarding Marlowe's attempt to ferret out smugglers from the Muscovy Company. At the time, of course, Poley hadn't known that Cecil was the primary suspect. Poley had also written that Phelippes, their arch foe, was behind the scheme to cast Marlowe in a torture chamber for the sole purpose of uncovering yet more damaging information on Cecil.

Up on the third floor, just down the hall from Cecil's rooms, Poley heard the soft hum of a hushed conversation. Taking care to remain silent, he made his way to the door.

" . . . likely I shall find Marlowe tonight," a voice was saying.

"If not?" Cecil inquired.

"Tomorrow, sir. It will be done."

Retreating, Poley turned a corner and slipped behind a wall hanging. Standing quietly, he took in the full measure of Marlowe's predicament — Phelippes determined to have him racked, and Cecil now plotting his murder. One wished him to speak, the other to be silenced. Two of England's most powerful men had set certain wheels in motion, could Poley turn them back?

Heavy footfalls crushed the hallway's new floor rushes. Peering out, Poley saw Cecil's assassin. It was Ingram Frizer, a businessman widely considered to be a loathsome swindler. According to rumor, Frizer and a partner had just duped a young gentleman out of thirty-four pounds through a commodity brokering deal involving a dozen wheel-lock pistols. Where he'd obtained the guns, Poley hadn't a clue.

Once a few minutes had passed, he stepped back into the hall and headed to Cecil's chamber. "You received my message?" he asked.

"Yes."

"I did as you required, sir. Marlowe is at liberty, and I made all the arrangements to secure his secret departure from England."

"You know where he is?"

"No," Poley lied, glad he'd omitted mention of Nelly Bull's home in his recent message. "Unfortunately Marlowe didn't think it necessary to leave just yet. Assumes Phelippes will give up his devious strategem now that—"

"Well, he's wrong," Cecil interrupted. "Phelippes is never so easily thwarted. It doesn't matter, though. I've chosen a different means of handling the situation."

"Let me guess. You've sent someone to kill him?"

Cecil nodded. "Yes. Marlowe is now too much of a danger. The coining—an inquiry into that, I could have withstood. But *this?*"

"Sir, I don't know what you're speaking of."

"Marlowe may soon have knowledge of an alliance I've forged with one of the Crown's enemies. A financial arrangement, nothing more. But as the trade involves English armaments, without the queen's knowledge . . ."

"I agree," Poley said. "That cannot be allowed to come out."

"I have a man familiar with Marlowe's various haunts who has sworn to find him within a day's time. And should Marlowe change his mind and try to quit England, he'll be detained. I've every port under watch. He won't pose a threat for long."

"You no longer fear implication in a murder?" Poley asked, resigned.

"No. This man will make it appear as self-defense. And his word won't be doubted. He's a gentleman. A property owner. With no known association to me."

"Even so, I think it might be best to shut down your . . . financial arrangement, sir. You may stop Marlowe, but surely another could expose it?"

"I don't believe so. It's too well designed. And none of the other spies at Phelippes's disposal are a tenth so clever as Marlowe."

"True," Poley replied.

"There is also the fact that it is enormously profitable, and winning the queen's favor is a costly business."

"Stealing from her to impress her . . . has a nice circularity to it, I admit," Poley mused.

Cecil, however, was not listening. He had been gazing absently down at the grounds, and a scowl had suddenly darkened his face.

Moving to the windows, Poley followed his employer's eyes. Elizabeth and Essex were strolling in the darkness hand in hand.

Gesturing to them, Cecil said, "He has his ways, I have mine."

SOUTHWARK — MORNING

The sword would have punctured Kit Marlowe's chest but for the safety button affixed to its tip.

Standing in the pit of the Rose theater, Ingram Frizer was watching Marlowe sweat over a mock duel with a young blond boy. Slashing and parrying, the two were zigzagging about the stage, wooden planks creaking, straw flying.

My, my, that lad knows his way with a sword. A change of venue is most definitely in order.

Seeing Frizer, Marlowe paused. "We're closed, if you haven't noticed."

"And rightly so," Frizer responded. Glancing about the half-timbered polygonal structure, he muttered, "Ungodly den of disease and corruption, this place is."

"I suppose you're not here for the entertainment, Ingram?"

He and Marlowe were vaguely acquainted. Frizer had bumped into

Marlowe at Tom Walsingham's country estate on a number of occasions. Why Walsingham was patron to such an impudent ruffian, Frizer couldn't figure.

"Master Walsingham requires a word with you, Kit. It's urgent. You'd best come with me."

At that moment, an irate voice boomed out from above. "Can you not see he's working on a new play?"

Turning to his left, Frizer looked up. A plump, ruddy-faced man stood in a doorway. It was Philip Henslowe, owner of the Rose, emerging from his office. No doubt he was intent on protecting his most valuable commodity: Marlowe.

"Do you see that fringed cloth-of-gold gown?" Henslowe bellowed, pointing to a heap of clothing draped across a pair of chairs at the edge of the stage. "That gleaming white silk petticoat? The red breastplate I just finished painting myself? He writes of Penthesilea, Queen of the Amazons! And not you, nor anyone, shall get in his way. Now, whoever you are, be off! Or I'll have you thrown from the premises."

Glowering, Frizer pivoted to leave. Then, to his surprise, Marlowe stopped him.

"Wait."

Frizer approached the stage.

In a low tone Marlowe said, "You may tell Tom he can find me in Deptford tomorrow morning. First thing. At Eleanor Bull's. I don't know exactly when, but I will be arriving sometime during the night."

"Oh, that will do, Kit. That will do nicely."

Exiting the Rose, Frizer was confident he'd be able to accomplish his deadly task with ease, that the illicit trade he was helping Robert Cecil facilitate would be able to continue unimpeded. Having left Marlowe sorting through bits and pieces of costumery, Frizer felt certain that Marlowe would not be making any further discoveries that could damage the trading scheme. And as a pleasant bonus, he thought with relish, the playmaker would be dead before his final bit of filth hit the stage.

Or so Frizer believed. He was a man of limited imagination, and it did not occur to him that Marlowe was doing exactly what he himself had done several days before—raid an armory. For the weapons Marlowe would be using to best his latest adversary were some of the props and items of clothing left behind by the Admiral's Men when they quit the city. Nor did it occur to Frizer that for his next drama, Marlowe had a much larger stage in mind than Henslowe's.

GREENWICH PALACE — DUSK

The shrill Arabic invective echoed throughout the great hall.

Befuddled, the guard at the door was not sure how to respond. He pointed out to the grounds, to the sea of richly costumed guests milling about—fireworks cracking and gleaming over their heads. Marble fountains rippled with colored water, acrobats tumbled, a juggler tossed up flaming sticks, who would want to come inside?

The dazzling young woman in the fringed golden gown stomped her feet. Yet more incomprehensible curses flew from her mouth. In a frenzy, she flung back her veil, tossing it over her jeweled crown.

She was a wealthy foreigner, the guard figured, judging by the richness of her dress and the strangeness of her words. But who was she dressed as? What kind of queen wore a sword and armor? *Red* armor? And more important, whatever could she want? But for three Privy Councillors interrogating a Bankside scribbler, the palace was virtually empty.

Then, during her next outburst, he made out two barely discernible English words: *bedchamber* and *maid*.

Ah, one of our royal guests, he realized. Nodding, he motioned her in.

Imperiously she strode down the hall and ascended the stairwell.

Minutes later she reappeared, with a stooped figure shrouded in a white wimple shuffling by her side.

In spite of the itchy fabric he'd just wrapped about his head, it didn't take Marlowe long to spot Robert Cecil. Faces might be concealed at a disguising, but misshapen shoulders were more difficult to hide. Marlowe also recognized the parrot perched upon Cecil's forearm. Dressed in the simple white robe of a Moorish falconer, Cecil had apparently used ash to darken the feathers of his normally white pet bird—ash that, Marlowe saw, was darkening the fabric of Cecil's sleeve.

The diminutive spymaster was standing upon a gentle slope chatting with a mermaid, a woman who was wearing a flesh-colored bodice and billowing blue silk skirts with an elaborate jeweled green tail suspended from her waist. Maneuvering between curious beasts sculpted of ice and real ones tethered by chains, Marlowe guided Helen toward their target. He watched one of the royal lions devour a live chicken, then attempted to catch a glimpse of his sovereign. Women in white face paint and red wigs abounded, but . . .

Where was the bowing and scraping? Where was Queen Elizabeth? Her great chair was empty, he noticed. And the lord-in-waiting was scanning the crowd, perplexed. She must watch from a window, Marlowe thought to himself. He'd heard many a tale of her penchant for taking steps to disarm guests and subjects. Most notably, the queen was said to have appeared before the French ambassador years before with her bodice gaping open, leaving him red-faced and stammering.

A few yards from Cecil, Helen paused, as if to admire a troupe of dancers. As she edged closer, straining to hear his conversation, Marlowe decided that a true maidservant would be doing something servile right about now. He moved off to fetch her a drink.

Surveying the offerings, he chose a goblet of what smelled like spiced wine.

"You serve your queen well," a voice behind him declared softly.

Marlowe turned to the tall, bony man who seemed to be dressed as Charon, the ancient Greek ferryman of the dead. Wearing a long black cloak with the hood pulled low, the man had on a black mask and gloves, which had a skull and hand bones painted on them, and carried a paddle.

"I've been at it for quite a while," Marlowe responded in his best falsetto.

With a wink, the Charon figure replied, "We know."

Stunned, Marlowe gaped in silence.

"Close your mouth at once!" Queen Elizabeth commanded. "And don't you dare bow, Master Marlowe. You'll give us away."

Breath stuck, he managed but one word. "How . . . ?"

"Sir Francis spoke so highly of your . . . *efforts*, we sought out your face at the Rose."

Collecting himself, Marlowe appreciated the irony of her choice in costume. The queen might not ferry them across the Styx herself, but a great number of souls were indeed sent to the underworld, on account of her.

"We assume you are here on such a matter today?"

Marlowe nodded.

"Then we shall leave you to it. But tell me," she said, looking pointedly at the ink stains on his fingers, "what is it you write of this time?"

"Hero and Leander, Your Majesty."

"A reckless swimmer and the halfwit who dove after him?"

"Your Majesty does not care for tragic lovers?"

"On the contrary, it is tragic fools we do not care for. And swimming at night during the height of a storm? Flinging oneself upon a lifeless body, to be dashed to bits by the rocks below?" The queen shook her head with disdain.

"Ah, but that is not how my poem shall end, Your Majesty," Marlowe said.

"Explain."

"Neptune allows Leander to reach the shore."

"Interesting," the queen said, nodding slowly. "In that case, we should like to see it."

As she finished speaking, a solid slap drew her attention. Several feet away, a heavily muscled man clad in the white tunic and plumed golden helmet of a Grecian warrior was attempting to kiss the mermaid Marlowe had seen earlier. The mermaid was having none of it.

Queen Elizabeth turned back to Marlowe. "We've a couplet you may use in your poem, if you like."

"I would be honored."

Very softly, she said, "Maids are not won by brutish force and might. But speeches, full of pleasure and delight."

"Your Majesty's words sparkle as brightly as the jewels in your crown, fair Queen. They shall light up my page."

"Well then, Kit Marlowe," she said, dropping her usual royal plural, "it is I who am honored."

"Have you gone deaf? Stuffed cotton in your ears?" Helen demanded, snapping Marlowe from his reverie.

"What?"

"You were right. The crookback. It's him."

Marlowe nodded. Since learning of the fifty thousand pounds Cecil had pledged to Ralegh for the Guiana voyage, he'd felt reasonably sure that Cecil was the smuggler.

"What next?" she asked.

"His house. He's a traitor. We seek out evidence for the queen."

Throwing back her shoulders, Helen sniffed, "I did not command—"

"The *other* queen," Marlowe said with a grin.

Adjusting his wimple such that only his eyes were visible, he followed her back to the river.

25

$\mathcal{T}$he Dickens Inn was overflowing. Every seat on its three-tiered wood-beamed veranda was filled, and dense clusters of bright flowers spilled out of every window box.

Cidro Medina was seated at one of the tables arranged out front near the water. He was within spitting distance of a gaudily painted black and yellow yacht lashed to the dock. Sipping a soda, he was looking out to the marina, a picnic basket at his feet.

"Hey, sailor, buy a lonely girl a drink?"

"I'm meeting someone any minute," Medina said, eyes traveling from her face down to the steel toes of her boots. "But . . ."

The snug hem of her black miniskirt now held his gaze. "But what?" Kate asked, laughing.

"Good God!" he exclaimed, recognizing her. He reached over to touch her hair. "Is this real?"

"No. A wig," she said, of the bone-straight, jet-black long hair shot through with chunky crimson highlights. Dark brown lenses were covering Kate's green eyes, her skin was several shades darker — courtesy of a sunless tanning lotion — and a fake barbed-wire tattoo ringed her right upper arm. The look, which was completed by Victoria's Secret's most miraculous bra, matched an alternate passport she'd brought from home. She'd used her real passport to fly from Rome to Paris's Charles de Gaulle airport, then had ducked out to make a few quick purchases and book a hotel for the night in order to leave a credit card trail. She'd then changed in one of de Gaulle's bathrooms and had flown to London under the alias.

"Remember that humdrum assignment I mentioned?"

Medina nodded. "Dodgier than you expected?"

"Right."

"Is it serious? Are you . . . ?"

"Looking like this, I should be fine."

"But we've been seen together for days. Whoever is trying to find you, won't they—"

"Hey, a guy like you—one of *Hello!*'s highest ranked eligible bachelors—anyone watching would expect you to be with a new girl today, right?"

He grinned. "Good point."

"Mind calling me Vanessa for the day?"

Standing up, Medina slid his hands around her waist and pulled her close. "Would Vanessa object if I do this?"

"Well, I'd be bringing up all the reasons it's a bad idea . . . but Vanessa? She's just plain easy."

Laughing, Medina kissed her. Tenderly at first. Then harder, with passion. For how long, Kate had no idea.

Picnic basket now full, Kate and Medina headed for Tower Pier. They purchased tickets from a booth, handed them to the captain, then found seats on the upper deck of the tour boat.

"You said we're plotting some kind of heist?" Medina asked softly, pulling her legs across his lap.

"Mmm-hmm."

"At Greenwich Park?"

"Yup."

"It's, uh, royal property."

"True."

"Guarded by some special royal police force, I'd imagine."

"And your point is?"

"You just don't strike me as the type to break that kind of law," Medina said. "Risking jail, I mean."

"Of course I don't," she said solemnly. "We at Slade's never break the law."

"But . . ."

"Vanessa Montero, however, is a bartender with fewer scruples. As far as my company is concerned, *I'm* on my way home. Which is good because *this*," she added, touching her forehead to his, "would feel a tad awkward if money were still changing hands."

The captain's voice interrupted their quick kiss. "Welcome to the *Millennium of London*," he declared over a loudspeaker. "'Bout fifty miles in from the North Sea, we are. Thames is a tidal river, rising and falling twenty-six feet. . . ."

The motor rumbled to life, and the boat pushed forward. "Just on your left," the captain continued. "Traitors' Gate. One of London's first one-way streets."

Hearing chuckles, Kate turned to look. The once-feared passageway was now sealed over with moss-covered stones.

"Also on your left, Executioner's Dock. Pirates and smugglers were lashed to it and left to drown in the rising tide. Captain Kidd was the last. Chained to the Dock in 1701, he was. And the half-timbered pub just beyond—Charles Dickens wrote many of his novels in the attic above."

Leaning back into Medina's arms, Kate watched decrepit wharves and warehouses zip past, along with the occasional set of luxury condominiums, which stood out from their surroundings like flying saucers.

"Now . . . *Vanessa*," Medina said, squeezing her shoulder, "are you going to keep torturing me, or are you going to tell me what you figured out last night?"

Smiling, Kate turned to face him. "Okay. Remember that numerical report we've been talking about? The final page of the manuscript? I'm pretty sure it's the one, and that I was wrong about Jade Dragon's intentions. He's not trying to keep information out of the public eye for fear it could hit him in the wallet somehow. His motive *does* seem to be about money, but it involves gaining a windfall, not preventing a loss."

"So the report itself is valuable somehow . . . and not as a tool for blackmailing anyone?"

Nodding, Kate slipped a piece of paper from a pocket in her skirt. "Remember how yesterday I told you that Christopher Marlowe was investigating the Muscovy Company in May 1593? And discovered that one of its higher-ups had an illegal trading relationship with a Barbary pirate?"

Medina nodded.

"Listen to this," she said, unfolding the paper. " 'Most beloved and mighty Queen, I must tell Your Majesty of a treachery. Your crooked back man—' "

Looking up, Kate explained, "Marlowe's referring to Robert Cecil, who was a hunchback. Also a top courtier and one of the directors of the Muscovy Company."

"Got it."

Kate continued reading the message. " ' . . . stole arms, which he then changed for treasure at sea. If you believe not me, then believe your own eyes. In the ground beneath the ship bottom near your tree, behold what was found in his river home, and ask of him, from whence did this come? A dutiful man, with looks like a great hill, will soon return you your filched arms . . . ' "

"Her tree?" Medina interrupted. "You know what that means?"

"Yeah. In the Tudor era, there was a royal palace at Greenwich where the Royal Naval College now stands. It was Queen Elizabeth's favorite residence. And in the grounds out back, there was an oak called *her* oak. Supposedly her parents—Henry VIII and Anne Boleyn—used to dance around it, and people say Elizabeth hid in its hollow when she was young."

"That tree is still there?" Medina asked.

Kate nodded.

"And you believe Marlowe's letter never reached the queen? Not even a copy? That whatever he buried is still there?"

"It's possible."

"What about . . . what was his name? Uh . . ."

"Phelippes?"

"Right. Surely if Marlowe revealed the location of some kind of treasure, Phelippes would have pounced on it."

"*If* he'd been able to decode Marlowe's message," Kate replied. "But I don't think he ever did. Because if he had, no doubt there would have been some kind of investigation into Marlowe's accusations against Cecil, and there's no record of any such thing. Cecil wasn't disgraced that spring, and he eventually beat out the Earl of Essex for the position of secretary of state. Was later made an earl himself. So, in my opinion, there's no way Phelippes ever read Marlowe's last report. In fact, it's possible that no one ever has."

"Until now. Good Lord. How'd you do it?"

"I had a *serious* advantage. Marlowe based his code on a poem he was working on around that time, which wasn't published till five years after his death. Phelippes probably never knew he was writing it. For me, it was right on the Internet."

"But to even think of it . . ."

Kate shrugged. "Lucky guess."

"What do you think the so-called treasure is?" Medina asked. "An actual jade dragon?"

"Could be. Marlowe did mention riches from the East, and in the Ming Dynasty, which was right around that time period, Chinese craftsmen used a lot of jade. Dragon designs were popular then, too."

"Why do you think he buried it? If he wanted to return it to the queen, why her backyard and not her . . . I don't know, lord-in-waiting or whomever?"

"Probably for leverage. He'd been arrested and was . . . out on bail, you could say. Certainly not off the hook for the atheism stuff. And at the same time, he was stepping on the toes of two of England's most powerful men. Phelippes must have been fuming that Marlowe wasn't providing him with the identity of the smuggler, and Cecil could not have been pleased that Marlowe had uncovered his secret and stolen his treasure. I'd guess he was trying to figure out a way to stay alive in the midst of all that."

"Having read Marlowe's final report, do you know who killed him?"

"I couldn't say for sure, but I have a better idea," Kate said. "I may have told you that according to the coroner's report, there were three witnesses to Marlowe's death? One was Cecil's top spy, another worked for Essex's network, and the third was a shady businessman—or con man, really."

"Two spies and a con man? Their word must carry some weight," Medina said wryly.

Kate smiled. "They'd supposedly gathered in a room at a Deptford inn for a day of eating, smoking, and walking in the garden. After dinner, they said, Marlowe was lying on the bed while the other three were sitting at a table—side by side, mind you—eating or playing backgammon, as a later account suggested. Then, Marlowe and the con man—a guy named

Frizer—are said to have started arguing about the bill. Marlowe grabs Frizer's dagger from his belt, slashes at the back of his head, and then somehow Frizer turns around, and in spite of the fact that his legs are under a table and he's sandwiched between two men, manages to wrestle back his knife and stab Marlowe through the eye socket. Frizer claimed self-defense, and the royal coroner ruled it as such."

"Sounds like bollocks to me."

"Tell me about it," Kate said, smiling. "I mean you've got that bizarre positioning—who eats or plays backgammon sitting three people in a row? And that physical behavior—from what I've read, Marlowe *was* handy with a sword and apparently had a hot temper, so if he'd wanted to hurt Frizer and came at him from behind, surely he'd have done some real damage. Instead, Frizer only had light flesh wounds and somehow managed to outfight Marlowe from a really awkward position, with the other two just sitting or standing there like paralyzed idiots. None of it makes sense. And then there's the fact that these were not people who normally got together for a good time."

"So . . ."

"I think the claim that they all spent the day together is a lie," Kate said. "They just weren't a bunch of buddies. I'd guess the killer got to Marlowe first, then the others showed up for some reason and agreed to help with the cover-up. Now, about who and why—"

"Cecil's spy? To keep Marlowe quiet about the smuggling?" Medina suggested.

"Nice work! You *have* been paying attention," Kate marveled. "And yeah, to me, Cecil's spy, Robert Poley, seems most likely. Or, Phelippes wouldn't have wanted Marlowe dead, I don't think, but no doubt he would have wanted his spy, Nick Skeres, to get hold of Marlowe's final report. Maybe they scuffled in the process of that. Now Frizer, he may've shown up to help Marlowe. He worked for one of Marlowe's closest friends."

"So why would he agree to take the rap?"

"Maybe the others pressured him into it. As the only non-spy, Frizer would have been the most believable. Deadly brawls were common back then, but with a spy doing the killing, a political motive would have been suspected. And with all three men seen entering that room that day, they all could have gotten in trouble if the self-defense story didn't fly."

Hearing the captain announce that they were passing Deptford on their right and the Isle of Dogs on their left, Kate glanced at the shorelines. They're so different today, she thought, seeing nothing but wharves and densely packed condominiums. The colors were all muddy earth tones, with hardly any green in sight.

Gesturing toward the Isle of Dogs, she told Cidro, "That used to be all forest. In the sixteenth century, it was a big hideout for fugitives."

As they neared Greenwich Pier, the captain directed their attention to a set of water steps at the top of which Sir Walter Ralegh had famously laid his cloak over a puddle so that Queen Elizabeth could proceed dry and unhindered.

Within minutes, Kate and Medina were themselves disembarking. Passing souvenir shops, pubs, and the National Maritime Museum, they made their way to the park, a vast green expanse dotted with trees and the occasional flower bed. Just inside the gated entrance, a large plastic map stood on display. The park, they saw, was a large rectangle with paved paths lining the edges and winding throughout.

Medina turned to Kate with a curious smile. "Remind me why you want to commit a crime tonight rather than inform the proper authorities?"

"If we go through official channels," she said, "red tape will hold up any digging for months, you and I will be cut out of the loop, and we'll be no closer to finding whoever's behind all of this."

"You have a point," he said, not fully convinced. "But I still—"

"We can find an anonymous way to get whatever we unearth to the Crown. I'm just impatient to verify that it's what Jade Dragon is after. If the chest is there and has a jade statue of a dragon in it . . ."

"We'll be sure."

"Yup." Pointing to a spot in the center of the map, Kate then asked him, "Can we meet here? At Queen Elizabeth's Oak?"

Medina nodded.

"I just need twenty or so minutes alone for this next part."

"Sure. I could use a nap."

Ten minutes later, it was time for her third attempt.

Strolling down the path along the park's western edge, Kate saw a middle-aged woman approaching from the opposite direction, walking her dog. Kate bent to pet it. Smiling up at the woman, she said, "He's adorable."

"Thank you."

"It's a beautiful park. I can't imagine having it in my neighborhood."

"It is very nice," the woman admitted impatiently, making it clear that she was not in the least impressed with Kate's outfit.

"I'm sorry to bother you. I shouldn't have, it's just that it's my first day in London, and I've never traveled alone. . . ."

"Not to worry," the woman said, warming up a bit.

Admiring the grounds once more, Kate repeated the same line she'd used on two previous passersby. "The local college kids must sneak in here at night all the time."

"Oh, no," the woman responded. "After dark, the park police drive around periodically and release their dogs."

The Queen's Oak, Kate saw, had long since fallen. A decaying carcass— about ten or so feet long—was resting on the ground, enclosed by a wrought-iron fence.

A few yards away, Medina was lying on the grass, too. His eyes were still closed when Kate reached him.

"Wake up, Sleeping Beauty," she said, kneeling beside him.

Reaching out, he pulled her on top of him. "How'd it go?" he asked, face inches below hers.

"Very well," she replied, hoisting herself back up. "Come with me."

Taking his hand, Kate led him to a massive, curiously shaped hole in the ground. A giant gully that resembled a ship's hull. "Now this, Cid, is where we'll dig."

"Every night for a month?" he asked wryly. The gully was more than a hundred yards long. "That letter doesn't give a precise spot?"

"The wording is a bit vague, but I think there are only two possible lo-cations."

"Seems doable."

"Yeah. Now let's eat and talk about how we're gonna pull it off."

Belvedere of Punta Cannone, Capri — 2:34 p.m.

"Where is she?" de Tolomei asked, entering his surveillance room.

"East London," his assistant answered. "In Greenwich."

"The team will be departing soon?"

"Yes, sir. In a few hours."

26

Go on, my lord, and give your charge I say,
Thy wit will make us conquerors today.

— MYCETES, in Marlowe's *Tamburlaine*, Part 1

LONDON — EVENING, MAY 1593

The two figures moved slowly along the Strand. One limping, relying on a stout walking stick, the other deliberately slowing his pace.

The man with the limp wore a dark gown and a matching flat cap. He had thick gray hair and a long scraggly beard and carried a wooden cross, painted red, in his left hand. His younger companion wore a white apron over simple attire and carried a stoneware jar.

Reaching the stoop of the brick and timber mansion owned by Robert Cecil's father, Marlowe used his walking stick to thump upon the door.

It cracked open, and a young maid peered out. "Who are you?"

"Physician, mistress," Marlowe replied. "I received a summons this morning."

"Why?" she asked, alarmed.

"A report of plague."

Terrified, the maid gasped.

"I bring a cross for the door," Marlowe continued, "and an apothecary with remedies so that the rest of you — God willing — may escape the disease."

"Mummy," Helen chimed in, proferring the stoneware jar. "Dead man's ashes. You stir four ounces into twice as much wine—"

The girl darted back inside, then reappeared moments later with another maid at her side—her sister, by the looks of things—and together, they tore off down the street.

Taking a seat on the stoop, Marlowe and Helen waited for the house to empty.

"Seems he doesn't keep written records of the alliance, Kit," Helen said, pushing the drawer shut. Their visit to Cecil's office earlier that evening had been equally fruitless.

They'd searched every corner of Cecil's bedchamber and had been scouring his study for the better part of an hour.

"Perhaps not, but surely he still has that jade dragon given him by your captain."

Sitting back against the wall behind her, Helen nodded. "The way he spoke of it, I'd not expect him to have sold it. But a man of his position, mustn't he have a country home? Which might be a safer place to—"

"I'd wager he prefers to keep it close," Marlowe cut in, peering behind a framed map of the world. He then began running his fingers along the wooden wall paneling. "Perhaps one of these conceals—"

"Wait, stop," Helen urged, excited. "Look down."

"They're scuffed, I know," Marlowe said, examining his boots. "I've been meaning to—"

"No. Beneath them."

He was standing on a small, richly colored carpet. An Egyptian Mamluk, Helen thought to herself. "In the hall, the parlor, the bedchambers, the fine carpets are draped over benches and cupboards," she pointed out. "They're placed as if considered too valuable for walking upon. But here . . ."

"Of course," Marlowe murmured, kneeling to the floor.

Together they rolled back the carpet, exposing three floorboards shorter than any of the others in the room. Taking her knife from her boot, Helen pried them up, revealing a compartment . . . and a small wooden chest.

Resting on thick, inch-high legs, the chest had elaborate floral carvings on the front and sides. Lifting the smooth, polished lid, they saw nothing but bunched silk velvet in a bold blood-red hue. Marlowe reached in. The first item he unwrapped was a fan of peacock feathers encrusted with sapphires and emeralds. Lifting out a velvet parcel herself, Helen found a delicate box, carved from ivory, and a set of ivory knives.

There were several pieces of Turkish porcelain—with intricate designs painted in royal blue, sea green, and ochre—a golden dish with a lotus design, a multicolored cloisonné spittoon, and, in several layers of velvet, the willow-green jade dragon with rubies for eyes. All resting on a bed of gemstones the size of robins' eggs.

"Infinite riches in a little room," Helen observed.

"Well put," Marlowe replied, grinning. The line was one of his. "How did you . . ."

"I saw your play February last as I was passing through London. Twice."

Marlowe's *Jew of Malta* had been performed at the Rose the previous winter. Helen was still marveling at what she'd learned that morning. Meeting at the locked, near empty Rose to fetch costumes, she'd assumed they would break in and was surprised to see that Marlowe had his own key. Had he stolen it? Or was he a player? she'd wondered. Then, once inside, she'd witnessed the reverence the theater's owner had heaped on him and was stunned to realize that Kit—the spy she'd spent several days with—was *that* Kit: London's most beloved playmaker.

"Might not be an admission in his own hand," Marlowe was saying, pleased. "But such treasures—with trading routes as limited as they currently are—will at least provoke questions."

He stood.

"Greenwich?" Helen asked.

Marlowe nodded.

"It's late."

"The perfect time to slip into the grounds."

"We're not marching up to the front door, are we?"

"It's too soon to reveal everything. Too much remains . . . uncertain. In the meantime, I know just the place."

As they headed along Ivy Lane down to the river, Helen tried to ignore the fact that she was falling for a man who smiled at her with nothing but friendship in his eyes.

DEPTFORD STRAND — NIGHT

Sword across his knees, Nick Skeres was sitting on a stump in the yard directly opposite Eleanor Bull's home. He had been peering through the hedge for hours. According to Thomas Phelippes, when Marlowe arrived he would be carrying some form of evidence implicating Sir Robert Cecil in treason. Phelippes had offered Skeres twenty pounds to seize that evidence. For five minutes' effort, it was an irresistible sum.

Ideally he would creep up behind Marlowe as he approached the door and strike him on the head with the hilt of his sword. Skeres was hoping to preserve their friendship, as well as Marlowe's life.

Not so Ingram Frizer.

Across town, in a lodging house near the opposite edge of Deptford's green, Frizer was sharpening his sword. He'd assured Sir Robert Cecil that Marlowe would be dead before sunup, and he meant to keep his word.

27

After stepping from their tour boat onto Westminster Pier, Kate and Medina did not go far.

Thirty minutes later, they were just across the river near the London Eye, the city's giant ferris wheel. It was a highly congested area, particularly popular with tourists.

"We might have found our decoys," Kate was saying. The three young Russian women she'd just introduced herself to were in their early twenties, and not one spoke more than a few words of English.

Speaking quietly to them in Russian once more, Kate explained the offer in greater detail. At first they appeared to be confused, but when she had finished, they were nodding enthusiastically.

In a nearby café, the five of them hashed out the details. Before the girls left, Medina handed each of them an envelope. A fifth now, Kate said, the rest later that evening.

Based on the money as well as the simple nature of the task, she and Medina did not doubt that the girls would come through for them.

"I'm terribly late," Medina said, his hands gripping Kate's hips. "Traffic looks dreadful and my meeting's in fifteen minutes."

"If you take the tube, Mr. Fancy-pants, you should be fine," she pointed out. They were standing near the entrance to the Westminster station. "This line goes straight to the City."

"Good idea. Hadn't thought of it," he admitted. "What are you going to do?"

"I was awake most of last night. Deciphering reports, changing my appearance, traveling . . . I need a nap."

"But you can't go back to—"

"There's a guest apartment in our office building," Kate explained. "And as of yesterday, it's free." Gemma George, the receptionist at the local Slade's office, had already collected her things from the Connaught.

"But if the Connaught's under any kind of surveillance, you'll be seen. Your office is just across the street."

"Yeah, but we've got a back entrance."

"You're welcome to come to my place," Medina offered.

"Thanks, but you're a distraction, and—"

"A good one, though," he said, pulling her up against him.

"Which is why I can't see you. I want to sleep till ten. You know, to prepare."

"We're really going through with it?"

"Cold feet, Cid?"

"A bit," he said sheepishly. "Arrest is an alarming possibility."

"Not when you're with me. And keep in mind that as far as the park police know, they're just guarding trees and dirt. Not priceless treasure."

"Good point. Call me when you wake up?"

Kate nodded.

"By the way, after this is all over, I'd like you to come on a holiday with me. It'd probably be a good idea anyway, what with this dodgy Italian after you."

"I'm flattered," she replied. "And I'd like to, but my father is . . . going through something. I'm planning to go to Washington to stay with him for a bit."

Remembering her friend Jack's invitation to go on a trip together soon, Kate made a mental note to ask him if he would settle for D.C. Jack had lived with them for a year during elementary school, and it might be a good time to fill her father's empty house with a familylike presence.

"Okay," Medina was saying. "But when will I see you again?"

"I'm here on business now and then. And in the meantime," she teased, "I don't imagine you'll have a major problem finding another picnic partner."

Medina shook his head slowly. "It's truly tragic," he lamented.

"What?"

He sighed. "I think you may have ruined me for empty-headed women."

Kate laughed. "Cidro, let me tell you a little story. Remember how Marlowe used one of his poems for his final code?"

"I do."

"Well, it was about Hero and Leander."

"The couple separated by a river or something?"

"Yeah. In the classical version, there was a storm one night, and when Leander was swimming over to see her, the lamp in her tower blew out. Totally lost, he drowned, and his body washed up against the shore beneath her window. She leaped out, onto his corpse. Died when she hit the rocks below."

"I take it you don't fancy long-distance romance?"

Kate put her hands over her ears and winced, as if hearing nails scraping a chalkboard.

"Vanessa?" Medina guessed, laughing.

Kate nodded. "She just screamed she'd rather eat spiders."

"Then tell her to grab a fork and get ready. She might be tough, but my powers of persuasion are second to none."

Once part of King Henry VIII's hunting grounds and stocked with deer, St. James's Park was now open to the public and stocked with sunbathers, nannies pushing strollers, and civil servants quietly debating affairs of state. It was one of Kate's favorite spots in London. Willows wept upon a lake full of swaying reeds and paddling geese, and the flower beds, though impeccably tended, were irregularly shaped riots of mismatched color.

Heading west along the Birdcage Walk on her way to her office, Kate left a message for Max, asking if he'd had any luck with the genealogical research—if he'd found any potential candidates for Jade Dragon.

. . .

The man Kate sought to identify was in his bedroom preparing for the evening ahead. With his family's treasure in hand, he'd be leaving for Bangkok before dawn.

As the means by which he'd built up his fortune were far from legal, he'd come under intense scrutiny recently. He'd successfully dodged the authorities for years, but now his accounts, including those offshore, were being monitored. He did not know which government entity had breached his security, but he did know they would soon freeze his assets.

Fortunately the previous week, through a stunning, truly serendipitous call, he'd learned of the discovery of a manuscript that very likely contained information for which he'd been searching his entire life. In that instant, he'd resolved to steal it.

According to an old family legend, Christopher Marlowe had stolen a chest of extraordinary riches from Sir Robert Cecil in May of 1593 and had written a report detailing its location shortly before his death. That report, it was said, had fallen into the hands of Thomas Phelippes, who had never been able to decipher it.

The theft itself had not been a grave disaster for his ancestor. Cecil had recovered financially, and whatever illicit activities he'd undertaken to obtain his treasure had never been exposed. His political career had continued on its impressive trajectory. Queen Elizabeth I eventually named him secretary of state, and James I had granted him an earldom in reward for his dismantling of the Gunpowder Plot. He'd outfoxed all of his political rivals—had lived to see Essex beheaded for treason—but apparently, until his dying day, Cecil had lamented the loss of one particular item from that chest. A beautifully carved, gem-encrusted jade dragon.

Feeling a twinge of regret about his friend Simon Trevor-Jones, Jade Dragon cursed aloud. He'd miss Simon. But time had been short, and he hadn't known any other capable thieves in London. Not that he'd needed someone of Simon's caliber, but he had needed a thief who, in a heavily patrolled neighborhood, could break into a home and crack a safe without setting off an alarm.

Physically shaking off the dark mood, he continued with his packing. Simon was good, but no one was invincible. Simon would have been caught eventually, and as it seemed he'd intended to commit suicide the moment he was cornered, his premature death was inevitable.

It had not, however, been in vain, Jade Dragon thought to himself. A stash of untraceable riches was hours from his grasp. It was also pleasant, he mused, that his ancestor's embarrassing loss would shortly be rectified.

Kate was crossing Green Park when Max returned her call. True to its name, the park was entirely green, with the exception of a single pink flowering tree and a few dozen dying daffodils.

"Slade's got me jammed, but I'll be able to start tracking down descendants of those guys soon," Max told her. "Robert Cecil, Ingram Frizer, Robert Poley, and Nicholas Skeres? That's everybody, right?"

"For now. I thought it made sense to start with the primary players in Marlowe's murder, with the exception of Thomas Phelippes," Kate said. "They're the most likely to have had access to the relevant information and to have passed it down through the centuries . . . you know, quietly."

"Got it. Also, I've been meaning to tell you. That cell number I haven't been able to trace?"

"The call placed to the Cat last week?"

"Right. Turns out the phone was only used one time, for that one call."

"Bought under the name of someone who doesn't exist?"

"Yeah. Probably disposed of by now."

"Fits Jade Dragon's style," Kate said.

"Hey, about tonight. Think he had you followed to the park today?"

"No. I didn't spot a soul. If someone tailed Medina from his office, they must've fallen for my disguise—decided Medina was off for a lunch date with a new girl and could be left alone."

"And tonight, how will you . . ."

"Medina and I will go to a dance club, then slip out the back."

"Sounds good. Even so, the idea of you going in without backup—"

"If I get caught, it's as Vanessa, New York bartender, with an authentic passport to prove it. I can't ask anyone from Slade's London office to break into royal property with me."

"True. Which is why you're not supposed to put yourself at risk for a private sector case. No client is worth it."

"Max, tonight is for me, not Cidro. I stopped billing him when I got back to London. The case is nearly over. As soon as we find out which of those descendants is desperate enough for money that he'd risk major jail time or, better yet, has a connection to Simon Trevor-Jones . . ."

"Okay. But I want you on the first flight out in the morning. I told Slade I'd keep you locked up here in the office, remember?"

"Not a problem," Kate said, climbing the stairs to their local office's guest room.

"Call me with the information, and I'll meet you at the gate."

"Yes, sir."

Having finished selecting the clothing he wished to take with him, Jade Dragon moved on to his study. Approaching his desk, he removed his favorite type of pistol from a locked drawer and attached a silencer. He did not tuck it into his travel case, however. He'd be using it that evening.

28

What strong enchantments 'tice my yielding soul?

—THERIDAMUS, in Marlowe's *Tamburlaine*, Part 1

DEPTFORD—NIGHT, MAY 1593

*N*ick Skeres smacked his forehead.

No good.

He tried again.

Head still foggy, eyelids even heavier. Sleep was creeping in.

Perhaps Phelippes was wrong, Skeres thought to himself. Perhaps Marlowe wasn't coming to Widow Bull's that evening. And even if he did, surely he would sleep well beyond dawn? Yes, Skeres decided. Dawn would be the perfect time to seize whatever evidence Marlowe had on Cecil.

To the left of the stump on which he'd been sitting, a thick patch of soft grass beckoned. Settling on it, Skeres shut his eyes, confident that the sun would awaken him.

As he drifted off to sleep, Skeres had no idea that Marlowe and the evidence were in a boat less than twenty yards away, moving swiftly along the Thames toward Greenwich.

When Marlowe arrived at Widow Bull's, the plump middle-aged woman welcomed him in and showed him to a spartan yet comfortable chamber on the second floor.

He was alone. After burying Robert Cecil's chest, he and Helen had parted. She was on her way to the village where she'd grown up, with a handful of Cecil's gems for her family. She would not be back until morning. Marlowe patted the inside of his left boot. He'd taken a number of stones as well. He and Helen deserved payment for their services, he figured. Besides, who knew how long he'd have to survive without money from plays or spying? Who knew if he'd ever return to England?

Taking a seat at the table positioned in the center of the room, he spread the pages of his poem before him. Withdrawing ink, a pen, and a fresh sheet of paper from his satchel, he began to write a coded letter to the queen.

LONDON — NIGHT

Thomas Phelippes was writing as well.

Hunched over his desk, he was recopying the missive he'd retrieved from the London Bridge chapel the previous day — Marlowe's account of the unnamed Englishman allied with a Barbary pirate. Though Phelippes had held the original to a candle, which had turned the previously invisible letters dark brown, it remained illegible, as Marlowe had used a simple cipher. Even so, it required recopying. The foul stench of onion was wholly unsuitable for Phelippes's secret compendium. This new version, however, would hold a place of prominence — the second to last page.

Finishing, he set down his quill, covered his ink, and burned Marlowe's original. His thoughts then returned to his need for a title. The decision had to be made by sunup. The binder was expecting him.

Phelippes reached for his list of possibilities:

On Secrets: Being a Distillation from the Work of Sir Francis Walsingham, Principal Secretary, 1573–1590.

Legerdemain Curiosities: Wherein Is Contained Selected Secrets of Sir Francis Walsingham, with Additions Annexed Thereunto.

A Catalogue of the Most Curious Secrets in England, Containing Selections from Sir Francis Walsingham and Thomas Phelippes.

Damn. Not one of them was right.

Phelippes wondered when Nick Skeres would arrive with the information for his dénouement. That should give him an idea for the title, he decided. No doubt reading Marlowe's last report would be a most inspiring moment.

Deptford — Night

Shortly after Marlowe finished penning his final sequence of numbers, a knock sounded on the front door. Hearing Widow Bull move to answer it, he gathered his papers and tucked them into his satchel.

The stairwell creaked. The door to the adjacent chamber opened and shut. Then, more footfalls.

Robert Poley appeared with a bottle of wine and two mugs in hand. "Ralegh's vessel is leaving with the next tide," he said. "Come morning, I will bring you to it, hidden in the back of a small cart."

Marlowe nodded.

"Shall we drink, Kit?"

"What else have I to do?"

"You came across proof of Cecil's complicity in the smuggling operation, as you anticipated?" Poley asked.

Marlowe didn't answer. His lips and tongue were tingling, and he was wondering why.

"The proof of Cecil's guilt," Poley pressed. "Did you find it?"

Against his will, Marlowe felt his eyes traveling to his satchel. With a concentrated effort, he managed to press them shut, but it was too late. What was happening to him?

"Unfortunately the situation has changed," Poley said darkly. He drew a dagger from beneath his sleeve.

Watching the candlelight glint upon the blade, Marlowe thought about his sword over on the bed. Could he swing his legs out from under the table and reach the sword before Poley reached him?

He tried to move, but his limbs would not budge. It was as if a blanket woven of iron threads had descended over his body.

. . .

The pain, when it came, was agonizing. Marlowe felt warm liquid spurt across his face, and his right eye seemed to have been thrust into the deepest fires of hell.

He heard a chilling scream and was trying to work out whether it had been his when everything went black.

29

RUISLIP, LONDON—12:53 A.M., THE PRESENT DAY

*A*t RAF Northolt, a private military airstrip used by royalty, politicians, celebrities, and other VIPs, a Gulfstream G550 recently in from Naples was resting upon the tarmac. Four fit-looking men emerged.

"We're boarding the chopper now, sir," one of them said into his mobile phone.

"Has she reached Greenwich?" came de Tolomei's reply.

"Not yet. We'll be there just after she arrives."

Sitting in their headquarters on the southern end of Greenwich Park, the two officers of the Royal Parks Constabulary looked at each other in confusion. What was that noise? Great squeals of young female laughter, by the sound of things. Were kids driving past with the top down? Piling out of a nearby party?

They went back to their reading material. Having returned from a round ten minutes earlier in which they'd let the dogs run loose in three different spots in the park, they considered the idea of intruders unlikely.

Then came a distant sound of splashing.

The river? Or the pool inside the north gates?

Kate and Medina were walking quietly along Maze Hill, the road grazing the eastern edge of Greenwich Park.

As soon as they glimpsed the police car zoom down the park's central avenue, they slipped in through Maze Hill Gate. Kate had unlocked it a few minutes earlier with Simon Trevor-Jones's pick gun to let the Russians in.

"You know what they say about Greeks bearing gifts?" she asked, breaking into a jog.

"Beware of Russians in bikinis," he chimed in softly.

In less than a minute, they reached the gully shaped like a ship's hull. With nearby trees blocking most of the moonlight, they descended the steep twenty-foot decline carefully.

"From here," Kate began, positioning herself at the base of the imaginary ship's bow, "Marlowe says we take 'one two' steps toward the stern. His poem doesn't have the words 'three' or 'twelve' in it, so I'm guessing he meant either of those. Let's start with three." She moved forward, using what she thought were man-sized steps.

Unzipping their tool bag, Medina withdrew a metal detector and held it over the spot she'd reached. Nothing happened.

Kate took nine more steps. Medina tried again. When a series of soft beeps sounded, they grabbed their trowels and started digging.

To the utter shock of the Royal Parks policemen, three young women in swimsuits were having some kind of splashing contest in the large pool.

"Excuse me. The park closed hours ago," one of the officers declared.

The girls didn't notice him.

He tried again. "Ladies, the park is closed! And swimming is most certainly not allowed!"

Pausing, they turned. With big smiles, the girls began speaking in what sounded like slurred, drunken Russian.

Medina's trowel struck something hard.

Digging further, he gradually exposed a smooth wooden surface about eighteen inches by twelve. "My God," he exclaimed with excitement, leaning across the hole to pull Kate into a kiss.

"Cid, we'll have time for that later," she laughed, nudging him off. She then joined in, scooping earth away from the edge nearest her. They eased the chest from the ground and set it on a patch of grass illuminated by a bit of moonlight filtering through the foliage.

Kate slapped Medina's hand as he reached for the lid. "Hold on, Mr. Skip-to-the-back-of-the-book."

Using a dish towel they'd brought from his home, she wiped away the bulk of the dirt. On the front of the chest, clusters of daisylike flowers had been carved into three evenly spaced framed panels, and surrounding them was a thick border containing a twisting, flowered vine that resembled a climbing clematis. The sides, she saw, were similarly decorated but smaller, with one panel of daisies in each.

"Are we about finished?" Medina inquired dryly.

Smiling, Kate nodded.

He lifted the lid, revealing crumpled, decaying red velvet. Gently he reached in and nudged the fabric with his fingertips. Reddish dust drifted upward, filling the shaft of moonlight like blood in a test tube.

A bit of pale green was now visible. A spike.

"The dragon's tail?" Kate suggested, near breathless.

Medina gestured toward it, palm up.

"Such a gentleman," she said, gently taking hold of the object.

Lowering her head as she peeled back the velvet layers, a sheet of black and red hair fell across her face.

In that moment, Medina reached around to the small of his back for the silenced Hämmerli 280 hidden beneath his sweatshirt.

30

O that his heart were leaping in my hand!

—a murderer, in Marlowe's *The Massacre at Paris*

DEPTFORD—NIGHT, MAY 1593

Dawn would soon break.

Ingram Frizer was crossing the quiet town green on his way to Deptford Strand. As he neared the river, the pleasant fragrance of the local plum and cherry trees was losing out to the stench of butcher shops, fisheries, and sewage. He turned onto a narrow dirt lane and paused, appraising Eleanor Bull's home.

All was silent.

The rear entrance was located within a walled garden. The gate was chained and padlocked. Frizer climbed over the wall, picked the back door's simple lock, and soundlessly eased his way in.

Standing just inside, he listened. Nothing. Carefully he began climbing the stairs.

He entered the first bedchamber. It was empty. Moving farther down the hall, he tried the second one. Empty as well. In the third, he saw embers smoldering in the fireplace and a body on the bed. Squinting, Frizer thought he recognized the doublet Marlowe had been wearing earlier that day at the Rose. The silver buttons down the front were catching a bit of firelight, and they had an odd, memorable shape.

Slowly he approached the bed, allowing his eyes to adjust to the darkness. Marlowe's sword lay on a table across the room, he noticed. Perfect. Frizer raised his own, then groaned with disgust.

Evidently someone had done his job for him. Marlowe's right eyeball was dangling near his ear, and a dagger protruded from the socket. Droplets of blood had dried upon his unnaturally pale skin, and a large stain darkened the pillow beneath.

Startled by a sharp noise, Frizer turned.

Robert Poley was entering the room. "Ingram, good timing," he said, unfolding a large white sheet. "Cecil tells me you're to make this appear as self-defense?"

Frizer nodded.

"Then we should work out the story straightaway," Poley said, laying the sheet across Marlowe's body. He then slid onto one of the benches at the table. "I was lucky enough to find him tonight, but you're the only one who can make this work. Have a seat."

Frizer did so. "Marlowe's temper is well known," he began. "Particularly when he's in his cups. I thought it fit to say that we'd been—"

Before Frizer could finish his sentence, a soft squeaking sounded from the floor below. It was the front door, he realized. Someone was on the stairs.

Nick Skeres came in.

Frizer could see that Skeres was trying to work out what he and Poley were doing together in *this* room, on *this* night. He knew Skeres quite well. They did business deals together regularly. Skeres also worked for Thomas Phelippes, but fortunately that would pose no threat, Frizer thought to himself. For he and Poley had stopped Marlowe before he could obtain his so-called proof of Cecil's illicit undertakings, whatever it might have been.

"I'm looking for Marlowe," Skeres said. "Phelippes wishes to speak with him. Is he about?"

Frizer pointed to the bed, to the unmistakable shape of a body beneath a sheet. "He refused to pay for his meal. We argued. He took his dagger to me."

Skeres shook his head in disbelief. "You killed him?"

"I'd no choice," Frizer replied.

Standing up, Poley took the leather satchel from the table and held it toward Skeres. "Belonged to Marlowe," Poley said. "I did see a coded message inside. Perhaps you'll find it's what you need."

Skeres extended his arm.

Poley took a step back. "*If* you'll return at midday and swear to the coroner that what Frizer says is true."

"Of course," Skeres said.

Watching Poley hand over the bag, Frizer marveled at how expertly the man had manipulated the situation. Whatever the contents of Marlowe's message, Frizer was sure that it couldn't be what Phelippes was looking for, but Poley had convinced Skeres otherwise. In so doing, Poley had secured another witness to bolster their case. Brilliant.

After Skeres had left the room, Poley turned to Frizer. "Would you mind fetching the royal coroner?" he asked. "Lives in Woolwich, five miles east of here."

"Not at all," Frizer replied. "I came by horse."

31

Cool, pale mint green with a hint of a shimmer. Flashing rubies set beneath angry brows. Small, embedded diamonds forming a pattern of scales. The wings and tail, curling upward, accented with delicate golden inlay.

The jade dragon was exquisite.

Sensing movement, Kate raised her eyes. Medina was in the process of standing up, with a gun pointed at her head.

"Cid? What are . . . all this time, it's been *you?*"

He did not reply.

"Jade Dragon—he was just an illusion," she murmured, rising slowly as well. "To create a false sense of danger, of urgency . . . to get me to decipher the manuscript without making it public."

He disengaged the safety on his pistol.

"You didn't even find the manuscript, did you?" she asked, voice shaking. "It was Andrew Rutherford. That file I came across in his office . . . the one that made it look as if he'd been working on it himself for a while . . . he *had* been. My God, you murdered him. A defenseless old man, poring over the discovery of a lifetime. How *could* you?"

"I prefer to think of it as alleviating his suffering," Medina said tightly. "And if you hadn't been so coy with the details in Marlowe's letter, I could have avoided doing this." Taking aim, he pulled the trigger.

• • •

"Got him," Detective Sergeant Colin Davies heard Max exclaim through his earpiece. As they all knew, a confession was the only way they'd tie Medina to the tutor's death.

"She's *good*," Davies remarked. "That quiver in her voice? My word."

"Tell me about it. And thanks, by the way. For everything," Max said.

"Likewise."

At first, Davies had been reluctant to go along with Kate's plan for the evening, saying it was too dangerous for her, but he gave in when she asked if he really wanted to let Medina get away with murder.

Eyes trained on the pool inside the north gate, Davies was watching the frustrated park policemen shepherd the Russian girls into their jeep. One of them said something about a translator due to arrive at their head-quarters within twenty minutes.

Perfect.

Jogging south, he headed for Maze Hill Gate.

Medina was confused.

He tried again.

Nothing.

The park police jeep roared past without pausing. Down in the gully, he and Kate were well out of sight. As he squeezed the trigger for the third time, she lunged toward him and slammed her right knee upward, driving it into his groin.

Kate had slipped the bullets from his gun an hour earlier. Not long after she'd fallen asleep that afternoon, Max had called to tell her that he'd begun the genealogical research and learned that Medina, through his mother, was an indirect descendant of Robert Cecil. It hadn't taken them long to put the rest of the pieces together.

Doubling over, Medina clutched his stomach and groaned in agony.

"That was for the Cat," Kate said coldly. "The so-called friend you be-trayed. And this," she said, unzipping her sweatshirt a few inches, "this is for Andrew Rutherford."

Looking up, Medina saw the wire taped to her chest. He was silent, but his eyes hurled daggers.

Kate whipped her head to the left. And as Medina followed her gaze—toward nothing—she pivoted on the ball of her left foot and slammed her right boot into the base of his skull.

"Now *that*, motherfucker," she told his inert, unconscious form, "was for me."

"The Russian girls will get a stern reading of the park rules and be sent on their way," Sergeant Davies said when he reached Kate.

"Cool." And Max, she knew, was hacking into one of Medina's off-shore accounts to ensure they received the remainder of their money.

Faintly a siren began to wail.

"Press will arrive soon," Davies then told her, as he snapped a set of cuffs around Medina's wrists.

"Then it's time for me to go," Kate replied, gazing at Medina for a moment. It was a nice bit of cosmic justice, she decided. Sir Robert's treachery finally exposed—his stolen treasure returned to the state—on account of the greed of his descendant.

"Not one for the limelight, are you?"

"Setting up a client for a very public arrest would not be good for company PR."

"See you in the morning," Davies said. "Nice work, by the way."

"Thank you." Kate turned and ran up the edge of the gully.

As she crossed a large clearing, two men materialized before her. Dressed in black. The Met police cars were still on their way, she thought to herself, still hearing the sirens approaching. And these were definitely not reporters, or officers of the Royal Parks Constabulary. Had Medina anticipated her plan? Had he arranged for backup of his own?

"Hello," she said calmly, slipping a tube of lipstick from her pocket. *She* might know they weren't on her side, but they didn't have to know she knew. "You must be Sergeant Davies' partners," she said, raising the lipstick to her lips. "I know I've got like thirty seconds before the press descends, so . . ."

Before either man saw fit to draw his weapon, Kate had fired tranquilizer darts into each of them. Almost immediately, they crumpled to the ground.

Behind her, a twig snapped. *There was a third*. Okay, she thought, trying to calculate how far back he was. Seven feet, maybe?

Taking two quick steps back, she then spun, bringing her foot around in a sharp, slicing crescent kick. She felt her heel connect with the man's skull before her eyes registered that he'd fallen to the ground.

Sighing, she turned to leave once more. But before she could take a single step, she felt a strong arm grab her and a piece of wet, pungent fabric press across her nose. Immediately her mind went fuzzy and her muscles limp and useless. *A fourth one . . . shit.* Kate felt herself being hoisted up and slung over his shoulder. Watching his legs move back and forth as he carried her—somewhere—she blacked out.

New York City—8:38 p.m.

Max knew that something was wrong. Kate should have been out of the park and checking in with him more than ten minutes ago.

Worried, he decided to at least find out *where* she was, if not *how* she was doing. Like all of Slade's field people, Kate had a tracking chip implanted in her shoulder. Max brought its signal onto his computer screen and saw that she was heading due west, fast.

Judging by the straight, crowlike movement where there was no direct road, he knew she was in a chopper.

32

Base Fortune, now I see, that in thy wheel
There is a point, to which when men aspire,
They tumble headlong down; that point I touch'd,
And seeing there was no place to mount up higher,
Why should I grieve at my declining fall?
Farewell, fair Queen, weep not for Mortimer,
That scorns the world, and as a traveler
Goes to discover countries yet unknown.

—MORTIMER, in Marlowe's *Edward II*

DEPTFORD—MIDDAY, MAY 1593

Six pallbearers, draped in black, were carrying the coffin toward the church of St. Nicholas. Dozens of mourners followed behind. There was a fight, people were saying. He had tried to kill a man. A lovers' quarrel, some thought. No, a dispute over a bill, another corrected.

Robert Poley followed the procession from a distance. The inquest had gone smoothly, he thought. Ingram Frizer was able to locate the royal coroner easily enough, and Nick Skeres had returned promptly as well. The coroner had interviewed the three of them out in the garden, then had taken his measurements of the wounds and the layout of the room. Sixteen jurors heard the evidence. Local men—landowners, bakers, and the like. The verdict was what Poley had expected. The story was declared accurate. Frizer had indeed killed Marlowe in the defense and saving of his own life.

It had all been fairly simple.

With pleasure, Poley recalled how he'd tricked Nick Skeres. He'd examined the contents of Marlowe's leather satchel in advance. Realizing that the numeric code for the message he'd found was based on the fragment of *Hero and Leander,* he'd taken out every page of the poem and slipped them into his doublet. It was the lone copy, Marlowe had said, and as a result, no one—Phelippes included—would be able to read Marlowe's letter to the queen.

Poley had only had time to decode the beginning. Frizer and Skeres had arrived sooner than he'd expected. But he'd read enough. "Most beloved and mighty Queen," the letter began. "I must tell Your Majesty of a treachery. Your crooked back man stole arms, which he then . . ." Although Marlowe had indeed learned of Cecil's illicit trading relationship, now no one else ever would.

Poley had had no problem letting Marlowe down in that regard. He'd never intended for his pledge to help the playmaker to endanger his own livelihood. And when that prospect had become clear, Poley knew he had to alter his course. It was a shame what he'd had to do to Marlowe, but it was the only way. His own interests came first.

In a few years, he would offer Marlowe's poem to a publisher. By then, he imagined, Phelippes would have forgotten the matter and would not think to test the poem against the coded message.

After what Poley had done to Marlowe, it was the least he could do.

Essex found his queen strolling along a secluded stretch of the riverbank. The cool breeze was rich with the scent of honeysuckle, strawberries, and salty gusts blowing in from the sea. Gulls soared overhead, and waterbirds flapped and warbled in the rushes by the shore. Sunlight danced upon the jeweled flowers and golden embroidery adorning her gown.

"Beloved, what is it?" he asked, sensing her melancholy air.

"Christopher Marlowe. He's dead."

Essex placed his hands upon her shoulders.

"He was to give us his newest poem," she continued softly, allowing Essex to draw her into his arms.

• • •

The funeral procession reached the churchyard at the edge of the green. The pallbearers set about lowering the coffin into the fresh grave.

Robert Poley found himself standing near a trio of poets.

"He was the muse's darling," one of them was lamenting.

"A truly nimble throat," another said sadly. "That so amorously could sing."

"One of the wittiest knaves that ever God made . . . pen sharp-pointed like the knife that slew him."

When the minister began to speak, Poley turned to leave. Finally, he thought, he could go home and rest. His work was done.

33

*N*o movement, Senator," Max said into his phone to Donovan Morgan.

He'd tracked Kate from RAF Northolt to Naples International and from there, on to Capri. She had not moved since.

"Which means he's got her drugged . . . or physically restrained," Morgan responded.

"Right." Max prayed that Morgan was correct, that de Tolomei had not killed her. "Slade will be there any minute, Senator. I'll call you as soon as I hear anything."

"Thank you."

Hanging up, Max wondered what it was that Slade and Morgan were keeping from him. For some reason, neither man doubted that de Tolomei wanted Kate alive. Max wished he felt as sure.

He also wished he had not allowed all of this to happen.

BAY OF NAPLES—5:03 A.M.

Two inflatable Zodiac speedboats zoomed southwest from the Sorrentine peninsula, disco music and lights fading behind. Four men were aboard each. Before long, the north face of Capri appeared before them.

To their left was the well-lit Marina Grande. Their destination was farther west. Within minutes, they were closing in on the island's infamous Blue Grotto. A grizzled Caprese stood waiting. He helped tie up their boats, and the eight men began climbing the rickety, zigzagging steps to the top of the cliff.

Dividing into groups of two, Jeremy Slade and his seven employees took off on different routes to Luca de Tolomei's home.

WASHINGTON, D.C. — 11:07 P.M.

He hadn't known until it was too late.

Kate had been mentioning a boyfriend, an archaeologist, for more than six months. He had a Welsh name, she'd said. Rhys, because his mother was of Welsh descent, too, like Donovan Morgan.

He'd never seen his daughter so happy.

Morgan was supposed to meet Rhys that first Thanksgiving, but Rhys had had to go into the field, to do some last-minute research to supplement a presentation he was giving. Something to do with ancient writing.

That same Thanksgiving, an American spy code-named Acheron had been sent into Jordan to neutralize a terrorist cell plotting to release nerve gas into the New York subway system.

Morgan had not made the connection. There were thousands of young men at Harvard. The possibility had never crossed his mind. Slade's spy had grown up in Egypt. Kate's archaeologist was Welsh.

Then came the New Year's invitation: Kate was going to stay with the Khouri family in Cairo. Morgan hadn't understood.

"Didn't I tell you?" she'd asked. "Rhys's father is Egyptian. He grew up there. Came here for grad school."

What were the chances?

Morgan had tried to discourage the relationship, telling Kate she was too young to be so serious with someone, but she wouldn't listen. And when he met Rhys and saw them together for the first time, he understood. Engagement came quickly. Rhys was going to tell Kate about his double life, but after Iraq, he told Morgan. After Operation Hydra. He didn't want Kate to spend those months worrying.

Telling her that he and his brother were going to the Himalayas had been Rhys's idea. He'd needed an explanation for why he wouldn't be able to contact her for a couple of months. And then he'd disappeared, and Morgan had kept quiet, not wanting to add to Kate's unhappiness.

BELVEDERE OF PUNTA CANNONE, CAPRI — 5:09 A.M.

De Tolomei was watching.

He'd had cameras placed throughout Donovan Morgan's home a number of years before. All for this moment. To see the familiar expression, the one he'd been wearing himself for so long. That blend of grief and intense, unmitigated self-loathing.

Jason Avera and Connor Black were the first to arrive.

Dressed once again as tourists, they were climbing the narrow, winding steps of Capri's Via Castello, passing white stucco houses and tiered gardens rich with palm and citrus trees.

De Tolomei's home was perched at the end of the road near the cliff's edge. It was surrounded on its three inland sides by a curving, ivy-covered stone wall with black steel railing grazing the top.

"Boss," Jason reported softly, looking at a glint in the wall. "We're being watched."

Slade, who was probably within shouting distance by now, did not reply. Cameras had been expected.

Moving slowly along the wall, Jason continued, "And there's enough Semtex around here to vaporize us all. I see one trip wire, and I'd guess there are others. Probably one or more detonators inside as well."

SOMEWHERE OVER THE MEDITERRANEAN — 5:16 A.M.

"A trap?" CIA Director Alexis Cruz asked Slade. Her private jet was beginning its descent into Naples International.

"Purely defensive, I'd say. I think he wants to savor this for a bit . . . not take us all out together."

"Unless they're already dead, and this is merely an exercise in tormenting Donovan for as long as possible."

"I don't think de Tolomei has a death wish, Lexy."

"Does he want a pardon? Money?"

"Perhaps both."

"You have a blank check, you know."

"Good. Have the medevac ready. We won't be long."

Blinking, Kate awoke. She was in a chair by a window in an otherwise empty room. Outside she saw nothing but midnight-blue sky.

"Coffee?" de Tolomei inquired, entering the room with a steaming mug.

Head still cloudy, Kate nodded warily. To her dismay, he had fixed it exactly as she liked it. How long had he been watching her? Listening?

Her eyes were burning. Remembering the colored contact lenses, she reached up and took them out. Her wig was on the table beside her, she noticed, and she dropped the lenses onto it.

"Not a bad disguise," de Tolomei said. "We might not have found you if—"

"You hadn't put a bug and tracking chip in my cell phone?" Kate finished.

He smiled. "My men never imagined that subduing you would prove so difficult."

Kate shrugged.

"Have you relayed my message?"

"I haven't spoken with my father in a few days, but I think you know that already."

"I couldn't be sure."

"So is this when you try to kill me? Or tell me what he did to secure your wife's testimony?"

"Neither. I'm not a murderer. I've killed one man, and you know why. As to the latter, if you must know, I was twenty minutes late picking our daughter up from school the day she was murdered. I told my wife that I'd been working late. Your father, however, revealed that I'd been involved in a brief affair with my partner—suggested that I'd been in bed with her at the time of the kidnapping."

"Was it true?" Kate asked.

"Yes, I'm ashamed to say. But a colleague and friend—a man with a child of his own, no less—exposing what I'd shared with him in confidence in order to get a conviction for *that* crime?" De Tolomei shook his head with disgust.

"You expected the U.S. Attorney's office to condone torture and murder? By a fed? To basically tell the public that vigilante justice is okay?"

"Given the circumstances, yes," de Tolomei said. "My own mistakes may have cost me my daughter, but your father's revelations cost me my wife. Ever since I've wanted him to experience the same heartbreak and regret over something he'd done—to be tortured by the threat of its exposure, fearing he'd lose what was left of his family."

"Good luck."

"Thank you, but I no longer need it."

"You can't possibly expect me to believe he's done something equivalent to adultery, child neglect, and murder. You know what kind of man he is."

"Some things speak louder than words, Kate. Come with me."

Max was riveted to his computer screen. Finally Kate was moving. It was possible that someone was carrying her, he knew, but he was hoping the movement meant she was walking.

De Tolomei led Kate up a flight of steps and down a curved hall, then gestured toward an arched doorway.

"The CIA sent their top operations officer into Iraq three years ago as part of a mission designed to unseat Saddam Hussein. Your father, then chairman of the SSCI, knew all about it. That spy was captured by Iranian intelligence and has been held in Tehran's most vicious prison ever since. Rescue was never attempted, was deemed too politically troublesome, I'd imagine. So his loved ones were told he was dead, and he was abandoned. The man who made those decisions was Jeremy Slade, if my sources aren't mistaken."

"They must be."

"Have a look."

Standing in the doorway, Kate peered into what resembled a room in a luxurious medical clinic. With the dawn light hitting the opposite side of the house, the room was still dark. Slowly her eyes adjusted.

On the far side of the room, she saw a very thin man lying on a bed, hooked up to an IV pole. But for the rising and falling of his chest, he was perfectly still. Not quite sure why, Kate felt compelled to move forward.

The patient's eyelids, she saw, were fluttering open. Seconds later, he turned to face her.

Elhamdulillah, he's awake!
Surina Khan was in the doorway of the adjacent wall. She was carrying a tray of new medicines, ointments, and IV bags. From where she was standing, she could see her patient and the young woman with the brown hair and strange tattoo.

They were staring at each other. In silence.

Without question, the woman recognized him. Her lips were slightly parted, her face pale, body frozen. She did not appear to be breathing.

At first, Surina's patient appeared calm. His expression was open, kind perhaps, but there was a blankness to it. Then, ever so slightly, he tilted his head and pressed his lips together.

Seconds later, a radiant smile began spreading across his face.

Looking back to the woman, Surina saw tears slide down her right cheek, pause briefly at her jaw, then plummet into the air.

And then the silence was broken. Her patient started to speak. At first only a soft whisper came out. Clearing his throat, he tried again. Looking into the woman's eyes, his voice was hesitant but warm. Hopeful. "Surina?"

For a moment, the word hung in the air. A leaf drifting in a gentle breeze.

Then, a crashing sound.

The young woman with the strange tattoo hadn't moved a muscle, but the real Surina had dropped her tray.

34

LONDON — EARLY AFTERNOON, MAY 1593

*T*homas Phelippes was at his desk, staring angrily at the numerical message Skeres had delivered to him that morning. He had been attempting to decode it ever since, to no avail.

"Marlowe," he spat. "Stabbing was too good for you."

Robert Cecil felt the same way.

He was peering into the empty hollow beneath the floorboards in his study. Fury had never burned so hotly within him. What a shame that Marlowe was now well beyond his grasp.

Had Cecil known what was happening downriver at that moment, he would have been doubly enraged.

DEPTFORD — EARLY AFTERNOON

With three customs agents behind him, Oliver Fitzwilliam was striding down the private dock toward the Muscovy Company ships. Kit had asked him to conduct an inspection just before they set sail, suggesting that a smuggling operation was afoot.

Fitzwilliam was crushed by his friend's sudden death and furious at whoever had brought it about. He did not for a moment believe the story about a quarrel over a bill. Surely the killer—or his paymaster, at any rate—and the man who'd orchestrated the smuggling were one and the same. Unfortunately though, with Kit dead before his investigation was complete, whoever it was would undoubtedly remain at large. But hopefully, as his means of transporting smuggled goods would soon be gone, the villain would not find his operation easy to resume.

"On the authority of the powers invested in me by the court," Fitzwilliam began angrily, "I inspect these ships for contraband."

Helen tethered Kit's horse at the Deptford stables, then headed for the riverfront. Apparently his friend Robert Poley had secured places for each of them aboard one of Sir Walter Ralegh's privateering vessels, the *Bonaventure*.

There was a great commotion on the merchants' dock, she saw. Four uniformed men were hauling crates off one of the Muscovy Company ships. She recognized the fat one. It was the customs agent who'd confiscated her papers and taken her money. He and his subordinates, she overheard in passing, were confiscating caches of stolen weaponry.

Her captain would not be pleased, Helen thought. But Kit would. She could not wait to tell him. They'd been apart for only a day, she realized. But she missed him all the same.

35

De Tolomei pulled the door to his surveillance room shut behind him. He found Kate in the hallway, wracked with quiet sobbing.

Noticing him, she used her sleeve to wipe her tears, then grabbed the front of his shirt. "You've kept him here, knowing what he's been through? He needs proper medical attention. He needs a doctor!"

Calmly looking down at the bunched fabric in her hand, de Tolomei said, "And he's had one. Three times a day since he arrived in Tunis."

Kate took a step back. "What did the doctor say?"

De Tolomei nodded down the hall, then turned and strode out into his garden. Though well-tended, it had a haunted, melancholy atmosphere. Pines and cypress trees cast long shadows. The lush greenery was dense and overgrown, and the flowers, mostly shades of blue and purple. Jasmine and aloe dangled from crevices in the mossy walls.

"Rhys is recovering well," de Tolomei said, as they moved away from the house.

"Is he —" Voice cracking, she tried again. "Is he in pain?"

"Not anymore."

"Will he . . . get his memory back?"

"He was drugged extensively for years. They don't know yet."

"How did this . . . all of this . . . happen?"

"Three years ago, someone at Langley leaked the details of Rhys's mission in Iraq to Iranian intelligence. Specifically, to a man I've gotten to know quite well. My friend had been planning to defect and thought if he had an American spy on his hands, he could negotiate a deal with Langley for protection. He wanted to issue himself an insurance policy. A few weeks ago, he asked my advice."

"But how did you make the connection? To my father? To me?"

"I've had surveillance conducted on both of you for years. When I saw the face of the spy my Iranian friend had imprisoned, I recognized him and . . . offered a sizable sum."

"How much?" Kate asked. She was nearly certain she knew the answer already but wanted to confirm it.

"Eleven million dollars."

"I know you didn't do it for Rhys or for me," she then said softly. "But thank you."

"You're welcome," de Tolomei replied, surprised that his words felt genuine. Even more startling, he felt a lightness in his heart and knew that it was not due to the anguish of Donovan Morgan. The look on Kate's face—of intense, even if conflicted gratitude—was the reason he had joined the FBI so many years before.

Kate opened de Tolomei's garden gate and walked toward the scenic overlook at the end of the Via Castello. Leaning against the railing, she gazed through the pines down to the bright turquoise waters below.

Before a minute had passed, she heard footsteps. She turned around and saw Jeremy Slade.

"Is he okay?"

"Recovering," Kate said.

"I thought he was dead. That it would be easier on everyone who loved him to have certainty. And there was protocol to consider. An incident had been reported in the Himalayas, near Everest, so . . ."

"That arm?"

Slade was aghast. "You opened the casket?" He shut his eyes for a moment. "We needed something for the funeral home people. It . . . belonged to one of the German tourists killed in the attack. Rhys's brother was near their camp, and—"

"He's the one who sent me the postcards."

Slade nodded. "You have to know, I questioned hundreds of Iraqi defectors over the years. And when Saddam emptied his prisons before the war—of everyone but spies—I sent teams in to make inquiries. For months. Just to be sure. It never occurred to me that—"

"I can understand what you were thinking," Kate cut in. "But if you hadn't lied, someone might have thought to look where you didn't."

Slade remained quiet.

His eyes, Kate saw, were haunted by guilt. "The leak, Rhys's disappearance—was this part of why you left the Agency?"

He nodded.

"How long have you known he was alive?"

"Your father received a videoclip five days ago, but—"

"My father has known for *five days*?"

"We wanted to find him and bring him home safely before telling you," Slade said softly. "De Tolomei sent you to negotiate?"

"No."

"What does he want?"

"Nothing. He already got it."

"He doesn't want a pardon?"

"He has no intention of returning to his Nick Fontana identity, or to the U.S. He said you can go in and see Rhys. And have a medevac land in his garden."

"You speak as if . . ."

"His guards were dismissed last night. And now he's gone, too," Kate said. Before she'd left his garden, de Tolomei had told her about the elevator shaft that had been drilled into the cliff beneath his basement.

"He doesn't have your level of training. . . . You could have stopped him."

"After what he did for Rhys?" Kate shook her head. "Besides, he has no intention of telling anyone what he knows."

"You believe him?"

"Yes. He's not a threat to any of us as long as you don't try to have him extradited or killed."

"Did he say who else knows the truth about Rhys?"

"Only Hamid Azadi, but Azadi defected. Has left the intelligence world behind him. He won't reveal anything."

Slade did not reply. He took his phone from his pocket. "We're ready," Kate heard him say. "In his garden. No, it won't be a problem."

· · ·

Thirty feet beneath the surface of the sea, de Tolomei was in a small, two-man submersible hydrofoil known as a Bionic Dolphin, speeding toward the mainland.

NAPLES — 8:04 A.M.

The sky was gray. A light morning mist filled the air.

Shivering, Kate watched as the gurney was rolled toward the sleek white Gulfstream, Director Cruz's private jet. Two men were wheeling it across the tarmac, and, on reaching the stairs, they lifted it, carrying Rhys aboard.

The young nurse, Surina Khan, followed them onto the plane. She had asked to go, and seeing how well Rhys was responding to her, Kate and Slade had agreed that it was a good idea.

Picking up speed, the jet took off down the runway and proceeded on its way to Washington.

Kate turned and started walking toward the airport's main terminal.

"You have to tell me *everything*," Adriana burst out as soon as Kate answered her phone. "Everyone's talking about Medina's arrest. Huge headlines in every paper, apparently. I haven't read any of the articles yet, but I thought I'd go right to the source. Or are you not able to talk about it?"

"Hey," Kate said warmly, relieved by the distraction. "As far as I'm concerned, when he pulled a gun on me, his confidentiality privileges went out the window."

"Oh my God! Are you okay? I didn't know you'd been in Greenwich Park! Everyone thinks it was just the police."

"I'll tell you about it. I'm . . . I'm fine."

"You sound sick."

"Yeah, bit of a cold."

"Can we meet for coffee?"

"That'd be great," Kate said. "My flight's about to board. I'll be back in London around eleven."

"What do you mean? Where are you?"

"Another . . . work thing came up. I'm in Naples."

"What's your flight number? I'll come get you."

"Oh, you don't have to do that. I need to go to my office anyway—take a shower, pick up some things . . ."

"How about we meet in Shepherd Market. The main square. Get something to eat."

"I'd like that. How's twelve-fifteen?"

"Perfect."

36

I go as whirlwinds rage before a storm.

—Guise, in Marlowe's *The Massacre at Paris*

LONDON—AFTERNOON, MAY 1593

He could tarry no longer. His compendium had to be bound and hidden immediately.

Phelippes looked out his window. Dark clouds were gathering. Rain would soon fall. Good.

Using a small blade, he carved Marlowe's numerical message into the sole of his left boot. He then slipped the vexing original into its proper place at the very bottom of the stack of reports in his pewter box. Phelippes was loath to have it bound before assuring himself that his final page did, indeed, provide evidence attesting to Cecil's treasonous liaison with a Barbary pirate, but he had no choice. As soon as Cecil discovered that he possessed such damaging evidence, men would be sent to his lodgings. Men who would not give up until every last crevice had been searched, and every seemingly solid surface had been tapped for a hollow. Not only would Phelippes lose his ability to vanquish Cecil, but his painstakingly accumulated arsenal of secrets would be ripped from his grasp. That must not be allowed to happen.

Time for the title.

Phelippes withdrew a sheet of paper from his desk and unscrewed his jar of lemon juice. Citrus was terribly expensive but for this, well worth it.

He gazed upon his list of possible titles one last time, then held it to a candle flame. Not one of them pleased him.

Too long, perhaps?

Because of that vile wretch Marlowe, he was being forced to rush a task he'd intended to linger over. Had Marlowe's death been quick? he wondered. Did a knife plunging through the eye extinguish life instantaneously? Or did Marlowe have a few moments to gloat, fancying he could take his secret to his grave?

Suddenly the title came to him. It was shorter than his others. More powerful, too. Like a dagger thrust. *The Anatomy of Secrets*.

Phelippes wrote out the words with lemon. He then uncovered his pot of ink, took up a second quill, and wrote out several lines of nullities above, below, and between the lines of lemon lettering. When the page was dry, only the lines of nullities were visible. Satisfied, he laid it on top of his collection, slipped his box into a large canvas sack, and stood to leave.

His binder was waiting.

Back in his study, Phelippes went straight for Marlowe's leather bag. He'd found something else of interest in it, something with which he could vent his frustration. It was a poem Walter Ralegh had written about his love affair with the queen.

Thousands of lines long, the poem had to have involved a great deal of effort. It was very likely the original, Phelippes thought, as a great many words had been crossed out and replaced.

"Well, then, he shall miss it." After lighting a fire in his hearth, he began tossing page after crumpled page into the flames.

In spite of the enormous popularity of Ralegh and Marlowe's written works, Phelippes felt sure that his manuscript was the only worthy creation. Their words, their pages, would quickly be forgotten. As would Marlowe, he thought, remembering that the poet-spy was being buried that day.

Phelippes had no way of knowing that centuries later, Renaissance scholars the world over would miss the lost Ralegh poem and lament Marlowe's premature death, while hardly a soul would even know his name.

His task finished, Phelippes lay down on his bed and closed his eyes. It should not be long now. Before nightfall, in all likelihood.

. . .

There was a great thumping noise. And another.

The door. Phelippes had barred it, but . . . with a sharp crack, it gave way. Cecil's men had arrived.

Phelippes was alone. If he'd changed his pattern and hired men to guard him on this day, Cecil would know for sure that he had something to hide.

"Where is it?" a big brute demanded.

"I've no idea what you're speaking of," Phelippes responded, attempting to appear bewildered.

There were three of them, and they strode in and began searching without preamble. They leafed through books, slashed his straw-filled pallet, checked beneath and behind everything.

Four hours later, they stopped. "Undress," the big one commanded.

Phelippes did not resist. He unfastened his doublet and removed his shirt. One of the men checked the pockets and ripped out his doublet's lining. The other two snickered at the childlike scrawniness of his body.

Phelippes then sat down to pull off his boots. Immediately hands reached inside them and checked to see if either of the soles was loose, if a folded piece of paper had been slipped beneath.

The boot-checker frowned. There was mud all over his hands. "A right pig you are," he grumbled.

Phelippes shrugged. He hadn't wiped his boots for a reason.

37

Jeremy Slade was pointing a silenced Browning automatic handgun at a man whose face was swathed in bandages.

"You're wasting your time," the man said. "Hamid Azadi is already dead. All I want to do is live in peace, by the sea."

"You really imagine I'd choose to trust you?"

"No. I'm going to trust you. My new name is Cyril Dardennes. I inherited money from a wealthy French grandmother, and I'm moving to Key West. I've dreamed of this for years."

"You don't deserve dreams, Azadi. You stole three years from someone I love like a brother. Not to mention the fact that if he'd been operational the past three years, who knows how many innocent lives might have been saved."

"I'm sorry your friend lost time. But don't forget that if I had not interceded, he very likely would have been captured and executed by the Iraqis."

"On the contrary, I believe he'd have prevented a war." With an audible clicking sound, Slade pulled back the hammer of his pistol.

"Your resources in my former country are slim. One day you'll need me. At the very least, you'll want to know who passed me the tip in the first place."

Slade narrowed his eyes. He'd assumed that the traitor would have kept his identity a secret. "You know who it is?"

Azadi nodded. "And I'll tell you . . . sometime when you don't have a gun pointed at my head."

Seconds later, Slade turned and left. He had not fired.

Mayfair, London — 11:54 a.m.

When Kate finished combing her wet hair, she unzipped her suitcase and pulled out her make-up bag. She wasn't ready to talk about what had happened on Capri, and didn't want Adriana to see the puffiness beneath her eyes or the blotches on her cheeks. Unwinding a stick of concealer, she used her fingertips to dab it where needed, swept a layer of powder across, then lined her eyes with dark brown and her lids with several shades of coppery gold.

After smoothing on a layer of lipstick, she examined her image. Only the redness in her eyes betrayed what was in her heart. She slipped on a pair of dark tortoiseshell sunglasses, reached for her shoulder bag, and headed down to the street.

Shepherd Market was not far from the local Slade's office. Within minutes, she was crossing Curzon Street and entering the market via a cozy corridor paved with large stone slabs and lined with sandwich shops. The quaint pedestrian enclave buzzed with life. From the main square, Kate spotted Adriana sitting outside a bistro with a bright red awning and matching tables.

"Thanks for coming here," she said, leaning in to kiss Adriana's cheek.

"Of course. I'm *dying* to hear what happened last night."

Kate slid into the wicker chair opposite her friend. "I'm starving," she said. "Order first?"

"Yes."

"What are you having?"

"Mmm, coffee and the feta tomato omelette."

"Sounds good," Kate said, not in the mood to peruse a menu. "I'll get that, too."

Adriana caught the waiter's eye. Once he'd come and gone, she turned back to Kate. "So about Cidro. I'm confused. People at work were talking about a pirate chest, which is exciting and who wouldn't want it, but for Cidro to risk jail when he's a top fund manager with money coming out his ears?"

"Actually, it only appears that way," Kate said. "His so-called Midas touch? That was a friend of his at a top accounting firm, who told him which companies were cooking their books so he could short them. When the accountant got fired, Cidro's fund tanked. Eventually, he started to recover by using front organizations to spread false rumors about companies he was planning to short. The Serious Fraud Office has been investigating him for a while. He's also near broke. Not too long ago, he shorted some companies whose stock shot up. He's facing massive margin calls and can't cover his positions."

"God, I had no idea."

"Neither did I. He kept the pretense up really well—of the blasé rich guy without a care in the world . . . I never doubted it."

"How did you figure out it was him?"

"I knew that the, uh . . . well, bad guy, was aware of certain historical information scholars today don't have a clue about. So I assumed it must have been some kind of family secret. In privately held papers, maybe, or just lore, passed down through generations. Max traced the descendants of the Elizabethans likely to have had access to the information back then, and—"

"Cidro was one of them."

"Exactly," Kate said. She'd known that Marlowe could have shared the location of Robert Cecil's chest with anyone, like a friend or a family member, but she'd been pretty sure that the Elizabethan in question was either Cecil or one of the three witnesses to Marlowe's murder. She believed Marlowe would have kept such information close to the vest until he found a trusty means of getting his letter to the queen.

The waiter returned with their coffees.

"When did you find out?" Adriana asked, pouring in milk for both of them. "That it was Cidro, I mean?"

"Last night. A couple of hours before we snuck into Greenwich Park."

"Cut it kind of close, huh?"

"I got lucky. Max wasn't even going to try to finish the research yesterday. Tracking down the descendants of four Elizabethans, researching them, and attempting to link one of them to the case? We thought it would take days. Even weeks, because so many of the necessary records wouldn't be online. But he had a free hour and decided to get started with the one aristocrat, a man named Robert Cecil. You know, because the guy's family tree would be all over the Internet. He traced the direct line but didn't find anyone with serious financial trouble or a connection to the Cat—the thief the mystery villain hired. When Max started looking into the offshoots, though—Cecil's indirect descendants—he eventually found Cidro."

"And that was it? You knew?"

"As soon as Max looked into his finances—the SFO investigation, the fact that Cidro was selling assets and moving the proceeds offshore . . ."

"So where did *you* come in?" Adriana asked, as she shook salt on one of the omelettes their waiter had just delivered. "Why'd he hire you?"

"To find the chest, he needed someone to decipher the manuscript he pretended to have found in the City."

"Pretended?"

"He sold his office a while ago, but that's where he said he found it last week. The manuscript really was found in that area, in Leadenhall Market, so it was probably the safest lie. Cidro bet, correctly, that with crime scenes to investigate and hundreds of reports to decipher, I wouldn't take the time to do something that wasn't advancing the case—like check out the phony discovery site."

"So who did find it?"

"A history tutor of his from Christ Church," Kate said. "A man named Andrew Rutherford."

After Max had told her what he'd learned about Medina the previous evening, Kate had assumed that to be the case, but she'd called Oxford's Inspector Hugh Synclair to be sure. Rutherford's will, she imagined, would make reference to the manuscript, if he'd found it himself. She'd been right. The will described how Rutherford had come across it a month earlier and asked his colleagues to forgive him for not making it public immediately. It was wrong, he knew, but he found the prospect of deciphering such a thing in the few months he had left irresistible.

It was a student, he said, who'd inspired the find. Fifteen years before, one of his tutees had told him about a mysterious letter that Christopher Marlowe had written just before his death that had ended up in the hands of Thomas Phelippes. The student had said that a major disaster could befall his family if that letter ever surfaced.

Kate knew that the unnamed student in Rutherford's will was Cidro Medina, and that the story about his family was just a shameless ploy to manipulate Rutherford into alerting him whenever new Elizabethan documents came to light.

Though it wasn't his official specialty, Rutherford had a pet obsession with Elizabethan espionage and was highly intrigued by his student's revelation. He'd been searching for the Marlowe letter ever since. He'd combed archives all over Britain for more than a dozen years and had kept abreast of all construction work done in and around Leadenhall Market. He knew Thomas Phelippes was in love with the tools of espionage, especially ciphers and secret compartments, and thought it a vague possibility that Phelippes might have hidden something in his home, which could then have been lost when the building was destroyed by the Great Fire. The previous month, a construction crew had begun doing structural reinforcement of one of the historic buildings in the area, and they chanced upon Phelippes's pewter box. As Rutherford had become friendly with the crew's foreman over the years, the man gave him the box as soon as it was unearthed.

"Rutherford invited Cidro for dinner last week," Kate told Adriana. "Which must be when Cidro learned about the manuscript. Later that evening, he went to Rutherford's office and killed him for it."

"Why not just steal it?"

"Because his tutor hadn't told anyone else about his discovery. He was keeping it quiet until he finished the book he was writing on it. Cidro had to kill him to keep the theft a secret."

"A murderer . . . it's hard to imagine. He was so charming."

"Trust me, I know."

Kate unzipped her shoulder bag's outermost pocket and held it so that Adriana could see Simon Trevor-Jones's pick gun. "When we're done here," she said, "I'm going to take you to his house and show you how to use one of these."

. . .

Kate led Adriana up to Medina's study. She pried up the floorboards covering his safe and began turning the dial.

"You know the combination?"

"We installed this," Kate said, as she lifted the safe door. She reached in for Phelippes's box and tucked it into her bag.

"You know, I could get used to this," Adriana said.

"Letting yourself into places you're not supposed to be?"

"Mmm-hmm. I've done my share of illegal things but never this. Which reminds me. That famous thief everyone's been talking about, the Cat, he and Cidro were friends, right?"

"Yeah."

"So why did Cidro hire him to break in here? His own home?"

"It was part of his plan to create the illusion of a fake villain out there so I'd decipher the manuscript quickly and quietly, thinking I was protecting him by finding some dangerous mastermind."

"But . . . the Cat died. If that was Cidro's intention, how did he convince his friend to walk into a death trap?"

Kate gestured to the walls around them. "Nothing personal, see? No photos of friends or family. No quirky stuff. It's a short-term rental. I bet the Cat had no idea it was Cidro who'd just moved in here. And I'm sure Cidro didn't tell him there was a security guard on the premises."

"Think he knew his friend would commit suicide when cornered?"

"No. That was a surprise to him, actually. Last night, I called the security guard who was here that evening. It was a young guy, new to the job. Not one of ours. He told me that Cidro said he'd been getting death threats, and that armed intruders could show up at any moment. Cidro needed to make him jumpy enough to shoot, because if the thief had survived, he would have learned he'd been set up and Cidro's game would have been over."

"So risky," Adriana said. "I mean, the guard would have wanted to protect himself but not kill the intruder, right?"

"Yeah. But the whole plan was risky. Seems to be Cidro's thing—huge risks for huge payoffs."

"I'm glad you never got involved with him."

Kate was silent.

Glancing over, Adriana read the chagrin on her face. "Oh my God. What happened?"

Kate looked at her watch. "Oh, look at that," she teased. "I've got to meet someone at two. Time for me to go."

"Don't even think about it," Adriana declared sternly.

Kate shrugged with mock helplessness as they headed for the stairwell.

"Where is this so-called meeting?"

"New Scotland Yard. The policeman I've been working with—we're taking the manuscript and the chest to the British Museum."

"You've got plenty of time. It's just south of St. James's Park, right?"

"Yeah."

"I'll walk you over," Adriana said, opening Medina's front door.

"Company? Can't say no to that." Kate locked the door, and they set off for the park.

"Well?"

"It was nothing, really," Kate said. "I wasn't falling for him or anything, but I did think he was sincere, that his interest in the manuscript was exactly what he said, idle curiosity. And I, you know . . . had some fun with the flirting."

"You had no reason to suspect him, though. Hasn't he been using your company for a while?"

"Yeah."

"Which means they did a preliminary background check on him, and you were led to believe he was everything he said he was?"

"Mmm-hmm. It's just humiliating to have your tricks turned on you. I had no idea he was coming on strong for the sole purpose of clouding my judgment. I've done that to people as part of my work for years, but I missed it when it was done to me."

"Maybe he seemed sincere because he *was* sincere. I bet he liked you, but just—"

"Ana, he tried to shoot me."

"Holy shit! How did you . . ."

"I'd taken his bullets out," Kate said with a smile. "Our plan last night was to go to a club and duck out the back, in case someone was following us. I imagined he'd be armed somehow but wouldn't carry a gun into the club for fear I'd notice. When he ordered drinks, I pretended to go to the restroom but ran out to his car. I found the gun beneath his seat."

"Wouldn't it have made more sense for him to go into the park ahead of you? Or send someone?"

"Without realizing, I made that impossible. He tried to get the exact location out of me — so casually I didn't even notice — but the language in Marlowe's letter was vague, and I didn't feel like explaining it at the time."

"Even if he'd managed to slip away last night, he'd have had your boss after him for the rest of his life if he'd shot you. Why not just knock you out?"

"Either he didn't have time to get his hands on the right tranquilizing equipment — it was almost six when we separated yesterday, and he had only a few hours to recalibrate his plan — or he just didn't care either way."

Kate sighed. It was time to confess. "If you can believe it, Ana, I made out with someone who had no qualms about killing me."

"*Finally.*"

"Excuse me?"

"I've known you almost ten years, and this is the first time you've got a bizarre sexual anecdote I can't top."

NEW SCOTLAND YARD, LONDON — 2:26 P.M.

"I'm shocked. Just shocked," Lady Halifax declared as she slipped her ruby ring into her purse.

Sergeant Davies was running late, so Kate had checked on the ring, then called Lady Halifax to let her know it was ready. With all of the necessary forms signed, they turned to leave police headquarters.

"Seeing Simon's gorgeous chum on the morning news jogged my memory," Lady Halifax continued. "I'd seen them about quite a bit. Thick as thieves, they were, I'd always said to myself. And how right I'd been . . . though for entirely the wrong reason. Whatever the case, though, I'd never have thought one would betray the other. And so ruthlessly."

"I know," Kate agreed.

"I'm sorry I wasn't able to help you. Ella and I simply could not recall his name."

"Oh, not to worry."

"I'm not. It's quite clear you did perfectly well without me."

"Thank you."

"Next time you come to London, I'll expect you to ring me for tennis," Lady Halifax said as Kate helped her into a cab.

Smiling, Kate nodded.

"But please, dear. If you don't mind. Some lessons?"

38

Are these your secrets that no man must know?
—GUISE, in Marlowe's *The Massacre at Paris*

LONDON—LATE AFTERNOON, MAY 1593

*P*helippes knew he was being followed. For hours, he'd been walking around slowly, allowing his watcher to keep him in sight. Easily. Phelippes wanted the man relaxed.

He'd gossiped in St. Paul's churchyard, then had ambled down Cheapside, making several purchases along the way. He'd asked questions of every shop owner. How was the wife? The son? By the time Phelippes reached the Royal Exchange, his pursuer was shifty and stifling yawns.

In the center of the courtyard, Phelippes paused, as if to adjust the packages he was carrying. The man behind him, he noticed, was waiting back by the front entrance. Relieved, Phelippes continued walking. His bookbinder was in the far corner, a few yards from an inconspicuous exit. Phelippes perused the wares of the adjacent jeweler. Knowing he was in full view of his pursuer, he picked up a miniature clock suspended from a chain, held it to the front of his doublet, and moved toward a mirror. As if dissatisfied, he shook his head and began examining a display of hat pins. The jeweler was helping another customer, and as soon as their backs were to him, Phelippes slipped out the back and darted left, into the closed tent of his binder.

"I need it now," he said, handing the man several shillings.

"I've just begun the design," the binder said. "I'll be able to finish in a few hours."

"I haven't even a minute," Phelippes said hurriedly. His watcher, he imagined, was by this time elbowing his way through the crowd to come find him.

"You cannot return in the morning?"

Phelippes shook his head. "A man is coming for me now."

Resigned, the binder went over to his desk, lifted a piece of fabric, and handed Phelippes his pages, now bound in black leather. "He shall not hear of it from me."

With his manuscript sealed in its fitted pewter box, Phelippes stepped from the tent and ducked low, using the crowd as a shield as he moved to the nearby doorway. He slipped through in a crouch, then straightened and broke into a run. He was two blocks from his building.

Another of Cecil's men would be waiting in his chamber, Phelippes presumed, but he was not going there just yet. Instead, he picked the lock to the rooms on the ground floor. As expected, they were empty. An old woman lived inside, and she took her supper at a nearby inn at this time every day.

Phelippes strode toward the hearth and knelt on the floor. Pulling a knife from his belt, he used the blade to pry up one of the large flat stones. Months before, he'd dug a hole beneath it. Roughly a foot square and five feet deep. He placed his pewter box at the bottom, then stood and went into the woman's bedchamber. A large, scuffed oak bed was positioned in a corner. Phelippes lay down on the floor and maneuvered his body beneath it. Edging closer, he reached out, waved his arm about, then grasped a sack he'd placed in the corner weeks before. He hauled it to the hearth, emptied the dirt it contained into his hole, and replaced the stone.

Before leaving, he checked the bottom of his left boot. Marlowe's numbers were still hidden beneath dried mud. Good.

He'd unravel them soon, Phelippes assured himself. He'd never failed before.

CHISLEHURST, KENT—DUSK

Tom Walsingham was sitting in his pear orchard. It was a beautiful day. The sky was clear, the air still warm, and birds were singing all around him.

It made him angry. His closest friend was dead, and such beauty seemed an insult. A mockery. The world should be sad, larks included.

When he heard hooves pounding nearby, he did not rise to greet the visitor. He did not wish to speak with anyone. Fortunately whoever it was did not linger. Within minutes, Tom heard the horse galloping away.

"Sir," he then heard. His page was approaching.

"Whatever it is can wait."

"Sir, the man said it was urgent."

Reluctantly Tom took the scroll and unfurled it. His eyes shot to the bottom. The letter was signed "Gabriel." He did not know a Gabriel. The courier must have made a mistake. He looked up, intending to hand it back to his page, but the boy was gone.

Tom then read the single paragraph. Doing so confirmed his suspicion. It discussed a mundane, meaningless matter—one of no concern to him. "My friend," the letter began, "I am writing to recommend an excellent type of wax I acquired from a shop in Canterbury. It is most durable. Yesterday I left it in a very warm room and it did not melt. Let us dine soon, and I will tell you more."

"Wax is wax. Why the devil would anyone . . . oh. Oh!"

It was a coded message, Tom realized, stunned. Delighted. It played on lines from Kit's *Dr. Faustus* in which the chorus forecasted the magician's tragic death by comparing him to Icarus. "His waxen wings did mount above his reach," they would inform the audience in the opening scene, "And melting, heavens conspired his overthrow!"

Poley was telling him that Marlowe, who was born in Canterbury and called an Icarus by many, did not really die. Because Poley, playing the archangel Gabriel—the purveyor of God's secret messages to his chosen ones—had somehow fooled everyone.

"Rob, you clever bastard. If you were here, I'd kiss you."

LONDON — NIGHT

Poley awoke in a sweat.

He had just seen Ingram Frizer stabbing Kit. My God, I failed, he thought, heart sinking. Then the nightmare faded, and the truth flooded his mind. Frizer had *not* reached out to touch Kit's body. He had not felt its warmth and learned he'd been tricked. Instead he'd turned away, sickened by the gruesome sight.

It was the reaction Poley had counted upon.

Poley felt bad about Marlowe's eye, but he did not regret having gouged it out. He knew Cecil would learn of the lodging arrangements he'd made with Nelly Bull, and it was imperative that Marlowe be declared dead that evening. He wouldn't make it out of England alive any other way, not with Cecil's men on such high alert. Thank God Nelly had agreed to help. Poley's plan had hinged upon one critical element — that Marlowe's injury appear so ghastly, so utterly deadly, that Frizer would not even think to test the body for warmth or breath. White makeup, a retractable stage knife protruding from the eye socket — even together, they would not have been enough. The possibility that theatrical devices had been used might have occurred to Frizer. And if that had happened, Marlowe would have been dealt a fatal blow, and Cecil, no doubt, would have made good on his promise and cast Poley in a torture chamber.

The dangling eyeball had prevented all of that from happening.

As soon as Frizer and Skeres had left, Poley and Nelly Bull had gone out to her garden to the cart he'd positioned just inside her gate. Beneath the sacks of garbage, Poley had hidden a lifeless corpse.

Locating a newly dead body in London should have been an easy task. Dozens were succumbing to plague every day. But finding one with no telltale sores or visible injuries had been a challenge. After he'd learned of Cecil's determination to have Marlowe killed, Poley had spent all night searching. Finally, by the following afternoon, he got word of a man — of the right age and height — who had just succumbed to falling sickness. Perfect.

He and Nelly Bull had laid that body on the bed and carried Marlowe out to the cart. The drug Poley had given Marlowe was strong, and he was still unconscious. Then there was just the matter of stabbing the corpse's eye socket and pouring a bladder of pig's blood into it.

When Skeres and Frizer returned for the inquest, it had been easy to ensure that they'd not view the substitute body. Poley had asked the coroner if he could give his testimony out in the garden, as the room above was filled with an oppressive odor. Skeres and Frizer had eagerly followed suit.

Thinking of Thomas Phelippes, Poley felt satisfied. This time, he had bested his longtime foe, along with thwarting the murderous demands of his own employer, Robert Cecil, sure to become England's next secretary of state. It was a stunning triumph. His most impressive to date.

Poley's only regret was that neither could ever know.

39

WESTMINSTER, LONDON — 2:48 P.M., THE PRESENT DAY

*H*e was alive. He was a spy. He did not remember her.

Kate was leaning against a stone pillar near New Scotland Yard's revolving front sign. A heavy shower had broken out, and rainwater streamed from the edges of her umbrella. The sky had darkened, and she couldn't see more than thirty yards ahead of her. How fitting, she thought.

A ring sounded. Her cell phone.

It was her father. She let it go. What could he say now that could make up for all he had not said?

An armored car pulled up from the garage, and Kate saw Sergeant Colin Davies through a window.

Turning off her phone, she walked over to meet him.

40

What is it now but mad Leander dares?
— Marlowe's *Hero and Leander*

The Mediterranean Sea — June 1593

*I*t was a gusty but warm spring afternoon when the skiff was lowered by rope and pulley over the starboard side of the ship. A young deckhand called Hal looked on, puzzled. The *Bonaventure* couldn't be more than half a league off the Barbary Coast, home to pirates so vicious they brought tremors to the knees of each and every English sailor, whether he would admit it or not.

Hitting the choppy waters, the skiff bounced and nearly capsized, then the two young men aboard steadied her and began to row. Straight for the enemy's lair. Were they mad? Hal wanted to inquire of someone, but the captain had forbidden any discussion of this event. On specific orders from their ultimate master, he'd said, Sir Walter Ralegh. Anyone who breathed a word would be run through and heaved to the deep.

Standing on the aft deck, Hal watched the little skiff shrink behind them, the heads of the two seamen now no larger than grains of sand. As they neared that faint, blurred line where the ocean meets the sky, he shook his head — with disbelief but also disappointment. He'd enjoyed their company. The smaller one, Lee Anderson, was an expert swordsman and had given him lessons, which was great fun, of course, but it was the one with the eye patch he'd truly miss. The fellow had saved his life. It was considered bad luck for sailors to know how to swim, so when a sail swung loose, knocking Hal overboard two days before, he was sure he was done for. Helpless and thrashing about, he'd been choking and spitting out his last prayers when he'd felt an arm grab him about the chest and begin hauling him to safety.

Back on deck, a grateful Hal had asked his name. Perhaps it was the chill of the sea or the shock of danger barely averted, but the fellow seemed to have forgotten it. He'd opened his mouth to speak, then had paused, a look of confusion on his face. No words came out. So Hal had spoken for him. "Whatever it may be, I do know one thing, by God. You're a true hero, you are. A hero."

"In more ways than one, you might say," his savior had said, glancing at his friend, Lee Anderson.

And then, to Hal's surprise, the young man had started to laugh.

41

The dragon stood on his desk.

"Most unusual," the curator said, examining it through a small glass suspended from his neck. "The diamond pattern, the golden inlay . . . I've never seen anything like it."

"Ming, do you think?" Kate asked.

The thin, balding man peered up. "The Chinese almost never embellished jade," he said, tugging on his yellow bow tie. "Particularly not with precious stones. It might be a Mughal piece. I'll need some time to make an assessment.

"Will you excuse me?" he then asked, reaching for his ringing phone.

Kate and Sergeant Davies both nodded.

Listening to the voice on the other end, the curator nodded excitedly. "Quite intrigued, you say? Oh, yes. It's lovely."

Then his mouth fell open. "She wishes to *what?*" he stammered, beads of sweat breaking out on his forehead. *"Today?"*

The bulletproof limousine glided to a stop before the gilded, wrought-iron gates. Two men in well-cut suits approached and conversed with the driver. A few minutes later, the heavy gates swung open, and the limo began moving across the forecourt of Buckingham Palace.

Kate and Sergeant Davies were sitting next to each other in the back-seat. "Might be a different one," she said, turning to him. "But the letter, the chest—they're finally making their way into the hands of a Queen Elizabeth."

"About time, isn't it?"

Author's Note

When I began working on *The Intelligencer*, I did not intend for Marlowe to survive the Deptford killing. Such speculation about the possibility of a faked death was, to me, the province of the Marlowe-was-Shakespeare conspiracy theorists. But after a former Renaissance literature professor of mine told me his theory about Marlowe's *Hero and Leander* — a theory readers may remember encountering in chapter 23 — I was inspired to change my mind.

Most people consider the poem to be an incomplete fragment — the opening of a tragic tale that Marlowe never had a chance to finish, perhaps because he was working on it at the time of his death. My professor, on the other hand, suggested that Marlowe may have kept his Hero and Leander alive deliberately. He may have been playing with the conventional form of tragedy, choosing to flout the overwhelming expectation of doom for his protagonists by closing the poem before the night of the fateful storm.

At first, I was intrigued by the possibility that Marlowe had used that literary technique, but I was not yet tempted to try the same thing with my own doomed character. I did not wish to end my Marlowe story before the night of May 30, 1593, as I was looking forward to dramatizing the still unknown events of that mysterious evening. But when I reread Marlowe's *Hero and Leander* some time later, it occurred to me that Marlowe might have done more than simply cut off the poem before the night of the storm in order to keep his tragic lovers alive. He might have veered from convention even more dramatically by depicting the fateful storm but changing the outcome, allowing Leander to survive his near drowning and reach the opposite shore.

In the classical version of the story, Leander swims the Hellespont to visit Hero every night for an entire summer, then drowns when a fierce fall storm hits. Marlowe's version dramatizes only a single crossing, but I think the poem can be read as a compressed version of the myth.

Marlowe's *Hero and Leander* does, indeed, feature a storm. The quote that opens my chapter 40, "What is it now but mad Leander dares?" comes from the moment in the poem when Leander is standing at the edge of the "toiling" Hellespont, staring longingly at Hero's tower. He then leaps in, begins to swim, and nearly drowns—"the waves about him wound, / And pull'd him to the bottom," where he is "almost dead." But then Neptune "heav'd him up," "Beat down the bold waves with his triple mace," and "swore the sea should never do him harm." I think it possible that this was *the* storm—that Marlowe's Leander escapes the fate of his classical counterpart.

Looking at the poem this way inspired me to employ the same technique with my Marlowe character—to depict the moment of certain, overwhelmingly expected doom, then allow the tragic figure to survive. The fact that the sea god Neptune allows Leander to reach the shore gave me the idea to use a form of pseudodivine intervention in *The Intelligencer*. The Tarot reader, you may recall, tells Marlowe, "Barring angelic intervention, you'll not live to see the next moon," and at the end of the novel, Robert Poley plays guardian angel, helping Marlowe escape Cecil's death warrant.

My decision to end the Marlowe story with his cheating death and heading out to sea was also inspired by his work. In *Dr. Faustus*, shortly before the devils arrive to take the magician to hell, he wishes that he might escape damnation by disappearing into the ocean: "O soul, be chang'd into little water drops, / And fall into the Ocean, ne'er be found." And in *Edward II*, when facing death, Mortimer refers to himself as "a traveler," who "scorns the world" and "Goes to discover countries yet unknown."

While the denouement to *The Intelligencer*'s Elizabethan story was influenced more by Marlowe's poetry than by historical evidence, the rest is grounded in fact to the extent possible, portraying the known events from Marlowe's final month. A poem signed "Tamburlaine" that threatened London's immigrants with murder was, indeed, affixed to the wall of the Dutch church on London's Broad Street on the evening of May 5, 1593. A special five-man commission—one of whom was, in fact, Thomas Phelippes—was charged with apprehending the unknown author. The commission's men did report finding a so-called heretical document in Thomas Kyd's lodgings, which Kyd said belonged to Marlowe. Kyd was arrested and imprisoned on May 11 or 12, 1593, and by many accounts was tortured. A warrant for Marlowe's apprehension was issued on May 18, 1593, and he appeared before government officials two days later. A spy named Richard Baines did write an informant report, entitled "A Note Containing the Opinion of One Christopher Marly, Concerning His Damnable Judgment of Religion and Scorn of God's Word," which is believed to have been delivered to the Privy Council on May 27, 1593. And according to the coroner's report, Marlowe was stabbed to death on May 30, with the inquest and funeral held two days later, on June 1. For dramatic purposes, I compressed the sense of time, so that Marlowe's final twenty-six days feel more like one week, and I also moved the delivery of the Baines's report forward, having it precede, rather than follow, Marlowe's interrogation.

Very little is known of Marlowe's career as a spy. In fact, a letter that was sent by the Privy Council to Cambridge University in 1587, in order to squelch rumors that he was a Catholic traitor and prevent his expulsion, is the only reasonably solid evidence that he worked for the secret service. The letter itself does not survive, but the Council's minutes describe its contents in considerable detail. Marlowe, the letter reportedly said, had no intention of defecting to the Catholic cause; rather he "had done Her Majesty good service, & deserved to be rewarded for his faithful dealing." He should be given his master's degree, the Council urged, "because it was not Her Majesty's pleasure that anyone employed, as he had been, in matters touching the benefit of his country, should be defamed by those that are ignorant in th'affairs he went about."

As no one can say for sure what affairs Marlowe actually went about, I relied on the speculations of Renaissance historians for my descriptions of Marlowe's previous espionage activities. For example, records do indicate that Marlowe was arrested for counterfeiting in the Netherlands in early 1592. That this incident was part of an intelligence operation is a theory put forth by Charles Nicholl in his essay, " 'At Middleborough': Some Reflections on Marlowe's Visit to the Low Countries in 1592" as well as in his wonderfully gripping nonfiction account of Marlowe's murder, *The Reckoning*.

That Marlowe was assigned to investigate England's Muscovy Company is pure invention on my part, as is the idea that Sir Robert Cecil, one of the directors, was using company ships to deliver weapons to a Barbary pirate. These choices did not, however, come out of thin air. There is evidence that Marlowe was aware of the Muscovy Company's illicit arms trade with Ivan the Terrible, and the general manager for the company's London operations was, in fact, a man named Anthony Marlowe, believed to have been a distant cousin to Christopher. Muscovy men were known to have engaged in smuggling operations quite frequently. It is certainly possible that Cecil, at some point, took part.

While *The Anatomy of Secrets* is also a fictional invention, Francis Walsingham's files really did go missing after his death in 1590, and they remain lost to this day. Thomas Phelippes has long been one of the top suspects. As to the contents of the manuscript, for the most part I gave imaginary solutions to unsolved Elizabethan mysteries. That Anthony Bacon was investigated on charges of sodomy in France is the one account in the fictional *Anatomy of Secrets* that is widely considered to be true.

Regarding Thomas Hariot's use of a telescope in 1593, I took a liberty. It is not known when he constructed his first "perspective trunke," but it is unlikely that he did so in 1593. The telescope is commonly believed to have been invented by Dutch eyeglass manufacturers in the early seventeenth century with the technology being disseminated immediately. However, in defense of this scene, Hariot published very little about his extensive scientific endeavors, and since he was an expert in optics and the intellectual equal of Galileo, it is possible that he had constructed a telescope by 1593, though highly improbable. Such an invention would have been an awfully big secret to keep.

Throughout the historical chapters, I tried to make the details as authentic as possible. The laments Robert Poley overhears at Marlowe's funeral, for example, were taken from poetry written about Marlowe shortly after his death. Poley *was* given a diamond by Anthony Babington, one of the young Catholic conspirators he helped send to the gallows when he was working as an agent provocateur in the 1580s. Poley's employer, Robert Cecil, did keep exotic birds from the East as pets, and he was, in fact, one of the chief sponsors of Walter Ralegh's Guiana voyage. He is believed to have contributed the bulk of the sixty thousand pounds Ralegh eventually raised. Regarding the Puritan preacher who grabbed Marlowe's arm in chapter 22, pamphlets warning readers against intellectual curiosity were in wide circulation at the time, and the image of Icarus plunging from the heavens was a common feature. And though Thomas Hariot left few records behind, evidence does indicate that he conducted many experiments to explore the nature of rainbows.

As a final note, I would like to say a few words about the real Christopher Marlowe. The mysteries surrounding the life and death of this controversial figure have been subjects of hot debate for centuries. Most of the historical records pertaining to his character, behavior, and beliefs convey the dubious statements of paid informants, literary rivals, and a victim of torture, and as Kate and Medina's conversation in chapter 25 makes clear, the royal coroner's account of his death is a very questionable document, depicting a highly implausible scenario. The facts, though tantalizing, are also open to multiple interpretations. That he appears to have worked for the secret service does not tell us he was a patriot of any kind; he may have been motivated solely by a desire for money and adventure. That he faced charges of atheism says very little about what his actual religious beliefs may have been; more often than not, such accusations were a political tool used to discredit an enemy. To be sure, his plays hint at a strong religious skepticism and suggest a profound disdain for his culture's orthodoxies. They also depict such savage violence and cruelty that many view Marlowe as having been mean-spirited and heartless. However, his plays were most certainly influenced by the competing needs to shock, titillate, and captivate jaded theatergoers in a bloody age; intrigue patrons; survive censorship; and perhaps enhance his pose as a political dissident. Using them to get a handle on the real Marlowe is a tricky enterprise.

Many Renaissance scholars believe that Marlowe was what we would now call homosexual—a term, as well as a concept, that did not exist at the time. Though no one can say for sure, based upon the homoerotic themes and imagery scattered throughout his poetry and plays, I would imagine he enjoyed both sexes, if not just males. In *Hero and Leander*, for example, it is actually "lusty" Neptune who instigates Leander's near drowning. Neptune pulls Leander to the seafloor because he thinks the dashing lad is Jove's immortal boy-toy Ganymede and heaves him back up only when he realizes that Leander is an almost-dead human. I decided to leave the question of Marlowe's sexuality out of this book, for the most part, because in the few days I was portraying, I wanted to focus on his final intelligence assignment and literary endeavor. Readers may, however, remember that in chapter 12, my fictional Marlowe had a brief flash of disappointment when he learns that the fair Lee Anderson is actually a girl.

As Marlowe the man is and perhaps always will be an enigma, it should come as no surprise that there are as many different fictional versions of his life and death as there are people who've written them. There will undoubtedly be more. But which is the most accurate, we may never know. Several documents came to light this century that added to his murky, fragmented biography, and perhaps more are yet to come. Even so, it is very likely that what happened on May 30, 1593, in that Deptford room will remain a mystery forever.

Acknowledgments

Above all, I would like to thank my literary agent and adored friend, Joanna Pulcini, and my wonderful editor, Greer Hendricks, for believing in *The Intelligencer* before most of it was written. Their vision, infectious enthusiasm, and unflagging support truly made it happen.

I am enormously grateful to everyone at Atria Books for championing this book with faith, patience, and style, especially Judith Curr, who loved it from the beginning. Many thanks also to Suzanne O'Neill, as well as to the outstanding art department, sales force, and publicity team.

For their exceptional editorial suggestions, I am deeply thankful to Liza Nelligan, Michele Tempesta, Ken Salikof, and Nina Bjornsson. Also to my admired friend and mentor, Jack Devine, a thirty-two-year veteran of the CIA, for his encouragement and guidance. And to my parents, sister, and all the friends who commented on draft after draft, particularly Christian D'Andrea and Priya Parmar. Thanks also to Sarah McGrath, whose thoughtful advice was so helpful at every step along the way.

For all their hard work on my behalf, I very much appreciate Linda Michaels and Teresa Cavanaugh of Linda Michaels Limited; Lynn Goldberg and Brooke Fitzsimmons of Goldberg McDuffie Communications; Matthew Snyder of Creative Artists Agency; and Linda Chester, Gary Jaffe, and Kelly Smith.

My heartfelt gratitude to the History of Science and English Departments at Harvard University. Especially to the brilliant Stephen Greenblatt, author of my favorite Marlowe essay of all time, for sharing his theory about Marlowe's *Hero and Leander* and inspiring the end of this novel. Thanks also to John Parker for so generously answering my questions and sharing some of his seemingly infinite wisdom, as well as Anne Harrington, James Engell, Katharine Park, John Guillory, and Steven Ozment for their kindness and intellectual guidance. For Kate's discussion of Copernicus, Bruno, and Galileo, I am very much indebted to the engrossing lectures of Steven Harris, historian of science extraordinaire. As with everyone I have mentioned above, any mistakes are mine.

Finally, I would like to sing the praises of Charles Nicholl's captivating and exhaustively researched nonfiction book, *The Reckoning: The Murder of Christopher Marlowe*, which was an invaluable help as I developed *The Intelligencer*, as was Richard Wilson's intriguing essay about Marlowe and the Muscovy Company: "Visible Bullets: *Tamburlaine the Great* and Ivan the Terrible."

The Intelligencer

Leslie Silbert

A Readers Club Guide

About This Guide

The suggested questions are intended to help your reading group find new and interesting angles and topics for discussion for Leslie Silbert's *The Intelligencer*. We hope that these ideas will enrich your conversation and increase your enjoyment of the book.

Many fine books from Washington Square Press feature Readers Club Guides. For a complete listing, or to read the guides online, visit www.BookClubReader.com.

A Conversation with Leslie Silbert

Q: One reason *The Intelligencer* is such an interesting read is that it transcends several genres—it's part spy thriller, part historical novel, with a splash of mystery thrown in. How do you describe it to people?

A: I say that it's designed to keep you highly entertained while you're curled up on a rainy night or in an airplane, but also that I wanted to do something beyond pure escapist fiction. My hope is that when you finish it, you'll feel like you learned something about an intriguing era and consider your time well spent.

Q: Though *The Intelligencer* is a work of fiction, it draws on your real-life experiences. Can you explain your move from the ivory tower to the world of private investigation?

A: As a grad student, I was studying ideas about curiosity in English Renaissance culture—specifically, the pursuit of secrets and forbidden knowledge. So there was *some* logic to the move, some method in the madness. Anyway, about six months into my program, I realized that the academic track wasn't for me, and I applied for positions with a number of private investigation firms. I loved school, but my subject matter had inspired me. I wanted to take my interests into the real world, to pursue secrets for a living.

Q: Which tempted you first, private investigation or writing fiction?

A: It's hard to say. Both interests sparked somewhere in grade school. I was a serious Nancy Drew addict as a kid and fantasized about doing what she did—the sleuthing that is, not kissing her blah boyfriend Ned. I also remember starting to write a Sidney Sheldon–ish novel in the seventh grade. I don't remember too much about it, other than the fact that there was a dashing but menacing Swede named Sven von Blixen. Though I didn't get past the first few chapters, the interest in writing thrillers lingered. The intent to actually sit down and do it, however, didn't resurge until after college. I was standing in line at a grocery store browsing the shelf of bestselling paperbacks. I picked up a few and began to read. I forget what they were, but let's just say they weren't among the greatest out there. I was thinking, "Man, I could do better than this." And then I had one of those moments where you step back and ask yourself, "Are you gonna go through life saying things like that, or are you actually gonna do it?"

Q: **Like you, the young heroine of *The Intelligencer* works for a top P.I. firm in New York City, under the guidance of a former CIA officer, and also has an expertise in Renaissance history and literature. How much of your own life have you written into Kate Morgan?**

A: An embarrassingly large amount! We also have similar interests and senses of humor, as well as past experiences and relationships. I confess I took the easy route here. I was completely new to fiction writing when I started *The Intelligencer*. I hadn't taken any creative writing classes, read any how-to books, or had practice of any kind since a short story I wrote in the eighth grade. It was daunting, so I followed one of the few adages I'd heard over the years: Write what you know. Instead of wondering if my main character was two-dimensional or spoke in a consistent voice, I could just think: What would I say? I have, however, made Kate much cooler than I am. Most notably, the company I work for does not double as a clandestine U.S. intelligence unit. My contribution to global justice is, unfortunately, quite limited.

Q: **In *The Intelligencer*, Kate assumes different identities to unravel the mystery behind the manuscript. Do you do this? Based on your experiences as a P.I., can you tell us a little about this?**

A: I always try to stay as close to the truth as possible. The more, ah, fibs you've got to keep track of, the easier it is for someone to trip you up and the less confident you tend to be. My great-grandmother grew up in a remote cabin in the Lithuanian countryside, and one day, an axe-wielding madman attacked her home. She and her sisters were running around, frantically locking doors and windows, and swinging fire pokers and frying pans to keep him at bay. Assuming a fake identity can be a little like that. If your cover is really far from the truth, you're like my great-grandmother on the day the madman attacked, panicked because you've got a whole lot of open windows and doors—you know, vulnerabilities. But if your cover is just a stretched and tweaked version of who you really are, you're more like my great-grandmother if her cabin had been Dick Cheney's secret bunker.

Q: While doing P.I. work, has anyone ever been suspicious of you?

A: As far as I know, no one's been suspicious of me . . . as a P.I. What's funny is that I *have* generated suspicion and been escorted off property, but that was as a writer, when I was being entirely straightforward—you know, using my real name, asking questions with no hidden agenda, etc.

I was doing research for *The Intelligencer* in London. There's a heist scene that takes place at the end of the novel, and I wanted it to feel as authentic as possible. So I went to the location—it was royal property, mind you—and I was out in a garden checking things out. A woman walking her dog came by and I said, "It's so beautiful here. The local college kids must sneak in all the time for late night trysts." And she replied, "Oh no. The Royal Park Police drive around and release their dogs at various times throughout the night." That seemed like good enough information, but I had the time and decided to be extra thorough. So I went up to one of the guards and said, "Hi, I'm Leslie Silbert. I'm writing a spy novel, and I've got a scene where two characters break in here. Could you tell me . . ." As I began asking my series of questions, the guard frowned. "I've never heard of you. How do I know you aren't planning to break in yourself?" I tried telling him about my novel and my publisher, but it didn't do any good. He thought I was lying and asked me to leave!

Q: The historical storyline in *The Intelligencer* focuses on the murder of the famous playwright, poet, and spy Christopher Marlowe. How did you come to choose Marlowe as your subject?

A: One spring morning a number of years ago, I was sitting in a Renaissance drama class listening to a lecture on Marlowe's *Dr. Faustus*, when a friend of mine leaned over and whispered, "You know, he was also a spy." I had a million questions, but my professor was looking right at me, and he was giving an awfully compelling lecture, so for the next forty minutes I sat there quietly, thoughts racing about Marlowe and his dangerous pursuits—of God's secrets in his intellectual life, and state secrets in his real life. Both of which were deadly at the time. Remember, this was an age when certain intellectual efforts were crimes punishable by death. After class, when I learned that Marlowe had been killed under mysterious circumstances, that in all likelihood he was murdered for one of his dangerous pursuits, I was hooked.

Q: Did your graduate work give you enough background for this novel, or did you do extensive research following school?

A: I began delving into Marlowe's life in grad school, then continued researching afterward until the last page of *The Intelligencer* was written. There is a lot we don't know about Marlowe's final days, but I wanted to make sure that what we do know would be accurately portrayed in my novel. Envisioning the historical record as a puzzle with missing pieces, I used my imagination to fill in the blank spaces, not alter accepted facts. I also consulted professors and grad student friends and had several read chapters or the full manuscript, because I wanted to make sure my Marlowe felt plausible to people who are considered experts on the subject. And then there were the other Elizabethan characters to consider: Queen Elizabeth, Walter Ralegh, the Earl of Essex—countless pages have been written about all of them. So yes, I did a lot of research!

Q: Since you're a Marlowe buff, did you find it difficult to figure out what an average reader might find interesting?

A: Yes, absolutely! That's why I enlisted friends and family to read multiple drafts and draw little sad faces wherever their interest started to lag.

Q: At one point, Sir Francis Walsingham claims, "Books, you see, are but dead letters." I would guess a Renaissance literature scholar would find his opinion blasphemous. What can you tell us about this statement?

A: I lifted this line from a letter the real-life Walsingham wrote to his nephew. And actually, after this comment, he goes on to explain that real-world experiences give life to those dead letters. So there's no blasphemy here. Walsingham's not denigrating book-learning in any way, he's just saying it isn't enough. For a full education, you need more. You need to travel and meet different kinds of people. So that's what I have Walsingham say to Marlowe in my novel, as he's encouraging his new recruit to stick with intelligence work. Interestingly enough, not only was "intelligencer" the term for spy at the time, but the word "intelligence" took on its espionage meaning during this period of history.

Q: Which author has had the greatest influence on your writing and why?

A: I'd have to say Tom Stoppard, because his play *Arcadia* inspired the structure of *The Intelligencer*, as well as the rest of my series. When I first saw *Arcadia* in 1997, I was captivated and awed at how Stoppard deftly interwove stories separated by centuries. Years later, as I prepared to start writing my first novel, remembering Stoppard's play convinced me to try creating a similar structure.

I had a series in mind at the time, featuring a young woman working for a boss similar to mine. I was excited to give a P.I. story the aura of authenticity I had yet to encounter in popular culture. I was new on the job, but it didn't take long to realize how wildly unrealistic *Charlie's Angels* had been. As I mentioned earlier, I'd also been kicking around the idea of a novel about Christopher Marlowe. But as I wanted to sell my first one and knew that, at the time, historical fiction wasn't the most commercial of genres, I decided to table Marlowe and write a modern-day page-turner. Then, when *Arcadia* popped up in conversation one day, it hit me. I could do both—tell a story about Marlowe's doomed final days as well as one featuring the twenty-first–century heroine I had in mind. The chapters would alternate, and the mysteries would intersect and unfold together.

Q: What can you tell us about your next Kate Morgan novel?

A: Like *The Intelligencer*, it will interweave a historical mystery with thematically linked modern intrigue. The theme for *The Intelligencer* was the pursuit of secrets and forbidden knowledge in the English Renaissance—specifically, what was the most dangerous type of knowledge to pursue in Marlowe's day and how has that, or hasn't it, changed today? The theme of my second novel involves the clash of civilizations, Islam versus Christendom—specifically, what sparked war in the Baroque period and how has that, or hasn't it, changed today?

Discussion Questions for
The Intelligencer

1. The action in this novel moves rapidly between Elizabethan England and modern times, shifting centuries with each chapter. How did this atypical structure affect your reading of the story? What does the juxtaposition of two time periods offer that novels confined to one period do not?

2. Christopher Marlowe is presented as a complex man: poet, spy, patriot, friend, and enemy. And while he doesn't follow many rules, his ultimate commitment to doing what he thinks is right never wavers. This becomes clear in chapter 6: "It was a delicate balance to maintain—satisfying his handlers while operating according to his own set of principles—but somehow, he was managing it." What do you think of this policy? Given that Marlowe knows his delicate balancing act is "doomed to an unpleasant end," why does he persist? Would you?

3. Kate admits that she has always admired "the Cat," the burglar who initially tried to steal the manuscript. The Cat was described as a modern-day Robin Hood, stealing from the rich and giving the proceeds to charity. Do you think Kate would ever change teams and become a thief herself? She seems to relish the thrill of thwarting the bad guys; do you see her getting involved in other, perhaps not so legal, work? Do the connections between her character and the character of Marlowe help to answer this question?

4. Talk about the way that human nature is portrayed in this novel. Does it seem to change between Marlowe's day and the modern era,

or do you see certain commonalities that transcend time? To what extent do you criticize a character like Robert Cecil, a man who will do anything to further his own interests? To what extent is he a product of his environment? What about his descendant, Cidro Medina? Do you consider it more forgivable to be a villain in what some might call a more villainous age?

5. While Marlowe and Kate are parallel characters in many ways, their cultures are not so similar. In fact, some might say that more comparisons can be made between Marlowe's England and Hamid Azadi's Iran. As noted in chapter 3, beneath the glitter, Elizabethan England was an "ugly police state," a Protestant theocracy similar in ways to the Islamic theocracy of today's Iran, which also represses and tortures religious and political dissidents. Discuss these parallels.

6. While backstabbing, thievery, and deception have been the norm for spies since the first days of espionage, there are glimmers of integrity in some of *The Intelligencer*'s most unscrupulous characters. Even Robert Poley, a man who seduces married women for sport, is often characterized in a somewhat positive light: "Betrayal might be his livelihood and greatest form of pleasure, but when it involved someone he respected, he lost interest. And beyond that, he wanted to help whoever was trapped in the tangle of government plotting." What is your impression of Poley — is he a good man, or an inherently immoral character? What about Luca de Tolomei? In many ways, his grief-induced obsession with revenge is understandable. By the end of the novel, do you think he feels satisfied, or rather, avenged? Did you still consider him a villain? Do you see similarities between his character and that of Robert Poley?

7. By chapter 24, it is clear that both of Marlowe's employers are trying to bring about his doom. It's a different story for Kate. There's no question that her boss, Jeremy Slade, values her and wants to protect her. Do you think this is a reflection of certain differences between the intelligence services in Marlowe's day versus those today? Also, while the actions of Marlowe's bosses are clearly unforgivable, what

about the lies that Jeremy Slade told Kate? Do you think Kate will forgive him in Silbert's next novel? What about her father, Don Morgan? Now that Kate has had her absolute trust in her boss shattered, do you think she'll keep working for the Slade Group? Do you think she'll take on Marlowe's policy of lying to his superiors and carrying out assignments how he sees fit?

8. Late in the novel, as Thomas Phelippes attempts to break into Essex's bedroom, we learn that "He liked to surprise people now and then because you didn't really know someone if you only saw them the way they wanted to be seen." In what ways might Phelippes's secret habit inform a discussion on the nature of truth? Is it possible to ever truly know someone you've never caught in a private moment? Silbert shifts points of view frequently in this novel, allowing us to get to know most of the main characters and see the action and meet others through their eyes. Did you like this narrative structure? What do you see as its advantages and disadvantages when it comes to novels of suspense? Do you think it allows you to more fully "know" the characters, than does a novel told entirely from the first-person perspective?

9. Kate told Medina that while in school, she studied the pursuit of secrets and forbidden knowledge in the Renaissance, focusing on the question: What type of knowledge was the most dangerous to pursue back then and why? Reflecting upon the story, and Kate's discussion with Medina from chapter 17 in particular, what would you say was the most highly protected secret knowledge in Marlowe's day and what is it now? Who pursues it and who is the most threatened by its exposure? What is at stake for the pursuer, the government, and the culture if it is obtained and revealed?

10. Do you think it significant that the object that sets the modern-day adventure in motion is nothing more than an old manuscript? In chapter 7, as Kate and Max consider who might be trying to steal it, they discuss secrets with the power to transcend time. Kate speculates that the manuscript might contain evidence invalidating

someone's claim to a valuable estate, while Max wonders if the secret in the manuscript is something that a government or church wishes to cover up. Were you surprised to learn what Jade Dragon was really after? In real life, do you believe there are secrets having nothing to do with the prospect of financial gain, for which people would kill, to keep quiet?